STEVEN MEEHAN

DEAD
MAN'S HAND

FORGER'S BOOK 1

SILVERSMITH
PRESS

Published by Silversmith Press–Houston, Texas
www.silversmithpress.com

ISBN 978-1-961093-69-0 (Softcover Book)
ISBN 978-1-961093-70-6 (eBook)

To my daughter, Fiona Lily,
for whom I would sacrifice anything.

ACKNOWLEDGMENTS

There are far too many people who have helped me bring this book to the world, from simple words of encouragement to the most brutal of criticism. However, I'm going to make the attempt. First off, I want to thank my father, who, when he was with us, read the first completed draft and started listing all the things I needed to fix to have a completed novel.

To my sister Jeanne and her husband Joe, who took time out of their busy schedule to read subsequent drafts before giving me their honest opinions and encouragement. It doesn't take much for a challenge to appear overwhelming, and writing a book, especially your first, is as daunting as it comes. You need plenty of support to help you whenever you're teetering on giving up. Thankfully, my older siblings, Chris and Katie, provided me with the support I needed to stay true to my goal. By embracing their advice, both current and from years prior, I kept myself on track with this dream. Friends are the family you choose. I'll always love my family, but sometimes I haven't been able to reach out to them, and thankfully, I have amazing friends. Regarding this process, Andrew, Tim, and his wife, Beth, were willing to read early drafts, and they didn't hold back in their constructive criticism.

Despite going back and redrafting my book, I want to express my gratitude to Erica Ford, who assisted me in drafting the first edition. She put in a fair amount of work to knock off a lot of the rough edges of my first novel. Yet as I poured myself into other work, I saw some of the more inherent flaws in that version. With that realization, I wanted to dive into the literary prose and fix the more blatant issues. Thankfully, I lucked into a webinar arranged by Dr. Steve Turley, which featured Joanna Hunt. The class focused on writing a novel, but Joanna and her team at Silversmith Press were more than happy to help bring this new edition to life. Everyone who I worked with provided me with wonderful feedback and helped strengthen this new edition.

I also want to thank my wife, Amanda, and Carl Keller my father-in-law, who tore through my updated manuscript with a red pen to help me smooth over everything from character traits to dialogue and everything in between. And to anyone else who either gave me advice or lent me a hand in keeping me focused, whom I have not named here, I thank you all for all the help you gave me.

AUTHOR'S NOTE

Despite my love for creating stories, I haven't always been an avid reader. To my shame, in my distant youth, every day sparked new ideas on how to skirt the tasked reading. In fact, during those days, I only wanted to *learn* by watching television or movies. After all, I didn't have to work to get the story. To a child who didn't enjoy working to be entertained, this was a very tempting and all too powerful lure for me to avoid. However, those wonderful Saturday morning cartoons conflicted with the prizes I could get from my local library, provided I did the reading. As a result, there were many times that I faked the reading just to claim the prize. A tactic that I adapted to deal with the pesky school summer reading projects.

Now, before I keep going, I should mention that I believe listening to an audio book is just as worthwhile as pulling a hardcover off the shelf and reading it. Regardless of how you consume the words, whether through letters on a page, pixels on a screen, or words through a speaker, the result is the same as long as you let the words take root in you and spark your imagination. And since I rarely have the luxury to pull out a book or Kindle to read, thankfully, I have access to Audible. With that service, I have access to all the literature I want. As a result, it's now my primary source of reading.

With the little mini rant done, let's talk about how my love of the written word sparked.

Despite my desire to avoid reading, one day, when I was still in high school, a good friend of mine recommended Wizard's First Rule to me. I figured since neither of us were avid readers and he was so excited about the book, to the point of giving me a copy, I read the first few pages. After reading those first few, I chose to read the next chapter, and then the next few chapters. Before I knew what had happened, I'd finished the story, and was eager to get my hands on the next installment in the series. That single book, well the complete series, in fact, was my entrance back into the wide world of literature that I didn't even realize I yearned for. If my friend hadn't suggested it to me, in just the right way, I would never have gotten back into reading. Let alone embrace my ability to tell stories.

And as the saying goes, *youth is wasted on the young.* Now that I don't have the time to read as much as I want, I keep discovering books and authors to add to my reading list. And I wish I could reclaim the time I wasted in my youth and use it to read or write, rather than being so obsessed with TV.

PROLOGUE

I've had my fair share of bad days, but I have to rank the last twenty-four hours as the worst. I mean, it's not typical to end up standing over your own bullet-ridden corpse. In case you're wondering, getting shot can put a damper on your day. However, as those recent events churned through my mind, I realized being shot was not the low point, simply the harsh termination of a series of choices. Despite the valiant effort of myself and Alexis, our current situation almost felt inevitable. While he had insisted we crafted the perfect plan, given the time constraints, we obviously had a massive blind spot.

A series of cracks ripped my gaze away from the trio of bullet holes in my body. As I whirled about, searching for the source of the commotion, Bertrand Dempsey's wild eyes snagged my attention and refused to release me. The portals to his soul overflowed with raw emotion, something conflicting with his storied reputation. Instantly, every story, rumor, or tale of this unflappable man filled my mind. When they'd all played through my mind's eye, their central theme loomed over me. He was a rational and dispassionate man who seemingly possessed omniscience. And with that overabundance of information, he utilized patience in dealing with any obstacle to his desires.

Yet, amidst the din from the raining debris, Dempsey's resolve lay among the wreckage of Alexis's home. I gazed into those tumultuous orbs, searching for the words to describe the man's mounting emotions. In the end, I could only force a single word upon that look: excitement.

There he was, looming over my corpse, with the actual smoking gun clutched in his whitening fingers. What was wrong with him? As he stood there, basking in what he'd done, his gaze shifted from my body to his next victim, Alexis. The excited gleam in his eyes grew from a faint spark as he studied the man standing beside my corpse. Was Dempsey demented? Never mind, of course he was demented. Unfortunately, if something didn't change soon, then I'd be as demented for agreeing with this joke of a plan. It had sounded like a good idea while we were discussing it. However, through the lenses of hindsight, my brain catalogued this scheme's every flaw.

With his chest swelling, Dempsey leveled the pistol on Alexis. And between a pair of moments, an explosion washed over everyone. Why did I flinch? Given how things turned out, I was beyond Dempsey's grasp, but I still reacted. I pushed the involuntary reaction aside and studied the room, finding Alexis on his butt. Blood seeped through his fingers as he grasped his upper arm. Dempsey inched forward, his lips curling upward. Why did he simply wound Alexis? Was he looking to torture him? If I had been able, I would have screamed.

Why'd Alexis think this plan was reasonable? Before Dempsey's specter descended upon us, Alexis assured me a noisy entrance would prompt a call to the police. Of course, considering the outcome, I could no longer help Alexis. And considering the taunting silence, Alexis's belief in his neighbors was also worthless. Despite the steady stream of commotion, the resounding din still lacked the telltale signs of the police's arrival or approach.

PROLOGUE

Dempsey's car had plowed through Alexis's front wall, spewing chunks of glass and wood throughout the room. Given Alexis's confidence, where were the comforting sirens? Despite the constant noises emanating from the wounded structure, nobody considered intervening.

As the sinister presence grew, Alexis's guarantee resounded through my mind. He was certain that a good neighbor would make a call. With every passing second, the lack of authorities kindled Dempsey's growing turmoil. Meanwhile, the color drained from his fingers, gripping the pistol.

When I suggested the police might not arrive until it was too late, Alexis had overruled me. He was confident in both his neighbors and his ability to delay Dempsey's actions. He was certain the police would swoop in and prevent the man from going too far. As the excitement in Dempsey's wild gaze intensified, I knew Alexis had been wrong.

And right then, the crazed gunman wanted to teach Alexis why interfering with Dempsey's business was always a fatal decision.

CHAPTER 1

As I leaned against the headboard, my eyes studied the unwavering image emanating from the remote camera I had installed upon my arrival in the city. Despite the very occasional tussle of the debris scattered about the asphalt, this solitary image was the only thing I'd seen since I had begun keeping tabs on the warehouse. When I laid the camcorder down to rub my eyes, my cell shattered the looming silence. With a groan, I pulled it off the nightstand and peeked at the name splashed across its screen. I took great care not to answer the call as I returned the phone and placed my feet on the carpeted floor of the hotel room, waiting for the silence to return.

After the final intrusive tone, a silence wrapped around my shoulders like a comforting blanket. While my hands soothed my weary eyes, another call yanked my attention back to the offending device. Why couldn't Matt take a hint? Given his immediate follow-up call, it was more likely the sun would rise, revealing a nice verdant color, than for Matt to leave me alone. As a result, I swallowed the curse that leaped to my lips, pinched the bridge of my nose, and answered the call. "How's it going?"

"Marcus, are you ready for this tournament of yours tomorrow?"

My eyes flicked toward the camera, registering nothing had altered in the last few heartbeats. A few seconds passed before

I pulled my attention away from the surveillance. While it was possible he would forgive the recent string of ignored calls since I answered this one, he rarely skipped the pleasantries.

Normally, he'd weave the verbal beating into the conversation. I'd have to remember his metaphorical baton was poised to bludgeon me upon my first misstep in the chat. I knew he'd be marching down this path. The sheer directness of his question was supposed to unsettle me. And truthfully, he'd succeeded. Matt's known how to wind me up from the day we met. I drew in a deep breath as I wiped my face and forced a smile upon my lips. "More or less."

"What!? You're running out of time. How could you not be ready?"

The corner of my lips curled up as I switched the phone to my other ear and rubbed the freed one. What was that tone? Had Matt allowed agitation to seep into his voice? Or was that bit of color because of some slow-burning rage? Frankly, it was too late for him to affect the outcome of the upcoming tournament. I licked my lips as I turned to pat the suitcase lying beside me. "I've collected my entrance fee."

"That doesn't answer my question."

I grabbed a laminated document off the nightstand and placed it on the case. Then I rested my hand on it and drew in a long breath. Why was he prodding? Did he find something out? I felt bad keeping the details from him, but that was only because he didn't need to know about all the minutiae. As I pulled my hand away from the sheet, it shrank into a paperclip. However, I couldn't let my guard down. Matt was skilled at eliciting a grin from anyone and then using that moment of pleasure to pry hidden truths out of them. I was certain he'd get me to smile as I stared down at my execution.

CHAPTER 1

I placed my hand on the paperclip and pulled it off a heart-beat later, revealing a small folding knife with a worn wooden handle. At that moment, I needed to keep some secrets from him, specifically what I'd discovered about the tournament. Before the building silence could intensify any more, I cleared my throat. "Yet it's the only thing that matters right now."

"Not true."

Those simple words slapped me across the face. Normally, my response would have been to laugh. However, as my eyes drifted to the camcorder, I found I couldn't force any mirth from my lips.

"Who's orchestrating it? Where's it at? Have you been scoping it out? I can think of even more questions to ask."

Despite barraging me with a litany of questions, he'd fired them off in such rapid succession that I knew he didn't really intend for me to answer them right then. "None of that is per-tinent to the game," I said, tapping the blade's handle with my knuckles. "The only thing that matters is that I finished collecting my fee and I'm ready to sit down and play."

"Did you just finish collecting your fee? The tournament is tomorrow, right?"

"I'm in a good place."

"Normally, when you need to raise capital, you're a little quicker. Is something wrong? Why have you been avoiding my calls? Did you scope out the location? Where is the tournament taking place?"

My head fell back, colliding with the bed's headboard as I closed my eyes. "Matt, if you want answers, focus on one question before skipping to the next."

"Then start answering them."

Poof. And just like that, all of Matt's whimsey vanished. My eyes drifted to the ceiling as my mind tried considering and dismissing partial and even complete answers. With a tense silence engulfing me, I eventually settled on the belief Matt wasn't completely serious about the interrogation.

"Give me a little credit. I've possessed the entire fee before I rolled into the city."

"When was that?"

Instantly, my hand pulled away from the knife, revealing a miniature copy of my friend's face laying upon the briefcase. It was a decent rendition, complete with a furrowed brow and a mouth pulled into a severe line. I covered the small model and pulled my hand away again, uncovering a small teacup. I'd offered more than I intended with that tidbit. Unfortunately, despite being able to dissemble my way out of most situations, Matt could always slice through my meticulously crafted narratives. Which meant I'd have to dance around the aspects I didn't want to share.

The only hope I had was to select a true and meaningless fact and then embellish it. While he'd sniff out an outright lie, I typically could slip massaged truths past him. So I gritted my teeth as I placed my hand on the small porcelain cup and smashed it. However, instead of shattering, the ceramic vessel changed back into the laminated document I'd plucked from the nightstand. I was going to tell him a partial truth. "I've been in the city going on three days now."

"What have you spent the last three days doing?"

Sometimes the world gives you what you're hoping for. As my lips curled into a warm smile, my friend's voice shattered the momentary pause.

"Wait, have you been using that glass circle trick of yours to get your surveillance?"

I mouthed the word yes. My gift was one of the very few things that distracted Matt. Whenever I flexed those muscles, it

CHAPTER 1

was like a dog seeing a squirrel scamper across the yard. I pulled my hand off the document to watch the large paper contort into a collection of sticky notes. Of course, the most memorable example of what I could do was the glass circle trick.

The first time I showed it to him, nothing really came of it. But with each subsequent use, he devised more lucrative ways to use that little sliver of my gift. Sometimes between the uses, I regretted showing it to him. Throughout the years, Matt asked me to place those eyes everywhere. At first, I was more than willing to create them. However, as he continued asking for them, I grew tired of dropping them. They made things far too easy, which was something Matt never understood.

Despite the constant slew of arguments, eventually I'd relent. By then, we must have experimented for days as we sought the best way to leverage that aspect of my power. Despite my frustration with the frivolous uses Matt devised, I usually relented simply because of how dear this transformation was to me. While I'd accidentally altered the world around me long before I devised this technique, that initial glass circle was the first conscious use of my gift.

That single instance of forcing my will upon the world crystallized the breadth of my abilities. All these years later, I remembered pressing my hand against a wall when suddenly the portion under my fingertips changed. It was a subtle change, hard to spot unless you were searching for it. The only difference to the wall was an extremely slight discoloration in an almost circular pattern. However, without a paired transformation, the first was useless. Yet when you looked through that second alteration, you could see out of the discolored section of wall, creating an undetectable surveillance camera, which would work no matter how far apart the items were.

As my lips curled into a broad smile, I picked up the camcorder and traced the piece of glass secured to the front of the device. "Yes, I'm using the glass circle thing. Can you think of a better way to get intelligence?"

"Nope. It's truly the best way to spy on people."

Closing my eyes, I laid the camera back down, making sure not to dislodge the bit affixed to its lens. While I endeavored to keep my abilities hidden, there were several times when Matt had been close to letting out the source of the interesting tools he'd used. "You haven't been talking to anyone about any of the equipment I've left behind for you, right? Not even indirectly?"

"Are you kidding me?!"

"Don't give me that," I said, running my fingers through my hair. "You know how many times I've had to stop you from blabbing."

"You've got to be joking. That hasn't happened in ages."

"Three months ago isn't ages, my friend." It took great effort to keep any tinge of sternness from my voice. Based on Matt's lack of reply, I must have blended my voice correctly. However, as the seconds continued to tick away, my eyes widened into saucers. "Matt, have you let anything slip?"

"No. No, Marcus, I haven't been talking to anyone."

As those words rebounded through my mind, my head swept back and forth. While I couldn't always tell if he'd been dishonest with me, there were times I was certain he was being honest, at least to me. And this was one of those occasions.

Normally, Matt wouldn't have objected to my prodding, but given the current circumstance, I shouldn't have pushed my luck. I'd ducked too many of his calls recently. I should have kept that minor fact in mind. Oh well, there really wasn't much I could do now except listen and wait for the other shoe to drop.

CHAPTER 1

"You've beaten that little fear of yours into my head often enough through the years that it has become one of my own. All your secrets will die with me. And before you have the chance to ask, there is no one in the house, so there's no chance that anyone is listening in on our conversation." With a sharp intake of breath, Matt paused as if ordering his scattered thoughts. "Do you have any idea how difficult it is to empty this house when I haven't had a successful conversation with you in over a week?"

Instantly, an answer swirled in my mind. Fortunately, I kept myself from letting it leap from my lips. Why was he pushing this conversation? Given I had mentioned the surveillance, Matt would normally end the conversation and let me continue scoping out the location before walking into anything. What happened to him not carrying a grudge?

"Marcus!"

"Sorry, did I miss something?"

"Why have you been ducking me?"

I rested my feet on the bed and covered the sticky notes with my free hand. "I've been busy."

"Did you find out who's orchestrating this little tourney?"

A hint of scorn laced Matt's words, and I knew the only reason he wove that into his question was to remind me of his frustration that I came here. It also made me realize I should've known better than to answer the phone. I should have stuck to my guns and ignored the incoming calls. If I had, I would have owed him a small favor, though the size was rapidly increasing with every question. I pulled my hand off the suitcase, revealing a deck of cards.

Of course, this was the one question I didn't want to answer. And with the directness of his inquiry, my mind raced. Frantically, it searched for partial truths Matt might believe. Matt had been wary of the need to have an invitation or a recommendation to come to this tournament. Despite getting my hands on an invite, though secondhand, Matt considered this to be nothing more than an unnecessary risk. Ultimately, I had overruled his objection, citing my need to test my skills in the tournament.

It didn't matter to me who was pulling all the strings. The access I had to the invitation presented me with an opportunity to test my skills with an array of highly skilled players. Unfortunately, I'd stopped taking Matt's calls when I figured out who was orchestrating this tournament. While I didn't care about this individual's involvement, I knew how Matt would react upon hearing the organizer's name. Or rather, I suspected. He'd either try guilting me out of the tournament, or he'd catch a redeye flight down to New Orleans and drag me back to the airport.

Given the long waiting list for this game, I could walk away without insulting anyone. But I wanted to remain, despite the man in charge. And it wasn't because of the prize. While that amount of money was enticing, I didn't need it, considering my ability to make more. No, the real reason I stayed was simply the allure of the challenge. I needed to confirm my skills, and going to local casinos didn't present me with ample opportunities to flex my skills, especially since it was getting harder to find games back home.

"You know, I haven't quite been able to track—"

"Not a chance Marcus! Who's running this tournament of yours? I also know that's why you've been ignoring my calls. So spill. Who are you going to annoy on this trip?"

That was quite a mental leap for Matt to make. There was no way he could know what I knew. "Excuse me—"

"Don't play games with me, Marcus!"

And there goes the hope I could skate around the truth. There was real ire in his voice now.

CHAPTER 1

"Not with me! You only beat around the bush like this when you KNOW exactly what you need to say, but, for whatever reason, you're unwilling to say it. Now spit it out."

Resigned that I tread upon a field of land mines, I took the time to prepare myself for the ordeal. With a long pull of air, I wove through some of the more obvious placements of potential pitfalls. "From what I have seen through my surveillance equipment and the rumors swirling about the tournament, my guess is that Dempsey is the puppeteer."

The lie here allowed for the possibility I was wrong about the puppeteer's identity. Hopefully, I'd rooted it in enough truth for it to slip past his notice. After a few moments of tense silence, I scratched behind an ear. When had Matt mellowed out like this? While it would mark a substantial improvement in his personality, there was no way he was this calm. With a twinkle in my eye, I pulled my phone away from my ear. Though my flittering smile soured when I saw the numbers continue to increase. For a second, I'd thought the call had dropped. Had I sent him into cardiac arrest or something? Why was he so silent? As I brought the phone back to my ear, Matt finally broke his silence.

"What in the name of all that's good and holy would convince you that walking into that tournament is a good idea?"

I yanked the phone away from my head as fast as I could, but it barely helped. I hadn't realized the speakers on this phone were so powerful or that Matt had that type of lung capacity. With my eardrum ringing, I latched upon the only positive aspect from his tirade. Matt had accepted the embellished truth. It wasn't much, but under the circumstances, I would take whatever he offered.

While his temper was a potential issue, he never remained irate for long. If I let him vent, I might have a decent conversation with him afterward. As the stream of words tumbled out of the phone, I was pretty sure he failed to notice the sound of it crashing into the carpet. As the harsh syllables reached my ears, I grabbed the camera and sighed when I saw a slightly different, unmoving image. Of course, during this conversation, something happened. Why was that a universal truth?

I had been watching the feed for almost three days and had seen nothing. It was entirely possible Dempsey's minions had completed all the prep work, if any, prior to my arrival. However, I'd hoped to see something, anything, that could provide me with an edge against my opponents. As I silently cursed over missing something, I realized Matt's voice no longer teased my ears. With a groan, I eased the camera down and plucked the phone off the floor. When had he stopped talking?

"Marcus, answer me!"

I was so frustrated with Matt's demand that a growl emanated from my throat. Given the phone's potential volume, I kept it a good six inches from my ear. "You realize folks in the surrounding rooms, and maybe the next hotel, could hear you, right?"

"Answer me!"

Another growl filled the room as my fingers whitened around the phone. "There is no reason to shout like that. And on top of the damage you're inflicting on my eardrum, I think you made me miss something on the video feed."

"No! You don't get to change the topic that easily, Marcus! I know you. You're planning to run some kind of game on Dempsey."

"No, I'm not."

"Don't lie to me! And don't think about poking the bear. Dempsey isn't just some local thug like you typically push around. The man owns almost everything and everyone east of the Mississippi and south of the district."

Because this conversation would determine Matt's upcoming

CHAPTER 1

choice, I couldn't blow him off. And given its potentially incriminating nature, I wouldn't transfer the call to the speaker. So I turned the volume down a little. When he cooled off and I couldn't hear him, I'd ratchet it back up. This was the reaction I had expected, though my original plans involved having it after the tournament. Either way, I took a deep breath and launched into an altered version of my well-rehearsed speech.

"Matt, you know the story, and that's all it is. While I'm sure Dempsey's influence is substantial, I am also sure it's been exaggerated."

"Really?"

"We've done it to boost our credibility."

"We're not in the same league."

I massaged my forehead as my eyes closed. "It's a common play to stoke wild rumors. Besides, even if, and I cannot stress that word enough, he was controlling an empire of that size. You remember who he engineered this tournament for, right?"

"Not the point."

"Have you forgotten how I got my invite?"

"You swindled it."

"The spoiled rich kid from one of our longer cons. When we finished with him, he just got the gilded invite and unfortunately couldn't raise the funds for the game. Thankfully, we bonded over poker, and he handed me his invitation. While I'm sure Dempsey will have a couple of goons and card sharks mixed in with the attendees, the majority will be like our friend, a gullible kid with money to burn.

"After all, who else can afford to throw that kind of money away on something like this? Now, also keep in mind that those very kids are by their nature not the most tight-lipped. They don't truly understand what they've received. Most of those people think money grows on trees. Dempsey has to know that this would eventually spill over and become known. I wouldn't be surprised if the local police knew about the tournament. Though I'm pretty sure they won't know where it is until after the fact.

"And one more fact for you to chew on. According to the kid who gave me his invite, this is an annual occurrence. Now, armed with all these tidbits, we can safely assume that Dempsey views these attendees as walking, talking piggy banks. Wouldn't you agree?"

"There's some truth to what you're saying."

"Then why did you jump down my throat?"

"Because you constantly flaunt your abilities while you're playing poker, especially when you're losing."

My friend liked to circle back to the handful of times I'd altered cards to ensure I won the last hand of the night. My forefinger rubbed my temple as a sigh tumbled past my lips. "If the orchestrator of the tournament thinks of these people as portable banks, what's wrong with me having the same assumption? Keep in mind, while Dempsey can break the little, well, in this case, I should say large piggy banks. If he does, do you think he'd be able to revisit them every year?"

"No."

"Exactly! Besides, nothing I'm bringing was made through my transformations or purchased from a use of my gift." I dropped my hand on the cards, holding it there for a moment before pulling it away, revealing a pair of sunglasses. Picking them up, I slipped the cheap shades onto my face and chuckled. "This is just a simple tournament, and you know that I'm more than a fair hand at hold 'em."

As I sat there waiting for Matt's reply, a sudden chill ran up my spine. Was he simply gearing up for another verbal assault?

CHAPTER 1

But that would be out of character for him. Then I remembered I'd turned the volume way down. So I cranked it back up and caught the tail end of his response. "—cut and run."

With what I'd already gleaned, it wasn't difficult to fill in the missing context. I pulled the sunglasses from my face and held them up. Instantly, the hunk of plastic contorted and formed into a metal pen. I twirled it through my fingers as I stared into the wall. "Listen Matt, you're worrying too much."

"No, I'm not! You aren't as talented as you think you are."

"That's not fair."

"Marcus, your skills only take you partway up the hill. You only win the battles because you use your gift to alter the occasional card. While you can skirt the issue with the local tables by the skin of your teeth. In a real casino with cameras on the cards, you'd be arrested so fast your head would spin. Though if you don't use your gift, you'd be bounced from the table as soon as the dealer collected your last chip. You can't keep relying on luck to avoid the trouble you're due."

"I'm better than you realize."

"No, you're not."

Clenching the pen in my fist, my lips pulled into a perfect line as I counted to ten. When I finished, I kicked off my shoes and socks and paced across the industrial carpet. While it wasn't soothing, there was something oddly distracting from the uniform, stiff strands of carpet tickling my feet. "Would it make you feel any better if I told you that Dempsey doesn't use cameras on his tables either?"

The rough scoff answered his question as succinctly as possible. As my sigh died, I bumped my fist against the television stand. "From the facts I've been able to dig up, when he first started this thing, yes, his tables were equipped with cameras.

However, five years ago, he stopped using those at the request of the participants."

"Are you telling me the crime lord bent his knee to anyone beneath him?"

"Why not, when your banks say they'll stop coming if he didn't rescind the use of the cameras?"

"How did you find any of this out?"

When I reached the door, I rolled to my toes and spun around. "A combination of the guy who's invite I used and his friends. They were more than happy to divulge plenty of information, though most of it wasn't particularly helpful."

"Just because he stopped doesn't mean he can't or won't bring them back."

"Matt, you just have to trust me. I'll be fine. Besides, I'll fit the part of a spoiled rich kid." As my words hung in the air, I bit my lower lip, mentally hoping his curiosity would latch onto that crumb.

"Yeah? And just how are you going to manage that?"

The resignation behind this question told me that while he was still reluctant to change the topic, he knew I would never back down and withdraw from the tournament. He didn't like it, but he accepted it was my decision. A decision I would probably pay for later.

"You'd be surprised just how far you can go with one million dollars, despite needing to keep half for my fee."

"You looted a million dollars on your trek down to New Orleans?"

Hopefully, his interest in that feat would be enough to hold his attention, especially since I'd only been on the road for a couple of weeks. As the words rebounded about my brain, I dissected the tones Matt used. While I could tell he was impressed with what

CHAPTER 1

I'd done, the disapproval of my choice lingered. He was still hung up on Dempsey's involvement. While I wanted to scream at him to forget the mob boss, I knew pushing him on this wouldn't go well for me.

Contrary to his assumption, I had earned the money on this trip. While I'm willing to attend Dempsey's tournament, I'm not stupid enough to try to fleece him with illicit money. So I'd stopped at casinos every night and built my nest egg. Granted, with all the jobs and cons Matt and I have pulled, we had enough money available to pay the fee and deck me out like any spoiled rich kid. However, every dollar had been linked to a use of my gift.

"Matt, not a single penny of what I currently have was the fruit of an illicit act."

"What about transformed goodies?"

A rough chuckle seeped through my lips as I continued pacing the length of the hotel room. I wouldn't have begrudged Matt the question if I hadn't just precluded it. Technically, I hadn't been explicit, but I considered those things to fall into the same bucket as an illegal act. Technically, the only thing that had to be real was my entrance fee. If there was anything wrong with my funds, Matt wouldn't get the chance to tell me I told you so.

Everything else was fair game to supplement with my gift, but where's the fun in that? Besides, it gave me a chance to hone my skills. And with all that work, I had earned enough cash to complete the ensemble, everything from the suit to the suitcase for my entrance fee and everything in between. I sauntered over to the closet and ran my fingers under the suit's lapel. "Aside from the funds used to start the nest egg, everything I have now is nice and clean, including the handmade silk suit that I'll be wearing."

"Silk?"

I pushed the charcoal gray suit aside and pulled out the shirt.

"It was worth the money, not to mention the time required to have it made. Same with the shirt. Silk is a luxurious fabric."

"How fancy do you plan on getting?"

"Just the shirt and suit," I said, as I rehung the shirt in the closet. "I have other important accessories like a fancy set of cuf-flinks, a fancy watch, and a truly expensive pair of leather shoes."

"Aren't you going a little overboard?"

I tapped the shoes resting on the shelf and shook my head. "As a spoiled rich kid, there's a certain image I need to maintain."

"Does that include your car?"

With a broad grin, I sauntered over to the nightstand and grabbed the keys as a soft, warm chuckle filled my suite. "That was an odd experience."

"What?"

I tossed the keys into the air and caught them as they fell. "I'm pretty sure this is the first car that I've actually ever legally purchased."

Matt's laughter mingled with mine as I tossed the key onto the second bed.

"That fact is as equally interesting as it is disturbing."

"Isn't it?" I pressed the phone to my shoulder with my head as I pulled my wallet out of my back pocket. I cracked it open and thumbed through the contents. "Given my role, I needed to get used to their behavior."

"Wait a second. What are you talking about?"

"The role I've slipped into requires me to hand out money like water. Since that's not something I normally do, I needed some practice, hence the car."

Another round of laughter drifted through the phone as my fingers continued to search through the money and scraps of paper in my swollen wallet.

CHAPTER 1

"What's so funny?" I asked as I withdrew what I'd been searching for.

"What was her name?"

Taken aback by his question, I tossed my wallet onto the mattress and laid the paper next to me. My tongue ran across my teeth while I ordered my thoughts and fought my swirling emotions. "What are you talking about?"

Unfortunately, I wasn't able to keep it from cracking ever so slightly.

"If you won't tell me her name, at least tell me you got her phone number."

For the briefest of moments, a dark corner of my mind wished we were still talking about Dempsey. Then I seized that foolish portion of myself and clubbed it into submission. I tossed the pen onto the bed. Instantly, it expanded, reforming the laminated document from the nightstand. Why would any part of me prefer to dwell on that piece of our conversation? Matt knew that there were only a handful of topics that I considered off limits with him, just a handful. And my love life, or lack thereof, was one of them. There were some things that we simply didn't need to share. He knew this would get under my skin, and I knew he was already trying to get payback.

"Who said the dealer was a woman?"

"Yeah and . . ."

A soft growl silenced Matt's thought. As the resulting silence lengthened, I cleared my throat. "Move on, Matt."

"So after spending all that money, you failed to get her number. No wonder you're a little cranky."

He clicked his tongue, and I could hear the glee in his voice. Unable to restrain myself any longer, I released a pent-up sigh as I pulled the paper up and studied Robin's brief message and number, written in clean, crisp lines. Given the rest of the conversation, it was better to allow Matt to pursue his faulty assumption. "If you're just going to give me grief—"

As if on cue, Matt broke in, satisfaction dripping from his every word. "You didn't need to acquire a new suit. You possess a few stock ones in your closet."

"Therin lies the issue," I said, laying Robin's information beside the room's phone. "What self-respecting, spoiled young adult wears something mass produced, if they have the money?"

"Someone with fiscal maturity."

I quashed the budding laughter as I rolled to my feet and once more sauntered the length of the suite. As the last chuckle forced its way out, I rounded the corner into the bathroom and stared into my eyes. "Are you asking me to model my life off unicorns?"

"You and your stupid challenges," Matt said, before blowing air through his lips.

I didn't think he was taunting me, but I also knew I was getting awfully close to the end of his patience. "What's wrong with pushing past your limits?"

"If you keep foolishly pushing up against people, eventually, you're going to end up on the wrong side of your quest to prove your worth."

"What's the point of life if you don't stretch yourself both mentally and physically?"

"Forget it, Marcus. We've had this debate countless times. I yield! Though I'm begging you to start taking the path of least resistance."

As I pinched my phone to my shoulder, I turned on the faucet and put a cupped hand under the stream of cold water. Once it spilled over my fingers, I threw it into my face. I turned the water off and grabbed a towel to soak up the liquid clinging to me. "Don't forget that my taking these challenges normally nets us with the greatest reward."

"Not the point."

"I can't walk away from this."

"Well, since I won't be able to talk you out of this nonsense," Matt said, all joviality draining from his voice, "can you at least tell me that your reconnaissance has been going well?"

When the towel fell onto the countertop, I turned off the light, sauntered back to the bed, and grabbed the camera. As I stared into the screen, I mentally reviewed what I'd seen over the last couple of days. Unfortunately, aside from the motion that teased my eyes earlier, it was an exercise in futility. It was unfortunate I was only able to get eyes from the single vantage point. I should have returned to drop another, but the men guarding the building were intimidating.

While only one of them interacted with me, it was enough. Afterward, I was able to pick out more of them. From the way they carried themselves, I knew each of them had exceptional training. They also managed to steer everyone away from the building while not making it obvious that's what they were doing. And they didn't discriminate. In addition to the spoiled-rich-boy persona I'd developed, I'd refreshed my homelessness persona, only to have my efforts wasted.

Typically, everyone leaves the homeless alone, and I planned to use that guise to plant a few of my surveillance cameras. With my skills, I simply needed to touch the building, and presto, my system would be embedded. Not only would I have been able to keep tabs on the comings and goings of Dempsey's employees, but also on what happened within. Unfortunately, when I tried to get close enough to place my first transformation, the guard materialized out of thin air.

Well, he didn't actually "materialize," that would have been quite the trick, but it certainly felt like he had. If he hadn't been carrying that rather enormous and lethal-looking firearm, I might have tried to place another somewhere else along the wall. But with the threat of impending death, I contented myself with a simple perimeter search, turning up a single entrance. The only visible door inside the building was next to its loading dock. Disheartened, I placed a camera pointing at the entrance before I gradually made my withdrawal.

I eased the camera back onto the bed and arched my back, resulting in a series of small cracks. "I think I saw the first movement since I created the feed while we were talking."

"What do you mean, you think?"

"It's hard to be definitive when you're consuming my attention."

"I must not have heard you correctly."

This time, the furious tones were clear in his reply.

"The Marcus I know wouldn't be so incredibly stupid as to even consider walking into an illegal poker game in some random warehouse without having secured ample video footage!"

Yup, zero to fight in less than a second. I was too tired for this, physically and mentally. Normally, I don't mind arguing with Matt. It can be fun, or as I like to see it, something to be overcome. But the renewed vigor in his voice told me that if I let this go on, fun would be the last thing gained from this conversation.

The game was tomorrow. I needed to rest and clear my mind. Again, I wondered why I had picked up the phone in the first place. But then, I already knew the answer to the question. I had felt guilty. Sighing, I made the argument I knew would get me out of this discussion, not that I was proud of what I was going to do.

CHAPTER 1

"Matt, where did you think a game like this was going to be played? Did you think an invitation-only poker game would happen in some rented office space? There is a reason I set up surveillance on the building." I had to be very careful not to confirm the lack of good surveillance. "No alcohol has passed through my lips for days. I know what I'm voluntarily getting myself into. I will be fine. Okay?"

"Was that supposed to be a hint?"

And like that, the fight was gone. Matt had resigned himself to the coming events. I must have sounded angrier than I thought because I have rarely heard him give up an argument so quickly. It made me feel like a heel, and there was no reason. I drew the curtain aside and stared out upon the sprawling cityscape. "I wasn't trying to be heavy-handed."

"But you'll use whatever you're dealt. Is that what you're saying?"

Either it worked or he knew what I was doing and let it pass for the moment. Fortunately, it didn't matter. "Something like that. Hey, I'm not expecting quality cell service during the game, so I'll call you when it's all over. And, when I get back, dinner will be my treat, so pick your favorite restaurant and meal."

"Sounds like a deal. Just do me a favor."

"What can I do?"

"Don't transform any of the cards you're dealt. I've enjoyed our friendship far too long to see it end at Dempsey's hands. Besides, I want that dinner."

A smile spread across my lips as his words settled into my mind, biting back the pithy retort swirling in the depths of my mind. I was ready for the conversation to end. "Would a promise not to perform any serious mischief satisfy you?"

"That's not the same thing. Remember what I said; this isn't some back-alley game, this is Dempsey you're dealing with. If you flex your abilities, you'll wind up in trouble, and you know it."

"Matt, he's not arrogant enough to make any of the attendees disappear without justification. Remember, they can afford to pay his entrance fee. He would rather keep them alive so that they will keep coming back for more."

"Marcus, you don't need to win."

While it sounded like a plea, his words were hollow. He was simply laying more groundwork to throw in my face later, if things fell apart. Any fire that had been coursing through his words was now gone. The curtain fell as I drew my thumb across my nose. "I'll see you when I get back, my friend."

And just like that, the call ended. There had been no last good-bye. No wish for luck, just the silence that comes when someone hangs up. Had I pushed him too far this time? Could this be the straw that broke the camel's back? No, I was reading too much into his momentary depression. Matt always got right back up and was stronger than ever. Once I won the tournament, I'd go home, and we'd spend the next two months plotting our next mark and having fun. At least once he got his revenge.

Besides, Matt was worrying about problems that would never come to pass. I would be very surprised if Dempsey showed up at the tournament. More than likely the game would be managed by some trusted lackey. Not that the possibility of his presence hadn't crossed my mind, but after thinking it through, it didn't make sense he'd attend the tournament. After all, with his sup-posed empire, he'd have more important things to attend to.

That thought reminded me of the halfhearted promise I had given Matt. I knew he had wanted more, but there was no way I'd handicap myself like that, not when I wasn't entirely certain what I was walking into. There were going to be too many goons, some obviously armed, others not so obvious, in that warehouse. And I would not enter a building like that unless I could defend myself. It just wasn't going to happen. Though truthfully, I was determined to win the game, no matter what.

I plopped into the serviceable chair beside the bed and resumed watching the video feed, trying to force the conversation from my mind. But after several fruitless minutes, I realized there was nothing to gain by continuing, not live anyway. Double checking there was enough memory for the night, I placed the camera onto the simple table and placed a hand on my rumbling stomach.

I rose from the chair and hopped over the bed and grabbed the phone. While I needed to keep my wits about me, I'll admit he was right about that, I needed something to occupy my mind. So I grabbed the hotel's menu off the bed and perused the options, selecting a meal catching my interest and what I believed would be a complementary cocktail. With my choices in mind, I picked up the phone and placed the order.

CHAPTER 2

With the steaming plate of eggs, bacon, sausage, toast, and biscuits arrayed before me, I drew in a sample of the mingling aromas. Instantly, my mouth watered as I rubbed my hands together. A slow breath rushed through my lips as I tore into my breakfast, slathering the first piece of buttered toast with strawberry jam. After biting into the sweet and creamy goodness, I sped through the last remaining footage of the previous night.

When I caught up to the live feed, I popped the last bit of toast into my mouth. And with that, I'd confirmed nothing had happened with the building in the last seventy-two hours, give or take a few. As the worthless feed continued mocking me, I pulled the plate laden with eggs closer to me and began slicing through them, spilling the yolks across the porcelain surface. With a false grin, I ripped a biscuit in half and sighed.

I dipped the fluffy bit of bread into the yellow pool, scooping up a small portion of it. As two thin streams raced for the impromptu utensil's edge, I shoved the laden morsel into my mouth, smiling as the buttery flakes of biscuit melded with the richness of the yolk. While my tastebuds were enjoying the complex flavors, I made a mental note to encourage Matt to choose a steak house for that dinner.

Despite being presented with worthless footage, I made sure I

CHAPTER 2

skimmed every second, even the bit I thought was going to provide me with a brief insight. Unfortunately, the supposed motion I saw while talking with Matt was nothing more than a trick of the light. Chasing that simple illusion cost me some sleep, but it shouldn't affect me too much. When the last bit of the egg and biscuits tumbled down my mouth, I grabbed a piece of bacon. Between bites of the crispy strip, I witnessed the first signs of movement.

The warehouse door swung open, and six men marched out, carrying a collapsable table and folding chairs. I dropped the remaining bit of bacon and leaned forward, licking my fingertips as I studied them. Where had they come from? Did Dempsey convert a portion of the building into a barracks? After a few moments, I dismissed those questions and others as foolish. In the end, it didn't matter if he'd converted a small section into a temporary home for some of his men. More importantly, it meant he'd already stocked the building with everything needed for the tournament.

As I chased the looming questions from my mind, the only one that lingered concerned their apparel. Even though anyone could have a nice suit, these employees were exceptionally well dressed. While they wore formal clothing, none of them could pull off the look. Given the quality of their garments, it was apparent they didn't dress like this normally. However, despite wearing unfamiliar clothing, they quickly arranged the table, the accompanying chairs, and even a miniature bookshelf I'd missed under the direct supervision of the largest lackey. Given the man's brutish stature, it was fairly evident how he'd risen in Dempsey's ranks.

The aroma wafting up from my remaining breakfast teased me, but I couldn't rip my eyes away from the flurry of motion. While this footage simply created new questions, it was a far cry more than what I'd had when I woke. When the formally dressed thugs finished their work, four of them walked back inside, leaving their supervisor and another block of muscle behind to wait, presumably for the attendees. They promptly sat down and started talking to each other.

Instantly, I slapped my forehead. One of these days, I was going to have to figure out how to add audio to this system. But in the meantime, I had a few things to take care of before heading out. I quickly wolfed down the last of my meal and promptly took a hot shower before removing the stubble from my face. As I slipped into my persona and the accompanying ensemble, I reviewed the footage, grinning when I confirmed Dempsey's doormen were the only people there.

While I slipped the cufflinks into my shirt, the first attendee stepped into view. In stark contrast to Dempsey's men, this fellow knew how to wear his immaculate suit. From his haircut to his shoes, this man oozed money. As I watched him interact with the doormen, a low whistle sliced through the suffocating silence. My hand reached for the briefcase containing my entrance fee. When my fingers brushed the luxurious leather, I was glad I had insisted on purchasing something gaudy to carry the fee.

By the time I finished getting ready, a dozen attendees arrived, and I watched the same repetitive script. The player would step up to the table and offer their fee to the muscle on the right, while they addressed the seemingly brash supervisor. After a brief exchange, he would rise and lumber around the table to pat down each guest, male or female. Obviously, Dempsey wanted to ensure his people held the metaphorical higher ground.

With a halfhearted laugh, I shoved everything into place and left the room. "It's time to get started."

As I rounded the corner of the warehouse, Dempsey's doormen locked eyes with me, sending a shiver down my spine. I

CHAPTER 2

wanted to stop and study both sets of eyes, but given who I was pretending to be, I rolled my head and strolled toward them. When I reached the table, I placed my gaudy briefcase onto the sturdy plastic table, gripping the handle with both hands.

Despite not studying their gazes, I was able to survey their body language. Even though I noted their unease from the video in person, that discomfort was amplified. And after another second's scrutiny, the quality of their garments snapped into focus. The feed had provided me with enough details that I knew their clothing was exceptional, but standing before both, I realized how immaculate their tuxedos were. While it's true, the addition of formal wear will elevate anyone, there are some like these two hulking brutes who should stick to wearing simple suits. It wasn't worth the expense to reach for this level of quality.

As a silence wound amongst us, I dismissed the trappings these two men wore. Like me, they were playing a part. Unlike me, the only layer for their guise was their clothing. In all honesty, I don't think there was any danger that'd fool anyone. Their harshness bled through their disguise with every motion. No one would confuse these brutish thugs for gentlemen. Don't get me wrong, the clothing did wonders to obfuscate a lot. But every motion promised they were not only ready but more than capable of inflicting harm in an instant. There wasn't enough finery in the world to camouflage these two as anything other than what they were. These gentle thugs proved my point about anyone owning a nice suit.

The man to my left shrugged, and the motion threatened to rip the sleeves from his coat. "This is a private event. Without an invitation, you'll have to leave."

"I have one," I said, reaching into my coat.

In the blink of an eye, both men produced guns, thrusting them toward me.

I'm loathed to admit it, but in that moment a squeak filled the air, and I was the source of the undignified sound. As I forced my lungs to draw in a fresh breath, my eyes started flickering between the firearms as I kept my hand where it was. "I'm reaching for my invitation."

"Make sure that's all you're doing," the supervisor said as he rose to his feet.

With a nod, my fingertips clenched the corner of the fancy cardstock. It took what felt like an hour to pull it out of my coat. But once it was free, the man snatched it from me and examined it. "I know who this belongs to, and you're not him."

"He signed his invite over to me."

The large man grunted as he holstered his pistol and plucked the folio off the table. "What's your name?"

"Marcus."

He grumbled something under his breath as he flipped through the pages, while his companion kept his gun trained on my forehead. After another subjective eternity, the supervisor stabbed the folio with his finger. He tossed it onto the table and waved at his companion, prompting him to lower his weapon. "You're on the list."

"That's a good thing." I licked my lips as I brushed off my clean shoulder. "Is this a normal hello for attendees?"

"Only those I don't know." The thug leaned forward, letting the stale, earthy scent of his breath wash over me. "Or people I don't trust. It just so happens that you fall into both categories." The supervisor straightened as he jerked a thumb over his shoulder. "Now pay your fee. Or are we going to have trouble after all?"

As I pushed the briefcase toward the other man, I shook my head. "Why don't you trust me?"

"I don't know you." The lead man said, blending gentleness

and ferocity in a way I'd never heard before. "Now, put your hands on the table."

As the words tunneled into my brain, another shudder raced down my back. While I didn't like the idea of him patting me down, I had a fairly good idea what would happen if I refused his command. So I shook my hands and placed them on the table's edge. "Do you think I'd be foolish enough to come here armed?"

"What you think doesn't affect my job," the man said as he stepped behind me. Without waiting, his hands flew up and down my body. When he brushed my pants pockets, a hand clamped around my neck as he reached inside. "What's this?"

"I carry a lot in there," I said, prying at the thick fingers squeezing my neck. "You'll have to be more specific."

"We don't have to accept your fee." The supervisor's grip tightened as he breathed down my neck. "And trust me when I tell you, it won't be conducive to your health to find out what happens then."

"Why would you reject it?" I asked as I continued my futile attempt to free myself.

The gentle thug withdrew the item from my pocket and placed it in my face. "What's this?"

My eyes locked onto my secret weapon, and I mentally cursed at the supervisor's attention to detail. A different thug might have recognized the device as an oddity and waved me through. Yet this one wanted to know more about it. I yanked the small device from his grasp and shoved it back into my pocket. "It's an electronic hand warmer. Would you like to borrow it?"

The supervisor shoved my neck as he lumbered back to his chair. He folded his hands and leaned forward with eyes dripping with white, fiery rage. "Why do you have it?! It's a pleasant enough day. And once inside, you won't need it!"

The toneless words were impressive. While he'd put some force behind his words, the malice from his eyes hadn't tinged his response. I rolled my shoulders and readjusted my jacket. As I flirted with studying the supervisor's eyes, I plucked the first comfortable misdirection from my mind. "Sometimes my body has trouble regulating itself, and I suffer from chills. It can happen on a dime, and that helps keep me warm."

The gentle thug leaned into his chair as he crossed his arms. "Really?"

For anyone else, a hand warmer would be nothing special. But for me, it was like a triple shot of espresso laced with amphetamines. Fortunately, since I'd never met anyone with my gift, it was unlikely any of Dempsey's lackeys would know why it was such a powerful tool. "It's a condition I've had since childhood. And while it's gotten better over the years, it seems to crop up at the most inconvenient times. So I've learned never to leave home without a few of these."

The gentle thug turned his hands toward the sky and offered me a false smile. "I'm sorry, sir, but I'm required to be thorough."

I shoved my hands into my pockets as I forced my lips to twist into a warm smile. "Everyone must work with the constraints of their job. Are we good?"

A chortle tore through the budding silence as the supervisor looked over his shoulder. "Is everything there?"

"To the penny," the other gentle thug said, sliding my briefcase onto the miniature bookshelf.

My gaze drifted to the door as I rubbed my neck. "Are you satisfied with your search?"

"Our employer isn't the most trusting individual," the supervisor said, folding his hands on the table. "Which means neither are we. I mentioned this earlier, but if we don't know you, there's

CHAPTER 2

no way we can trust you. Though even if you become trusted, we always verify that trust."

While the supervisor's words dripped with that odd blend of gentleness and ferocity, the gentle side of the blend was waning. I doubted anyone ever dared insult or question him, and I'd done the latter. And with a man like this, there was always a reckoning. As I studied his eyes, I saw two swirling forces battling each other. The first was his desire to teach me how to respect him, while the other factor was his loyalty to Dempsey. Luckily, his leash would keep that initial motive checked.

With a glare that could slice steel, he rose to his feet and leaned over the table, shoving his face into mine. "Your fee has been accepted, sir. Welcome to the game."

The second thug opened the door. "Right this way, sir."

I stepped into the doorway and turned to face the two gentle thugs and bowed my head. "Thank you both for the pleasant conversation, not to mention your attention to detail." Before they could respond, I spun about and dashed through the darkening hallway.

CHAPTER 3

The moment I pushed through the inner door, my feet stopped moving, and I barely managed to keep myself from kissing the floor. Before claiming my spot in this tournament, I had researched the location, and while I thought it odd Dempsey would select a warehouse for his walking piggy banks to gather, the gentleman whose invite I'd commandeered assured me it wouldn't interfere with the experience. Based on his assurance, I had assumed the crime lord would spruce up the interior, but I hadn't expected this. I had expected to see the stereotypical aesthetics of a warehouse.

Or rather, what television and movies have made me think of as typical. Where were the unfinished walls and an endless array of shelves with their uniform wooden crates? It would have been easy for Dempsey's minions to move everything to the side and set up the required tables. If that was all Dempsey's team had done, it would have been fine. While it would be far from comfortable, we could play like that.

However, the elite who could afford to be here wouldn't have been as agreeable to the arrangement. I'd just underestimated the lengths the crime lord would take to ensure his portable banks would be happy and willingly return to stuff his coffers. But as I stood frozen in the doorway studying everything arrayed before

CHAPTER 3

me, those assumptions died. After a few moments, I walked inside, letting the door close with a whisper. Somehow, Dempsey had created a portal leading from the industrial surroundings to the lobby of the most opulent hotel on the planet.

Even though the décor commanded most of my attention, I felt the eyes of the other players and staff linger on me. Their piercing gazes sized me up and then dismissed me, just like I would treat a mark. With a mental grimace, I forced a smile to my lips and sauntered away from the entrance, studying the people milling about the room. Given the attire of the employees gliding through the sparse crowd, Dempsey's intention for these men and women became obvious. They were here to provide another layer of opulence for his piggy banks. The crime lord certainly knew how to staff his events. Everyone served a purpose, especially the contrasting pair of doormen who welcomed me.

As I strolled past the initial collection of tables and a couple of chatty players, I realized nobody, including Dempsey's workers, thought much of my entrance. While I'd felt everyone register it, none of their body language screamed they were lingering upon it. Even the couple who were in deep conversation weren't discussing my gaff. It was as if it was the expected reaction to someone's first appearance at one of these events, and based on the door-men's reaction, everyone understood I was new here. Mentally, I released a sigh of relief as I strode through the tables, looking for an adequate place to perch and study the already-present players.

With half of the room behind me, I headed for the wall and leaned against it. My eyes flittered about the room, itemizing the extravagant trappings. After finishing the initial catalog, the only thing tumbling through my mind was Dempsey didn't understand or comprehend restraint. Each of the four walls reflected the light with a golden hue. As I drew a finger along the surface, I doubted he had achieved the color with gold paint. Rather, it felt like lacquer, and the texture appeared to be that of gold leaf. While I'd have to be too obvious to know for sure, the walls had the shiny factor you expected from precious metal. The only break in the golden chamber was the rose chair molding, which to my thumb felt like granite.

When I ripped my eyes away from the opulent walls, I started gauging distances. Based on my initial walk of the building's perimeter, I was fairly certain this room represented only half of the interior space. Perhaps my recon hadn't been as fruitless as I'd thought. What else did it give me? The only way in or out was the loading dock and entrance. Which meant that one of these golden walls, most likely the one opposite the doorframe, contained a hidden doorway, despite its nearly uninterrupted nature.

The only other embellishments to those smooth walls were a pair of bars built into each corner opposite the entrance. To highlight the elegance, the bars lined up perfectly with the exquisite molding. Aside from the opulence, the structure of this partial chamber screamed that everyone inside was trapped. This wall had more in common with a Venus flytrap than the hotel it pretended to be.

The bars, molding, and walls would have made the room comfortable for even the most pretentious member of the elite. But If Dempsey stopped there, it would have shown a semblance of restraint. Besides the luxurious surroundings, the man ensured people could wait, eat, and drink while catering to their every need. Scattered throughout were twenty-four circular tables, complete with five chairs. The man loved his stone surfaces. At least that's what the tabletops appeared to be hewn from, based on what I'd seen as I walked past a few of them. They also appeared to have been hand carved from either marble or granite and perched upon sturdy metal legs.

CHAPTER 3

As I stood there watching the elaborate motion, I watched several members of the wait staff deliver food and drinks to the scattered players sitting around the ornate tables. And judging by the collection of aromas woven through the air, Dempsey had contracted a kitchen to provide decadent meals. Given the work needed to prepare everything here, how had Dempsey made a dime on these tournaments? While he collected half a million dollars from each player, there was too much on display to justify the opulence.

After a few tranquil minutes, a couple of probing eyes drifted back my way. Immediately, I pushed off the wall and strolled to the nearest bar, plopping onto the first open stool. While one bartender worked with another guest, the second one cleaned a tumbler. I leaned forward, extending a couple of fingers as I waved at the unoccupied employee. Unfortunately, the man continued wiping down the small glass. I dropped back onto the stool to study him and saw through his guise at once. This man was not a real bartender, at least not by trade. Despite his larger frame, he fit the formal wear shared by the other man behind the bar. I raised my hand and cleared my throat.

Promptly, the faux-tender returned the glass to its place, tossed his cleaning cloth onto his shoulder, and approached me with an artificial smile. "What can I do for you?"

Based solely on his build, it was easy to lump this thug up with the two doormen. However, his warm voice belied his brutish frame. Despite possessing a pleasant demeanor, I didn't understand why Dempsey would place this man behind the bar if he wanted to pacify the high-end socialites who would be attending. Why had he stocked the bar with one of his goons? Was he as skilled with making cocktails as I imagined him to be at breaking limbs and collecting debts? I placed my elbows on the bar and leaned forward, wringing my hands. "What would you recommend?"

A blank stare latched onto me as the faux-tender scratched his head. "Excuse me, sir, but I'll need you to tell me what you'd like to drink."

Was he being serious? I ran my tongue across the back of my teeth as I hemmed and hawed. As the burly man stood there with a false smile, I scratched bartender from the list of skills. With my elbows firmly planted on the bar, I leaned forward, wrapping my spoiled rich kid persona around me. "It's my first time here, and I don't know what you have. Can't you think of something that would be an adequate starter?"

"Would you like a whisky on the rocks?"

Surprisingly, the faux-tender kept his cool. Despite my jab, small as it was, he kept his composure as he offered a suggestion. I had to give Dempsey credit. His goons appeared to be well trained, and that was not cheap. Had I been looking for a drink, I probably would have said yes, but that wasn't the point. I wanted to test his composure.

My hands started teetering up and down like a set of old-fashioned scales as I muttered gibberish. Eventually, I snapped and thrust a finger into his chest. "That might be a decent first drink on any normal day. However, today isn't a regular day. At the moment, I'm looking to try new things. Can you make me a Sazerac?"

"What was that?"

He's cracking. "A Sazerac."

The faux-tender pulled a reference guide out from under the bar and thumbed through it. After a brief search, he returned the sheets and excused himself. A few moments later, the other bartender approached, his hands cleaning a small tumbler.

"I'm sorry, sir, but we don't have everything required to make a Sazerac?"

"What are you missing?"

"The absinthe," the bartender said as he placed the clean glass beside the others. "And since you don't really want it, can I interest you in something else?"

"Are you a mind reader as well?"

"While I've heard of people who like that drink, the vast majority can't stand the hint of black licorice that comes from the absinthe."

Not only did this guy know the obscure drink's ingredients, but he also knew its flavor profile. Dempsey definitely had to be shelling out serious money to employ this fellow. Turning my hands up, I offered a genuine grin. "Bartender's choice will be more than sufficient."

With a nod, he looked me over and went to work, deftly mixing my cocktail. His hands whirled about in a state of controlled abandon. It was a mesmerizing show. When he finished, he cracked the shaker and poured the cocktail into a long-stemmed glass. As he shoved the glass toward me, he spooned a little olive brine into the glass and mixed it with a few speared olives. Then, before I could grab it, he dropped a bit of lemon peel into the glass.

"You should give the drink a moment to mellow before tasting."

I pointed at the sliver of the yellow rind. "Is this how you make martinis?"

"Everyone has their own take to the drink," the bartender said as he cleaned his tools. "It should be ready to drink."

I picked up the glass and gave it a cursory inspection before taking the first sip. I let the alcohol flow over my tongue as I absorbed the flavors. This was without a doubt one of the best martinis, if not the very best, I'd ever tasted. If I hadn't needed a clear head, I would have drained the drink in a single gulp, but I had my priorities. With a broad smile, I carefully placed the glass down on the counter and withdrew my wallet. I thumbed through the bills and withdrew a one-hundred-dollar bill, offering it to him. To my surprise, he looked absolutely offended I offered him money of any kind.

"Sir, in case you didn't know, prior to the tournament, the bars are open. You can have as much as you'd like."

That was a useful fact. So I filed it away for future reference and did my very best to contort my face to look disgusted by the bartender's actions. But instead of arguing, I reached out and stuffed the bill into his shirt pocket. "I don't recall asking how much I owed, do you?"

The bartender nodded as I picked up my glass. The drink was truly a masterpiece. But I couldn't let the alcohol affect me. So I summoned a bit of body heat and focused on the drink. In my mind I imagined it being exactly as it was, without the intoxicants. When the image crystallized, I poured the collected warmth through the mental image. Instantly, the intoxicants were purged from the martini.

That was another excellent use of my gift. The ability to encourage people's assumptions about your sobriety was a useful edge to have. When I took another sip, my smile widened. Sometimes when I stripped the alcohol from a drink, the taste suffered. When it happened, I typically didn't mind. But if I had butchered this cocktail, while a necessity, it would have also been a tragedy.

"I didn't ask the cost of the drink because that was a tip, nothing more, nothing less."

"Thank you, sir," the bartender said, patting his pocket.

After taking another sip, I swirled the drink as I gathered the stray droplets clinging to my lips. "What's your name?"

"Simon," he said as he picked up another dirty glass. With a nod, he turned to walk down the bar.

He understood. More importantly, he accepted the burden of being the only bartender I'd use for the day. "Thank you for the drink, Simon. You're a magician with those bottles."

Just as I took another sip of the drink, a clipped voice in a thick Russian accent barked at me from just behind my right shoulder. "You know, you just make all of us look bad."

Before I could turn around to ask the man what he was talking about, another voice came to my rescue from behind my other shoulder. In contrast to the first, this voice, while smooth, had a faint accent I couldn't place. "Wrong, it only makes you stiff-necked and greedy people look bad. Personally, I see nothing wrong with that. There are those of us who are willing to tip the staff for their hard work."

The man who had leaped to my defense leaned down and asked me a question, speaking quietly enough so only I could hear him. "But between you and me, that was a hefty one. You didn't start your drinking before arriving, did you?"

I didn't need this right now. I just wanted to be left alone to enjoy my drink and continue examining the room and the other attendees. But I supposed some of the social niceties needed to be observed. With that in mind, I took another sip as I turned toward my defender. "No. I have had nothing to drink so far today. I'm just well-off, and the drink put me in a generous mood."

Even though I could tell my answer confused him, the stranger was willing to accept it. This man was truly one of societies' elite. A pompous and spoiled individual who never had to work for anything in his life. He could never understand or appreciate anything other than his desires. So I twisted my words into something he should be able to understand. "Swift service that's poor is worse than a quality service that takes ages to come to fruition."

"What does that have to do with the tip?"

I lifted my martini and flashed a broad smile. "That tip ensures that I'll have quality service that's prompt for the rest of the day."

I watched the understanding unfurl in his eyes as he matched mine, though could see his generosity wouldn't increase any time soon. From behind me, I heard a grumpy harrumph and footsteps stomping off. I turned around and caught sight of a slightly stocky gentleman heading to the other bar. Presumably to get as far away from me and my ideals as possible. Watching the man stride off, all I could think about was that this was going to be a challenging day.

As I turned back to the other gentleman, he slapped my back and pointed at the other bar. "Don't worry about Nicolai."

I spun to face him and noticed, by the look on his face, he was in the middle of a strenuous mental debate. "It's just that his wallet is tighter than an oyster's shell. He also cannot abide people who freely share their wealth, even if you had a decent reason."

With a chuckle, I looked into the man's eyes. "He's crazy. You know that, right?"

"Yes, he is, but that doesn't mean he's not a good person, mostly," the man replied as he stared off toward the other bar. Before I could respond to this apparent contradiction, he moved off and chased Nicholai's retreating form. Finally left alone, I turned my back on the bar and resumed studying the gathered players. When my eyes fell upon the mystery man speaking with Nicholai, I thought of something I should have thought of before.

CHAPTER 3

Most of whoever came would be self-centered, spoiled millionaires, which made them entitled. And that entitlement certainly made them dangerous. Just like a shark in a feeding frenzy, these children would never see past their own entitlements if I stripped away their money. I was going to have to be even more cautious than I had thought. That or Dempsey had arrangements to keep their baser desires at bay—namely, his goons. While that certainly made sense, I wished there weren't so many holes I'd ignored.

With the revelation in mind, I put a pause on studying the spoiled children and scattered professionals. I needed to know about the room I was in. Armed with the knowledge there had to be at least one door, if not a pair, I started walking along the wall, searching for the seam. As I walked along its edge, I thought about the way the room was shaped and filled out. There was another reason there had to be a door along this wall, and that was because the room was a lounge. There was no way to rearrange the tables here so we could play. Which left me asking a couple of questions. First, where were we going to play? And second, where was the door we'd end up using?

By the time I had given the wall a cursory examination, I had found nothing useful, so I could do one of two things. Either I could keep looking for the door and announce to everyone I was up to something. Or I could sit down at one of the tables and study my competition. So I quickly scanned the tables and found one positioned well enough for me to see most of the room, the occupants, and the entrance.

Within moments of claiming a seat at the empty table, a waitress came up and asked me if I needed anything. I looked down and found a mostly empty glass, so I told her I would need another martini. But before she could retreat, I told her to get it from Simon. It took me another moment to convince her it would be very beneficial for her to take the time to find my requested bartender.

As the last drops of Simon's masterpiece tumbled down my throat, I resumed my examination of the attendees. As the seconds ticked by, I instantly spotted the professionals from the spoiled children. They were the ones drinking as little as possible, and what they were drinking was soda or water. They also blatantly didn't care what the elite thought of them. In fact, the only thing they did care about was collecting the money from the rich patsies. I could tell a few of them lumped me into that category, and I didn't want to separate them from the misconception. As far as I was concerned, it would just make it easier for me to take them out of the game.

The room was just large enough people wouldn't feel cramped, even once all the players arrived. That feeling would encourage everyone, or most everyone, to spread out, which would keep me from getting a reliable read on them. Fortunately, I was a jack-of-all-trades. While I only had mastery of a couple of things, I sought to know something about most topics, especially if it had the potential to be useful. But just before I could start another trick, the waitress returned with my fresh martini. I plucked the fresh drink off her tray and flicked the rim of the glass.

I thanked her for her diligence with a fifty-dollar bill. It's amazing how easily cash can win people over. The waitress left with a warm smile. With my drink in hand, the chair beside me dragged across the floor. I turned my head to examine the intruder. As far as intruders go, I could have done much worse. The woman standing above me was quite striking.

CHAPTER 4

She looked down at me with a very warm smile, and before I could speak, her silken voice, colored with a hint of sweetness, broke the silence. "Would you mind some company?"

My fingers tightened around my martini's stem as it hovered under my nose. While the soft hints of citrus and salt tickled my nose, I purged the intoxicants from my glass, losing a trivial amount of body heat. After taking a sip of the non-offensive drink, I placed the glass on the table and clapped my hands together as I lost myself in her tranquil gray eyes. I wanted to say no. But those soft pools of gray soothed my inner voice. So I gestured at the chair she'd claimed. Besides, I could learn a lot through some friendly banter. That she was one of the more attractive women in the room was simply a bonus.

"You would be a very pleasant addition to my table."

She slipped into the chair almost before I finished speaking. While she settled into the chair, I reclaimed my martini and took another sip. My gaze followed her every twitch as she composed herself. Despite the wonderfully balanced flavors of Simon's work, she stole my attention. And it wasn't simply her striking eyes captivating me.

Given some of the more flamboyant clothing worn by the present elite, her simple garb suggested she was a professional.

The clothing had been selected for comfort, not to impress. However, that didn't mean her selection was incapable of serving both purposes. The sleeveless teal shirt was so rich that it bordered on a deep blue, which only emphasized her pale skin. Despite the lack of color, this woman wasn't sickly. Rather, it was reminiscent of a porcelain doll.

As my eyes dipped, I noted the elegant pair of gray slacks and sensible shoes. While they were more formal than a set of sneakers, you wouldn't have expected to find them on someone in this ornate waiting room. But the most shocking contrast was her strawberry-blond hair. Heavy strands cascaded over her right shoulder, landing atop her bare arm, creating a trap that would ensnare even the most hardened. As she twisted in the seat, the light reflected off her flowing locks, and I noted the slightest touch of honey to them.

I pulled my gaze away from her exposed shoulder and studied her face. It took me a couple of passes to realize she hardly wore any makeup, but what she did wear was strategically applied. Despite the subtlety, she was stunning, and more importantly, she knew how to use her looks to manipulate people. She was going to be a challenging opponent. With a silence settling in between us, she pursed her lips as her legs crossed.

I'd like to say her lures didn't affect me.

I really want to say that.

Unfortunately, that would be a lie. This mysterious woman captured my attention, and she seemed capable of wrapping me about her little finger, if that's what she wanted. With all those facts swirling about my mind, I tried to think of something clever to say. But the first thing that had popped into my mind slipped out.

"Though I hope we won't sit together when the tournament begins."

CHAPTER 4

As another silence swallowed my comment, her genuine smile wavered. And her obfuscated glare confirmed my supposition about what she could do if she put her mind to it. The icy glare coming solely from her eyes could have pinned a tank in place. And since there wasn't a metal hull protecting me, I didn't stand a chance. Her words, despite the harshness behind her eyes, were still wrapped in the cheerful tone she'd used moments ago. "So you're one of those players."

"I think you misunderstood what I was saying—"

However, she didn't seem to be all that interested in letting me finish.

"No, I understood perfectly. You don't like women intruding into your precious game." Despite the fire hidden behind her radiant smile, she kept that pleasant tone in her voice, which contrasted perfectly with her icy gaze as she pushed away from the table.

Forcing my body to relax, I shook my head and clarified my position. "Not at all. I love playing with anyone who's willing to sit at the table. I just don't like the thought of separating a beautiful woman from her money." For whatever reason, I was attempting to keep her from leaving, and it certainly helped I was being sincere, though perhaps a bit too specific. Matt and I would run scams on just about anyone, but I had a couple of guiding principles. One of them prevented me from targeting women or children. In fact, sometimes, especially when they needed help, I would enlist women or children and let them in on the take.

Early on, I needed to enforce the rule with Matt. He believed everyone was fair game. Who they were didn't matter, which meant I had to tamp down his enthusiasm from time to time. Nowadays he's mostly adopted my rules, though I could tell when he thought about going after the occasional rich woman. When those thoughts started creeping in, I took steps to present him with a better alternative, and after a spirited debate, he typically agreed.

My words must have registered with her because she froze halfway out of her chair. And her smile reasserted itself. The implied flattery probably helped as well, though I could still sense a little wariness behind those fierce eyes. After another moment of consideration, she slid back into her chair and gave me a tiny nod. "I'll assume you don't have the same sentiment for men." She paused, pursed her lips a bit, and asked, "Or ugly women?"

Nodding, I told her the rule I lived my life by. "My dear lady, men are easily parted from their money. But should anyone dare to try to part a woman from hers; that poor fool will suffer for a lifetime."

This time, she laughed as she pulled her chair forward. "Should I take your flattery as an attempt to force me off my game? Is that the kind of player you are?"

"No, the flattery was sincere. Despite the surrounding opulence, you're the most stunning thing in this room."

Ducking her head ever so slightly, she attempted to hide her blushing cheeks. She failed, of course, but since she'd made an attempt, I felt obligated to oblige her and pretended not to notice the rosy coloring that enhanced her beauty. Once her embarrassment had subsided a bit, she tilted her head back and asked, "Why not pick on women? Men can be even more vindictive than us."

Her words held a little fire. She must love arguing with people. But I could tell from her tone she was only half-heartedly pursuing the point. "For the most part, a man will be singular in his vengeance. But a woman, well now, they typically possess the imagination and the drive to truly put the fear of God into any heart. As we all know, 'Hell hath no fury like a woman scorned.'"

She smiled and lifted her finger in a chiding motion. "You have a point."

Ignoring the finger, I returned a smile as I lifted my glass in a salute.

A slender finger beckoned me closer as she asked, "So does that mean when the two of us meet at the tables that you will willingly surrender your chips to me?"

It surprised me she'd accepted my comment and thrown them back so deftly. She was quick-witted. That was not an ideal quality to find in potential opponents. I hesitated a moment, letting her see a sense of confusion on my brow. It was always prudent to lay false tells even before the first hand. "Just because I don't like to separate a woman from her money doesn't mean I'll hesitate to do so if she's insistent." I leaned back and spread my arms out as I finished my train of thought. "And I can only assume that since every woman present came willingly. Which means they're insisting I separate them from their funds."

"Smooth recovery, sir, very smooth. I applaud you."

"Thank you," I said, raising my martini and taking a small sip.

For a moment I felt her eyes examining me, trying to decide if I was worth any more of her time or if I deserved to know her name. But then the moment passed, and with that beautiful smile, she announced her decision. "My name's Bella. What's yours?"

"Marcus."

"Marcus," she said, letting my name roll across her lips, "the name suits you."

"Thank you, Bella. And I have to say it's a pleasure to share some time with someone as witty as you before the game begins."

"Thank you, but so far, the pleasure has been entirely mine."

As the martini swirled in my glass, my eyes drifted up to her gray eyes. Why would she assume that? Wasn't I smiling? Didn't

I look to be having a good time? Or was that how she disarmed her opponents? I swallowed another taste of Simon's work and licked my lips. Let's see if I can get a sense of her style of play. "That's unfortunate."

The cheerful twinkle behind her eyes vanished with a pair of words. Two innocuous words undid what the friendly banter had accomplished. Was she oblivious to her effect on people? Her gaze drifted about the room, presumably scanning other tables where she could find more stimulating conversation. "Why is that?"

She could slip between emotions about as easily as I could breathe, which was a crucial piece of knowledge to have before our upcoming battle of wits. Yet the calmness she spoke with belied the simmering rage burning behind her eyes. Was this an act? Could she be probing me, looking for how I would react? I sipped my drink, letting the martini wash over my tongue, sending subtle hints of salty citrus through me. If she was playing with me, it meant she was skilled. And given why we were here, I planned on holding onto that assumption, which meant the best next step was to pretend like I had offended her.

I swirled the dwindling drink while laying an ankle across a knee. "You're attempting to rob me of my pleasure from meeting you."

Her responding chuckle was as equally forced as it was genuine. She must not have expected my response. With a smile, I placed my drink on the table and leaned forward, propping my chin on my folded hands. "I'm sorry if you took my previous comment the wrong way. However, let us dwell on better topics."

"Such as?"

"Your simple name does nothing to highlight or enhance your beauty."

Her reaction was another sign she was incredibly skilled. It took a lot of practice to alter all the little details that could betray your thoughts. Somehow, she managed to hit them all. From tamping down the brewing storm behind her gray eyes to letting the corners of her mouth drift up. Dropping her hands into her lap, a solitary eyebrow rose as she leaned forward, speaking in a whisper. "You're aware that the name comes from an Italian word that means beautiful, right?"

"That's news to me," I said as a laugh teased my lips.

Her eyes bulged hearing my confession. Her back fell into the chair's embrace as she raised her hand. "You're either a brilliant flirt—"

"Or?"

"The luckiest man alive who continues to stumble into the right words to appease my growing anger."

"Did you think I was going to say something else?"

With a wry smile, she laid her arms across her chest. "Marcus, Marcus, Marcus. We've only just met. Is there any way I could have drawn that conclusion?"

"Have I been rude?"

She laid her hands on her lap as she leaned against the table. "The day's still young. Though you have been making the most pleasant contradictions, I guess I should have had a slight clue. But do you know what you've shown yourself to be an expert at?"

I swirled my martini as a slow smile spread across my lips. "Please tell me what I've let slip."

Her lips curled into a devious grin as she shrugged. "You've shown yourself capable of provoking powerful emotions from me, despite having never met me." Her eyes drifted away as her fingers clenched. "That's gotta be the basis of your play."

"Well, you're not going to get a confirmation out of me that easily," I said, placing my glass on the table. I pressed my fingers on the bottom of the glass and slowly spun it around as I studied her profile. "However, you'd have to provide me with some context so I can know if eliciting those feelings is something I'd regret."

"How can it be a good thing?" Bella's back straightened as her face hardened. "I only see that being a detriment for you."

I took another sip of my delightful cocktail, letting a momentary silence blossom. With an explosive sigh, I leaned into the chair's grasp and unleashed a playful smile. "Given that you're still here, I must have done something smart to captivate your attention. Wouldn't you agree?"

"Touché," Bella said, covering her face with her hands. "But what makes you think that's a good impression? Perhaps I'm trying to investigate the competition."

Unfortunately, or fortunately, depending on her motives, her slight fingers couldn't prevent me from seeing the rosy hue bloom across her face. Given the gambit of emotions I'd seen, I figured some of them were real, but I needed confirmation.

"The fact that you're still here." As the words hung in the air, I drained my drink. I placed the empty glass on the table and waved a finger at her. "You appear willing to just get up and leave if someone offends you. And while some of my words appeared to have done just that, you're still sitting with me. Besides that, you also accused me of being filled with pleasant contradictions."

"That's a lot of supposition. It doesn't mean much."

"True," I said, laying an arm on the table. "You could have joined me, hoping that I'd either prattle on or you could encourage me to do so. All the while looking for any potential tidbit to wield against me in the tournament."

"Are you dismissing that valid option?"

"Certainly not. People can achieve multiple goals during any action." Her slight cough, paired with her darting eyes, confirmed a portion of my assumptions. "I wouldn't say you're here just to try to work me over. But either way, you're mostly a good person."

"What do you mean, mostly?"

I placed two fingers on the bottom rim of my glass and moved it in circles, as if it were a spoon mixing a larger concoction. "People are people. While anyone can be good, an individual is never wholly good or bad, we simply have a predominant leaning."

"Is that so?"

My lips curled into a coy smile as I abandoned my empty glass and scratched behind my ear. "There are exceptions."

"What makes you think that I'm not an exception?"

"Personal experience."

"Are you sure about that?"

"I am."

"Have any of your initial assumptions ever been wrong?"

"Of course, but if you go about in life expecting the worst, then when things don't go the way you expect, you'll only ever be pleasantly surprised."

"That's a depressing way to live."

I shoved the empty glass to the middle of the table and clapped my hands. "Let me see how well I've read you. I'm sticking to my assumption that you're mostly a good person. Which means that you wouldn't only be looking for tells of your opponents. Rather, that's a part of your motivation. The broader reason you're here is because you're looking for pleasant company to pass the time till the game."

Her head bobbed up and down, causing her strawberry blond hair to cascade around her shoulders. "That's not a bad interpretation of my actions."

"Was I close to hitting a bull's eye?"

"However, you're far too arrogant." Bella slumped into her chair, folding her arms across her chest. "That said, you're in the general neighborhood of a perfect shot. I'll give you that."

"I never thought myself arrogant," a slightly raspy voice said as the metal legs of the chair slid across the floor. "Would you all mind if I joined you?"

My eyes flicked to the man as he filled an open seat. Based on his voice's roughness, my guess was that he was getting over a cold, flu, or some other minor bug. Though there was a chance this was his regular voice. Either way, it sent a shiver down my spine, especially when paired with his haggard yet professional visage.

While he objected to an accusation of arrogance, his actions proved worthy of the definition. My eyes drifted to him as I studied the newcomer. Despite the cleanliness and caliber of his clothing, they clashed with his unkempt hair and five o'clock shadow. Even if he'd splurged and gotten something on par with the elites, he still wouldn't look right wearing them. That placed the man firmly in the bucket of professional players or one of Dempsey's plants. I lifted a finger, twirling it as I clicked my tongue. "By all means, join us, mister . . ."

"Patrick Wallace," he said, offering me his hand. "Now I've met Bella before, but you're a fresh face. What's your name?"

I stared at his offered hand and blew across my fingertips. Brushing them against my suit, I shifted my eyes to his. "Name's Marcus."

He reclaimed his snubbed hand as he laid his brew on the table. "With the introductions out of the way, can we become friends?"

"You're full of yourself," I said, looking for a roaming server.

"Feel free to ignore his sarcasm," Bella said, laying a hand on his arm. "Though you already know the limits of our friendship."

As I turned about in my chair, searching for anyone on the

CHAPTER 4

waitstaff, I twisted my lips into a false scowl. "I'm eager enough to make new friends. After all, Bella, that's why I didn't object to you joining me. Your politeness didn't affect my decision."

Bella scoffed and repositioned herself equally between us. The message was loud and clear. She wasn't going to get involved in our exchange. It also encouraged the idea that Patrick joined us to scope out a new player for this tournament. With that bit of confirmation, I turned, giving this card shark every bit of my focus. Patrick drew his thumb across his lips and forced a smile. However, the lifeless green eyes staring back at me told me that his smile was false.

"Marcus, I did ask to join." Patrick swallowed a swig of his brew as the corners of his lips quivered. "Didn't you hear me? Since you were speaking with Bella, I assumed you weren't deaf. Though maybe I spoke toward the wrong ear."

My eyes whipped about the unkept yet immaculate man sitting across the table. Once again, I studied him, though this time I was searching for future leverage. Unfortunately, aside from his impish face, I found nothing. Though the lack of anything provided me with an insight into his behavior. It told me he was used to this kind of introduction. He was happy to toss verbal jabs, hoping for reactions, all while he secured his defenses. He must have practiced this routine every time he sat down at a table. With that realization, I added Patrick to the list of players to avoid at the onset.

There are times when you just know something about someone, despite not having the ability to justify the belief. And at that moment, I knew deep down Patrick was going to be one of the better players attending this tournament. While I kept tabs on the top players out there, I'd never seen this man's face. Despite my lack of familiarity with Patrick, his body language oozed confidence with every motion. I'd hoped never to find such a player. Not only did I find one, but he had also sought me out and said hello. Hopefully, somebody would knock him out before I had to sit across from him.

I dropped into my seat and steepled my fingers under my chin. "I heard you, but you didn't wait for a reply." It was time for me to make a move. Given his introduction, I didn't think he liked people abbreviating his name. However, there was only one way to determine if that petty slight would influence him. "You simply pulled out the chair and sat down before we could answer, Pat."

He pursed his lips and took a pull from his beer. A sigh broke the silence as he gently laid the mug on the marble. "While that would have been the polite thing, it wouldn't have been as much fun."

Patrick's false smile was infuriating. In most sports, that false grin would have been grounds for taunting. However, given the lack of officials here, that kind of thought wasn't going to help. I took a deep breath and placed two fingers on my empty glass. "Being rude is fun for you?"

"It wasn't for you?"

Warm, giddy laughter washed over the table as soft hands rested upon our arms. "It was certainly fun for me, since I netted a couple of tells."

My smile tugged at the corners of my eyes as I waved at a nearby waitress. "I'm glad you found our banter entertaining."

Unfortunately, the young woman who I tried to divert to our table sauntered to another one. However, as I sunk in my seat, another fetching lady stepped up beside me, her hands folded in front of her chest. "How can I help you, sir?"

Turning toward the warm voice, my smile deepened. It was the same waitress who had fetched my first martini. My tip apparently smoothed over any sour feelings she may have had. I handed her my empty glass as my mouth curled up. "My dear, I'd love another martini from Simon." I leaned forward and tapped Bella's forearm. "Is there anything you'd like?"

"Did you place an order for your bartender in addition to your drink?"

I nodded.

"All right." She laughed as she brushed the hair hanging over her shoulder with her fingers. "That's an oddity worth investigating." Bella touched the waitress's arm as her smile brightened. "I think I'll have the same."

"Yes, ma'am."

I glanced over at Patrick, offering a forced grin. "I know you're already working on something, but would you like this lovely waitress to top you off? Or would you like to sample Simon's work?"

The stoic man shook his head as he lifted his drink. "I'm still working through this one, and I wouldn't think of ordering another while I still have a fair amount left."

"Very good, sir," the waitress said, nodding her head to Patrick. She turned back to me and beamed down at me. "Is there anything else you require, sir?"

I shook my head as I replied, "No, I think that should be all we need for now."

"I'll be right back with your drinks."

As the waitress vanished, I looked at Patrick and thumped out a steady beat on the table with my index and middle fingers. "I'm sure you act this way so you can provoke your opponents into revealing things they shouldn't."

Patrick sipped his brew and leaned against his chair.

Even though he remained silent, that silence was as good as

any confirmation. My lips drew into a sinister line as my fingers hastened their beat. It was wise to lay something down as a false trail. That way, I'd be able to leverage it to my advantage if I had to face either of them later. "While effective, your bombastic attitude makes you as obvious as a rampaging bull."

"Is that so?" Patrick leaned over his knees, gripping the rim of his mug, and swirling the brew inside.

I forced my smile to warm as I tipped my head. "I'll grant you that'll help you learn about your opponents' thoughts and tells, provided they're unable to control themselves. While I've used such tactics myself, I've found them to be less reliable than you appear to."

"Maybe," Patrick said, gripping his mug with both hands, "or maybe you're wrong about my intentions."

A second later, I shook my head as my tapping fingers stopped moving, letting a small silence slither between the three of us. As it constricted about, I studied Patrick's lifeless eyes. "If you say so, but may I offer you my thoughts as to why it's a flawed tactic?"

"It's a free country."

"The flaw centers around being unable to provoke genuine emotions. While the everyday gamblers aren't all that well guarded, most professionals aren't swayed by the bombastic behavior, giving them the advantage."

"You seem to be employing the very tactic you're suggesting I stop." Patrick shrugged as he took another pull of his brew.

The level of control this man possessed was inspiring. He dismissed everything without admitting to anything, whether in words or body language. However, this man had challenged me, and I was willing to accept defeat. "It's a clever tactic when it works, and you get an honest reaction."

Patrick clutched his bottle to his chest as his gaze flitted about the room. "I'll be the first to admit that there are some who can wrap themselves in an alternate persona, rendering that technique useless."

Well, that was nicely worded. He never admitted or denied his actions. To hear him speak, you would think from his tone he was merely chatting about the weather. Though his acknowledgement did show me a glimpse of something I could latch onto and assault. It wasn't a big target, but any weakness was better than nothing. "Every trick has its own weakness, that's for sure. But that's the very reason I find this stratagem inconsequential. I have come across too many people capable of nullifying it."

In the blink of an eye, I found my victory. If I hadn't been searching for it, I would've missed the subtle twitch in Patrick's left eye. He'd attempted to swallow the harm to his pride in an exaggerated eye roll. It was nearly a perfect obfuscation, but I was hunting for it. While I appreciated his skills, that mistake was all I required. He had a weakness, his pride. Unfortunately, Patrick had ample reason to be proud.

Patrick drained his drink and thumped it on the table. "Do you simply prefer trying to discover what you can with a smile?"

I tapped my temple as I offered the man a lopsided grin. "Observation has always worked well for me."

Patrick's arms extended like a bird of prey descending upon its next meal as his smile widened, revealing his canines. "While that's a solid foundation, when you're not given adequate time, the ability becomes fruitless."

"I won't argue that the lack of time does play against me." With a shrug, I leaned into the chair's comfortable embrace. "Like I said, every option has its flaws, but those with sharp eyes can pick things out that most people would miss a thousand times over. Wouldn't you agree?"

"Not in the slightest," Patrick said with a false grin.

Waving away the disagreement, I pressed my back against the cushion. "Besides, I've found that it works against those who, as you've said, wrap themselves in false personas."

Despite his attempt to blank his face, I saw the wrinkles in his defenses. Unfortunately, in the next instant, his eyes resumed their lifeless nature, and I knew he caught me marking his flaw. I wasn't sure he realized what I'd seen, but I knew he knew I saw something I believed I could exploit.

"Excuse me, gentlemen," Bella said as her glare bounced between us. "The two of you seem to have forgotten where you are. We're not sitting at the tables. This room is about letting our host pamper us while we prepare for the game in our own way. Can't you two simply agree to disagree?"

"She's right," Patrick said through an expressionless face.

With a halfhearted grin plastered, I buffed my fingernails with my coat's lapel. Once I finished, I extended my hand to this masterful pro. "I can do that well enough."

A raspy chuckle tore its way out of Patrick as the stoic man glared at me with his lifeless orbs.

I wrapped my fingers around an imaginary shot glass and raised it. "I know that I'm shy about one drink to make a toast, but I have some wise words I'd like to share. May we find our way to the tournament's final table, and may we never run afoul of those better than us."

"Here, here, Marcus. That's a delightful thought," Patrick said with a pleasant voice despite the dead gaze. "Each of us can only perform with the gifts with which we were born. And unfortunately, not all gifts are equal. In fact, some strategies are far too difficult and should only be attempted by a master."

The man was desperate to gain something after losing a

skirmish with me. If Patrick was indicative of the caliber of players I'd find here, I would need to focus on shoring up my mental defenses. However, as a tense silence settled upon us, I leaned forward and shattered the uneasy tranquility. "Patrick, while I'll agree that you're a skilled player, it would appear that we won't be able to honor Bella's request."

"I'm sorry," Patrick said, collecting Bella's dainty hand. He drew it to his lips, kissing her knuckles.

I didn't want to anger Bella, but I needed to confirm how to position Patrick to exploit his weakness. So I kept my eyes focused on the man's face as I brushed my lip with a thumb. "However, contrary to your assertion, dissecting an opponent's body language isn't difficult. In fact, it's something that people learn early in life. Unfortunately, we stop practicing, and the ability withers away from lack of use. Fortunately, for me, I've never stopped flexing that skill."

As my words vanished, I saw another twitch in Patrick's eye before an exaggerated roll swallowed it. Just as before, if I hadn't been looking for it, I would have missed it altogether. It was an extremely slight motion, but now, after repeating its production and capture, I knew I'd be able to leverage this mistake in a game. From how Patrick carried himself, I knew this man normally possessed an endless supply of patience. However, when something he cultivated was attacked, that vast reservoir vanished. Yet his self-discipline was so regimented that if it disappeared, he would instantly patch the damage and refill the supply through a sheer act of will. Nothing else mattered. This hustler had a weakness, and I'd found it.

"You're right, of course, Marcus. A skill that's not properly trained is quite useless. Now, if you'll kindly excuse me, I see some other old acquaintances." And without another word, Patrick stood up and left the table, leaving his empty mug behind.

"Did you have to provoke him?"

I pulled my gaze away from Patrick as he disappeared into a small crowd and propped my head on my arm. "Do you think I intentionally tried to provoke him?"

"Absolutely." With an insincere scowl on her face, she licked her lips. "I enjoy spending time with him. Besides, I need a better read on him."

Time to drop another false trail. Thinking of a funny story, I covered the resulting laugh with a hand. "I got the impression he was trying to fill any gaps in his course on you."

Flashing a coy smile, she twirled a finger. "Of course, he doesn't understand how I think, and it just drives him crazy." Her smile warmed as she laid a hand on mine. "But I've never intentionally annoyed him like that. He likes to hold grudges."

I looked into her wondrous gray eyes and winked. "While I don't linger on painful memories, I rarely forget anything."

"I'm just saying there will be a reckoning."

"That'll keep things interesting." I pulled my hand out from under hers and bounced my fist against the table. "Don't forget, he was slinging insults my way as well."

Bella stared back at me with a mischievous smile and tucked a loose strand of her strawberry blond hair behind her ear. "Marcus, you continue to impress me. I knew there was a reason I liked you."

"Is it my charming smile?"

Laughing, she shook her head as her finger waved back and forth. "It's more than that. It's your confidence, the way you carry yourself. I know you couldn't tell, but Patrick's smile is vastly more charming than yours. But you don't need a mesmerizing grin when you're gliding over your competition, and Patrick saw that too."

CHAPTER 4

"I wouldn't say I'm that far above him."

"Which is why you are."

The waitress stepped between us, our martinis resting on her small tray. "Here are your drinks."

With a broad smile, I grabbed both glasses while she collected Patrick's empty mug. Before I could look back at her, she'd vanished into the mingling crowd. I promptly cleansed mine of its intoxicants as I slid the unadulterated one to Bella. As we sat in silence, I took a sip of my martini and grinned. It was even better than before. That or was I simply riding a high from successfully beating one of the better players present at his own game?

CHAPTER 5

The conversation with Bella had blinded me to time's steady march, and with every question we posed, we would reply with an interesting tidbit from our past. While I can't speak for her, I believe her answers were as genuine as mine. Yet despite the honesty, neither one of us offered anything that might hamper our ability to compete in the tournament. In fact, the only sour notes from the chat were when other players popped in to introduce themselves and/or to offer well wishes.

The most egregious of those interruptions followed the example set by Patrick Wallace. However, since I'd chosen to spend my time with Bella in lieu of studying my opposition from afar, I wasn't as prickly with them as I'd been with Patrick. Instead, I quickly welcomed them to join us so I could get a gauge of their skill level. Out of the dozen or so people who joined us, only a couple were part of the elite. The rest were professional gamblers, and I recognized a couple of them from televised tournaments. Thankfully, none of them shared Patrick's skills.

By the time my mental count of attendees reached one hundred, I popped the last bite of steak into my mouth, searching for signs of motion. After a few seconds, Bella laid her hand on my arm and gently squeezed. "Given the compliments you've passed along to the chef, should I assume the confusion coloring your expression is from something other than your finished meal?"

I scooted closer to her and pointed at the men lingering near the entrance. "By my rough math, the last player has arrived. Shouldn't the staff start closing things down and getting the game started?"

With a slight chuckle, Bella placed a palm against my chest and leaned forward, speaking right into my ear. "I'm not mocking you, Marcus. I simply forgot this was the first time you've attended this annual event."

"What does that have to do with anything?"

Bella leaned back into her chair as she claimed her tea from the table. With exaggerated motions, she stirred the drink with her straw while draping her right leg over her left. "While all the players have arrived, we're still missing the most important person for this undertaking."

After wiping my lips with the napkin, I tossed it onto the remnants of my meal and shoved the plate into the center of the table. While I kept my focus on her, I grabbed my unoffensive martini and mixed it with the skewered olives. I knew she was baiting me, hoping I'd ask the obvious question. For a few tense moments, I chewed my inner lip as my gaze focused on Bella. "If we're still short, please tell me who we're missing."

Bella's head swept back and forth as her face underwent a subtle transformation. In between moments, a building blaze consumed the playful cheer oozing from her eyes while her normally pale face darkened ever so slightly. Her slender finger reached out and beckoned me to come closer. After pulling an olive off its skewer, I dropped the remaining ones back into the martini and leaned toward Bella.

"Do you know whose tournament this is?"

With a wry chuckle, I tossed the olive into my mouth before leaning back in my chair. Once more, my idle hand swirled the martini about as I forced my lips to curl into a warm smile. "I'm well aware of Bertrand Dempsey's support of this opulent event."

She halted my drink's motion as she lifted my chin with her other index finger. "If you knew that, then why'd you ask who we're missing?"

Bella's gaze held mine for several tense seconds until she released my hand. A moment later, she patted my cheek and sipped her tea. My eyes drifted to my whitening fingers and suddenly the throbbing reached my brain. It took me a couple of seconds to force my fingers off the glass's stem. Thankfully, it wasn't damaged.

A small silence settled between us as I rubbed my temples. Eventually, when I trusted my voice not to crack, I turned to Bella and licked my dry lips. "There's no reason for Dempsey to join us for this tournament."

"Why would you assume that?"

My mind took her question and started retrieving the list I'd given Matt. Though they flew to my mind quickly enough, the moment I saw the look of shock and disappointment swelling behind Bella's gray eyes, I realized how hollow they'd been. Unfortunately, I'd bought into my convictions so much that I knuckled down and tried to justify my original position.

Bella's slender finger swished back and forth in time with her clicking tongue. When the melodic admonishment ended, she took another sip of her tea. "I'm sure your initial thoughts revolved around the idea that a man of his stature has more important things to worry about than a card game."

Latching onto the metaphorical lifeline she'd tossed, I scooted forward, perching on the chair's edge. "This game isn't entirely legal. There's no way he'd want to risk being here. He needs the deniability."

Bella shook her head as her fingers tightened around her glass. "Do you know how much Dempsey makes from this tournament?"

I spread my arms out as my gaze swept across the room, highlighting the ornate décor. "Given the grandeur of this lounge, I don't see how he makes a penny."

Once more, Bella's finger swished about like a conductor leading the ensemble. "He takes half of every fee right off the top. That's twenty-five million dollars per player. There's plenty of money there to finance this portion of the event, not to mention some of his other more elaborate and dubious activities. So, while he spends the money up front, before we play a single hand, he's been reimbursed a few times over."

"That looks like lacquered gold leaf," I said, pointing at the nearest wall.

"It probably is," Bella said, shrugging her shoulder. "But even with all the elaborate trimmings to accommodate the elite guests, he probably makes twenty million, give or take a couple."

"What about exposure?"

She placed her hands on my cheeks and stared into my eyes. "Given how lucrative this event is, do you honestly think he has other places to be?"

"Wouldn't a trusted underling be able to represent him? That way he'd maintain a level of deniability?"

Shaking her head, she patted my cheek. "If you were receiving all that money, would you snub the guests by not making an appearance?"

I slowly shook my head.

With a wink, she pulled her hands away from me as she grabbed her tea. "Then why would a man as savvy as Dempsey risk offending the people who fund his activities? It's expected from his clientele, and as far as the authorities are concerned, he doesn't fear the law, be it local, state, or even federal. He has enough people on his payroll to keep the location from them until he's cleaned up."

She licked her lips as she stirred her drink. "Every official east of the Mississippi knows about this tournament. They're even aware that it's an annual event. But his clout and influence prevent anyone from making a move against him. He enjoys flaunting that invincibility. So I'm sorry to burst your bubble, but nothing is going to stop him from greeting the people who line his wallet."

I scratched the back of my head as I thought about how to counter her points. Unfortunately, I couldn't think of a single argument. Resigned to accept my chiding, my head fell against the chair as I stared into the wall. "When you put it like that, I have to admit my assumptions were based on substantial flaws."

"It's nice to know that there are still some naïve, innocent men around," Bella said, winking as she lifted her glass to cover her laughter.

As my shoulders fell, laughter tumbled out. She and Matt were right. I'd been incredibly foolish. If Dempsey had federal employees on the payroll, then the rumors of his empire stretching to the capital were true. Or was that a fresh assumption? What if he really had an empire as big as the rumors? Was it possible for him to control an entire city? Could his influence spread to an entire state with enough loyal lieutenants?

What was Dempsey's official business? Biting my lip, I grabbed my martini and scoured my memories, searching for how he made money, aside from overseeing a criminal organization. I thought I remembered his core business, but every time I reached through the jumbled thoughts, the concepts' shadowy edges eluded my fingertips. I had already shown a certain level of ignorance that could get me killed had I been talking to the wrong person. As it was, I preferred not to rely on luck anymore, and since no one here was surfing the web, I guessed this topic would remain out of reach. Hopefully, it wouldn't come up in natural conversation.

That was until I looked into Bella's eyes, where I found a sea of questions straining to escape. As another sip of my martini bathed my tongue, I sat up, forming a question I hoped would plug the leaking dam. I eased my glass onto the table and leaned toward Bella. However, before the hastily gathered words could emerge, the lounge's entrance swung open. Instantly, my gaze flicked toward the sudden motion, and my eyes bulged once I registered who'd arrived.

I moistened my dry lips as I patted Bella's arm and jerked my head toward the doorway. "Is this our esteemed host?"

"Yes."

My gaze snapped back to my companion to find a scowl marring her features. "I take it you're not a fan of his."

"That's a safe assumption." The fire filling her words matched the harshness of her cold eyes.

At that moment, my fingers reached back and scratched my neck as I hoped to never offend her. After an awkward moment, I scooted away as anger and hatred oozed out of her. Her reaction was so visceral, I thought the temperature rose a couple of degrees.

With an audible harrumph, she snatched her tea and stared into the icy drink. "Though I'm certain 'esteemed' isn't an appellation he deserves."

"Personal grudge?"

"My dealings with the host are my own." Bella's icy glare

flicked up to me, and I saw the seething anger ready to escape and consume anyone who got in her way. "Don't push me on this."

With a nod, I put her issue with Dempsey out of my mind and resumed studying him. His reputation was larger than life, and at first glance, it felt wrong to apply that reputation to this man. The image I'd painted from those stories didn't match the man looming in the entryway. He was nothing exceptional, at least physically. The only thing about him stressing his place in society was his clothing. Every piece of his ensemble appeared to be the epitome of fashion and elegance. The contrast between the extraordinary wrappings and the ordinary individual was stark.

Aside from being of average height and weight, there wasn't a physical trait marking him as special. If pressed, I would say that he was lean. Built with muscles crafted from a life of constant running. He had close-cropped black hair contrasting perfectly with his pale skin. In fact, Dempsey was so pale I wondered if he ever ventured into sunlight. I had the idea Dempsey had little desire to do anything that didn't directly benefit him, like ensuring a healthy dose of vitamin D.

Then I caught sight of his innermost thoughts through his pale-gray eyes. If I had been standing when our gazes met, I would've collapsed like a house of cards. Fortunately, the chair kept me from making a fool of myself. After taking a sip from my martini, I resumed studying those gray pools. While they were colder than ice, they also exuded a strength that would rival any hardened steel. Despite their dispassionate demeanor, they also captured my attention, promising nothing but trouble if I ever crossed him. That unspoken promise was the most prominent of all the rumors I'd heard. Well, that is aside from his patience and wisdom. And given his stature, those whispers had been accurate.

Despite his eyes elevating his status, his clothing skyrocketed him to new heights. While I can't remember who told me that a man's wardrobe will betray his secrets, I've proved the saying right too often to ignore it. Granted, if I were to steal them, I wouldn't find Dempsey's account numbers or passwords anywhere in or on the fabric. Yet they revealed so much more about him. With the correct point of view, you could learn so much about who you were dealing with. And none of what I saw put me at ease.

After a few seconds, a pair of henchmen removed his scarf, overcoat, cane, and hat before his emotionless gaze swept through the lounge, registering and cataloguing his portable accounts. As he took everything in, I could see why a handful of rumors claimed he was omniscient. While the look on his face boasted knowledge of everything unfolding before him, nobody could read another's mind. However, this appearance, when coupled with a vast team of dedicated researchers, something he had the money for, would complete the hint of those tales.

While I attempted to follow Dempsey's example of being well informed, holding onto all those facts was difficult. It takes a special mind to store, let alone recall, specific details at the drop of a dime. But there he was, his mind busy crunching the numbers, so to speak. Instantly, I knew he'd spent his lifetime training himself to handle whatever his spies collected. Even worse, he could find relevant details to help guide his actions in real time.

That assurance played with another aspect of his reputation. Dempsey rarely made mistakes. Though when he did, the ramifications didn't reach far or last long. As the weight of Dempsey's persona overwhelmed me, I regretted not following Matt's advice. A compulsion to cut and run swelled in my chest. Reflexively, my mind toyed with the idea of leaving, despite knowing it would be without the entrance fee. While I'd already written it off as a loss, it might be the best use of the money. Unfortunately, leaving would probably mark me as something to be pruned as quickly as possible.

No, I couldn't leave. I had to see this through to the end. If Matt were here, he would have poked my stomach as he said something like this is your mess to deal with. All I could do at that moment was accept my fate and follow Matt's other bit of advice about transforming my cards. Despite my friend's opinion of my ability, there were times I couldn't help but tweak whatever the dealer had sent my way. My problem came with losing. At that moment, I promised to fight my baser instincts and accept whatever came my way.

Once Dempsey adjusted his blood-red tie, he stepped clear of the doorway and spoke with a booming voice that certainly carried to everyone present. He must have arranged for the room's acoustics to amplify the voice of whoever spoke from that spot.

"Welcome to my tournament. It is good to see so many returning faces, not to mention the new ones. I hope all of you have been enjoying my hospitality." Dempsey clasped his hands together as his smile widened. "Now there is still time left before we begin, so please continue to mingle while we wait for the tournament's start. Also, be sure to enjoy the refreshments while the bars and kitchen are still open. Thank you all for coming."

Wordlessly, his hands fell to his sides as he stalked to the closest group of players. He promptly separated the best-dressed individual for a private conversation. Upon its conclusion, he crossed the room and selected another of the elites. When that brief conversation ended, he crossed the lounge for a third time to engage in a personal chat. Since no one complained, they must be used to it. But why was he bouncing about the room?

The next time he passed over an available player, I realized what he was doing. He was highlighting the targets for the professionals and whoever he employed. The simple meet and greet served two purposes. First, it made the elites feel good. However, that was just the icing on the cake. He was curating a list of approved targets. This was a masterful demonstration of his will.

"Marcus, are you there?" Bella asked, as she jostled my shoulder, spilling a bit of my martini.

My gaze whirled toward her, and I flinched. Despite the gentleness of her words, the scorn whirling behind her eyes threatened to consume me. I eased the glass back on the table and grabbed a spare napkin to soak up the spilled liquid. "I'm sorry. It would seem Dempsey's arrival spooked me more than I thought."

"Would you rather scurry off and have a conversation with him?"

Despite the simplicity of her comment, I could feel the searing rage boiling inside her. She definitely had a grudge against Dempsey. And based on the intensity of that contained rage, it was personal. Though I couldn't see what these two had in common. Based on what she'd shared, Bella was a professional card player. While Dempsey was the head of a sophisticated criminal empire.

What could be connecting them? She obviously knew he was going to be here, so why did she return if she had this much anger toward him? Ultimately, her reasons didn't matter to me. I would not become the lightning rod sparing Dempsey from her fury. Biting my tongue, I reached for Bella's hands, but she pulled them away from me.

"I'm sorry." I turned my hands and inclined my head. "That was rude of me." As a handful of tense seconds passed, I realized how much I'd genuinely enjoyed our brief conversation. This was a friendship I'd want to continue past the current moment. "I hope you'll forgive my brief obsession with him."

"You're acting like you've never seen him before."

With a shrug, I thought about spinning a lavish story, but ultimately, I kept to the truth. "I haven't. While I've heard of him and his reputation, I've never even seen a picture of him. Even though I probably could have found one before coming, don't forget I assumed he wouldn't show."

Her soft chuckle deflated the building anger as color flooded back into her fingers. "Every time I think I have you figured out, you do something or say something that invalidates all my assumptions."

"I'm good at that," I offered quickly. But after a shared moment of laughter, curiosity won over reason. "I understand Dempsey isn't your favorite person, but how many times have you met him?"

Her slender finger rose, swishing through the air. "More than you."

Something about her forced cheer got under my skin, so I took a different path. "How many of these have you been to?"

As I watched her stir her tea with her straw, I had trouble gauging her reaction. From our conversation, I knew she thought me intelligent, or at the very least, she respected me enough not to berate me. But now that I continued to push a topic she didn't want to have, I could see doubt trickling through her mind. However, she'd witness me trap Patrick with a few simple words. I could see the two warring thoughts battling in her eyes. Eventually, she lowered her drink and sighed. "This is the second time I've come."

"How'd you do last year?"

"I did well enough to secure my place."

"Could you be a little more specific?"

"No. After all, a girl needs to guard her secrets." And that was all she was going to say on the matter. It was one of the nicer denials I'd ever received.

I lifted my glass to take another sip while I tried to think of a suitably clever response. Unfortunately, I couldn't, so I offered her the first reason that popped into my head. "Except that's not much of a secret, considering other people would know how well you did."

With a sigh, she leaned over and beckoned for me to do the same. Once I was beside her, she tapped my nose. "Then feel free to find your source. Otherwise, you'll have to learn how to deal with a lack of knowledge."

"A woman of mystery, indeed."

"And don't you dare try to pretend that you're not thrilled by that fact," she said, giving me an enchanting wink.

"I wouldn't dare argue with you." While I tried to avoid thinking of the crime lord, that was when he walked right through my line of sight. Without conscious thought, I traced his gaze, finding Patrick on the other end. Had he spoken with him already? I don't think he had, but I could have missed the conversation. It wasn't much, but I recognized that expression. I'd seen it several times from Matt. That was the look of two friends with an inherent understanding of each other. Entire conversations could occur without having to rely on a single word. So what had those two friends talked about with that glance? Of course, I had no way of knowing, but the mystery teased me, like a prize just out of reach.

With thoughts of Dempsey on my mind, I looked back to Bella as I asked a follow-up question. "I'm sorry to bring Dempsey back into our conversation, but since you've had the privilege of being here before, does he talk to everyone, or just a select few?"

Bella thrust her jaw forward as her eyes drew to slits. "Why are you so interested in Dempsey?"

"I've already made one false assumption. It would be nice if I could correct that ignorance." I tossed the napkin onto the plate as I shook my head. "You've already seen how naïve I was, so I'm attempting to rectify that as quickly as possible."

"While not a terrible excuse, it's barely a justifiable one."

"I'm not trying to be rude." I plucked the skewer from my drink and ate all three olives. As I chewed them, I tossed the empty stick onto the plate. "It's just a bad habit I've carried around since my youth. When I'm ignorant on a subject, I physically cannot stop asking questions."

"You're blaming your curiosity for this series of unwanted questions?"

I couldn't fault her for questioning that excuse. While there was some truth behind it, I was stretching it out a bit to make it fit. Ultimately, my curiosity wasn't dependent on my lack of familiarity with the subject. I was just naturally curious. "Yes, and before you ask, I'm well aware how batty that can make people."

While she was still hesitant to respond, I desperately flashed her my most ingratiating smile. I guessed it helped because as she folded her arms across her chest, she gave a curt nod. "Last year, he met with everyone before we started."

"And the years before that?"

"You're lucky I like you. But that won't save you for long if you insist on this conversation." She drained a third of her tea and sighed. "Since I didn't attend his previous tournaments, I don't have firsthand knowledge of what happened. But from what the other players said, that's the norm for him."

Only a blind and deaf fool could mistake Bella's feelings for Dempsey. And since our conversation had taken quite a few twists and turns prior to Dempsey's arrival, I knew she didn't have a problem with my curiosity. Her disgust with Dempsey went beyond his criminal ties. And I didn't want to fall into the crossfire between these two. I wrung my hands as my eyes flicked from her to the prowling Dempsey. "Why don't you like our host?"

Bella doubled over in her chair. To anyone watching our conversation, it would have appeared I'd punched her in the stomach. As she straightened, she put her purse on her lap as her quivering lips stilled to a tight line. After several tense heartbeats, she'd banished the fury, replacing it with a mask of calmness. "What makes you think I don't like him?"

"You mean apart from that reaction and the anger that's radiating off of you every time he comes up?"

For a long time, she stared past me into nothing as her fingers tightened around the straps of her purse. So I focused on her rising and falling chest. There was no way I was going to take my eyes off of her, not after that reaction.

Eventually, she released another sigh and glanced up at me. "I have my reasons, and I'd rather not go into them. Now don't ask me any more questions about him. If you have questions regarding the tournament, ask. But you better think long and hard before your next question comes out of your lips." She leaned forward and thumped my chest with her fingertips. "If the question even remotely revolves around Dempsey, you will regret it. Is that clear?"

"I'm sorry," I said, wishing I'd mustered a better reply, but there was something familiar behind that glare.

"Good."

The lump that appeared in my throat threatened to choke me. So I took another swallow from my martini, washing it away. "I wasn't trying—"

"Welcome back, Bella." I recognized the voice instantly. The one man who infuriated Bella finally made his way to our table. I was too nervous to turn around, so instead I focused on Bella, as Dempsey's soft voice continued teasing my ear. "I hope this gentleman isn't bothering you."

Prior to his greeting, I wouldn't have thought Bella's face could rival the hardened steel of Dempsey's. But I would have been wrong. Her fierce glare sliced through the host as she rose. With a halted tilt of her head, she forced a false grin to her face. "Despite his occasional lack of restraint, Marcus has been a complete gentleman. In fact, he's kept me quite entertained as we waited for the tournament to begin." She placed a hand on my cheek and spoke with a warm smile. "Marcus, that bartender's name was Simon, correct?"

I nodded.

"Well, if you would excuse me, I need a refill, and I think you'll need one by the time I get back, so I'll bring one once you're free." With that, she whirled around and marched toward the nearest bar in search of Simon.

With Bella's chair vacant, Dempsey walked around the table, claiming it. "I hope you don't mind if I sit down and talk with you for a little while."

"Please do." I mean, what else was I going to say? I may have been willing to give Patrick some grief about what he did when he joined our table. But this man had enough influence to make me disappear if I offended him. And I wasn't interested in a firsthand example of his creativity.

As I sat there, I could feel the stoic man weighing me up as he looked at me. With a grin, he pointed at Bella. "Thank you for entertaining my niece."

Did he just say niece? Bella was Dempsey's niece? What? No. That had to be wrong. As my stomach hit the floor, I thought luck had abandoned me right there. Of all the people here at this tournament, how had I spent all my time talking with Dempsey's niece? There was nothing I could do to stop the panic rising inside me. And to make matters worse, I could see the glee in his eyes that he had rattled me. There was no reason I had to give him any more than necessary. I needed to reign in my panic. With a focus of will I borrowed from somewhere, I turned toward him and smiled. "Your niece is a wonderful woman, and she is one of the brightest people I've met."

"I would agree with you," Dempsey said, his voice lacking any emotion. "Though I believe my brother indulges her far too much."

The sterile voice was not the creepiest aspect to Dempsey. While it contributed, his willingness to treat a stranger like a life-long friend threw me for a loop. Since I didn't want to look into Dempsey's eyes, I focused on the tip of his nose. "I wouldn't be able to comment on that, Mr. Dempsey."

Dempsey rubbed the bottom of his chin as his lips curled into a slight grin. In a fluid motion, he folded his hands on the table as he leaned toward me. "You're a very careful man, Marcus. Normally, that's a wonderful trait to embrace. It's unfortunate that few strive for it. But please call me Bertrand."

"I'll do my best, sir."

Dempsey let the silence linger just long enough for it to become uncomfortable. "Is that normal for you to be so respectful?"

"Given your reputation, I'd rather err on the side of respect."

"If you didn't have to worry about that, where would that put us?"

"What do you mean?"

"Would you still guard your comments like a warden watching over his prisoners?"

"That's been a lifelong rule for me, with someone's family. You never know how anyone will react when it revolves around familial bonds."

With another nod, Dempsey seemed to approve of my response, or at least concur with his earlier measure of me. "Just between you and me. My niece appears to be smitten with you."

"What do you mean?" I asked as my head whipped toward the bar, looking for Bella. When I couldn't find her, I looked back at Dempsey. "She couldn't possibly be interested in me in that way. I think I'd have noticed."

"No, you wouldn't." Dempsey said with a shake of his head. A second later, his smile widened, threatening to crack his emotionless mask. "Trust me, men never see the signs that women shove into our faces. Which is entirely fair, considering they seemingly can't understand ours."

I swirled my martini as I drew in a long breath through my nose. "What leads you to assume she's infatuated with me?"

The host leaned back as he crossed his legs and placed his hands in his lap. "First, I said smitten. But let me assure you, the only reason you can't see it is because you don't know her."

"What?"

Dempsey lifted a finger as a smile reemerged. "I thought you were careful with family."

"I am," I said, putting the martini back on the table. "But how would my knowing her change my opinion?"

"The biggest challenge most men face with my niece is keeping her in one spot for any length of time."

With a scoff, I turned to the other bar, searching for Bella. "She got up and left."

Dempsey's finger swished back and forth. "Remember, my niece isn't here right now because it was time for me to say hello. Though from what people were telling me, you've come close to chasing her away once or twice."

"The conversation circled around you, honestly."

"That's not surprising." Dempsey's back straightened as he studied me. However, he was no longer weighing what he saw. Instead, he seemed to relax. But that just made me even more confused.

"Since this is your first tournament, you should have been one of the last people I met with."

"What interrupted your ritual?"

A chuckle washed over me as Dempsey snapped at a passing waitress. When she came by, it was the waitress who'd been taking care of me. "I'll take whatever you've been serving him."

The moment the waitress left, he immediately repositioned himself and stared into my eyes. "I was told by a few of the regulars that my niece had been sitting with someone for almost two hours, and he was about to chase her off."

"I take it Bella's not known for having lengthy conversations with other attendees."

"That is contrary to her nature."

Stunned by Dempsey's response, I took a moment trying to reclaim my scattered thoughts. Once I'd reclaimed most of them, I cleared my throat. "So you disrupted your ritual to save me from myself?"

"No," Dempsey said, shaking his head. "In fact, what I want is to see the man who's skating on thin ice with my niece. Remember, I'm not doing you any favors sitting here chatting with you. Now, that said, my niece is very picky about who she'll spend time with. Despite our troubles, which stem from the less savory aspects of my business, she is, as you said, family, and I want what's best for her, whatever that may be."

Leveling his gray eyes at me, I could see the change from a benevolent uncle to those of a cold-blooded crime lord capable of ordering someone's death as easily as most people breathe.

Somehow, I skipped the official queue and raced right to the front of the line. Those are cardinal sins while trying to keep a low profile.

"Be careful not to cross me here or anywhere. If you ever accomplish that, then there is no hole small enough for you to hide in. My wrath will tear the world asunder in order to balance the scales. Do you understand?"

"Yes, sir."

"Good." The sheer terror-inducing look vanished in an instant, once more leaving me to stare into the face of a kindly uncle.

At that moment, the waitress returned and placed a martini on the table. "Here you go, Mr. Dempsey."

"Thank you, my dear." Dempsey withdrew his wallet and handed the girl a pair of bills. She took the tip and bowed before rushing off to her next table. He lifted the glass to his nose and drew in a deep breath. With a smile, he sipped the drink. "I'm glad someone else has discovered Simon's magic touch."

"I lucked out in finding him."

"How's that?"

"I placed an order with one of your less-skilled employees. When he couldn't work out how to make the order, he dragged Simon over, and the rest is pleasant history."

Dempsey sipped more of his martini and pulled the skewer from the glass. He pulled both olives from it and grinned. With a laugh, he dropped the empty stirrer onto the table. "That's a similar experience to me. It seems my friend enjoys rescuing people from mediocre service."

"Excuse me, sir, but I want to ask you a question about Bella."

"You should ask her."

"I tried, but she didn't want to answer it." My head bounced between my shoulders as I drew in a sharp breath. "I'm fairly certain the answer is connected with you, and she really doesn't enjoy discussing you."

Dempsey took another sip as he stared down at me. "You want to know how she raised the funds to enter my tournament?"

"Do you know? I only ask because your reputation doesn't paint the picture of a man who's willing to give family members a break."

"You're right," Dempsey said, swirling the lemon peel in the glass. He took another sip and grinned. "I'm not one to break the rules for family when it comes to business. However, as I'm sure you guessed, my little niece has become quite a skilled gambler. And as you said, she is a very smart woman and capable of taking advantage of all her resources, including her looks.

"Now, don't twist that into thinking she's a vain woman; she's not. In fact she's unaware of just how much leverage she wields over her male opponents." He lifted his glass off the table and drew in another lungful of the drink's competing notes from the citrus and olives. "She won this tournament last year, which is how she earned the fee to be here today. But as far as how she earned last year's fee . . ." Shrugging his shoulders, he sipped more of the exquisite martini. "I don't know how she earned that fee. Though she had to learn those card skills somewhere."

I looked over my shoulder and caught sight of Bella at the bar, her foot tapping a rapid march while she clutched two glasses.

Dempsey rose and inclined his head to me. "Well, I'm afraid I have to leave before Bella lumps you in with me. If that happens, she'll never come back. Best of luck to you, Marcus."

Dempsey offered me his hand, and I took it and held it as firmly as I could, only to be surprised at how hard the other man's grip was. When he released me, Dempsey spun about and disappeared into another small group of players.

CHAPTER 6

A few seconds after Dempsey disappeared into the crowd, a feminine hand laid a martini down in front of me as strawberry blond hair brushed my cheek. "You two seemed awfully chummy. Should I move aside to make way for his return?"

"Absolutely not." I plucked the martini off the table and removed the intoxicants with a force of will. Bringing it to my lips, I drew in a sampling of the drink's competing yet balanced aromas. With a smile, I grabbed the skewer and stirred the contents. "You're far better company than your uncle."

"Oh," she said, covering her mouth with her fingertips. She returned to her seat, sipping her drink. "I didn't think he'd tell you that."

"Any reason you concealed the relation?"

With a shrug, Bella traced a fingertip around the rim of her glass while the corners of her mouth curled up and her eyes narrowed. "What were you two talking about?"

Wry laughter trickled past my lips as I rubbed my eyes.

"What's so funny?"

After taking a sip, I put my martini down and dropped my hands on my lap. I lost myself in her fiery eyes. She was awfully skittish with her uncle. For a moment, I toyed with the idea of mentioning her uncle approved of me, or at least didn't object to our lengthy conversation. That lasted for about a second because that scenario continued to end with her getting up and leaving. And I had a fifty-fifty shot of getting her drink tossed in my face. However, there was one key aspect of the conversation I could relay to her.

"Honestly, he was shocked to discover that you'd stayed in one place for so long."

"Excuse me?!" She drained her drink and turned, latching onto her uncle.

As she stared the crime lord down, I tried to catalogue her response. While I thought I'd heard a tinge of curiosity, when I caught sight of her eyes, the emotion didn't fit. It looked to be equal parts curiosity and anger, or was it indignation? Either way, it didn't matter. Ultimately, the source of the emotional outburst was a deep outrage at her uncle and his opinions. Despite those emotions, she wasn't willing to avoid the tournament.

"That man doesn't know me, no matter what he says."

"You may choose to disregard my words because of their source, but according to Dempsey, those who know you believe you to be a bit of a wallflower." Instantly, her hand flew to her mouth as her cheeks colored ever so slightly, but with her fair complexion, she may as well have been beet red. "Based on your reaction, I'll assume it's a fair description of your behavior."

Her brow furrowed and eyes narrowed to points.

My hands shot up as I shook my head. "Don't shoot the messenger. I'm paraphrasing your uncle."

Her harsh gaze softened briefly before crystalizing into the same icy, measuring gaze belonging to Dempsey. Considering the man must have patented the look, I idly wondered if she had to pay him a royalty whenever she slipped into the familial expression. However, before I could make a joke about it, she leaned forward.

"I don't want to talk about that relation anymore." She kept her fearsome gaze upon me, and that underlying rage seeped into her voice. "Do you understand?!"

With a sip of the cleansed martini, I held her fiery gaze. Contrary to her pleasing exterior, this woman could, with the flip of a switch, become a clone of her uncle. She'd inherited the family's intimidating streak. Despite the recent sip of my drink, it took me a few moments to work some saliva into my mouth. Strangely enough, the familial expression was more terrifying on her face than Dempsey's. I mean, you expected to see it on a crime lord, but it was odd gracing Bella's soft features. Once I replenished the moisture in my mouth, I nodded. "If that's what you want, I'll do my best to abide by your wishes."

"Thank you."

With a sigh, I eased forward and rubbed my chin. "Hopefully, this has enough separation to accommodate your request, but I have to know."

"Be careful with your question."

"Why are you here, considering you don't particularly like your uncle?" I spread my arms wide as my eyes flicked about the ornate fixtures looming about us. "Given what your uncle did with a warehouse, I'm fairly sure you could live a life of ease and luxury."

With a heavy sigh, she raised her empty glass over her head. "The only way I'd have that would be to accept and agree with the family business. Unfortunately for me, I know where his money comes from, and that's enough to keep me away from those kinds of obligations."

"Then why are you here?"

"To win the tournament." As our waitress plucked the glass from Bella's hand, she grabbed the woman's wrist. "Same drink from the same bartender."

The waitress nodded. "I'll be right back, ma'am."

Bella's eyes whipped back to me as she snapped her fingers and leaned forward. "Isn't it the same reason you came?"

"While the money is a nice perk," I said, reclaiming my drink, and tipping it toward her, "I'm really after the bragging rights."

"If you win this game, you'll have plenty of both."

After sipping my martini, I placed it on the table and scooted to the seat's edge. "But with your distaste of the organizer, wouldn't you be able to accomplish your goal of severing that relationship if you simply didn't come to his events?"

"Here you go, ma'am," the waitress said, placing a fresh martini in front of Bella.

"Thank you," Bella said as she sampled the cocktail. "I never knew how talented that man was."

Bella slumped into her chair as she pulled the glass to her chest. Holding it there, she peered into the cloudy pool of liquid, letting an awkward stillness engulf us. Seconds stretched into what felt like minutes as she traced the rim of her glass with her forefinger. When it stopped moving, her gaze crept up to mine. "While I'm not fond of my uncle or father, it doesn't change that they're my family, and you only have one, and there's nothing you can do about who they are."

"There's truth to that cliché." I sipped my drink and scooted back in my chair. "But that's not the real reason you tolerate them, is it?"

Once Bella placed her drink on the table, her hands dropped and tussled with her gray slacks, as if they were an assailant. Despite the frantic motion of her fingers, all she accomplished was to rustle her pants slightly. Was this an act? Or was the fiery passion I saw earlier the actual performance?

I leaned against the table and pulled the skewered olives out of my drink. "Based on the conversation I had with your uncle, I'm going to assume you consider him to be a little overprotective."

Bella nodded.

I pulled an olive off my skewer and brandished the remaining ones at Bella like they were a baton. "That's why you choose to deal with them at all, isn't it?"

It was small, but I saw a slight quiver in her jawline. While it confirmed I was on the right track, it also highlighted she was uncomfortable with the whole topic. "Fine, we can explore this a little. Yes, both he and my father are overly protective of me. While their attention makes me feel special, it comes at a terrible price."

"You could have the positive feeling without the price anytime you want."

Bella scoffed and leaned over her knees, clasping her hands. "If that's so, please explain. I'd love to hear about it."

"Certainly," I said, nodding my head as I dismissed her attempt at sarcasm. "Go on a handful of dates, and you'll experience the same feeling. I can't think of any reason a man wouldn't lavish his attention on you. Even if you ended up on a date with a blind man, the moment you started speaking, your voice would convince him of your beauty."

Despite expecting a reaction to the blatant flattery, I hadn't expected to see shock. That is until I remembered another of Dempsey's comments about his niece. She isn't fully aware of the effect she has on other people. Initially, I'd dismissed the idea, but the shock slathered across her face was indisputable. Was her uncle correct? How could she be so unaware of the impact her looks had on others? Perhaps her attitude was just a mask she wore. But if it was, how did Dempsey fail to see through it? And what might motivate her to create that kind of persona? Was it possible she believed it was her relationship with Dempsey that affected the people in her life and not her looks?

Either way, aside from a slight insight into her psyche, the shock looming in her eyes told me little. After a few moments, she batted the stray emotion from her face and snatched her drink, gulping a mouthful. A forced scoff broke the tense silence as she batted my comment away with a hand. "You're far too kind, but men don't show me genuine kindness based on my merits."

Her eyes darted toward her uncle as her fingers whitened around the stem of her glass. "The only reason people are nice to me is because they're afraid of my family. Well, specifically, they fear finding themselves locked in a box with only my father or uncle as company."

As the last word tumbled from her, a single tear streamed down her cheek. And with that, everything clicked. Contrary to her uncle's opinion, she knew how her beauty affected people, but she was so blinded by her family's influence that she couldn't trust her looks. I couldn't blame her for making that assumption, not with her family.

I pushed off the chair and leaned forward, clutching my martini with both hands as it dangled over the floor. "Would you mind if I asked you a question?"

"It depends on what you ask," she said through clenched teeth.

"Do you believe your uncle influenced how I've treated you?"

"I don't know," she said, lifting her olives out of her drink. She bit down on the one closest to her fingers and freed both from their skewer with a fluid jerk. "Though, based on all my previous experiences, I'd have to believe you were trying to score points with him."

"Have you forgotten that I assumed your uncle wouldn't be here?"

Bella shook her head.

"How about the lack of knowledge concerning your relation to Dempsey?"

"That could be true, or a small white lie. I don't know what's going through your head."

I placed my drink on the table and rubbed my eyes. "It's the truth. I just about had a heart attack when he addressed you as his niece. But aside from that, don't forget all we hear on the west coast about your uncle are the rumors around his shady business, not his family."

Bella laid her drink down as she swallowed the olives. "Is that so?"

"Has your uncle ever lied to you?"

She shook her head as she gripped the glass with her delicate fingers.

"When you get the chance, ask him about my reaction when he informed me you were his niece. If I'd been eating something, you would have noticed emergency services getting the food out of my trachea."

"Really?"

"Has my position toward you altered since Dempsey skipped the line to talk with me?"

In a rapid transition, her face went from restrained sadness to utter confusion. "Are you seriously telling me you didn't know about that relationship prior to him informing you?"

Her uncle truly blinded her. No wonder he described her as a wallflower. She had no way of knowing who was genuinely friendly versus who was trying to gain some brownie points by using her. "Yes, I am, but that's not all I'm trying to tell you. I'm telling you that who your uncle is simply doesn't matter to me. You're a good person, and I have honestly enjoyed our conversation with all its highs and lows. Whatever he's done—and by the stories I've heard, it's a vast array of questionable acts—it doesn't need to define you. Your words and actions do that. How would you like to be defined?"

A warm chuckle leaped from her mouth as she shifted in her seat and straightened her back. "I like that. Though with that commentary, you sound a bit too much like a fortune cookie."

"Clichés aside, the fundamental truth behind the words is still there. We're not the sum of our parents' actions. Whatever they do, or did, it's their past. We don't inherit their sins or consequences. While we can and should learn from their choices, those actions ultimately hold no sway over our lives."

Another bout of laughter bubbled out of her as her tongue slid along her teeth. "Unfortunately, for you, that argument might hold more sway over me, if my father and uncle weren't still around trying to decide my life. Honestly, it's hard to discern my footprints from the mess littered behind me."

"Have you tried outracing them?"

More laughter washed over me as she shook her head.

"Given Dempsey's obligations to his organization, he can't be as nimble as you. If you wanted it, you could outrun his influence."

Her smile widened as she scooted her chair closer to me. "You're a good one. A little naïve, but you're a wonderful man." When her chair bumped against mine, she laid her head on my shoulder. "There is no running from this family. All you can hope for is to survive it. Hopefully, you'll find someone worthy of standing by your side, even if it's only for a moment."

Pleasantly surprised by both her words and her head lying on my shoulder, I took a chance and draped my arm around her, giving her a comforting squeeze. "You mentioned that you have to pay a price when you take their affection." I felt her soundless reply, and knowing this was a sensitive topic, I lowered my voice. "If you don't mind me asking, what is it?"

She kept her head on my shoulder as she released her breath. "For that fleeting moment of happiness, I come out feeling dirty. I'm sure I would feel the same way if I swam through a sewage drain. Unfortunately, those moments of joy become shorter every time I attempt to seize them. Given enough time, those moments won't move the needle at all."

"It can't be that terrible."

"Says someone who's never had to suffer through that burden."

With another gentle squeeze, I pulled the last olive from my drink. "If you can't stand either your uncle or father, why do you even come to the tournament?"

"It's not to please them."

"They don't like how skilled you've become at playing poker, do they?"

"No. Neither of them considers my becoming a card shark a worthy pursuit."

As my smile widened, I took another sip of my martini. "So is the rebellion the only reason you attend?"

"It's a reason," she said, shrugging her shoulders. "Though as you said, the money is a pretty good perk."

There it was. I'd known she'd be looking for that payday. Most professionals would angle for that chunk of money. But given she won this thing last year, she could claim that kind of money throughout the year at casinos throughout the nation. What's the real reason she was here? As my mind toiled over the question, she reached out, grabbing her drink.

"I mean, anything I can do to keep prize money flowing back to my uncle is better than the alternative."

CHAPTER 6

"Excuse me?"

"My uncle employs a handful of highly skilled players for this tournament. So if I can carry some of the entitled nitwits he invites to the final table, I would consider it a win."

That was an impressive attitude. Here she was, not exactly terrified, but lacking any affection for her own family and actively working against them. I idly wondered what Dempsey would do if he ever realized his niece's true intentions. She was a good person, even if she couldn't or wouldn't see past her family's shadow. Though her voice lost its joviality, replaced with the emotionless tone of her uncle.

"That's a decent goal." I took a swig of my drink and smacked my lips as the complex flavors tumbled down my throat. "I'll do what I can to join you at the final table. That way, we can double our chances of keeping him from getting a secondary windfall."

She turned her head, locking eyes with me as her grin tugged at the corners of her eyes. "I made it there last year, and so help me, I'll do it again. Though that won't guarantee we'll be able to keep my uncle from capitalizing on one of his secondary schemes. All I can do is secure my position in the top ten and hopefully drag one or two of the pampered elites with me."

After taking another swig of my drink, I placed it down and brushed her cheek with a knuckle. "What's the big deal about that achievement?"

She swatted my chest as she sat up and repositioned her seat. "Reaching the last table guarantees you at least a refund of your entrance fee."

I felt my eyes grow as I processed her words.

Suddenly a full body laugh, emanating from her belly, broke the rising tension swirling about us. She reached up, covering her mouth. "I'm sorry, Marcus, but this isn't a winner take all tournament. Everyone in the top ten will take money home. While the tenth place slot reclaims your entrance fee, the prizes grow from there."

"Huh."

Her smile widened as she played with her hair. "You thought whoever won would get all the money Dempsey didn't claim, didn't you?"

Despite the mounting embarrassment, laughter spilled out of me. "Well, not really. I knew Dempsey took a portion of the entrance fees. . . ." When I caught sight of her eyes, I knew any excuse I could provide would make me appear more foolish. I gripped the stem of my glass and thumped it against the table, swallowing the fledgling thought. "Yeah, I thought this was a winner-take-all tournament, less Dempsey's hefty share."

"It takes courage to admit it when you're wrong." Her smile widened as she tucked her hair behind her ears. "It's good to know you're willing to do that."

"The smile looks good on you."

Her grin intensified, and just like that, she found a crack in my mental armor. Was she good at reading people? Was I just not defending myself effectively? Once she saw me notice, she silenced her laughter and forced the smile off her face to appease my bruised ego. "That was how my uncle ran these tournaments, originally."

"When did it change?"

"The second year, when the professionals refused to return. As I'm sure you can imagine, they didn't enjoy walking out of here with nothing, despite reaching the top ten."

"Yeah, that would be infuriating."

"Well, my uncle quickly found out he needed the pros more than they needed his tournament."

CHAPTER 6

"Why's that?"

"It was the only year when there wasn't a waiting list. It also affected the betting that takes place during the tournament as more of the spoiled rich made it to the top ten. My uncle, ever the savvy businessman, quickly changed the rules and sent out a profuse apology to the professionals. However, it took a couple of years to undo the damage completely. But eventually, the pros returned, and Dempsey tamped down on the plants. But after so many years, everyone is happy, and Dempsey's money streams continue to churn, though I enjoy doing my part to blunt them."

While chewing the edge of my thumb, I released my glass and shook my head. "Obviously, I know your uncle's role in the tournament, but does your father find his way to these events as well?"

With a warm, though rather unsettling smile, she laid a hand on my knee. "You really didn't know about my family before we started talking."

"I really didn't."

"Well, they both meet everyone who comes to the tournament. Only my father does it at the front door. Good old pops, he and his underlings pat down everyone who comes inside. Well, almost everyone. It's another perk of being in the family, I suppose. They trust me."

I leaned over, lifting a finger toward the door. "Your father is one of the men guarding the entrance?"

She did a horrendous job of hiding a laugh behind her hands. When she finished, I still couldn't get anything past my lips, so she pushed my arm down and patted my cheek. "Yes. In fact, I sought you out because you made an impact on my father. As such, I needed to meet with you."

As she spoke, I watched a smile break out on her face, which threw me even more off balance. "And I'm sure good old pops told my uncle about you as well. Oh, you should have seen my father's face when my uncle shook your hand and left you intact. I'm certain he would have preferred seeing you trussed up and roasting on a spit."

I had thought I had seen her biggest smile earlier, but somehow it was still widening. My laughter joined hers, surprising us both. Seconds later, her face went red. Before she could say anything, I leaned forward, grasping her hands.

"Here you thought I was trying to curry favor from you, because you thought I knew about your father and uncle, like everyone else probably does. But I honestly had no clue. And to top it off, all this time you were using the anger I brewed with your father to make him and your uncle uncomfortable." She didn't offer a different explanation, so I just sat there dumbly staring at her. She was very good. It never crossed my mind she had a hidden motive for joining me.

When I looked back at her face, I saw the color receding, which was unfortunate. That blush suited her. But I could tell she was trying hard not to rejoin my laughter. "You have to admit, this is absolutely hilarious."

She nodded as pops of laughter burst from her lips.

As I forced the laughter away, I took a swig of my martini and sighed. "Without a doubt, I can say you're one of the most complicated people I've ever met."

Eyeing me with the same type of measuring stare her uncle had used earlier, she eventually replied. "Thank you, I think." She watched me nod before she repositioned her chair to lay her head back on my shoulder. "That's the closest anyone's come to offering me a genuine compliment in quite some time."

"There's a chance that I can offer you more if you'd like."

CHAPTER 6

She leaned back in her chair, pulling her folded hand up to her stomach. "Is that so?"

I clinked her glass with mine and looked down into her eyes. "Rather, I'll offer you the chance after the tournament."

"My oh my." She perked up, her eyelashes fluttering.

There was no turning back now. Amidst the fluttering butterflies, I emptied my glass and set it back on the table. With a slight hitch to my breathing, I clasped my hands over my knees. "Would you like to accompany me for a meal once the tournament is wrapped up? My treat, of course."

"Marcus, are you asking me out on a date?" Her voice was thick with playful teasing, letting me know my question pleasantly surprised her.

In response, my grin widened. "I believe I just did."

"Just avoid sitting at my table when we begin. I would hate to ruin our first date by taking your money so early."

CHAPTER 7

After a brief respite, Bella grasped my hands and whirled around, shoving her face into mine. "Can you do something for me?"

My mouth widened as a hesitant laugh escaped me. "It would depend on the request."

"It's important," she said, her nose inching closer, almost brushing against mine. "I need you to pay attention to me."

I extricated my hands from her grip and brushed a lock of her strawberry blond hair behind her ear. "You've had it for some time now."

Her lips curled into a devious smile as her eyes drilled through me. "Whatever happens, don't win my money."

A horse chuckle tumbled through my lips as I grabbed my drink. I shoved it toward her and shook it back and forth, doing what I could to prevent any of the sloshing liquid from escaping. "You realize that all the attendees here are hoping to knock everyone else out of the game, don't you? I mean, this is how the tournament works."

She playfully punched my stomach as she rolled her eyes. "While that may be true, if you knock me out, I don't think I'd be willing to accept your offer for a date."

The mix of playful and serious tones running through her voice told me far more than her words. While she might not like it

CHAPTER 7

if I bounced her from the tournament, it wouldn't keep her from accepting the date. Leaning forward, I brushed her cheek with my knuckles. "I'll do what I can to avoid ruining your trip." With a broad smile, I took a sip of my drink and settled back into my chair. "However, once we reach the final table, all bets are off."

A chuckle flowed through her lips as she mixed her drink. After a few seconds of pensive thought, she stopped swirling the liquid and latched onto me as she offered a knowing wink. "I suppose that's a fair arrangement. At that point, while you might prevent me from claiming a larger prize, the worst you could do would be to send me home with my entrance fee refunded."

"Seems more than fair," I said, sipping more of Simon's work.

She grabbed her clutch and patted my arm. "Thank you for this."

"For the conversation?"

"That and more." After draining her glass, she thumped it on the table and looked at me with warm eyes. She tucked her purse under her arm and flashed me a warm smile. "Given our recent conversation, I'll assume you can appreciate that what you've given me is more valuable than a diversion while we wait for the tournament to begin. Though I doubt you can understand what your kindness means to me, or how good it makes me feel."

"Bella," I said, placing my martini on the table before collecting her hands, "don't forget, with the proper mindset and focus, you're not bound to your family. There's always a way out, provided you're willing to find it."

Her gaze drifted away from me as she slipped her hands from my grasp. "There are moments when I think you might be correct, and right now, I think one of those crossroads could be right down the road."

My lips twisted into a lopsided smile as my eyes slid to the wall that I believed held a secret doorway leading to wherever we would play. With a heavy sigh, I tapped Bella's shoulder as a wry chuckle eked out of me. "Mind if I asked a question that'll high-light my ignorance?"

She fanned herself with her clutch as she batted her eyes. "I didn't think you were someone who would offer an opponent such a valuable insight into any of your weaknesses."

"While there's a chance my ignorance may impact me," I said through a broad grin, "the likelihood of that is highly improbable, considering my poor judgment and naivety aren't connected to my play. As a result, it's unlikely to give you much of anything that you can use against me." I wrung my hands as I leaned into my chair. "Granted, I wasn't planning on converting anyone here into a confidant. However, given everything we've talked about, I'm glad you gave me the opportunity to confide in you."

Her smile twisted into an impish grin as she poked my side. "Are you sure about that? Maybe you regret all the accidental insights you've surrendered to me." With a wink, she jabbed my stomach. "Either way, your willingness to give me insight into your mind is a bold move."

After swallowing a quiet laugh with my hand, I leaned onto my knees, clicking my tongue. "That decision holds true for you as well, but let's put that aside for the moment. Since you're aware of my ignorance, would you mind another potentially silly question?"

Her smile tugged at the corners of her eyes as she crossed her legs. "Why would I mind?"

I spread my arms out like a bird of prey circling its next meal, as I straightened my back. "While this room is brimming with all the opulent trappings that the elite could hope for or want, it's missing the most important piece."

CHAPTER 7

"What's that?"

I rubbed my lips as my eyes flicked to what I assumed was the false wall. "Given everything here, I doubt this is where we are going to play."

She folded her arms across her chest as her head bobbed slightly. "So far I'm not sensing any ignorance, just a well-thought-out assumption."

"My question," I said, dropping my hands to my lap as I turned toward her, "is where will we be playing?"

Bella raised her hands to her chest, clapping them a few times as her eyes flicked about the chamber. "Honestly, I'm not sure. Don't forget, while this is your first tournament, this is only my second one, and it's not providing me any insights."

"How's that? Even if your uncle rearranged everything, you should have a decent guess." I placed an arm on the table and whirled my index finger about the room. "Surely, with this kind of ambiance, you would have asked about the history."

"I did," she said, nodding.

"If that's so," I said, leaning over my knees as I lowered my voice, "then why don't you know how your uncle laid out the building?"

She lifted a swishing finger as laughter rang out in time with each flick of her hand. After a few seconds, she folded her hands and tipped her chair onto its front legs. "There's the ignorance I expected to find."

As my fingers massaged my forehead, a scoff slipped out of me. During the next handful of frantic seconds, my brain whirled, looking for what would have been a less foolish question to ask. Unfortunately, no matter how I examined the situation, I kept coming back to the same and apparently flawed conclusion. Of course, as I was about to object to her admonishment, the obvious answer slapped me in the face. Instantly, my shoulders slumped as my gaze fell to my martini.

"Would asking if we are in the same location as last year have shielded my naivety a bit more?"

She reached forward, tapping my nose. "That's a small step of redemption."

I took another sip of the drink and held her eyes. "Well, is this the same place?"

"No," Bella said, thumping the table with her knuckles. "Last year's tournament took place in a different warehouse. And according to the more seasoned players, my uncle has yet to recycle a location." She spread her fingers wide and placed her palm against the smooth stone as she eased her chair back onto the ground. "While there's a chance that he might be forced to leverage a previous building in the future, I don't think that'll be a problem in this decade."

The muscles in my neck quivered as I drew several conclusions from that piece of information. While I'll admit I was wielding assumptions, they were fairly well-grounded by the rumors about Dempsey and what I saw here. Though, as I shifted my focus to the ornate décor, it was hard to balance the extravagance with Bella's ordinary tone. If I ignored the content of what she said, I could have imagined her placing an order for a hamburger at some fast-food joint. But then, for Dempsey and his kin, those two thoughts could be equivalent.

Once again, I leaned back and studied the surroundings, though this time it was with a fresh perspective. While the majesty of the room was inescapable, the sheer opulence was something else. I took another sip before using the glass to point at the more opulent aspects of the room.

"The cleanup must be even more intensive than the setup."

CHAPTER 7

One of Bella's eyebrows rose as her smile curled into a mischievous grin. "Why would you say that?"

"Reclaiming all of this can't be easy." I put my drink down as a free finger whipped over my head, encompassing the entire room. "Unless you're telling me he leaves it all in place as he resumes storing random goods on the premises."

Bella draped an arm on the marble slab and instantly started tapping out a dull march. As she continued authoring a stilted beat, her grin softened as her head tilted to a side. "Here's another example of how you're benefiting from being a genuine friend."

While she continued the march with one hand, the other swept about, highlighting the various attributes of the room's grandeur. "You think this costs my uncle a veritable fortune, don't you?"

"Yeah."

"Well, if he didn't possess his influence, authority, and power, it would."

"How can all this not be expensive?"

"Because," Bella said, as her drumming fingers quickened their pace, "he's managed to sink his hooks into several master craftsmen over the last decade or two. While they don't all share the same skill set, the array of knowledge covers everything needed to produce this chamber."

"Everything?"

The march slowed as Bella nodded. "Everything from the woodwork to the metalwork and even the paintings. Based on previous conversations and my experience, he refuses to recycle anything."

"That's ridiculous."

Continuing the beat, Bella whirled a finger over her head, dragging my attention to the grandeur looming over us. "You might want to guard that foolishness a little better. Once you understand that Dempsey owns the craftsmen, you can appreciate that, aside from buying the materials, he doesn't pay them much. In fact, he encourages them to consider their effort here as a price for his benevolence."

My eyes bulged as a soft whistle teased my ears. Once again, I pulled my gaze away from Dempsey's niece and studied the room's details. After a moment, I felt the weight from the opulence weighing on me like a lead blanket. Despite knowing a number of stories that detailed Dempsey's ruthlessness, his abuse of master craftsmen bothered me. Granted, I didn't afford them the same guaranteed protection I provided women and children, but I did my best not to harm anyone with that kind of mastery.

Bella gripped my chin and pulled my gaze back to her. Her sorrowful eyes appeared to swell with tears, which refused to flow. She released me and laid her hand on mine. "Does any of that really surprise you?"

"It shouldn't," I said, licking my lips. "Though I'll admit I'm slightly shocked by his brazenness."

"Considering how new you are, I suppose I should be fair with what I tell you."

"What do you mean?" I asked, as I inched toward the edge of my chair.

"From what I've heard, the craftsmen don't mind my uncle's demands."

"That can't be right," I said, bolting upright as I searched for the crime lord. "Why would they be okay with that kind of yearly theft?"

"It makes enough sense once you understand how massive this affair really is." Her fingers intensified their beat as her eyes narrowed. "Each of the craftsmen considers their donation to be a perfect way to advertise their skills to the elite."

CHAPTER 7

"The tournament actually improves their bottom line?"

Bella leaned back into her chair as her fingers slowed their haphazard beat. "Technically, I should correct what I said about my uncle refusing to pay them. While he doesn't compensate them in full, he gives them something for their work besides the free publicity to potential clients." She thumped her knuckles against the hard stone as her grin soured. Closing her eyes, she huffed as her fingers stilled. "Take these tables and chairs, for example."

"What about them?"

She leaned forward and brushed the table's rim with her fingers. "Unfortunately, for my dear uncle, he doesn't have access to quality stone masons yet. Which means he most likely had to purchase these, and their matching chairs, at their full price."

"That's got to hurt his ego."

"Not really."

"How could he possibly not—" She reached up with her left hand and laid a finger across my lips, bringing my protest to an abrupt halt. When I looked down at her, she was smiling, and I could hear the words she was thinking. *You're being foolish again.*

After a few seconds, she withdrew her finger. "Do you remember me mentioning that he has multiple money streams for this event?"

I nodded.

"Well, once he crowns the winner, my uncle sells these collaborations," Bella knocked on the table, "of art and function to the participants, at a price where he only needs to sell a handful to recoup his losses."

I grasped the table with both hands as I studied the expertly carved stone. "You can't be serious. Who would pay that much for these?"

"He's not marketing them to the pros. He's aware they won't consider the price worth it. However, enough of the spoiled elite consider it an excellent purchase, and with those foolish investments, he makes a tidy profit."

With another half-hearted smile, she brushed my cheek. "Don't forget that this is a unique experience for the young socialites. Also, the constant change in design keeps them interested every year. With all those lures, it's not surprising that they consider the tables a worthy consolation prize."

"Talk about your expensive trinkets."

Bella's lip quivered as she ran a finger along the smooth stone. "While these are far plainer than last year's, they're still remarkably ornate."

"How many of these does he manage to sell?"

"Last year, I think he sold almost half of the inventory."

"What does he do with whatever stock he can't sell?"

"Once he's secured a healthy profit, he leaves behind whatever he can't move."

"For the police to find?"

Over the course of our conversation, I'd seen a range of Bella's smiles, from the forced, to the genuine, and many in between. Yet the one gracing her face was the oddest mix of emotions I'd seen. Before I could catalogue what I found, she quickly pushed the unfamiliar emotions off her face as she reached out to tap the tip of my nose.

"Am I being foolish again?"

"Got it in one." She brushed my nose with a couple of fingers as she leaned back into her seat. "Don't forget the authorities know about this game. They're simply delayed long enough for my uncle and his lackeys to remove any evidence they were here, and all the guests have left. When the police eventually arrive, they find the furniture with an anonymous note gifting everything to whoever wants them."

I sat there, staring at the furniture, silently calculating what the price tag of these tables and chairs were. I gave up when I realized that whatever their cost, a policeman's taxes would be destroyed by such a gift. "The cops have got to hate these presents by now."

"That's precisely why they constantly donate them to charity, and since everyone knows my uncle commissioned them . . ."

"Don't tell me he gets a tax write-off to boot?"

A hearty laugh tumbled from Bella as she shook her head. "No, he hasn't decreased his taxable income yet. Though I'm sure he's tasked his accountants to look for the loophole that would allow him to write them off. But that wasn't what I was going to say."

"I'm sorry, I couldn't help myself. What were you going to say?"

"The charities that receive the donations love my uncle."

How did such an unassuming man insulate himself so well? How could the people who he exploited be thankful for anything? As my mind raced to find answers, Bella poked my stomach. When I glanced down, she twisted my gaze toward what I'd assumed to be a false wall. "Pay attention now."

Her uncle stood between the two bars with his arms clutched behind his back, waiting for the room to fall silent. After several seconds, under nothing but his watchful glare, the room's din succumbed to his mighty will, and a silence settled among the gathered throng of players. He took a single step forward as his arms spread out, like a father preparing to embrace his children.

Bella prodded my stomach with her finger as her mouth drifted toward my ear. "It looks like he's ready to get started. Don't forget to pick a table other than mine."

When I turned my head, our lips almost brushed together. "This tournament doesn't prearrange the tables?"

With a warm smile, Bella forced my gaze back to Dempsey. "My uncle doesn't believe in micromanaging these tournaments, which means he allows us to influence how the game plays out. Personally, I'm hoping my first table is filled with nothing but the elite."

Before I could reply, she leaned back into her chair and poked my back as Dempsey took a single step forward. He turned his head and coughed behind a loose fist, shattering the charged silence. Given what I'd learned about the craftsmen, I realized the crime lord had to have his claws sunk into a handful of quality engineers, considering that was the second place where sounds projected throughout the chamber.

I brushed my lips with my thumb as the attendees in the building turned toward Dempsey. Once everyone was focused on him, he clicked his heels. "With all the pleasantries observed, we can turn our attention to the crux of what brought us here."

A few of the more spirited billionaires responded in excited affirmation, again allowing the professionals and his men to tag the cannon fodder. However, the most chilling aspect to their outcry was Dempsey's timing. This was one of those stories that would only emphasize his legend. Somehow, he ensured the timing of an uncontrollable exultation with the opening of the hidden doors behind him.

They swung away from him as if they were gliding across a field of ice. I rubbed my chin as I perched on the edge of my seat, lost in thought. Even though I scoured that stretch of wall as best I could, I hadn't been able to find any trace of the door. Though given Dempsey's access to master craftsmen, it didn't surprise me I'd missed their work. Which just confirmed Dempsey controlled some of the best.

CHAPTER 7

As the two doors finished their journey, another one of Dempsey's traits snapped into place. He was a master showman. The only way he could have timed that exchange was if he'd scripted it. It wouldn't take much for his plants to rile up some of the cannon fodder. Since the doors ran the entire height of the wall, it also appeared like some unseen figure had ripped the wall in half. Dempsey was leaning into his myths, and while it wasn't likely to impress the professionals, it impressed the entitled rich.

When they stopped moving, Dempsey's lips curled into a false smile as his arms stretched out. "If you would all please come this way. We will begin just as soon as everyone selects their seat." Instead of waiting for the players to enter first, Dempsey turned around and walked through the doorway, flanked by his personal attendants.

"Well," I said as I turned toward Bella, "I guess that means we have to get up."

With a slight chuckle, she rose and arched her back. "Only if you want a chance to play."

After standing up, I offered her my arm as I inclined my head. Her cheeks reddened ever so slightly as she latched onto it. Given how quickly she entwined her arms around mine, it was obvious she was desperate for a bit of pampering. I patted her hand as we sauntered through the newly opened doorway. While I'd thought the outer chamber was over the top, this new room revealed the restraint Dempsey had when designing the lounge.

Bella stepped in front of me and poked my stomach.

My fingers rubbed where she'd prodded me as I flashed her a mock sneer. "That wasn't nice."

"You need to keep moving." After several more pokes to my side, her grin warmed. "Don't worry. I won't tell anyone how new you are."

"No, you don't have to." I extracted my arm and rubbed my sore side. "It would seem I've done that for myself."

As I drew in a deep lungful of the stale air, I stared into her eyes and saw she was just as impressed as me. She simply buried it better than I could. I only saw it because of our conversation. Given she was Dempsey's niece, she must have grown up exposed to this kind of opulence, but even this room was too much for her. I took an uneasy step forward as my eyes whipped about the room, cataloging everything.

Five minutes alone with these riches would allow me to buy a private island anywhere in the world and disappear. How much money did Dempsey pour into these tournaments? Was any of it reused? While he might get away with discarding the entire lounge, if he did that with this room, he would go broke the next year.

Stepping away from the crowd, I pulled Bella close. "You mentioned Dempsey reuses nothing in the lounge, but how about this arena?"

"Mostly, I think."

Licking my lips, I pulled her hands to my chest. "You don't sound so sure about that."

"If I had to guess," she said, rolling onto her toes, "I'd say he reuses the materials. But he's fond of the décor being different every year, according to the attendees who've become a staple here."

With a partial understanding, I released her hands and spun around, absorbing everything. "In other words, he takes these decorations down, dismantles them, and has his craftsmen rebuild them into something fresh every year, while keeping a sense of familiarity."

"Sounds about right," Bella said, laying a hand on my back. "I had the same thought the first time I saw this room."

CHAPTER 7

The room was massive. At least that's what it looked like. However, based on my initial observations of the building, I knew this room couldn't be as big as it appeared. I'm sure the crime lord's engineers did their magic to trick the eye, but I felt like an ant staring up and wondering about the odd moving mountain heading my way. In the middle were ten full-sized poker tables.

If you picture the ones from Vegas or from a televised tournament, you'd be in the general vicinity of a good comparison. Yet, that mental image can't relay the sheer amount of wealth Dempsey was displaying. While the former tables are elegant, they're also very utilitarian. On the flip side, just like the ones in the lounge, these were more works of art than anything else. The bulk of the mass appeared to be polished silver. That would have been enough of a flex, but Dempsey wanted to go a step above. Each table had a series of gemstones inlaid into the visible legs. While I couldn't see the playing surface yet, given everything else I'd seen, it had to be just as over the top.

When I pulled my gaze away from the tables, I noticed the walled off observation deck lining the room. As I rubbed my forehead, I felt more like a gladiator entering the Roman Coliseum than a poker player getting ready for a game. Though, given our dramatic entrance, we certainly made interesting stand-ins for the gladiators of old. As we marched toward the open seats, I wondered who would want to watch our battles. But my eyes quickly found the answer as I registered the people milling about the seats. Indeed, we were a fresh take on the ancient warriors. "Where did they come from?"

Again, my guiding light saved me from further embarrassment. Bella tugged my arm as her finger swept across the spectators. "Given the massive waitlist for this little party, there are too many people who want to be down here. Unfortunately, there are only a limited number of seats available. So what's an innovative criminal mastermind to do? Open the tournament up to those who can't participate while creating another stream of income."

"But they weren't out there," I said, jerking my thumb over my shoulder. "How'd they get in here?"

Bella reached up and gripped my face with her slender fingers. "In case you failed to notice our entrance," she jerked her head toward the doorway we'd walked through. "My uncle is fairly good at hiding and obfuscating doorways."

I closed my eyes and sighed.

She patted my cheeks as her smile grew. "When you consider where we came from, is it surprising we didn't see them enter?"

"I guess not." Despite my preparations, this warehouse had more than one entrance. Well, I had really screwed up this time. How did I miss an exterior door? While Dempsey's security prevented me from getting a decent look upon my arrival, I should have made other attempts to get the intelligence I required.

"Remember, Marcus," she said, winking at me, "we agreed to begin the tournament at different tables." And with that, she turned on her heels and went off to her right in search of an open seat.

As she disappeared into the crowd, I studied the rest of the room. The walls were just as ornate as the ones in the lounge, though their glint was a different hue. Other than the crowd, the wall's only other adornment was the singular bar. Normally, I wouldn't mind a little consolation. However, this wasn't a regular situation. This time, all that came from the move was a declaration that the free ride was over.

But the attribute that put this room over the top was the dangling chandeliers. Each of the half-dozen light fixtures appeared to be a handmade work of art. Yet somehow here I was, so close

CHAPTER 7

I could have snatched a single strand of metal and stones. While they provided some light, that wasn't their quintessential purpose. This was simply one more flex of Dempsey's wealth and power. And for the first time in years, my knees quivered.

A few settling breaths later, I sauntered through the tables and found one with four attractive ladies. I claimed the seat across from the dealer and studied the opposition. Two appeared to be professionals, while the others appeared to be easy marks. We sat in silence as other players joined us. Eventually, a somber man claimed the last seat.

The dealer prompted the newcomer and the player next to him for their opening bets, and once they surrendered their chips, the dealer began the tournament at our table. When I received my second card, I lifted both corners up and inspected the initial hand, finding a pair of aces. An excellent sign of things to come.

CHAPTER 8

After a stretch of bad hands, I lifted a corner of my latest one and mentally grinned at the suited nine and ten. I pinned the cards onto the table as my gaze drifted to Johnathon, who was still examining his own. Though after a few seconds, he slid his cards back to the dealer. Before the cards could be claimed, the living mountain, otherwise known as Tyson, tossed a few chips into the pot.

"Tyson raises the bet by three thousand dollars," the dealer said as he placed Jonathon's cards beside the deck.

"Too much for me," Kelly said, shoving her hand toward the dealer. Her fingers drummed the back of her cards as her eyes narrowed. "I'd appreciate some better cards. You've been giving me nothing but garbage so far."

"I'm sorry, ma'am" the dealer said, swiping the cards as Kelley's fingers rose and prepared to strike the discarded hand. As he placed her cards onto Jonathon's, he turned to the next player. "Sir, the action is to you."

Gregory slammed his cards onto the table before sliding them toward the dealer. "I'm afraid I'll have to follow Kelly's example."

The dealer turned toward Simone and offered her a friendly smile. "Ma'am, how would you like to proceed?"

However, instead of answering, Simone turned to her neighbor, Tiffany, and the pair quickly delved into a private conversation.

CHAPTER 8

Those two had to be friends outside of this tournament because they constantly launched into chats before either made a move. Fortunately, their antics proved they were members of the elite who'd secured a pass to play with the professionals from the initial hand. The sooner someone bounced them from the table, the sooner I could flush their tells from my mind, not that I needed them. Though I'd like to siphon a bit more before they left.

As I leaned over my cards, I stared at the two piles and mentally cheered. If these two kept up their reckless pace, they might present me with an opportunity to claim additional money this round. While we all took turns relieving them of their chips, Tyson had been the most recent recipient of their foolish decisions. Though given that he'd raised the bet for the flop, I wasn't sure I'd want to continue with this hand. When I looked back at the two socialites, I realized they were still in the early stages of their deliberation. So with a sidelong glance at William, I noticed a small stack of chips in his hand. And based on the rough number and denomination, it looked like he wanted to match Tyson's bet, provided these two didn't up the ante too much.

Eventually, the two women separated, and Simone split her stack in half before sliding it toward the dealer. "I think this is about fifty thousand."

With a smile of her own, Tiffany isolated a stack of equivalent value and added it to the pot. "That looks right to me."

William, myself, Malone, and Allison all folded in unison. Yet as the dealer settled our discarded hands in the growing discard pile, Tyson plucked one hundred and fifty thousand from his own stack and slid it toward the dealer.

The dealer leaned forward and roughly counted the stacks for Simone and Tiffany. "The bet will put both of you all in. Would you all like to proceed?"

Both women looked at each other and nodded as they moved their remaining chips forward. In unison, they flipped their hands over, revealing the garbage they went all in on. One of them had an unsuited deuce and seven, while the other held a mismatched eight and nine. I was so floored by their stupidity that I didn't pay attention to the community cards. All that mattered was that Tyson's ace and king took the round.

As he collected his fresh chips, one of Dempsey's goons stepped up to the table and escorted the two socialites to the seating looming over us. Shortly after their relocation, I caught sight of Simone interacting with someone, though he didn't appear to be a waiter. Rather, he looked like a classy bookie. Was she placing bets on the outcome of the tournament? It certainly looked like it. And considering I noticed other players noticing her actions and not commenting, I assumed it was standard procedure.

Of course, as my bad hands continued, my brain toiled through the reasons Dempsey would allow the spectators to bet on us. Honestly, it took me far too long to connect the obvious dots, but as one round finished, the truth slapped me across the face. This was one way Dempsey controlled his elite guests. It also crystallized the feeling I'd felt yet could not identify from the moment I saw the spectators. He turned us into modern-day gladiators. While we weren't engaging in the traditional blood sport, we were competing for the amusement of the elite.

This whole tournament was nothing but a spectator sport for the elite few who attended. While he allowed a few of them to take part in the tournament, if only for a short while, it provided them with an escape from their routine. Even if someone got lucky and knocked out a pro, it would only heighten their excitement. After the goons escorted the eliminated elite from the arena, they would join their own people and mingle, sharing their experiences with the rest. More importantly, they could place bets on the outcome of the tournament or whatever else they wanted to gamble on.

When Dempsey's control became clear, it revealed his real purpose. This enterprise wasn't about making money, not that he didn't. It was about social networking. Dempsey was slowly merging his business interests with society's elite. Sure, he made a healthy profit along the way, but even if Dempsey ran this tournament for a loss, he wouldn't stop, not when it provided him with the opportunity to influence the next generation of business leaders.

It was impressive how far out the man planned everything. He was running a game of his own, and everyone involved was a valid piece to move. He was teaching these future leaders to trust him; to lean on him; to come to him for everything. With that, it was no wonder Dempsey's sphere of influence was rumored to be as large as it was. And he was expanding it across the United States, one company or leader at a time. The companies represented here by their leaders wouldn't strictly belong to him, but they would still be his, or more importantly, under his influence. And because of the limited number of seats, the popularity of the event kept increasing. I could feel the weight of Dempsey's cold intellect just as much as Tyson's chip count, and they were both staggering.

Even though I'd folded a hand or two that could have turned out well for me, I didn't mind losing out on those situations, considering what I'd gained. In the larger scheme of things, understanding the truths behind the tournament and the man behind it would net me far more than a couple of early wins. As I refocused on the game, I watched as Tyson eliminated Malone and took a small chunk out of Gregory's stack. Fortunately, before Tyson could add another victim to his tally, I knocked Gregory out of the tournament. While my read of his tell was more of a hunch, it allowed me to capitalize on my straight and his bluff. However, Tyson's lead allowed him to bully everyone at the table, even me.

Half a dozen hands after bouncing Gregory, I studied Jonathan as he contemplated his options in response to Kelly's bet. If he'd spent more time scrutinizing the players both before the tournament and during the initial hands like I had, he would know she was bluffing. Though given the garbage in his hand, he should have folded anyway. Kelly's trash was better. Truthfully, I doubted I'd have isolated Kelly's tell if I hadn't pursued a few terrible hands myself. That was an excellent way to confirm speculations or plant false tells, provided the cost wasn't too high.

While I'd catalogued a solid dozen of Kelly's tells, the one I latched onto for this hand wasn't used often. True, she had hundreds of other mannerisms, but they were all derivatives of that core set. A few were obvious omens of an excellent hand, while a couple of others were used for laying traps for people like me. However, the vast majority were precious tools I or any of her more observant opponents could wield against her.

The slight twitch in her right eye was such a signal. It was easy to miss, unless you were looking for it, but it was a dead giveaway she was trying to bluff her way out of nothing more than a modest pair. While there were subtleties to the motion, all they did was intensify or lessen the need to bluff. Based on those nuances, I knew she'd been chasing either a straight or a flush. Unfortunately for her, the last of the community cars ripped that crutch away from her. Her pair, while it might be serviceable, was the weakest hand available with the cards in play. Not a good place to be when she jumped into the round with Tyson.

Out of all the players at the table, he was the only one I hadn't gotten a read on. As the seconds continued to draw out, Jonathan tapped his cards with his index and middle fingers. Nervous habits like that were a liability when it came to playing poker. On its own, that nervous tic meant little. However, after my crash course with these players, I knew he was going to fold, based purely on the speed of the tapping. In fact, I probably identified his course of action before he was consciously aware of his choice.

So, after several tense heartbeats, Jonathan confirmed my hunch when he shoved his hand toward the dealer. And then there were two. Kelly's bet passed to Tyson, and the man wasted no time re-raising. With that maneuver, Tyson secured one of two outcomes. Either he would eliminate her, or she'd fold. While she wasn't the most skilled player I'd met, Kelly was more than competent, which meant she'd reach that conclusion on her own. Her brain just had to get the message to her hands. Yet she sat there staring at Tyson's fresh raise, contemplating whether she'd go all in matching him. Had she somehow found a tell amidst Tyson's chiseled façade? Or was she frustrated with his bullying?

With another silence settling around the table, the analytical portion of her mind must have kicked in because she surrendered the hand to Tyson. The silent juggernaut smiled as he flipped over his pocket kings, revealing his winning hand, a kingly three of a kind. I could feel the blend of anger and frustration radiating from her. Was it possible that she could have won the hand if she'd stayed in? While a distant possibility, the more likely cause was the frustration with Tyson winning another hand. Begrudgingly, I had to admit Tyson was a very good strategist, though his steel etched face certainly helped mask his plans.

I rose from the table and arched my back as I rolled my shoulders.

"Giving up so soon, Marcus?" Allison asked with her sweet tones.

Despite her clumsy attempt to burrow under my skin, a raspy

chuckle washed over the table as I continued my stretch. When I was done, I placed one hand on my chair and grabbed my foot with the other, stretching my tightening quad. A few seconds later, I switched legs and answered her taunt. "Perish the thought, Alison. No, I'm simply stretching my stiff body. I was getting a little sore. I don't know about you, but after sitting down for this long, I need a stretch."

William grabbed enough chips to cover his blind wager and thumped them down in the middle of the table. "I don't care what the two of you do, provided you don't interfere with the ongoing game."

After securing Kelly's blind, the dealer dealt out the fresh hand, and when the final card settled in front of Tyson, six sets of eyes bored into me as I stretched my legs. A sigh tumbled past my lips as I dropped into my seat and peered at the corners of my cards. An ace and a seven were not much by themselves, yet they were both spades and that was worth pursuing to the flop, provided it didn't become too expensive. I sat there for a minute and tapped the table with my fingers, pretending to think about the odds but eventually matched the big. "They're good enough for the flop."

Allison propped up her cards, threatening to put a crease in them as she studied us, searching for any reaction. While she mentally ran through the odds for her hand, my eyes wandered around and ultimately landed on Tyson's cold and steely blue ones. Reflexively, I tried to look away, but I couldn't avert my gaze. It was as if his eyes produced their own gravity well, and I'd fallen into it. Something about them was off, and no matter how much thought I gave it, I couldn't isolate what was bothering me. A fact that only served to further unnerve me.

When I looked at something alive, I expected to see signs of life staring back at me. Especially when I focused on someone's eyes. Normally, I could tell when someone was driving the bus, so to speak. But whenever I stared into Tyson's eyes, I couldn't see the slightest sign of life. If the eyes truly are the windows to one's soul, then at that moment I would have shouted to the world that Tyson was without a soul. Truthfully, he might be proof the research into artificial intelligence had made a frightening leap, but I knew better. Robots didn't exist. So why was his gaze so lifeless?

As I worked on that question, I realized Tyson was silently and unobtrusively studying me. He took in absolutely everything about me, trying to build himself the perfect cheat sheet for future use. The fact I had caught him doing it didn't faze him. To the contrary, I thought I saw a shimmer of a smile as he continued collecting his precious data. And right then, not only did I feel incredibly exposed but I also knew Tyson was going to be at the final table. And I worried about making it there myself.

I had been so focused on Tyson's silent study of me, I almost missed Allison's announcement. But thankfully her clearing throat was the lifeline I needed to escape the influence of Tyson's eyes. I turned to her, catching the tail end of her words. "—can't justify moving on."

She was disappointed. At least I thought she was, not that I was able to correctly judge her emotional state, having just surrendered precious knowledge to Tyson.

With a scoff, Allison slid her cards toward the dealer. "I don't think anything would have helped that nonsense, and I'm not as foolish as Tiffany to chase a terrible hand."

The jest drew smiles from the entire table. It even cracked the stoic faces of the dealer and Tyson. Unable to stop from piling on the absent Tiffany, Jonathan calmly added his own thoughts.

"That may be, but I'm sure you would have been able to convince her otherwise."

I was certain his quip was just an attempt to deflect from his own dissatisfaction with his cards because he followed Allison's lead, tossing his hand to the dealer as well.

"True enough, but then where would the challenge have been?" Allison asked, but before anyone could respond, she stood up and inclined her head toward us. "I think I'll follow your lead, Marcus, but I think my stretch will take me over to the bar. I need a drink." She whirled about and sauntered off, waving her hand over her head. "Enjoy the round, everyone."

Without wasting his breath on unnecessary words, which meant he was his stoic and mute self, Tyson covered the blind. Despite my earlier thought, I regretted not folding my hand, despite just covering the blinds. Tyson's stare was just that unnerving. It was obvious he was just trying to bully the rest of us with his ever-increasing stack. Just like every other time Kelly had had the small blind, and no one raised, she paid the difference to see the flop. Finally, William checked away his opportunity to raise the buy in.

With the initial round of betting closed, the stern dealer quickly burned the top card before dealing out the first three community cards, and my mind danced a merry little jig. In the center of the table, the seven of hearts split the duce and jack of spades. So far in the tournament I'd caught three flush draws just like this. I was going to run with my past luck and wipe that expressionless look off Tyson's face; well that was my hope. But in truth, I wasn't going to exclude anyone still involved.

Kelly started the round with a check, meaning she wanted to see the rest of the table's interest before announcing her own, that or she was trying to bait an aggressive gambler. As the attention of the entire table turned to William, he reached for his chips. However, instead of making a bet, he played with his stack. After taking another look at his pocket cards, he slid the stack across the table.

"I think five grand will be a good first step."

After studying his face, I couldn't find a single tell. Truthfully, William did a decent job of hiding his emotions behind an unreadable mask. Yet, that didn't bother me since I studied players from their face down to the tips of their fingers and everything in between. And William's hands were not as schooled as his face. To anyone with enough knowledge of him, his fingers revealed everything. A few seconds of false consideration later, I tapped my largest stack of chips. "You must have something special to make a starting bet like that."

While not entirely true, considering his bet wasn't all that lavish, at least not for the moment, I was trying to bait him. You'll never hear me complain about free information, though it does make me yearn for more. Every tidbit was a potential weapon, and I was always seeking the best arms for these battles.

With an emotionless face, William turned to me and shrugged. "That's an interesting theory, Marcus."

William's words were a little too rushed, with too little force to be completely true.

"If you want to see what I have," William said, as he tapped the backs of his cards, providing some emphasis, "then you'll have to pay like anyone else."

His unschooled hands told me that while he had nothing solid, he was chasing down a better than decent draw, like me. Could he be hoping for a flush? It was possible, but that slight hesitation before his bet made me think the chances of that were unlikely. Even if he was after a flush, it made little difference. There were still two cards left to shape the game, and I was holding the better flush draw, since I held the ace. I had the best flush, so I might as well see just how far he was willing to go. "Let's make it eight thousand to see what's next."

Of course, the living statue tossed in the required eight thousand. But Kelly took a long look at what was out on the table and then thought about what she was holding before looking back at the rest of us and said, "Looks like it's time for me to get off this ride." Then she slid her cards toward the dealer before mumbling a curse under her breath. She needed to learn a little more control.

Once I raised his bet, William's hands had been busy with a small stack of chips, and as soon as Kelly folded, he asked the dealer, "That leaves me owing three grand, correct?"

"Yes, sir."

"There it is," William replied, as he added the required chips into the pile.

I kept my eyes on William, so I was barely aware of the dealer's motions. But since I needed the information to proceed, I watched William's hands. After I registered his reaction, my gaze drifted to the new community card, and I mentally jumped for joy when I registered the four of spades. While the spade should have completed his flush draw, he was still searching for something. While a straight flush was technically possible, I didn't think he was chasing it.

Yet William was playing with another stack as his gaze drifted from the community cards to me, then to Tyson, and back to his cards. Despite several more repetitions, I knew all of it was for show. He had already decided what his bet would be. He was trying to distract us with a show of indecision. He must have caught the flush and was now leaning into a potential straight flush.

"Hmmm . . ." he lifted the stack and let them slip through his fingers. "Well, I think I'll start this round out with ten thousand."

William's words were as calm as someone sitting at a bus stop, waiting for his ride without a care in the world. He was so confident, but how could he be if he was really chasing down a straight flush? In play, we all had access to the two and four of spades. I suppose he could have two low-value spades. If so, all he needed was another low spade. Could he really be chasing a straight flush? If he was, he had the flush to fall back on. Normally, that was an excellent fallback, but not when someone else was holding the ace.

"You said ten grand, right?" I asked, studying William's fingers as a chip flowed across my knuckles.

With a nod, William answered, "It's not too rich a bet for you, is it?"

He was certainly full of himself. It was time I cured him of that. "Certainly not, Willie," I said, using a familiar form of his name while I collected fifty thousand. I positioned the stacks in front of me and slid them across the table. "Not with my re-raise. You'll have to cough up an extra forty grand to stay in."

"Marcus," William said, with annoyance dripping from each syllable of my name. "You won't bully me out of this hand."

"Let's see how Tyson plays," I said, gesturing at the stoic sentinel. Yet William's outburst confirmed he was fishing for a straight flush. Despite my confidence, I couldn't explain it based on his tells. The only concrete thing I latched onto was his words. William needed a single card to achieve a straight flush, which was one of the best hands possible, given what was in play.

The stoic machine shoved his chips forward as a grin cracked his lifeless demeanor. I thrust a finger at the addition to the pot. "Willie, I wouldn't dream of it, though by the looks of it, our friend Tyson must have quite the hand since forty thousand is of no concern to him. And that short-lived smile is fairly frightening."

Allison swirled the contents of her glass as she reclaimed her seat. "I'm glad I bounced when I did. I dislike giving my money to Tyson."

A blustery William looked away from me and stared her down. "And just what makes you think he'll win this hand?"

"Well Willie, I think Allison is basing that statement on the fact that our apparently mute friend here has yet to actually lose a hand he's pursued." As I looked from William to Allison, I knew my logic had been sound. Once she gave me a slight nod, I grabbed a chip and walked it across my knuckles.

"Oh, Willie," Allison said, covering her mouth with her dainty finger. "I like that nickname, Marcus." She took a small sip of her drink and leveled her playful eyes on me. "While you're not wrong, I'd appreciate you letting me answer for myself. After all, I'm a big girl."

I knew she was only slightly serious, so I accepted the verbal slap. "I'm sorry, Allison; it won't happen again."

Scoffing at my mock apology, Kelly rolled her eyes. "Oh, please. We're all professional liars. Why should we believe anything you say?"

"Kelly dear," Allison said, running a finger along the rim of her glass, "just because you don't trust anyone doesn't mean I can't. I'm well aware of how skilled we are at bluffing and misleading each other. But his promise has nothing to do with the game, so I'm willing to trust him." She turned her head toward me and gave me a teasing wink. "Well, at least until he proves himself a liar away from the game."

"William, the bet is to you." Everyone, including the dealer, turned around and looked at Tyson.

The shock of someone we all thought of as mute speaking must've scared Kelly witless because she jumped out of her chair, breaking eye contact with Allison. When her heart stopped racing, she turned to face the steely eyed man. "It talks."

I was sure she had not meant for everyone at the table to hear her, but with the sudden silence, we could've heard a pin striking the floor across the busy chamber. Fixing her with his emotionless glare, Tyson shook his head. "Yes, I talk. But unlike the rest of you, I prefer to hold my tongue while I play. However, none of you have your attention where it belongs, which annoys me."

"Well, this should satisfy you, Tyson. Here is my extra forty grand." William placed his bet in front of him. He was playing it very calm for someone fishing for a straight flush.

While I knew what William was looking for, I attempted to read Tyson's body language. But it was like trying to climb a cliff upside down and, without a safety line, suicidal. But I needed something useful to attack him. Unfortunately, the stony visage betrayed nothing as the dealer revealed the last card of the hand. When I looked at the newest card, I found the three of clubs, and mentally whooped for joy. If it had been the spade, I would have lost.

My best guess for William's hand was the five and six of spades, which meant he fell into an inferior flush. As a result, I was going to beat him, but I needed to work on the mystery that was Tyson. What did he have? His icy gaze kept me at bay like a castle's moat. When I glanced back at William, he was busy counting over his chips, and as he went, he glanced at the piles in front of me and Tyson. "Well, since I'm the low man at this table, I think I need to rectify that. I'm all in."

I examined the cards laying in front of us, and a flush was the best hand, and I held the ace. I only thought about it for a moment before separating my chips. "Well, Willie, I think I'm going to follow your lead." When I had finished separating the piles, one covered William's bet, while the other stack would force Tyson to pony up a good chunk of his. "Well, my reserved friend, it's four hundred and fifty-three thousand to you."

Tyson stared at me, not with the lifeless eyes from earlier but with a measuring look, as if I was the point of interest in an internal debate. The duration made me think he was up to something, since he wouldn't be toying with folding if he had something. That or he was trying to place doubt in my mind for later. One thing was certain, he was a very skilled player. However, after a few tense seconds, he slid his cards to the dealer. "Not this time, Marcus."

As I pulled back the pile dedicated to Tyson, William's face was eager as he flipped over the five and six of spades. It was nice to get confirmation that I was right; too bad he was going to join the audience here in a moment.

The smug player reached forward as a smile slipped out. "Beat a flush, Marcus."

I reached out, pushing Marcus away from the pot. "It's too bad the river was the three of clubs. If it were the spade, you would have gotten a straight flush."

William rubbed his chin as his tongue slid across his teeth. "It's nice to hold a winning flush while you go fishing for something better."

I tapped my pocket cards as I leaned back in my seat. "That would have been the best hand if you had the right card." While it was mean, I enjoyed toying with William and the other players.

"I know that, Marcus," he said as he folded his hands right in front of his chin, and as he looked down at my cards, his mouth curled into a devious grin. "Show us what I beat."

With a broad smile, I revealed the seven of spades. And in that instant, the smug look plastered across William's face faltered.

Since the jack of spades was one of the community cards, he knew the next highest spade would decide the winner if we both had a flush. If I had another spade, he would lose everything.

I let the time stretch out for as long as I could, but eventually, the dealer prompted me to show my last card. While I focused my eyes on William's sweaty forehead, I lifted a corner of the card. Had William acted more like the gentleman he was supposed to be, I wouldn't have put him through this misery. When I had the card in front of my face, I turned it over so everyone could see and with a smile of vindication said, "Better luck next time, William."

Before anyone could really process William's coming departure, two of Dempsey's goons appeared out of thin air on either side of the eliminated player. One reason Dempsey used such a thuggish method to remove all the defeated players was because sometimes one of those players would try something. I had seen it once today, and it had been when Bella bankrupted Nicolai. As stupid as it was to assault Dempsey's niece, the man had made an attempt. And the pair had quickly stepped in to remove the flailing professional from the hall. Dempsey even apologized for the outburst before we got back to the game. The pair wordlessly helped William in his transition from active participant to sullen observer.

Tyson looked over at me and again I saw something alien in those eyes. What was it now? Why was that interesting? Had my petty act with William peaked Tyson's interest? If I kept this up, I would break him down in about, oh I don't know, maybe fifty years. Though the fact I'd bled the stone, even by as little as that, was a good enough reason for me to be pleased. Unfortunately, he saw it too because he cracked a little smile, which did more to unsettle me than any of his dead stares ever could.

"You played that well, Marcus," he said.

"My hand?"

Widening his smile, Tyson shook his head as he replied, "Not just your hand. The revelation was well played. It allowed William to think he might win while, in the end, you crushed his spirit."

I looked down as the dealer finished sliding the pot toward me.

For a second, we all thought Tyson had finished speaking, but I guess he just had to say one more thing. "Though I must admit, I thought you were bluffing. I'm very glad I didn't call you on that."

"Why's that?"

With his face falling back behind his stone etched mask, he spoke in an emotionless tone, "My flush would have lost to yours."

As Tyson's words sank in, I started idly fingering my stack. I quickly decided I needed to get out from under Tyson's glare. With a glance at the dealer, I asked, "Do I have the small?" When he nodded, I picked up the required amount and tossed it into the barren pot before standing up. "If you all would excuse me, I think I'm going to follow Allison's lead and get myself a drink."

CHAPTER 9

After the consistent drain of my stack, it was nice to finally win a pot. As I collected my winnings, I studied the remaining tables. With each clank of the stacking chips, I remembered how Dempsey's gentle thugs would approach and resettle a table's victors. Yet with every resettlement, they seemed intent on keeping everyone from joining our open seats. However, the moment the last individual was resettled, they would escort the vacant table out of the room as if it were a guest of state. When I placed the final chip on the small tower closest to me, I rubbed my eyes. Hopefully, that simple motion would plant a seed in the minds of everyone around me, and they'd try exploiting it later.

"That was nicely played," Allison said, resting her cheek on her fist. "Considering your recent play, I'm surprised you pulled it off."

I glanced from her warm yet devious smile to the chip smoothly flowing about her knuckles. As I forced my mouth into a complimentary grin, I snatched the top chip and flipped it like a coin. "Ever since William's departure, it seems everyone has taken turns courting lady luck." I caught the chip and laid it atop a pair of even stacks. "Keep in mind that we haven't lost someone in oh . . ." I glanced at my watch and tried some simple math, but dismissed it before getting the answer. "Let's just say it's been a while, wouldn't you agree?"

"Stealing little pieces of each other's pile has proven to be quite the killjoy," Kelly said in a dry voice as she tapped a chip against the table. She was either planting a wonderful false tell, or the monotony was getting to her. Personally, I was leaning toward the latter.

"Has it really been that long since you eliminated William?" Jonathon asked, rubbing the bags under his eyes. He must have had a late night before arriving, which meshed with his late arrival.

Though no matter the source of his exhaustion, mine was threatening to make my false tell a reality. I grabbed my drink and forced another bit of warmth through a mental image into the drink. Once the heat seeped out of my fingers, I sipped the altered water and felt a sudden surge of adrenaline and caffeine. I was going to have to flaunt that use of my skills to Matt, considering he claimed I wasted my time learning about the makeup of those chemicals.

"Yes, it's been a while!" Kelly, who'd been the solitary player who hadn't had a turn with luck, slammed her hands onto the table. "And since we've all grown cautious, it means we're unfortunately due for more of the same!"

Leaning back in my seat, I took another swig of my liquid sleep and nodded. "You are right that we've had to endure a rather tedious stretch, though some of us have found ways to occupy ourselves." And since I really didn't care about her reaction, I shifted my gaze to Tyson. "However, as the player most annoyed by our dithering, I figure you must be going absolutely stir-crazy sitting there and waiting for something to happen."

The closed-mouth Tyson looked up at me and asked, "Can I assume that the meaningless chitchat is finished for the time being?"

Every time I tried to stare down those lifeless eyes, a chill ran down my spine. The living statue still unnerved me, and I did my best to guard all my known tells. As those big dark eyes loomed over me, I hoped I'd been half as good as him. I cleared my throat as I scrubbed most of the emotions from my voice. "Despite your skills, your laconic nature makes me wish you'd joined another table."

For a second, I thought I'd rattled him. I saw a hint of confusion cross his brow. But as quickly as the expression had appeared, it was gone. Why had my statement gotten a reaction when all my deliberate attempts to poke the proverbial bear went unnoticed? I guess Tyson had prepared himself for everything other than a sincere statement. Before the silence could stretch much longer, Tyson nodded in acknowledgement before placing a neat little stack of chips into the pot. Immediately, Kelly added her small pile as she waited for the next hand.

Given the stagnant stretch of hands, I couldn't help but wonder why the blinds hadn't knocked someone out, since they were large enough. While they'd taken a chunk from Kelly, the rest of us had a turn or two courting luck. Still, I would have expected them to cause a little more havoc. The simple exchange of money was dreary and didn't seem to happen anywhere else. The other tables had been eliminating players. Aside from the initial purge, our table seemed unable to follow suit.

"Are you going to deal?" Kelly asked, rapping the table with her knuckles. Her eyes flicked to Tyson as her lips curled into a faint smile. "The walking mountain wants you to get moving."

However, the man's face didn't betray a single emotion. Granted, the remark wasn't one of Kelly's better verbal jabs, but he'd successfully ignored her every quip. To have enough control to prevent your face from dropping any hints meant he'd been playing for a long time. It also meant he had spent a majority of that time perfecting his mask.

While I'm sure she'd hoped for something, the impassive nature of the statue's face wasn't shocking. It would have been easier to coax blood from a stone, but that was Kelly's style. She was a bombastic player, and she played that stereotype perfectly. Fortunately, there are a couple of ways to deal with those kinds of players. First, you could ignore everything, though I'll admit that's easier said than done. If you can't block out the chatter, that left the other option, to twist their banter back onto them. While I'd opted for the latter, Tyson had chosen the wiser path, even though I hated admitting it. The man was like a piece of stone, just sitting there waiting for the next round to begin.

As the dealer's smooth motions delivered our hands, I studied him, since Dempsey seemed to like cycling through them. Shortly after Simone and Tiffany joined the spectators, our initial dealer was replaced. We also had fresh dealers shortly after each elimination, and then this individual joined us just a few hands ago. Apparently, Dempsey liked to keep his players strung out while his dealers remained fresh. Still, after we'd been playing this long, I found myself wishing for Dempsey to call for a break. It didn't need to be much, but something would help break up the grind.

Thankfully, I'd kept that desire to myself, because shortly after it popped into my mind, one of the spoiled elites voiced the same desire. That newbie had indeed been given what he asked for, only it was a more permanent version. His chips had been seized and redistributed amongst his opposition before the well-dressed goons escorted him into the stadium. My eyes drifted to the spectators, and I quickly found the man Dempsey had snubbed. His eyes burned with a white-hot rage threatening to incinerate the warehouse if he lost control.

I was thankful I had kept my mouth shut as another dose of my liquid sleep coursed through my veins. However, as time continued its steady march, I realized each dose wasn't producing the same effect as the previous ones. With each swig, I needed to intensify the stimulants lacing my water. Despite the diminishing returns, every time I sipped at my drink, I kept sleep from overtaking me, while other participants were overwhelmed by the exhaustion. Unfortunately, the chemically induced sleep was not as effective at muting the strain from mental exertion as it would have been against a lack of sleep. But I would take any edge I could get as I fought against exhaustion's efforts to drag me into the ranks of the overtaxed.

The dealer reached out and tapped the table in front of me as he said, "Sir, would you like to cover the bet or fold your hand?"

With my attention yanked back to the present, I bent down and examined my cards. When I lifted the corners, I discovered the king of spades and the ace of hearts. While an unsuited ace-king was a decent hand, I didn't want to overpay for the flop. Thankfully, it appeared no one else was willing to push the pot either, an example of the table's rut, so I added my chips to the pile. To my surprise, both Allison and Jonathan paid to stay in the hand, though they seemed to be weary that Tyson might raise the cost. Fortunately, he simply covered the difference between the blinds.

As we all prepared to see the flop, I gave a quick glance around the room, catching sight of a few displaced players heading our way. I silently cursed fate for not displacing them a good five minutes earlier. We were finally going to get some fresh players. Hopefully that would break up this five-way stalemate. When I took a closer look at the new arrivals, I noticed Bella was amongst them and she was scrutinizing me.

I gave her a small wink as I forced my attention back on the round. When the dealer revealed the flop, my clenched muscles kept me from betraying my emotions. The trio was a wonderful sight. The ace of spades and the six and eight of hearts gave me some powerful options. Not only had I grabbed a pair of aces, but I had a flush draw. I quickly shifted my gaze to the players and saw Tyson reach towards his chips as he began making a pillar. Once he finished, Tyson pushed it forward, ensuring the dealer could easily count the bet.

It didn't take long for the dealer's voice to announce the amount. "Tyson opens with one hundred thousand."

"Well, the flop didn't help me," Kelly said, shoving her hand back to the dealer as her shoulders fell.

Tyson's decision really didn't take all that long; he must have gotten something good on the flop. Or for all I knew, he was bluffing. Who could tell with body control like his? Maybe Tyson had the flush draw as well. Yet again I wished Tyson had any tell, no matter how slight, but I quickly dismissed this useless train of thought as it didn't help. I considered Tyson's style of play for a bit. Had he tried to bully people out? He might have. That was the problem. I just didn't know.

As the seconds drew out, I realized I'd been sitting there longer than I meant because the next thing I knew, Allison's soft voice pulled me from my thoughts. "Those cards won't change, no matter how intently you stare at them."

My eyes drifted across the table while a knot ran up my throat, almost choking me. While I narrowly avoided a coughing fit, I summoned all the confidence I could muster. "I'm aware of that, my dear. Besides, that's not what I'm doing."

With a snap, I grabbed a small stack and played with it. "Though that would be a cool trick." The last words seemed to come out on their own, and I cursed the mental smile it provoked. If they only knew that was within my ability.

"If you could manage that, you'd never find a seat," Kelly said, lifting her drink.

After the chips fell from my grasp again, I started picking through my pile for the money to cover the bet. "It's not something that can happen, Kelly." My gaze flicked to Allison as I raised a twitching finger. "Besides, I'm running the math, not hoping for a miraculous alteration of my hand."

"Are you going to cover or raise?" Jonathan asked as he drummed his cards.

I kept my breathing calm and deliberate. With the fresh infusion of talent waiting to join us, I wanted to shatter the stagnant streak we'd fallen into. There was something about the makeup of the hand that made me think something special was about to happen. "For the moment," I said, pressing my hand to my chest as I slid my chips forward, "I'm simply going to match Tyson's price to see the turn."

Allison wrinkled her nose as her fingernails struck the backs of her cards like a set of miniature jackhammers. While it had taken me a while to catalogue her tells, this was one she'd used somewhat regularly, and it never varied. She was going to cover the bet, though she'd make a show that she was debating on folding the hand.

Sure enough, a few seconds later, she shook her head and stared at the dealer. "I'm going to agree with Kelly. That flop wasn't all I hoped it would be. But I think I have something worth pursuing." She extracted the necessary chips and tossed them into the pot. "I guess I'll pay to see the turn as well."

"Unlike the two of you, I'm not willing to stick with this garbage," Jonathan said, sliding his hidden cards toward the dealer.

"Two down and two to go," Allison said with a wicked little grin. "I do hope you'll provide us with an interesting card, my good sir."

And as if on cue, the dealer discarded the top card before placing the ace of spades next to the other community cards. My trip aces with a king high was an excellent hand. I flicked my eyes over at Allison and noticed the slight gleam in her eye that she couldn't conceal. So far today I had learned a lot of things about her, but chief among them was her skill.

While she wasn't as skilled as Tyson when it came to hiding her emotions, though I seriously doubted anyone was, what she excelled at was working out the odds. She was quick to calculate them and know what the best hand was in any given situation. Which meant that for her to be this excited, she had to have the last ace. But what was her other card? That was the only mystery currently hiding behind her mannerisms.

I turned from studying her to the cards and once again ran through what was possible at this stage of the hand. There was no chance of someone having a royal flush, though I would love to see that hand once in my life. A straight flush or even a straight was almost just as improbable to find, given what was available. Thankfully, with the ace under my hand, there was no way anyone could come up with four of a kind. Unfortunately, both a full house and a flush were still very much in play, and both would beat my trips.

That river card was still a cause for concern, though not from Allison. She was riding the same hand I was, trip aces. She couldn't get a flush, not with the ace of clubs in her hand, and she wasn't reacting like she had a pair to compliment her trips. The only thing she had to compliment her three of a kind was a high kicker, either a king or a queen. Either way, her betting would confirm her hand.

However, Tyson was the first to make a claim, and he made quite the bet with another hundred thousand. He was being aggressive, but my first instincts had played exceptionally well for me today, so I raised him, bringing the new price tag for the river up to one hundred and fifty thousand. Let us all see just how in love you are with that hand, Tyson.

Everyone turned to look at Allison, who, without hesitation, reached for her own chips and calmly made her choice clear. "Well, I think I'm just going to raise you both, let's say, double. Three hundred thousand dollars to stay in and see the river."

As Tyson sat there thinking over the bet, she flashed us both a smile that seemed to offer greater rewards if we just submitted to her will. But Tyson wasn't willing to surrender, as he re-raised her by fifty thousand. This left me owing an even two hundred grand to the pot. Could Tyson have something of value? My gut still said no, but those lifeless eyes gave me pause. I closed my eyes as I took a deep breath and ran through everything once more. I knew I had Tyson beat for this round, but I was uncertain about Allison. She was betting like she had the best possible hand, but that didn't seem likely.

Despite her betting big, I was sure she didn't have the full house, so I called and presented what I owed to the pot and waited for her to do the same. For a second it seemed like she was going to demand even more, but after a moment she thought better of it and supplied the pot with the fifty thousand she owed. With the betting closed for the moment, the dealer discarded the top card before revealing the jack of diamonds.

As I ran my right hand through my hair, I began going through the available options. The fact that we received a diamond prohibited a flush of any kind and a straight was unlikely given what had been dealt. No one could have a four of a kind. Did Tyson have a full house? It was possible that his pocket cards were a pair turned into trips to complement the pair of aces available to us all. Was this the hand where my instincts would fail me? No! They were right. They had to be right. Yet the living statue made a modest bet of fifty thousand.

Clenching my jaw, I separated a couple of stacks from my chips and pushed them forward. "I think I'll go in for another two hundred thousand."

Allison, while not visibly staggered, wasn't as completely sure of herself as she was a few moments before. She carefully counted her chips before looking back up and settling her gaze upon me. "If either of you wants to see my hand, you'll have to match what I have left, and that comes out to be two hundred and twelve thousand above Marcus's raise."

The stone-faced and decisive Tyson hesitated. I saw there was a part of him that wanted to call, thinking Allison was bluffing, but there was a larger side wanting to protect his slightly dwindling stack. Eventually, he tossed his cards to the dealer. With Tyson out, I quickly added the chips required to knock Allison from the tournament.

"I'm not backing down," I said, thinking that I'd been correct in my read. "Your hand, while I'm sure it's impressive, can't win."

"What do they say about pride?" Jonathan asked, leaning forward on his elbows.

"Something about a fall," I said, tapping a chip against my cards. "However, my prediction doesn't stem from pride."

"I think you'll find you were mistaken." With her lips curling into a wicked smile, Allison turned over her cards as she described them to the table. "Trip aces courting a single lady."

I had been right, trips with a high kicker. My eyes flicked to the Jack as I licked my lips. She'd almost landed the full house. I reached out and tapped the community card as my head swept back and forth. "Allison, it's too bad you didn't catch a queen,"

I said, flipping my ace over. I then took hold of my king and revealed it to the table with a flourish. "Because the companion to my trips holds a greater value."

Her smile fell for a moment, but as it returned, her eyes darkened just a hair with frustration and anger. "Of course you would have the king." She shook her head briefly before standing up to greet her chaperones. "Oh well, the best man won. That was well played, Marcus. Let me be the first to congratulate you."

"I'm sorry to cut your time short with that close of a hand."

Allison laid her hands back on the table and leaned over, all the while staring at me the way a starving eagle would observe a field mouse. She took a calming breath before speaking. "No Marcus, you're not sorry. You won, and that means you're still in the tournament. You may be sorry for the heart-wrenching way you won, but in the end, losing is losing. It doesn't matter how close you are." Her look softened, if only just by a bit, before she added, "While I appreciate the attempt, I should have followed Tyson's lead."

"Not that I did it soon enough," Tyson offered as he looked down upon his stacks of chips, now simply just a shadow of their once-former glory. Not that he was in any danger of being eliminated.

Allison leveled a stare at him that could have melted stone. "Tyson, considering your stack, you'll forgive me for not weeping at your loss. Since you're in no danger of being escorted to the stands anytime soon."

As the two goons reached for her, she whirled her arms just enough to keep them from grabbing her. "I know you two are there, and you can simply wait another minute. There's no risk of any unpleasantness. After making my goodbyes, I'll accompany you to my new seat."

She leaned over and gave Jonathan a quick hug, while she

simply waved in Kelly's general direction. Then Allison rounded the table toward me and leaned over my shoulder and spoke so only I'd hear her. "You better not lose my money. I'm looking forward to getting it back."

Even though her face was out of my sight, I could hear the ever-so-subtle threat mixed with a promise of pleasure if I cooperated. So I just smiled and said, "I'll do my best."

"That'll do, Marcus." And with that, she turned and escorted her two guides to the audience above.

As I collected my chips, Bella came and sat down next to me. "Were you here to play or to find dates?"

Forcing a smile onto my face, I looked over at her and told her the truth. "Her name is Allison, and unfortunately for her, I just eliminated her. Between you and me, she didn't take it all that well. Has anyone ever told her that this is just a game?"

"Marcus, I saw the hand. Besides, how well would you have reacted if your situations had been reversed?"

"I wouldn't have made a veiled threat," I said with a shrug. "Not that I wouldn't mind returning her entrance fee to her." I tried to force some indifference into my voice, but I could not keep the smile off my face.

She saw my smirk and laughed as she leaned in and asked, "So you're going to give in to her threat?"

I kept my voice to a whisper as I replied, "Don't you remember what I told you about women and their money?"

Bella's face took on a hurt expression. She needed practice if she ever hoped for that look to fool anyone other than family. "You just admitted that she threatened you. Why are you treating her so nicely?"

"I follow my convictions. Besides, have I taken any of your money yet?"

With an ear-to-ear smile, she concurred in a silky voice that let me know she was only teasing. "No, not yet, but you haven't exactly had the opportunity."

"Well, aside from meeting you prior to the final table, it is good to finally get some new players over here."

"This is the group you started with?"

"Yup," I said as I scanned the faces of the newcomers and smiled when I realized Patrick wasn't among them. While I hadn't played against Patrick, I had the feeling he and Tyson were the two best players here. Between the two, it was a coin toss. As I studied the other fresh faces, I asked Bella, "Where's Patrick? I thought I saw him join your starting table."

She sat there, frozen and unmoving. I nudged her shoulder and repeated the question. This time she heard me, and after clearing her throat, she responded, "Patrick was at my starting table, but fortunately enough the rest were chumps. So we kind of fell into an unspoken alliance. We wouldn't go after each other while we had such easy pickings. After about an hour, when we dropped to four players, our table was scrapped, and we were plugged into other tables as seats became available."

"So once you two separated, you didn't meet back up?" I pulled my gaze back to her eyes and realized the distraction swirling behind them. "That's good." I folded my arms across my chest and asked, "What about our solitary existence bothers you?"

"Everything," she said with her voice void of emotion.

Only when I thought she fell back into herself did I prompt her with a question. "This is only your second time here. Do you really think that it is that unusual?" I tried to keep my tone conversational, attempting not to spook her further down a rabbit hole she plainly didn't want to go down.

She shrugged and pulled on my shoulder, drawing me closer

to her. "Even though this is only my second tournament, I've never heard of one of my uncle's tables going this long without other players filling the open seats."

I simply sat there for a moment, chewing the inside of my lip. I raked my left hand through my hair as I slowly let out a pent-up breath. "Well, it would seem we have a little mystery for another time." I needed to change topics. The last thing I needed to think about was how Dempsey might be trying to isolate either my table or someone at it. Though the most terrifying thought was he was isolating me. I looked around the room, again taking in its extravagance before blurting out another question. "Was last year's arrangement as spectacular as this one?"

"The room is a little worse," she said, her voice thick with indifference, "though that comes with jumping locations the way he does. But everything else is just as nice."

"Is he that aggressive about not reusing a property?"

"Even though my uncle owns just about everyone everywhere, he's just as careful. So after the authorities have raided the by then old warehouse, my uncle scratches them off of his list. He would rather find another place than reuse one. He figures that some overenthusiastic rookie or cop might try something by staking out the old locations, waiting for him to press his luck. No, as far as my uncle is concerned, every year deserves its own home."

"Your uncle is a very meticulous man."

"You've no idea."

I looked at the dealer's idle hands and asked, "Bella, did we miss something?"

"It looks like we're set to be the blind bets for the round."

She lifted her required small blind and eased it forward just a little, a move that required the dealer to collect her bet.

I restrained myself from pointing out the dealer should have attempted to get our attention. I simply extracted the required big blind from my stacks and tossed it into the center of the table. Once both blinds were given, the dealer dealt out the round, leaving me time to think about what I'd learned from Bella.

With my first card firmly under my right hand, I turned my attention to the stadium seating and saw Allison having what appeared to be a civilized conversation with another former player. The pair quickly called over one of the waiters; no, not a waiter, they called over a bookie. In addition to everything else Dempsey did here, the money he could make through extracurricular gambling was staggering. This was quite the elaborate scheme concocted by Dempsey, and it was one that had to have made him a ridiculous amount of money. No wonder he made a personal appearance at this event.

CHAPTER 10

The fact Tyson was collecting another pot highlighted the man's skill. As he regrew his stack, it felt like he never lost, and that's despite me getting the better of him a couple of times. The man's determination and will hammered mine, threatening to drag me under. As always, I quickly shored up my defenses and subdued the sliver of my mind questioning my ability to win. The only thing those thoughts did was depress me, and given the competition, I couldn't afford the liability. I twisted in my chair to stretch my sides to escape those lifeless eyes for a moment. While the stiffness in my side lessened, I saw Dempsey saunter into the chamber.

He ambled toward the center of the space and spread his arms out wide as he slowly turned about. "Ladies and gentlemen, at long last, we have whittled down our field of one hundred players to the elite ten. We will now take a brief break while we prepare a special table for the event. While my people finish their work, please help yourselves to refreshments." With that, he spun about and glided across the floor toward a stairwell leading up to the elite voyeurs. But after a handful of steps, he stopped and lifted a steady finger. "For the duration of the break, the bar will be open and the meals free. Please enjoy yourselves."

Turning back to Bella, I rubbed my neck as I stared down at the remnants of my water. "That's generous of your uncle." I down the last of my laced beverage and wiped my brow. "Would you like to join me for a martini?"

I waited almost a minute for her answer before I tore my gaze away from her retreating uncle to look at her graceful face. Her features, which had exuded calm serenity from the beginning, were now contorted with confusion. It was not a flattering look for her, and it startled me.

"Bella, what's wrong?" As she sat there, motionless, I grasped her shoulder and gently rocked her back and forth, breaking whatever trance she had fallen into. She looked up at me quizzically, so I shook my head as I released her. "Is something wrong?"

Her panicked gray eyes flitted about as she registered my reaction to her demeanor. She raised a finger as her breath settled into a steady rhythm. Once she dropped her hands into her lap, the impassive façade she wore for the game was thoroughly wrapped about her.

I knew something was off, so I leaned into my chair and dropped my folded hands onto my lap and waited. A few moments, the last player rose from the table, leaving the two of us there in silence. As the ice from my cup melted, I leaned forward, but she reached out, placing a finger across my lips.

Bella's eyes latched onto mine as her mouth curled into a wan smile. "As far as I know, my uncle has never had a break during one of his 'oh so precious tournaments.'" The volume of her words rose with each syllable until she reached a near shout to complete her thought. "Not once!"

I was uncertain how to respond to the information she offered, but I tried to offer the first excuse that came to mind. "Maybe this year's tournament is just running longer."

Her head instantly started sweeping back and forth, and I couldn't blame her. It had been a feeble excuse. Yet with each passing second, her eyes took on a hue of fear I couldn't understand. From our brief conversations, her decisions appeared to be rooted in common sense. While it helped keep her on a rational path, it encouraged her to be cautious. Was this just her taking that inherent cautiousness to an extreme?

She waved a dismissive hand at my suggestion as words poured out of her mouth in a rush. "No, Marcus, you don't understand. After last year's tournament, I asked him why he didn't offer a single break." She gripped my jacket and pulled me closer. "Don't get me wrong; I can handle a long time at the table, but even I was exhausted. While I don't remember the details of his answer, it revolved around what he considered sound business decisions. Whatever you think of his morals, he's driven by growing all his businesses. There's no way he'd upend a sound financial decision, without a compelling reason."

I eased her hands off my coat and gathered them up in mine. As I flashed her a false smile, I pressed her hands to my chest as I brushed her cheek with a knuckle. "What exactly do you think is going on if this is so unordinary?"

Bella took a series of deep breaths, imposing her will over her body. Once the steadfast calm settled upon her face, she licked her lips and scooted forward in her chair. "I'm not sure." She freed one hand and rubbed the back of her neck as her head rolled from side to side. "And to be honest, that's when my uncle is most frightening."

"Isn't it possible that you're overreacting just a little?" I asked as I placed my thumb and index finger just a hairsbreadth apart. "Let's focus for a moment on the positive side of things. For instance, I'm fairly certain your uncle no longer has any of his men in the last group of ten, so his payout is already as small as it can be."

Then I remembered the betting going on above our heads.

"Well, minus the gambling going on above us. But best of all is the re-opening of the bar, even if it was mostly an afterthought. And to tell you the truth, since he forces everyone to stay here, he should have left it open for the whole time."

"That may explain his opening the bar." Bella's back straightened as she leaned closer to me. "But the bar is a nice shiny toy to distract from the genuine surprise, which is the break. Why did he call for a break? That unknown reason bothers me."

While I could see the panic fighting to embrace her, I brushed her cheek again. "I'm not saying I fully believe what I said, Bella. After all, your uncle's reputation is known far and wide. However, there's no use worrying about something we have no control over. That's about as useful as trying to argue with a hungry grizzly bear. All it'll do is keep us from playing our best game, which is something we can't afford right now. I understand your worry, but we can't do anything about it."

When the tinge of panic gripping the edge of her eyes vanished, she looked past me, presumably to stare at her uncle. "You're right. This is not the time to let my uncle's actions dictate my options."

As her concern thundered through my mind, I scratched a temple. She was right. Dempsey was up to something, but there wasn't enough information available to draw a reasonable conclusion. Though it wasn't a terrible idea to highlight the differences between this year and the historical norm. While things like that were useful to know, you needed to understand when to use the knowledge. "Bella, information is always useful. It's simply a matter of when and how."

She opened her mouth to speak, but before a sound passed through her lips, I gently placed a finger on her lips. "Yes, information is useful. But information overload is potentially fatal. I will not let it rule my thoughts or actions during this break or once play resumes."

I kept my attention focused upon her beautiful gray eyes and just held them for several heartbeats. "Divergence from the norm is always useful to know about. You just need to figure out why things deviated from the well-worn path."

With a shy smile, she looked up into my eyes. "You really are an interesting mystery, Marcus."

My knuckles brushed her cheek again as my smile widened. "Well, would you like to accompany your man of mystery to the bar for another drink, courtesy of Simon?"

A smile wormed its way across Bella's face as she released her breath. Her hand grasped mine and offered me a wink. "One of his drinks might be the perfect way to steady my nerves. Let's go."

I offered her a smile in return as I rose and pulled Bella to her feet.

The moment she was on her feet, her arms wrapped around mine while she laid her head on my shoulder. My fingertips traced her brow before I gestured toward the bar. "It'll be nice to share a drink with you while we wait for the game to resume."

When we returned to where our table had been, I helped Bella back into a seat. After she reclaimed her drink, I sat down and removed the pesky intoxicants from Simon's work. However, as I held the drink under my nose, I sent another pulse of body heat through a mental image and altered the drink to have a stiff dose of adrenaline. I took a long pull of the martini while Dempsey's goons scurried out with the last of the extraneous furniture. When the final minion disappeared, only Bella's, mine, and eight other chairs remained.

I grasped the speared olives and stirred my drink as I examined the mounting worry on Bella's face. After a few silent heartbeats, I reached forward, tapping her shoulder. "Is there anything wrong with the tables they removed?"

"I doubt it," she said, pulling a booze-soaked olive off her stirrer with her teeth. She tilted her head, letting it fall into her mouth. "My uncle is a highly organized man. He is a poster child for the saying 'a place for everything and everything in its place.' However, despite his attempts at varying his actions, he is a person of habit. So, again, here's another example of him doing something that he's never done before. I was trying to reason out why he's doing it now when he's never done so in the past."

"Maybe he has something special in mind for the final table."

Even as she nodded her assent, I could tell she wasn't satisfied with the explanation, though she would accept it. "Hopefully, that's all it is. Either way we'll see soon enough."

Despite her timid agreement, I wasn't satisfied with my explanation. That she abandoned her conjecture so quickly just highlighted her eagerness to flee from the puzzle of her uncle's recent actions. While I would have appreciated following her lead, my mind refused to settle down. With each sip of my martini, my mind took the available facts and wove a new narrative. In the end, I may have soothed her frayed nerves, but I'd tattered mine.

I couldn't say why I was so determined to figure out what was prompting all the drastic changes in Dempsey's typical routine. But with all the odd behavior mounting up, I was having a hard time convincing myself nothing abnormal was going on. And I had a sinking suspicion I was at the center of it all. As the break wore on, my body started losing its fight with exhaustion. Why was Dempsey normally so opposed to a break?

He had to know how a break would affect the players. If it

hadn't been so haphazard, I would have congratulated Dempsey on his tactics, rather than question them. As the adrenaline in my system waned, my exhaustion grew by leaps and bounds. I quickly dosed my remaining martini with more adrenaline. Fortunately, just as I hit my biological snooze button, several of Dempsey's lackeys entered the room, carrying a grand table.

Neither Bella nor I detected anything that distinguished it from the ones that had been removed, despite our intense observations. There were zero visible differences. This new table could very well have been any of the previous ones. However, I had a bad feeling this unscheduled break resulted from Dempsey's desire to have this specific table for the ten of us to play on.

Once the table was positioned in the center of the chamber, ten minions came out bearing our consolidated chips, while another ten came to collect the chairs. Everyone rose as Dempsey walked up to the table. This time, he didn't need to silence the players or the observers. The activity and his showmanship did that for him. "Ladies and gentlemen, we have prepared our battleground. Please allow me to introduce the combatants."

There he went, playing up the comparison to ancient gladiators. As he listed off a few names, I drained my martini and peeled both olives off the stirrer. After swallowing the flavorful olives, I shoved the stick into my mouth, treating it like a toothpick. After the third name, Dempsey called Bella to the table, and she kissed my cheek before collecting her chips and claiming an open position.

Two names later, the crime lord introduced me, and after trading my empty glass for my stack, I claimed the empty chair nestled between Bella and Tyson. While a looming mystery was to my right, on my left, I ensured a steady supply of pleasant conversation between hands.

CHAPTER 10

After placing my chips on the table, I rolled my shoulders backward. Once I'd settled my nerves, I searched the grand piece of furniture for anything out of the ordinary but came up empty. Despite that, I was convinced there had to be something special about it. Why else would Dempsey break such a fine tradition of his? But before I could perform a more intensive search, Patrick claimed the last seat, completing the table.

I shelved the questions for the moment and followed the same advice I gave Bella, the best I could. It was time to ignore the differences and focus on how I was going to win.

CHAPTER 11

If finding the ten best players in the original field had been a marathon, then the battle among that elite group was a sprint. Within the first five or six hands, the fierce competition forced three of our number into the crowd. One could blame their downfall on the fact they had the least amount of chips, but in the end, the speed of their elimination was remarkable. While I had siphoned a decent chunk from that trio, the rest of the field received roughly equal shares.

Of course, with the next hand, Patrick baited the silent statue and Bella into a poor position. While Patrick failed to tempt them into betting everything, he enhanced his lead while dragging me into second place. Unfortunately, between the two, he'd suckered Bella out of a larger percentage of her stack. With a swig of my water, I studied my pocket cards and stared at my pile. If I chased this hand, my tenuous grasp on second place would vanish, so I did the smart thing and folded. That left everyone but Patrick, Tyson, and me vying for the hand as the dealer revealed the first trio of community cards.

There are some flops that scream 'Watch out! I'm a trap' at highly skilled players. One such collection was what just came: the king of hearts and the ace of spades and diamonds. If you ever see something like that, proceed with caution. You better be sure of

CHAPTER 11

what you hold. It certainly wouldn't have helped the garbage I had folded, but it had helped Bella.

Though based on what I read around the table, the players still in the round missed it. She calmly began the round with a check to Constantine, who aggressively pushed a large bet into the pot. David made a show of deciding whether he should call, but I could tell he was eager to continue with the flop, and he eventually matched Constantine's bet. Thomas pushed the round farther without even cracking a smile. However, it was Bella who amped up the intensity with a mighty raise. Eventually, the other three covered their differences, and we all waited with bated breath for the next card.

It was the jack of hearts. I could see the barest hint of a glimmer in Bella's eyes. Despite that betrayal of emotion, her mental discipline reestablished its dominance, smothering all traces of glee before it could betray her. This time she was the one who hemmed and hawed about what she was going to do before eventually placing a substantial starting bet into the pot. I wondered what she held. Though more subdued this time around, the other three matched her wager to see the last card.

When the dealer revealed the nine of hearts, Bella did an admiral job of hiding the sudden burst of glee. Despite the giddiness I knew swirled throughout her, she checked the action to an eager Constantine. He must have loved the card because he upped the ante by going all in. While his stack wasn't all that impressive, it would force both David and Thomas to risk their futures on this hand. As they agreed to continue the dance, Bella's eyes sparkled.

The moment the action came to Bella, she made a pile that would cover the active wager. Finally, she loosed the inner smile as she placed her hands around the bulk of her chips. "Thank you all for joining me in this dance."

"Does that mean you're in?" David asked as he brushed the corners of his cards.

"It does," she said as she shoved her chips into the pot. "What does everyone have?"

"I'll start," Constantine said as he revealed the seven and duce of hearts.

A flush? He was that aggressive chasing down a flush. Not only that, but he was that forceful when he didn't have it till the river. I knew he was desperate to rebuild his stack, but that was ridiculous. Granted, he caught it, but he should have realized there were better hands available. It was highly unlikely he'd survive the round.

"You shouldn't have chased such a weak hand given what's in play," David said as he turned his cards over one at a time. The first highlighted a pair of jacks, while the second cemented it as trips, giving David a full house, jacks over aces.

Instantly Constantine slumped in his chair, burying his face into his hands.

Thomas tsked as he waved a finger toward David and said, "My friend, one good turn deserves another."

"What are you talking about?"

Thomas grabbed a card and used it like a shovel to flip both over, revealing the other two aces and his four of a kind. And just like Constantine, David collapsed in his chair, lamenting his defeat.

I shook my head at what I just saw, a flush losing to a full house, which lost to four aces. Despite seeing her opponents' hands, Bella's smile widened. And that could only mean she wielded a straight flush. Nothing else could defeat Thomas's four aces.

Unfortunately for the arrogant fool, Bella picked up both of her cards and then laid them down on the pot as Thomas wrapped his hands around the scattered chips, revealing the queen and ten of hearts, a.k.a. a straight flush. If Thomas hadn't received the ace of hearts, she might have been able to play the best hand in all of poker, a royal flush. As a result, she ended up playing the second-best hand, a king high straight flush.

Bella reached forward and batted Thomas's hands away from her winnings. "I'm sorry, gentlemen, but you have to admit, it's something special to lose to one of the best hands in all the game. How many people can say that?"

"Aside from those three," Patrick said, playing with two small stacks of his chips, "I can't think of anyone I know who can make that claim."

"Exactly," Bella said, raising a chip in the air at their retreating forms. "They lost out on making bank, but they left with a story more precious than the prize."

"I doubt they would agree with you," Tyson said as he pointed at Bella's new pile. "Though it looks like you've regained what you had when we started."

"It does at that."

As the sounds of stacking chips filled the room, I leaned back in my chair as I thumped a chip against the table's edge. As the remarkable trio climbed the stairs, I couldn't help but think about what I'd just witnessed. Out of all the hands available in poker, we watched four of the best drop one after the other, in ascending order. It was unreal. I felt like I was watching an orchestrated movie rather than experiencing a special turn of events.

When Bella stopped organizing her winnings, I realized the silence gripping everyone. There wasn't a person here who didn't understand the sheer ridiculousness of what just played out. The uneasy tranquility lingered for a few more seconds before the dealer started dealing out the next hand. As the cards fell onto the table, I couldn't help but contemplate how quickly we were whittling down the competition. Now I had to deal with the real cream of the crop: Tyson, Patrick, and Bella.

Of the four of us, Bella had been toward the bottom, but with what she had just gained, she was roughly equal to Tyson, who had about half my stack. My eyes flicked toward the observers as the silence thundered over the din of shuffling cards. I would have thought someone up in the arena would have been saying something about what had happened or placing revised bets. However, an eerie silence reigned in the room. When the last card hit the table, the dealer pointed at me. "Given the radical change, the small blind is yours, sir."

Once Bella and I added our bets to the pot, Patrick checked the action to Tyson, who made a sizeable wager. He must have gotten an extraordinary starting hand. As the chips fell from his hand, Patrick and I slid our cards toward the dealer, while Bella raised Tyson's bet. With an uncharacteristic grin, he covered Bella's raise.

With the flop, we saw a pair of nines and a very lonely lady. Instead of pressing, Bella checked the action to Tyson, who checked into the turn, a two of spades. Satisfied with the current situation, Bella repeated her action. However, Tyson immediately made a sizeable wager, which Bella immediately called. What could either of them have with the current cards in play?

After the dealer revealed the four of diamonds, Bella checked for the third time. As she was rapping the table with her knuckles, Tyson made a bet forcing Bella to go all in if she wanted to finish the round. She took a bit of time examining the living statue and her hand, but she must have thought she had something because she called the bet with a big smile on her face. In fact, it only grew as she revealed her pair of aces, netting her two pair. It wasn't a bad hand considering what was in play, but Tyson's normally lifeless eyes signaled it wasn't enough.

He only flipped over a single card, but considering it was a nine, he didn't need to do more. His trip nines bested Bella's two pair. He tapped the hidden card and shrugged. "Do you need to see this one?"

A hoarse chuckle passed through her lips as she pushed away from the table. "No, I don't." She shook her head as she patted the table with her palms. As the goons approached her, she looked like she was thinking of something witty to say but found nothing and instead let out a rather undignified harrumph. "What can you say? I reached the greatest high I've ever had and the lowest low in consecutive hands. It really stinks."

After taking a moment to calm herself with a series of deep breaths, she stood up. I could see the frustration hanging off her like a cloak, and it took a moment for her to regain a mask of serenity, but then that was probably because of the smug look on Patrick's face.

Once again in complete control of herself, she turned to Tyson. "Well played. I'd say best of luck, but I'm sure you appreciate my preference that you lose." She pivoted around to face me, and before the pair of hired muscles could grab her, she leaned down and wrapped her arms around my neck to whisper her farewell. "I hope you can teach him one hell of a lesson, Marcus. I really wish you the best of luck. On the bright side, you didn't knock me out, so we can still be friends."

When I looked into her eyes, I saw the playfulness that had so quickly captivated me. "Thank you, Bella. I think I'm going to need it."

Without another word, she collected her drink and made her way into the audience to watch the outcome of the game. I could tell she hoped for me to take the statue and the smug man for all they were worth. I certainly hoped I was up for the challenge.

Then there were three.

Due to the limited number of players, I started holding onto hands I would have otherwise discarded because, at this stage of the game, too few cards were played. Fortunately for me, after a few more hands of nothing, Lady Luck kissed my forehead once more when the dealer gave me a pair of kings. I quickly raised Tyson's wager by a substantial amount. Unfortunately, Patrick folded his hand in response, but Tyson decided to bully me out by doubling my wager.

If I called his new bet, I would risk all but a handful of my chips. I had pocket kings. What would he have to justify that extravagance? Could he have pocket royalty like me? Queens or jacks would be a strong position, but aces would be the best hand leading into the flop. Despite the unreadable nature of his face, I had a good feeling in the pit of my stomach with this hand.

I leaned back in my chair and peered up into Tyson's eyes. "Are you sure about that raise, my silent friend?"

"Yes, Marcus, I'm sure. How about you?" Tyson's lifeless eyes flicked to Patrick as his lips teased a rare smile. "It's late, and I need to face Patrick in the showdown now rather than later."

"Careful, Tyson," I said, bouncing one of my chips against the table, "you're showing a little emotion."

The dig may not have been the best move to make, since I couldn't help but color my words with a hint of excitement. However, I think they struck a chink in his mental armor. For a split second, I saw the hue of eagerness bleed into irritation before being swallowed entirely.

The silent sentinel cracked his neck and stared over his

shoulder at me. "You are a skillful player, Marcus, but you aren't in the same league as Patrick or me."

"Then again, Tyson, you're not in my league either," Patrick said, turning his hands toward the ceiling.

"We shall see who is better after I knock our friend out," Tyson said coolly.

How comfortable was I with this hand? I had to remember I had never seen Tyson lose when he was involved in a hand where someone went all in. Did I want to tempt fate? After a moment of indecision, I pushed the worry aside and slid everything into the pot. "Well, Tyson, you will not get away with the bullying this time."

No sooner were the words out of my mouth than Tyson added his remaining chips and revealed his pocket pair of kings. While I had the spade and club, he had the heart and diamond.

"That's incredible," Patrick said, slapping his hands.

Tyson jumped to his feet, slamming his hands onto the edge. "We can't have the same hand!"

"Oh, this is exciting," Patrick said, as he wrung his hands together.

Tyson and I looked over at the dealer and watched as he revealed the flop, the seven and queen of spades, along with the five of diamonds. And just like that, I had a possible flush draw. Giving me the only path away from a split pot.

"Well, Tyson, it seems this hand just got more interesting," Patrick said with a smile. He could have been a little less obvious regarding his desire to play me rather than the living statue.

"The odds still favor a split, Patrick."

"We'll see what happens in a moment," I said as I motioned for the dealer to reveal the next card, a ten of spades.

"He only needs one more spade, and you're eliminated, my silent friend," Patrick said as he inched closer to the table.

"The odds are not in his favor."

Please, just give me one more spade. One more spade is all I need. All I need is one more. I watched the dealer discard the last card for the hand, and time seemed to slow down to a crawl. As the card crept to the table, I could have killed a thousand flies if they'd zipped in front of me. In a painful motion, the dealer pulled the last community card from the deck. All I needed was any spade to face Patrick heads up.

I could almost see the face of the card. Was it black? Move faster, you stupid dealer! And as if on command, time resumed its normal speed, revealing the ace of spades. I caught my flush! Tyson lost the hand! I looked over at Patrick and promised myself I would do the same to him.

"Congratulations on the pure luck, Marcus," Tyson said with what seemed to be petulance or would be if it had come out of anyone else's mouth. But when I looked over, Dempsey's minions had already collected him.

I shifted my gaze back to Patrick and smiled my warmest smile. "And then there were two."

"May the best man win," Patrick said, wringing his hands under his chin.

CHAPTER 12

When I tore my gaze from the community cards, I found myself staring into Patrick's joyful eyes. Mentally, I scolded myself for flirting with this hand with a litany of curses that would make any sailor blush. After deftly weaving my way to the final showdown with ample skill and a decent shot of luck, I ended up pursuing a terrible hand. I'll never be able to explain why. All I could say was I chased down my worst hand of the tournament.

I should have folded from the start. Normally I'd never chase the eight of clubs and the nine of diamonds, especially when dealing with a full table. However, since fewer cards came out of the deck in heads-up play, sometimes bad hands were worth pursuing. Unfortunately, I don't know what possessed me to follow Patrick's lead on this dance instead of jumping to the next hand. Despite gaining a flush draw with the flop, it was also available to Patrick. Over the next couple of rounds of betting, I should have pulled the ripcord to escape this terrible mess, but I didn't. For the first time that day, I was in a foul mood because of a looming defeat.

Once more, my gaze drifted to the community cards, as if hoping they would change. Unfortunately, they stubbornly refused to obey my wants. So I looked up to find Patrick's eyes boring into me. Why was he studying me? I could tell by his demeanor he knew I couldn't win this hand. While I could fold this garbage, I was far too invested in this exchange. This hand was my tournament. If I folded now, my stack would be so diminished it wouldn't be long before Patrick bullied me out. The other option was to leverage everything on this hand and advertise how foolish I'd been. For a moment, I considered a third option, but it didn't take long for me to dismiss it. I would not alter a card to escape this nightmare.

With the only two real options laid out before me, I weighed them again. Yet, because of my stubborn refusal to lose, my mind railed against those choices, looking for another path. Matt was right. Neither was acceptable after coming within spitting distance of winning. How had I fallen into this trap? I'd been playing so well that day. Despite the mounting frustration, I pushed everything from my mind and soothed my frayed nerves. At least I tried.

As I mentally tried to relax, I caught sight of Bella lounging in the stands. While I'd avenged her loss to Tyson, I got the feeling she was rooting for me, maybe even placed a small wager on my victory. However, given the garbage I held, I seemed doomed to disappoint her. With a deep breath, I rubbed my eyes as I studied a distracted Bella. It was odd she wasn't watching the game play out. She studied something else.

Even though we'd only spent a short time together, I felt like I had gotten to know who she really was. And when she joined my table, I saw a fresh aspect of her persona. She loved hold 'em. I mean, she had a passion for the game that went beyond playing. She enjoyed everything about it, including watching it unfold before her. Especially if she could learn something about a future opponent with no danger to her. However, instead of adding tells to her list, her attention was elsewhere.

When I traced her gaze, I found her uncle on the other end of her scrutiny. Why would she be staring at her uncle? Or was she trying to identify the man Dempsey was talking to? Based on how that stranger looked, he wasn't a member of the elite. My best guess was one of Dempsey's lieutenants. Though from this distance and without my enhanced tools, there was no way for me to understand what they were talking about. So I pushed the oddity from my mind.

As I returned my attention to the hand in front of me, Bella loomed in the corner of my eye, and I thought I saw confusion contorting her features. My eyes flicked back to her, and even from this distance, I could see the uncertainty swelling up inside her. It was the same expression I saw when Dempsey called for a break, and unlike the rest of the emotions I've seen her wear, this one didn't flatter her.

But her odd behavior wasn't my primary concern. Instead, my focus was on my decision to follow my instincts. While they'd helped me catch flushes at least five different times throughout the tournament, like when I knocked Tyson out, they were too easy to derail. When it mattered most; the river swept me under its surface and lady luck, my constant companion for most of this run, was no longer there to grab my outstretched hand.

My day came down to this unfortunate and unmatched pair of cards and they wouldn't support my ambition. Unless I did something drastic, this was going to be the end of the night for me, and I doubted my exit would be any more elegant than Bella's had been.

While I yearned to see something different staring up at me, the community cards refused to help me. Laid out in a straight line were the ace, six, and nine of clubs, paired with the ace of diamonds and the eight of spades. They sat there, mocking me as

I scrutinized them. And for another fleeting moment, I debated altering one of my pocket cards. If only the dealer had dealt an ace or an eight in place of the nine under my fingers, I would have had a full house, one of the better hands, given what was available.

As the silence lingered, the dealer cleared his throat and locked eyes with me. "Sir, the bet is to you."

Right then, I made an incredibly stupid choice, not to mention break the promise I made with Matt. There was no way I'd allow Patrick to walk out of this building as the tournament's winner. I pushed the last of my chips toward the center of the table. "I'll call Patrick. What do you have?"

With a wicked grin splitting his face, Patrick shoved the last of his chips into the pot as he turned over both of his cards, revealing the queen and ten of clubs. As I sat there studying his flush, I saw Patrick's mocking smile. With a pair of fingers resting on my cards, I tapped them for a moment before I withdrew the bottom one, revealing the eight of clubs. Instantly, the cocky player's smile cracked.

I plucked the image of the ace of spades from the depths of my mind and held it fast, while I rested my fingertips on the back of the nine of hearts. As my lungs swelled, I mingled a bit of warmth and my fierce will and poured it through the image. Instantly, the invisible energy flowed through my fingers and slammed into the card, transforming it into the required ace. I only poured enough heat for a temporary alteration, and based on my experience, the card would revert to its original in a half hour or so.

"Sir, if you'd please, show us your last card," the now dour-faced dealer said.

Well, if nothing else, I was giving the spectators a wonderful show. But since I didn't want to annoy the dealer anymore, I firmly took hold of the corner of my last card and flipped it over.

I'd been hoping for a perfect transformation and judging by the reaction of both Patrick and the crowd, I knew that's what I got. It also meant I won.

When I opened my eyes, the first thing I saw was a perfectly formed ace of spades. Then I shifted my gaze to Patrick, who had slumped into his chair, acknowledging his defeat. The dealer shifted the pair of aces and the eight away from him ever so slightly as he drew in a deep breath. "Aces over eights. Marcus wins the hand and the tournament."

I forced the uneasiness over changing my original card down and looked across the table. With a straight face and calm voice, I broke the silence. "Patrick, you're an outstanding player, and you had quite the run. Though I'm sorry to let you twist in the wind like that."

Instead of snapping back at me, which would have been understandable, Patrick rose, walked around the table, and offered me his hand. In a voice belying the venom oozing from his eyes, he spoke as I accepted his offering. "I could have sworn you didn't have anything that strong. I was certain my read on you was perfect." He paused, taking in several deep breaths. "But I guess I was wrong. Congratulations."

With that, Patrick pulled his hand out of mine and walked toward the bar, no doubt hoping to drown his sorrows in something strong. Despite altering the single card, I won Dempsey's tournament. When I pulled my eyes from Patrick, I scanned the stands for Bella. When I found her, she still had a look of confusion on her face, and she was staring at her uncle. This time, several apparent goons flanked the crime lord, and they all were deep in conversation.

Obviously, this bothered Bella, but with my triumph, I didn't have the mental capacity or the inclination to deal with the puzzle.

So I plucked a five-thousand-dollar chip from the pile in the center of the table and tossed it to the dealer. "I hope you can cash that in."

As the chip landed in the dealer's left hand, I thought I saw the briefest of smiles before it vanished, as he replied. "Thank you, sir." With a slight nod of thanks, he stuffed the chip into his vest and collected the few cards that were on the table before shuffling them, as if he had nothing else in the world to do.

Before I could stand up, Dempsey walked beside me and enveloped my hand with his own as he spoke with a reserved firmness. "Congratulations, Marcus. That was quite the display you put on for us. I can't say it was sportsmanly to let Patrick think he had won, but it was an excellent show none the less."

I had little choice but to tighten my grip on his hand and flash him a warm smile. "Thank you, sir." I looked past Dempsey and towards the dealer. "Will he be able to keep that?"

Without turning toward the dealer, Dempsey pulled me to my feet. "People tip my workers every year, though only those achieved during the events of the last table can share any real wealth. You just gave that man five thousand dollars from your winnings."

I thought about that for a second but just shrugged as I spoke without thinking, "I can live with that."

Dempsey's eyes looked down at me, screaming that he could see past my façade, which sent a shiver running down my spine.

The crime lord pulled me into a hug as he thumped my chest. "Don't sell yourself short there, Marcus! You convinced Patrick to march into that hand with what turned out to be inferior cards."

His head twisted back to Patrick, who was deep into drowning his defeat. While I continued to watch Patrick take robotic gulps from his drink, Dempsey squeezed my shoulders. "That's not a minor achievement, considering his expectations and history here."

"What do you mean?"

With a slight grin, Dempsey looked back at me. "He was quite upset about losing last year." With each word, Dempsey's smile spread wider until I was surprised he could speak at all. "I will say he looks to be taking his defeat better this year."

"Last year," I said, putting some facts together, "he lost to your niece, didn't he?"

I could feel the man's attention acutely focus on me before his head bobbed up and down. "That's right, she did, and she took great pleasure in doing it in quite a similar way, though she lacked your flair for the dramatic."

"It's hard to win a tournament like this, year after year."

"True enough." Dempsey clapped my chest as he guided me away from the table. "However, keep this in mind. Patrick won my tournament the previous three years. He hoped last year was an anomaly, but you knocked him off yet again. Ever since he started coming to my tournaments, he's made his way to the top ten, and more often than not, he has reached the final showdown."

Silently Dempsey turned away from me and stared into the crowd, where he instantly caught sight of Bella. She still had that expression of shock on her face, but now she focused it on the two of us. I suddenly felt an urge to consider her fear as a sign I should leave. However, before I could break away, Dempsey gripped my shoulder. "Well, we have to reward our victor, don't we?"

The crime lord gestured to the man behind him and said, "If you would please follow my associate. He'll make sure you get your reward."

Before I turned my attention away from Bella, I saw her mouth a single word repeatedly. And if I read her lips right, she was mouthing 'no.' Her fear and confusion were infectious, so I worked on the puzzle that Bella had introduced me to, piece by piece. As my mind was actively trying to work through everything, my subconscious compelled me to follow Dempsey's request.

I wordlessly turned around and followed the goon Dempsey had pointed out. As I trailed behind the slim man, I pieced together the various things that had apparently put Bella on edge. First there was the fact my table went so long without getting a new player, while we had multiple dealers. Then there was the break that would normally never have been called. Not to mention the impression that, as a winner, I was being handled differently than Bella had been last year. Did he embed cameras into the table during the break? Was it possible Dempsey knew what I had done with the last card?

The goon opened a door and ushered me into the warehouse I had expected to find upon entry. As shock registered in my eyes, the heavy door abruptly shut, engulfing the room in darkness. A second later, I felt an eerie sensation crawling down my spine. Then a pair of sharp prongs pierced my neck, followed immediately by a surge of electricity. The current quickly coursed through me, overwhelming my body, causing me to crumple to the ground, dazed and immobilized. As the electricity abruptly ceased, a sinister force coiled around my neck, constricting my breathing, and plunging me into a hazy realm of darkness.

CHAPTER 13

As I regained consciousness, my mind raced into action, taking stock of my body and the surroundings. Unfortunately, it didn't take long to realize my eyelids weren't cooperating, hindering my potential investigation. While I needed to know where I was, without the use of my eyes, that was not going to be a simple task. It would be far easier to discern my physical wellbeing. So in the artificial darkness, I catalogued every pain, no matter how slight or imagined, from my head to my toes.

Throughout my life, I'd been in unpleasant situations before, and in each of those instances, knowledge was the key helping me wriggle free. I needed to become a sponge for information. I couldn't allow anything to pass me by without analyzing it, no matter how trivial the tidbit appeared. At that moment, every fact was as precious as a drop of water to a man dying of thirst. You could never know which fact or detail would be the cornerstone for survival. The more you acquired, the better chance you had of collecting a handful of nuggets amongst the useless debris.

The first ailment I itemized was the overbearing darkness. The last thing I remembered was every muscle in my body contracting. After colliding with the ground, but before I could recover, something had wrapped around my neck. That combination meant I'd been tased and then put to sleep with a choke hold. But neither should be interfering with my eyes. Couple that with the fact there was no pressure around my head meant I wasn't blindfolded. Which told me Dempsey's goons had more than likely drugged me.

However, that was a rabbit hole that wouldn't be fruitful to explore since I'd just started cataloging my situation. So I pinned that mystery out of the way and continued exploring my circumstances. In addition to a chill coursing through my body, I could feel several bands of pressure. A handful ran across my chest while a few more secured my arms and legs to the chair. With a grunt, I twisted my shoulders, or rather, I tried. Turns out whoever secured me didn't believe in the definition of overkill; that or we weren't using the same scale. Without being able to see what they'd done, it felt like they'd welded me in place.

As I released a captive breath, I brushed my cheek against my shoulder. At that moment, I realized the cold assaulted me on multiple fronts. First, whoever had bound me had stripped me out of my jacket and dumped me somewhere chilly, like a meat locker or an industrial freezer. On the heels of that discovery, my eyelids began responding to my efforts. Which was a fancy way to say they started fluttering like a bird's broken wing. While I couldn't get many clear images of my surroundings, I saw several shades of gray.

So far, aside from the initial assault, I didn't feel anything indicating Dempsey's hired muscle used me as a punching bag while I was unconscious. While that wouldn't be a pleasant situation, I think I would have preferred it over whatever this was. I mean, typically, I'd dance a little jig if I woke up this healthy after an attack. However, this was far from a normal situation, and I still had more to itemize.

When I turned my attention to my arms, I ignored the soft pressure securing my biceps and forearms and instead focused on the bite of something unrelenting and cold, most likely metal handcuffs. Despite the bindings, the other piece of crucial information I'd gleaned was the twin needles jabbed into my elbows. That tidbit answered a few questions as it clicked into place.

I realized why I was so cold. Most likely, whoever had secured me hooked me up to a pair of IVs. I've been prodded by doctors often enough to recognize the feeling, especially when a sadistic nurse or goon jabbed them into your elbow. You only insert those shunts when you must pump fluid into your patient, or victim in this case. In addition to whatever saline and nutrients they might be pumping into me, I'm sure this is how they were administering the chemical handcuff. Did I mention these people didn't understand overkill? Even room temperature fluids will conflict with the average body temperature, and the liquids were a bit cooler than that. Whatever their purpose, it was obvious they wanted me docile and frozen.

When there was nothing left for me to discover from my arms, I turned to my legs, finding more bands of pressure and another thin band of chilly metal digging into my ankles. Between the chill and the snugness of the cuffs, numbness threatened to consume my toes. The only part of my body that had any kind of range of motion was my head, and my eyes were still fighting me. Though the trivial images I'd seen led me to think that Dempsey had locked me up in a walk-in freezer. Oh, and let's not forget that an over eager goon didn't know when enough was enough.

With my list completed, I summed up my predicament. I was relatively uninjured, drugged with an unknown concoction, trussed up like an animal waiting to be sacrificed, and shoved inside a walk-in ice machine. That was a truly depressing summation. Firmly discouraged by my inability to affect my bonds, I shifted my efforts to my surroundings. However, my eyes were still on strike, so I pitched my head forward and listened. As I tried isolating hints and whispers, a solitary question tumbled through my mind like a tumbleweed from an old western. How was Dempsey able to get the drop on me like this?

I should have paid more attention to just how freaked out Bella was by all the inconsistencies. Especially since they all revolved around isolating the mysterious new player on a ridiculous lucky streak. But that's what the intelligentsia would call hindsight. In the end, I had been so wrapped up in my own arrogance I'd dismissed every clue. Conversely, Dempsey was a man who sought every possible opinion and fact before acting. But what else had I missed? To those who studied Dempsey's reputation, he didn't appear to be willing to risk offending his walking piggy banks on nothing more than a hunch. Or would he?

And of course, that's when another piece fell into place, the break prior to the start of the final table. When Bella voiced her unease, I'd dismissed her worry. But now, her comments about the uniqueness of her uncle pausing the tournament should have put me on edge. Unfortunately, I'd been a little too cavalier about her secondhand knowledge. There was only one way for Dempsey to ensure he wasn't acting rashly. He had to have used the break to embed several cameras into the table. And with those in place, he would have seen my cards before and after the last community card. That alteration was all the proof he required.

If I lived through this, Matt would kill me. Though, given Dempsey's reputation, I doubted Matt would get the chance to extract his pound of flesh. With each passing second, a rising sense of panic flooded through me like a raging river, tossing me about. While those thoughts weren't helping me, corralling and dispelling them was proving difficult. As the mental storm raged, I started counting as I drew in deep and slow breaths.

CHAPTER 13

One, calm down and clear your head.

Two, think about how you are going to get out of this mess.

Three, what do you have to work with?

Four, you're still missing something.

Five, what was it?

Six, it's something painfully obvious.

Seven, what was I missing?

Eight, does it matter?

Nine, could I overcome this without it?

Ten, fight for everything you have.

Once I finished, I held my breath for several more slowing heartbeats before resuming my observation. I knew neither panic nor second guessing my decisions were going to help. After all, if they could, I'd be a millionaire. If I could invent a way to influence past decisions with hindsight, those riches would multiply by a million times. But that was a useless pipedream to explore. All that mattered was to learn from my mistakes and move on.

What was the first step to move on from this debacle? Of course, my first thought flittered back to the recent past. I made a vow to figure out how I could protect myself from guns, darts, stun guns, and any other projectile weapon. Even though such a discovery wouldn't help me now, it would go a long way in preventing this situation from occurring again.

After dispelling most of the mental conflict, I resumed listening to my surroundings, searching for anything that might help me survive. Unfortunately, wherever they shoved me, there wasn't a lot for me to hear or smell. And since my eyes still stubbornly refused to cooperate, I stretched my ears to their limits and waited.

An eternity later, hints of a conversation teased my ears, and my entire mind focused on the scraps, and I listened harder than I ever had in my life. Unfortunately, instead of growing easier with use, I struggled to keep the hints flowing to my ears. It was as if something was fighting me. As I fought against my struggling body, something else crystalized in my mind. Whatever they were pumping me full of was most likely designed to keep my mind clouded and ponderous.

Once again, I railed at my situation. What was I forgetting? I knew it was something, and it had to be simple. I couldn't explain why I was so sure about its simplicity, but I believed it. Something inside me screamed I was forgetting something as common to me as breathing. So why was it eluding me like a greased hog? My head twisted about and stared at the IV running into my right arm. Could I transform that scrap of plastic into something else?

Wait! My gift. I'd forgotten about my abilities. What were they pumping into me? An idle thought pulsed through my mind before I abandoned everything and flexed as many of my muscles against my bonds while forming an image of them turning into tissue paper. With the mental image firmly entrenched, I searched for body heat, and that's when everything made sense.

My body went slack. The chill nipping at me from inside and out was intentional. How did Dempsey know about my weaknesses? Despite seeing my pocket cards during the last round of the tournament through the cameras, there was no way he could know how I did it. Let alone that freezing me would inhibit those abilities. The latest realization also bolstered the shaky evidence of my eyes as far as where I was. With the conflagration of data, I was certain Dempsey ensured I woke up where they could freeze me.

Given the assault from the environment, there was no source of heat to power my abilities, and with the fluids seeping into me, he ensured I couldn't trade a little warmth for a single transformation. After all, you could only strain your body for so long. Without an ample supply of heat, I'd die wielding my gift or it would simply refuse to assist in my death. Either Dempsey somehow learned how my gift worked, or he'd gotten lucky that his standard method of detainment kept me from flexing my skills. What was the saying? It's better to be lucky than good. It wasn't fair Dempsey was both.

I pushed the tangential thoughts from my mind and latched onto the sounds. With each passing second, I could make out the shapes of words as if the speakers were getting closer, but I couldn't translate those rough concepts to a concrete example of language. As my mental strength waned, I stopped trying to pluck words from the haze and returned to my bindings. Deep down, I knew I couldn't break them. But could I loosen them enough to slip free?

Though after a few rounds of failed and painful attempts to loosen my bonds, I realized they were turning into just another nightmare. I'd never bothered learning how to slip out of bindings. Rather, I'd always leaned on my gift for whatever the world threw my way. Which meant that when I couldn't bypass the issue, like I've always done historically, I was left staring up at an insurmountable burden. I sucked in a lungful of frigid air, closed my eyes, and took an inventory of my dwindling heat.

Halfway through the internal checklist, I realized that while my core temperature was falling, there was still enough there I should have been able to trigger the transformation of my bindings. However, something prevented me from accessing the heat. Granted, if I'd been able to do it, I'd be right on the border of hypothermia, based on several troubling experiments, but I wouldn't be trussed up like a holiday roast ready to cook. Right now, something other than the cold kept me from freeing myself.

And I figured it had to be the drugs from the IVs. A flare of anger erupted from deep within my mind at the neutralization of my gift. Ever since I first discovered my ability, I've never been without it, no matter how cold I got.

As the seconds ticked on, my mind twisted from the inability to free myself to hopefully being able to pick up some helpful information. My imagination latched onto a stray memory of ear trumpets, and I manipulated the concept into an invisible cone to funnel stray sounds right to my ear. With the picture in place, I gathered the required heat and poured it through the mental image. Instantly, the strange sounds I'd isolated crystalized into the occasional word, though it had cost me more warmth than I wanted.

"... cameras were ..."

Thank you for proving my assumption right, Mr. Thug. While it was too late to help me, it was still gratifying my mind could work and connect stray thoughts. But it prompted a more dire question. Why was Dempsey allowing me to continue breathing?

Across all the rumors swirling about my mind, Dempsey didn't look kindly upon cheaters, period. So as I sat in the frigid room and attempted to glean more of the conversation, the stories highlighting the man's ruthlessness emerged. Of all the ones I had heard, the most horrific stemmed from the tournament six years ago. While I didn't know if the story was true, it didn't matter. Ultimately, I didn't know who to sympathize with, the poor fool or the animals who assisted in the eradication. I quickly clubbed the memory down, since I didn't need to depress myself any further.

As I thought about my situation more, I realized that if I was right and Dempsey ordered the cameras to be installed for the game amongst the top ten, then it meant my original information concerning the tables had been right. There weren't any cameras prior to the break. Which meant Dempsey altered everything off nothing more than a wild supposition. Dempsey stopped the game, insisting on a chance for top talent to mingle and discuss the odd- ity. What had I done to warrant that kind of scrutiny? Had I really been that lucky? Or had it been how I revealed my winning hands, the production involved, that motivated Dempsey's actions?

Replaying the tournament's highlights in my head, I could see how some of my winning hands might seem very suspicious, especially to a man like him. That Dempsey's actions were based on a false assumption bothered me. Yes, he actually caught me cheating, but until that last hand, I'd been playing an honest game. That he suspected me of cheating when I was playing hon- estly irritated me. If I had taken what the dealer had given me, then I would have honestly taken second place.

While I wouldn't have collected the reputation I'd been seek- ing, I would have gotten a boost, and the money wouldn't have been too bad. Given my troubles now, that would have been pref- erable. Unfortunately, hindsight being what it was, I couldn't help but chastise myself as these inconsistencies continued mounting. When observed holistically, they created an inescapable truth that made far too much sense after the fact.

Despite the challenge of seeking loose words from my captors, my brain continued to circle around to my present condition. This time, it highlighted another source, leeching the warmth from my body. The metallic seat beneath me. When you considered the temperatures surrounding me, the silk shirt and slacks provided virtually no protection for my skin. They probably left the chair in the freezer, just to get a jump start on the torment. It also made me think he was looking to add me to his collection of ice stat- ues. While I created some low-tech hearing aids, I didn't have the focus or the warmth for something more substantial.

With my current predicament in place, I started groping for any heat in my body. Despite gathering enough to dispel the ear funnels if needed, I had nothing else. But as the seconds continued ticking away, I realized that aside from dismissing the hearing tools; I didn't have the mental clarity of any transformation. That realization brought a renewed chorus of mental curses regarding Dempsey's ingenuity. How could Dempsey know how to neutralize me this effectively? I'd spent my entire life hoarding this ability from everyone except Matt. And I'd never stumbled onto anyone who shared it.

How did Dempsey have the perfect containment setup for me? When I opened my eyes, a small ray of hope crept forward. I could see just fine, too bad my assumption had been right. This was an empty walk-in industrial freezer. It didn't take long to itemize everything in view. The only thing I saw were three walls, not even a door. Here I was sitting in a freezer alone, two IVs pumping drugs into me, mentally clouded from said cocktail, and immobilized from the neck down. So far, Dempsey's thugs were doing a first-rate job of keeping me contained.

After another subjective eternity, as I strained to pluck more words from the swirling haze of confusion, something reached me as clearly as if it had been spoken into my ear.

". . . fool . . ."

While I only made out the single word, there was something off about the rest of the comment. It was as if whoever was speaking was being muffled. And given my present location, it probably meant the goons had propped open the door to this chilly prison. Had the circumstances not been so dire, I would have been inclined to praise myself for improving a skill. As it was, there was no reason to celebrate anything.

However, given my imprisonment, it didn't take me long to

figure out who the goons were talking about. After all, had I been in their place, I'd be tossing that word about. In fact, I'd probably be flinging harsher terms about someone in my situation. In fact, just because I couldn't make out their insults didn't mean they weren't laughing as they condemned my stupidity.

With each passing second, I was able to hear more words, though I still couldn't capture a complete thought. But the failure simply compelled me to redouble my efforts. I hoped to gather something that would give me some hope, and the current conversation was the only thing I could latch onto. Unfortunately, my situation changed, and the mutterings grew harder to understand. It was as if they started speaking another language. As the difficulty continued, my opinion on the door changed from slightly ajar to shut, though if that was the case, I didn't know how I captured anything.

I took a deep breath and closed my eyes.

". . . don't know why . . . boss . . . with him . . ."

Wait, I heard a mostly intact thought. My mind tried inserting some of the missing words. The first word to slot into a missing spot was the word was. I quickly dismissed it, since it didn't seem like it fit. After all, what did Dempsey want from me? If I kept having this kind of trouble following the conversation, I would probably go insane long before they got around to killing me. But I couldn't let something so trivial bother me.

A moment later, I plucked another word from the din, and I recognized that it came from a different person. "Shut up. . . ."

The other goon or goons quickly obeyed the terse command, highlighting the power dynamic between whoever was talking outside of the freezer. And while the foolish and ignorant corner of my mind wondered if that was something I could exploit, the more rational and intelligent portion overruled it, saying Dempsey would have trained disobedience out of their existence.

After a brief pause in the conversation, I caught a few words of the first goon's retort. "... guy ... palmed ..."

Did Dempsey's lackeys know what I'd done? Somehow Dempsey understood enough about my gift to imprison me like this, but he refused to keep his men informed about what they were guarding. While interesting, all that mattered was the confirmation that this was because I'd cheated. This goon appeared to think I simply palmed the ace, giving me potentially useful information. First, it let me know there was a good chance these guards hadn't been at the tournament. If they had been there, they would've known about the fresh deck.

It also meant they probably didn't understand why Dempsey wanted me trussed up like this. That realization gave me a glimmer of hope I might talk my way into a heat source, especially if they were supposed to be in the freezer with me. That gave me a sliver of hope, despite my situation being horrendous. The slight chance of escape teased a smile out of me.

Of course, it didn't take long for the rational part of my mind to extinguish that fledgling hope. It insisted the far more likely outcome of pestering the guards for anything would be their carrying out my execution. Fortunately, it also reluctantly admitted my being bound and alive was probably a sign Dempsey, or one of his lieutenants, wanted to have a brief chat with me. I mean, there are easier and crueler ways to kill someone.

When my focus returned to the conversation, I caught a few more words.

"... you need to ... you ... watch ..."

If I couldn't start catching more of what they were saying, I was going to lose it. The only thing the piecemeal words told me was I had been correct in my assessment of goon number two. He was devoted to Dempsey. He was the more traditional 'do as you are told without question' type of henchman. He would be more difficult to sway. This left goon number one as my best means of escape since he was a 'curious' henchman.

". . . know why . . . we . . . toss . . . end . . . to the other."

Speak and ye shall receive. That broken response belonged to Mr. Curious. This was getting ridiculous. Did he want to toss me around? Was that a possibility? If it was, he would have to be built from solid muscle to achieve it. Instantly, my mind conjured a large and muscular man beating me to a bloody pulp. With a deep breath, I forced the rising lump back down my throat, chastised myself, and added 'learn how to fight' to the list of things I had to do after I escaped. After all, what good would it do for me to learn how to shield myself from projectiles but not be able to defend myself in a fistfight?

A shiver ran down my body, and I pulled my attention away from the conversation to focus on a more immediate problem. While I had never studied to become a doctor, I'd learned a few things about the human body. Particularly how it interacted with cold. Every transformation consumed a portion of my body heat. Which meant in the early days, I flirted with hypothermia often. Occasionally, I even forced trips to emergency rooms. Since I made a point of living in temperate climates, none of the doctors could explain my sudden symptoms.

With all the times I teetered between life and death, I knew the limits of my body regarding hypothermia. And at that moment, my body was slowly approaching a dangerous temperature. I needed something warm, and I needed it soon. Maybe the part of my mind which assumed I was going to die had been right. It's possible I'd misinterpreted the goons, and Dempsey didn't want to meet me. Should I risk calling out to them? Were they waiting for me to break the silence? If I called out, what would they do? Well, nothing would happen if I remained silent.

As my lips wriggled, I plucked a couple of words from the loyal one. ". . . witch . . . him . . ."

Given the drugs, my mind was hazy. Couple that with the possible obstruction between them and me, I debated on what I'd heard. I doubted the thug actually said witch. While my skills could let me imitate real magic, I'd never encountered someone else like me, much less anyone flying about on a broomstick. I must have misheard what they said.

". . . the other witch . . ."

There it was again, but this time I didn't catch which goon had spoken. The surety I'd embraced a moment ago vanished like ice thrown into an inferno. And as my assurance ebbed, a bitter sense of dread bloomed in my chest, competing with the frigid chill.

". . . witch . . . this . . ."

To mishear the same word three separate times, while technically possible, was highly unlikely. Did that mean there were others like me? How? Despite my travels, I'd never come across anyone with my gift. While I wasn't a world traveler, I'd spent most of my life drifting across the West Coast and the neighboring states.

Considering the nonchalant tone in both voices, it felt like these two professionals had dealt with this woman many times before. Did both believe in witchcraft? Or was it only one of them? If one or both believed, they must have witnessed a genuine display from someone flexing our shared gift. The revelation dropped another piece of the puzzle in place.

I wasn't unique in the world, and Dempsey had his hooks embedded in someone like me. Based on conversations with Matt, what I could do was often mistaken for magic. If someone was so inclined, it would be easy to embrace the witch or wizard motif.

CHAPTER 13

In fact, it took me a long time to get Matt to stop calling me a wizard or mage. If I didn't know how to wield my gift, I'd consider it magic.

As my mind raced with the confirmation I wasn't alone, a litany of questions emerged. Were we the basis of magic in all the ancient myths? Were the ancient gods and their children, people who shared my gift? Was Merlin someone just like me? While I yearned for those answers, I pushed them aside and focused on the conclusions. I doubted I'd ever find out how Dempsey found someone like me. But it made sense he'd experiment with his 'witch' to be able to trap others he'd come across.

But why would this witch be interested in me? Had she thought she was unique in this world, like me? If she did, was she, like me, jealous of her lost uniqueness? Was this the person who wanted to meet with me? Were they planning to hand me over to her? Would I become a living experiment for her or Dempsey? In answer to those questions and others, my mind spun up, explored, and discarded multiple scenarios, each worse than its predecessor.

Sitting in the dry and frigid room, I tried connecting the dots from everything I'd collected or experienced. Dempsey either employed or had a solid relationship with a woman who shared my gift. My guess was they had an amicable relationship. My bonds and the IV spoke to just how entwined they were. Nothing else explained why I was so locked down. As is usually the case, the answers generated more questions. Was Dempsey a genuine believer in witchcraft? Or did he simply refer to her as a witch to keep his men in line? I dismissed the questions and focused on what mattered. This woman gave, either directly or indirectly, Dempsey and, by extension, his men, the knowledge of how to detain me.

I drew in a deep breath, steadying my nerves as I closed my eyes and dismissed the ear trumpets. "Is anyone there?"

The din vanished as my words echoed off the freezer's walls. I hadn't raised my voice all that much. How could I struggle to understand their words, but they heard me so easily? I cracked my eyes open and searched for a microphone but couldn't find anything. As the silence stretched out, I worried calling out was a mistake. However, a few moments later, squeaking hinges shattered the silence, announcing someone's entrance.

Light flooded through the opening, throwing the men's shadows over my body. Once they were within striking distance, they stopped. They stood behind me and waited. Which, of course, prompted fear to bubble up in my chest. Despite being ready for someone to make a move, I wasn't ready for that. So when a goon grabbed my head from behind, I tried to leap from the chair, though I didn't scream. While my body couldn't move, my heart beat so fast it threatened to fail. As my heart struggled to fall into a regular beat, a goon pulled my head back, forcing me to look up into the shadow-covered face. He held me there for several moments, letting the silence wrap around me till my lips quivered. "It looks like our guest of honor is finally awake."

I could safely say I didn't like the fact Mr. Loyalty was as smart in person as he had seemed through the snatches of conversation I'd overheard. Now that I could clearly hear the thickly layered accent of this stranger, I guessed he was from France.

"The boss will be happy to hear that," the curious one said with a chuckle.

Now that I was being given a bit more of their attention, I began to have second thoughts about calling out for it. But since their focus was now on me, I figured blacking out, or at least pretending to black out, would only make matters worse. "If I'm supposed to meet your boss, could I have something warm? If I don't get something soon, I'll freeze to death."

Another awkward silence filled the freezer as the loyal one slapped my head with his other hand. When he stopped treating my head like an anvil, he yanked my hair back and positioned his mouth next to my ear. "Our boss gave us very specific instructions when dealing with you."

"Am I supposed to meet him before I die?"

Mr. Loyalty clicked his tongue. "We were told to keep you from any kind of heat source. So if you ask me that again, there will be consequences." A moment later, a cold bit of metal pressed into my temple.

The man was threatening to shoot me.

A clicking tongue symbolized the gun's firing, making me flinch. The goons let the tense silence build before the curious one pressed the gun into my temple as he said, "Ask for heat, and I pull the trigger."

Well, apparently my assumption about him was slightly off.

Within a few seconds, the pressure against my skull vanished as Mr. Loyalty said, "I'm sorry for my associate's behavior."

He must have pulled the man's gun arm away from my head.

"But I'm afraid my companion is correct. We have the strictest instructions on how to deal with you. And unfortunately for you, one of those instructions is to keep your body temperature as low as we can without killing you."

I started clattering my teeth for show. Unfortunately, I quickly realized I couldn't stop. "Do you have experience in keeping people on ice?"

"Some," the man said, tugging my hair.

I closed my eyes, attempting to ignore the pain. "I know my body's limits, and right now, I'm approaching the point where I'll die without some heat. Do your orders include letting me die?"

"We're to do what we can to keep you alive," said Mr. Curious.

"Stop talking with him," the loyal one said, shaking his head as he tossed mine forward. "We are intimately aware of the healthy temperature range of the human body." A couple of clinks rang out from behind me as a sinister chuckle washed over me. "While you're uncomfortable, you aren't in any danger of freezing to death."

"Not everyone falls into that normal range," I said through clenched teeth.

"If you're too weak to survive, we won't be chastised," he said, flicking my ear. "If we were trying to kill you, we would have soaked your clothes before locking you in the freezer."

"The saline will do the same thing," I said through my clattering teeth.

With an exasperated sigh, a foot started tapping against the ground, while Mr. Loyalty said, "Since you can't see everything you're hooked up to, I can understand why you'd think we're trying to kill you. Ignorance truly is the bane of people like you, but I'm feeling benevolent today, and it doesn't matter if you know, but you're connected to a high-end thermometer." He paused for a moment and sighed. "Currently it's reporting that your body temp is eight-nine point seven degrees. I suppose we do need to raise the room's temperature slightly. Would you be so kind and see to it?"

"Sure," the curious one said.

Once the retreating footsteps vanished, Mr. Loyalty leaned down, placing his mouth beside my ear. "We were told to keep your body as close to ninety degrees as possible, so that's what we're going to do."

Needing more answers, I clenched my jaw and pushed my luck. The worst they could do was kill me a little sooner, but I might get lucky. "These IVs have got to be doing more than helping you regulate my body temperature."

CHAPTER 13

"What of it?"

"What are you pumping into my body through those shunts?"

Mr. Loyalty flicked my temple as he inched closer to me. "Marcus . . ."

The fact that he knew my name shouldn't have rattled me. But given the totality of the situation, it sent a severe shudder down my trapped spine.

". . . I know what you're capable of, even when you're chilled to this extent, without certain restraints in place," he said, his voice thick with mirth. "While the boss would prefer you to be alive when he arrives, he won't bat an eye if we tell him we had to make a corpse out of you, even though we know your potential value. Now, be quiet and wait for the boss to arrive and explain everything."

With another flick, he rose and vanished behind me. As the door slid across the floor, a snap thundered through the freezer as he said, "I almost forgot to give you this accessory. It's very stylish. I do hope you enjoy the . . . privacy this piece provides."

Before I could reply, a blindfold fell across my eyes, once again plunging me into a world of darkness.

Sick to my stomach from the isolation, an over-beating heart, and information overload, I sat in my chair, sifting through the brief conversation, seeking the gems from the muck. After the search, my shoulders collapsed as if a massive weight had fallen onto them, threatening to press the air out of me. I didn't think I was asking for much, just something to keep me afloat in this endless sea. Unfortunately for me, Mr. Loyalty was one of the most tight-lipped and careful men I'd ever come across. He could teach politicians a thing or two about providing useless answers. I sat there lost and alone, with only my thoughts to mark the passage of time or keep me company. This was going to be a long wait.

CHAPTER 14

Time's passage can be cruel. While certain days evaporate like water droplets falling onto a hot skillet, others seem to stretch out indefinitely. In the frigid chamber, every second seemed to be contorted into eons. With the loyal goon robbing me of my sight and the freezing temperatures and drugs stealing my gift, all I could do was linger on the events leading me to this prison. I didn't think I could continue scouring my recent memories without losing my sanity. Yet, each time I remembered receiving the blindfold, I bit my lip and went searching for fresh tidbits.

Despite the constant redoubling of my efforts, each pass through the recent events failed to reach the scrutiny of the previous one. In fact, every time I remembered Mr. Loyalty covering my face with the blindfold, the worry lines framing my face intensified. Despite dispelling the negative thoughts looping through my mind, Dempsey's cruelty loomed over me. I'm sure his walking piggy banks needed to be stroked, but this wait was designed for a singular purpose. He wanted the extreme conditions and time's creeping march to shatter my will.

Even though closing my eyes was pointless, thanks to the blindfold, I did it anyway as I sifted through the demeanor, actions, and words of everyone I'd met. And the most jarring statement the loyal goon made popped into my head.

"Marcus, I know what you're capable of, even when you're chilled to this extent, without certain restraints in place."

It wasn't much, but the first time I heard that qualification, a seed fell into a fertile corner of my mind, despite my ignorance. And with every repetition, the sprouting thought tripped me up. Whether the goon knew the inner workings of my gift or not, the phrasing implied neither was an adequate protection from my abilities, at least on its own.

From personal experience, I knew changing the world around me was possible even if doing so risked a severe case of hypothermia. But whenever I tasked my body to that degree, I needed an ample amount of mental clarity. Which appeared to be the purpose of the drug coursing through my veins. On the flip side, there had been a few times when my mind was racing, incapable of forming solid images, but an overabundance of heat would bypass that stumbling block.

To build a prison based on one of these restraints would have been equivalent to swatting a fly with a cannonball. However, when used together against someone of my skills, they transformed from the ridiculous into something more adequate for the job of eliminating pests.

And like that, the mystery of the goon's words became clear. Though I wasn't sure what help that tidbit would be, but I was a junkie for random pieces of information. While some facts might appear useless in the moment, you never knew when they would transform into the critical bit of intelligence that would save your life.

In that moment, understanding did little to help. In fact, it simply added to the dread coursing through my veins. While my physical status screamed my life was in danger, another comment hinted at Dempsey's true purpose.

"While the boss would prefer you to be alive when he arrives, he won't bat an eye if we tell him we had to make a corpse out of you, even though we know your potential value."

When you coupled that statement with Bella's comment about having hooks into masters, it made sense Dempsey would want to stake his claim to my skill, especially if he already had someone like me. Having a spare was never a bad idea. A second person capable of altering the world would be a tantalizing target to sink his talons into. But how could I be valuable to a criminal kingpin like Dempsey? Scratch that, my gift made me valuable to anyone who knew about it. My surprise of another person like me existing proved the worth of my abilities.

It wasn't just the threat thrown in my face. I'd heard bits and pieces of their conversation, and from what I'd heard, Dempsey valued me, as ridiculous as that seemed to me. He already had someone who presumably was already compliant to his whims. Or was she? Did Dempsey need to replace his witch? Was that why he wanted me alive and unharmed? As more questions floated through my hazy mind, I buried them with the others.

The speculation wasn't helping me. Ultimately, I believed what the goons told me. Dempsey valued me, or my gift at the very least. Every time my mind faced that fact, fresh chills, more intense than the freezer, filled my body. As I slowly accepted the prevailing scenario, the prison took on another degree of menace. Besides the physical and mental anguish, he ensured I'd know what would happen if I ever stepped out of line. He possessed the knowledge and the will to keep someone like me detained indefinitely.

While I'm willing to bend or break the occasional law, ultimately, there are lines I'm unwilling to cross. I'd like to think honoring those boundaries would give me the strength to refuse a deal with the devil. But I'd never been in this situation before. I had always been able to leverage my gift, my wits, or some combination of the two to sidestep every problem threatening me. Sadly, Dempsey had blocked every avenue of escape and prevented me from blazing a trail to safety. The man wanted me, and based on his reputation, whatever he wanted, he attained.

As the dread swelled within me, my desperation for a heat source overwhelmed me. Something as simple as a lighter would grant me everything I'd need to escape. Yet, in this arctic simulation, such a precious piece of contraband was not to be found. And my core temperature was far too suppressed to help me, even if my mind wasn't derailed from the drugs. At that moment, I finally acknowledged the fear swelling inside my chest. I had statistically no chance of escaping this room or Dempsey's wrath.

The stray thought sparked a war between the swelling dread, the mounting fear, and the creeping anxiety. As each emotion lashed out against the other, a small corner of my mind seized upon the fact I wasn't alone in the world. If there was someone else, there was a chance others existed. Right then, I only knew about Dempsey's witch. Did Dempsey have other people like us on his payroll? Truly, this drug's existence made more sense if others like his witch and me existed. Based on his reputation, Dempsey didn't like being out of control, and if there were more of us, he'd want an edge over all of us.

I pulled out my mental to-do list and thumbed through the entries until I found recent ones. Under the one directing me to find others like me, I added another. Inquire about this drug and other ways to subdue people like us. With the fresh note added, I shoved it back into the recesses of my mind and resumed observing the mental battle. Between the volleys, I wondered how many of us there were if Dempsey's witch and I weren't alone.

However, while I didn't stop the mental skirmish raging on, I pushed thoughts of others into a different patch of my mind. It would be nice to fantasize about new friends, and even mentors, but greater concerns loomed over me. Such as not freezing to death. Right now, I could see only one slim chance for survival, and I was hanging all my hopes on that treacherous and circuitous path.

Despite my hatred of the concept, I ultimately knew it was the only option available. Yet, with Dempsey's apparent omniscience, I worried he already knew how I'd try to escape, and instead of freedom, I'd find fresh obstacles blocking my path. Either way, if, and I couldn't stress that condition enough, I survived the night, it would mean becoming Dempsey's puppet for as long as I proved valuable. The risk in accepting that offer would be I would lose myself. There was a strong possibility I might have to abandon my principles, but I'd be alive. Hope existed beyond the reach of the dead.

A loud crash shook my wandering mind. "Is everything okay?"

"Do you really care?" the curious goon asked.

I'm not sure why, but the Minotaur from Greek mythology popped into my mind when the curious goon's voice reached my ears. Aside from the terrifying image, an idea wormed its way into me. I shook my head as I licked my lips and said, "I'm a helpful guy." This probably wasn't going to work, but sometimes people could and would surprise you if you gave them a chance. "In fact, if you released me, I'd be more than happy to lend you all a hand."

A deep, guttural growl answered, and I thought it came from the curious bull-like goon.

But instead of any kind of rebuke, all I heard was a soft whack, followed by a contorted laugh. As I tried to twist my head toward that eerie sound, Mr. Loyalty's cheerful voice cut through the chill air. "We don't require your assistance. Though if you really want to assist us, my companion would be more than happy to put a bullet through your head."

"That's a little extreme, isn't it?"

"Not at all," Mr. Loyalty said as footsteps echoed off the industrial surface of the freezer. "Don't forget, when dealing with you, we were given very precise directions as to your accommodations."

"Is shooting me on that well-ordered list?"

"It's at the top of the list, especially if you ever escape your bonds." One goon, presumably the loyal one, traced the lashings as his creepy chuckle washed over me. "Are you eager to experience that outcome?"

With my ability sidelined, my body restrained, and the looming threat of death, I wasn't left with many options. Yet I couldn't help but try to wriggle free from the numerous bindings. After the brief struggle, my shoulders slumped as I released my breath. "No, I can't say that's something I'm eager to experience."

A firm grip grabbed my shoulders as Mr. Loyalty's breath assaulted my nose. "Marcus, you are a clever child, but you don't know anything about what's happening to you. So allow me to paint you a picture. If you force us to kill you, my companion is faster than me. And he won't necessarily reach for his gun. Rather, he'll simply rip you from this chair and snap you in half. And given your unique skill set, he'll be overly cautious in defining what is or isn't an attempt to escape."

While the goon continued squeezing my shoulder, he patted my cheek as if I were a puppy learning a new trick. "Remember, the boss is looking forward to his conversation with you. However, he won't bat an eye if we have to deal with you in a way that prevents you from ever being useful to him. Do you understand?"

I licked my dry lips as my head bobbed up and down.

"Good. Now you should also know that neither of us is fond

of this kind of assignment." The loyal goon squeezed my shoulder with the strength of a vise. "Let us finish our work in peace, and you'll live to have your candid chat with the boss."

As soon as the pressure vanished, I nodded once again. While he wasn't a stupid fellow, Mr. Loyalty could learn a few things about veiling his threats a little better.

After several eternal minutes of grunts and scrapes, the room fell into silence, and the last vestige of hope for an escape vanished. There was no chance I'd warm up enough to break my bonds, which meant this meeting was going to happen. When they removed the blindfold, I would be sitting in front of either Dempsey or one of his lieutenants.

The clattering of my teeth was the only sound filling the room.

After what felt like the passing of an eon, a hand slammed into my chest, knocking me and the chair over. Though instead of slamming into the ground, a set of hands caught me.

"Tuck your head," Mr. Loyalty said.

I wordlessly obeyed the command as the goons lifted me up and carried me out of the freezer. After the brief trip, they dumped me back onto the floor and slammed something into my gut. Based on its unyielding pressure, I assumed the thing digging into me was the edge of a table. The discomfort lasted for several seconds, intensified by the lingering chill, but as I was about to break the silence, the pressure vanished as the table's feet dragged across the floor.

A hand rapped the table a moment before the loyal goon barked an order, "Get the boss's chair."

A series of thumps, scuffs, and curses announced the Minotaur's difficulty as he struggled to move the boss's chair. The piece of furniture must be large and unwieldy to give the beast who could fold me in half trouble.

Clack.

The vibrant sound cut through the din of the bustling goons and approaching footsteps. But what was that? It sounded like something metallic struck something hard but not metallic.

Clack.

There it was again, and it was closer than before.

Clack.

Each strike was crystal clear and somewhat symmetrical. It almost lined up with one set of the approaching footsteps.

Clack.

There was a rhythm behind those strikes. What caused the repeating sound? Was someone wearing tap shoes? No, not tap shoes. Yet, it was connected to someone's gait. Was a cane announcing someone's arrival?

Clack.

Yeah, that fit the scenario better than anything else.

Clack.

A cane was a good indicator of importance or injury. However, the reverence these goons used when describing the boss made an injury seem unlikely. Which meant that whoever approached was important. At that moment, I remembered seeing a cane recently. Someone had entered Dempsey's warehouse with a cane. But who? I quickly ran through everyone's arrival, looking for the potential owner.

Clack.

Halfway through the entrances, I started doubting my memory. Even if I proved my recollection true, it didn't mean that person would be whoever was walking toward me.

Clack.

I swallowed as I sped toward the end of the entrances.

Clack.

That came from just to my right. Come on, I needed to confirm my memory before my blindfold was removed.

Clack.

My mystery guest was rounding the table.

Thwack.

Had I not been so tightly bound to the chair; I would have leaped roughly ten feet into the air. Whoever just entered slammed their cane onto the table, obviously wanting to set the tone for this exchange. I pushed my memory to go faster. Suddenly, in the corner of my mental eye, I caught sight of something. I quickly took a few mental steps backward and saw the tantalizing image. As the main door swung open for the last time, a man with a cane walked in.

As my shoulders slumped, one of Dempsey's goons ripped the blindfold from my head. Not to mention some hair, roots, and all. When my eyes adjusted to the onslaught of light, I saw a wintry smile staring down at me. A moment before my eyes were freed, I'd seen a warmer version of that smile in my mind. However, those cold, emotionless gray eyes were the same. Despite what I'd overheard the goons say earlier, at that moment, staring into those impassive eyes, I was convinced Bertrand Dempsey came to watch me die.

CHAPTER 15

With each passing second, I stared up into Dempsey's unwavering eyes. Behind those gray orbs, I saw the calculating mind behind every rumor I'd ever heard. While I'd tried to explain away his apparent omniscience at the tournament, sitting under that scrutiny proved how foolish my supposition had been. After a few seconds seemingly stretching into millennia, I pulled my gaze away from his face, only to catch sight of his suit.

While there were similarities between what he wore now, I could tell that he'd changed since the last time I'd seen him. Typically, a change in attire would indicate a substantial passage of time. However, it's possible that's simply what Dempsey wanted me to think. However, despite his fresh and immaculate suit, he let us linger in silence, with his cane rolling between his hands. Aside from the soft scuffing of the cane's tip as it twirled against the floor, that stillness intensified, gaining substance. It didn't take long before it loomed over me like a predator circling its prey. Just before the silence engulfed me, Dempsey, ever the showman, twirled his cane overhead and slammed it against the table. The crash echoed off the rest of the room, creating a chorus of discordant notes.

When the last note of that impromptu beat vanished, the crime lord's fingers wrapped around his cane like a snake encircling its dinner. "Good afternoon, Marcus." With his free hand, he gestured at the open freezer behind him as his lips curled into a fatherly smile promising great suffering. "I'm sorry for forcing these conditions upon you, but we needed to have a candid conversation, and I required your complete attention."

There was no reason that grin should have put me at ease, yet it did. Despite all the evidence and conjecture, a part of me wanted to shake the man's hand and ask how I could help him. You might think it was fear prompting that desire, but you'd be wrong. Even now, I can't explain why that desire filled me. All I can say is there was just something behind that expression that comforted me. And with the perfect vision of hindsight, I realized I'd seen this expression at the tournament.

Unfortunately, I'd underestimated him, and now I was completely under his thumb. Based on those rumors, Dempsey would destroy me. If I had a single wish, I'd use it to trade places with someone tied up in front of a ravenous lion. I'm pretty sure those odds would be better, and if lady luck spurned me, my end wouldn't be as painful.

As I kept myself from looking my personal grim reaper in the eyes, my dry tongue dragged across cracked lips. Every time I came close to locking gazes with Dempsey, Matt's rebuke popped into my mind, and I swallowed a mental curse as my gaze fell. With Dempsey's omniscient glare boring through me, I hoped Matt got the chance to chastise me for my decision, despite the dread my arrogance had dug my grave.

Dempsey snapped his fingers, and a thick-fingered goon stepped forward, putting a bottle to my lips. He tipped it up, dumping water into my mouth.

"With all the fluids you've gotten intravenously, I'm sure you're hydrated." Dempsey laid his cane on the table and crossed his legs. "However, it's amazing what fear can do to the body. Hopefully, this will loosen your tongue."

When the goon removed the water, I swished the liquid in my mouth, stalling for time. A childish tactic, but it was all I had. Once I'd swallowed the cool water, my tongue moistened my lips. "Is this how you treat all your victors?"

Dempsey clicked his tongue as he folded his hands onto his lap. "While I'm sure you're anything but comfortable, Marcus, please don't insult my intelligence. We both know you're not here because you won the tournament." He picked up his cane and probed something over my left shoulder. "Annabelle, this is running a little low. Do we need to replace this before we go any further?"

Who was Dempsey addressing?

"It depends on how long you plan on talking with the boy," a feminine voice said from behind my right shoulder. "How long will this conversation last?"

"We should be fine," Dempsey said, with another gentle thrust of his cane. He eased the tip onto the floor in front of him and leaned over it. "I'm sorry for your discomfort, but it will be over soon." The formality behind Dempsey's words vanished as his passionless eyes fixed on me. "However, given your abilities, it's best that a conversation surrounding your future takes place while I have all the advantages."

As my teeth joined my quivering body, I focused my eyes on Dempsey's chin in a vain attempt to avoid his omniscient glare. "What abilities warrant this abuse?"

"What did he just tell you?" Mr. Curiosity asked as he smacked the back of my head.

"Dante!" Dempsey slammed his cane against the floor, his eyes burning with fury as he studied the Minotaur looming behind me. He curled his hands over the cane's head and spoke with a voice reminding me of a disappointed father agonized by his child's behavior. "I appreciate your disdain for lies, but I don't want you bruising our young friend. Is that understood?"

"Sorry, boss," Mr. Curiosity, I mean Dante, said.

"Isaac, can you and Dante take a few steps back? I don't want Marcus to worry that you're going to abuse him every time he speaks."

"Yes, boss," Mr. Loyalty, or rather Isaac, said as he and Dante obeyed the boss's command.

Dempsey was as masterful at wielding silences as Picasso was at laying brush to canvas. The crime lord not only had an inherent understanding of when to brandish them, but for how long he should allow them to linger to elicit the most of the desired emotion. As the terse stillness reached a deafening crescendo, he stamped his cane three times and leaned forward.

"Marcus, neither I nor my employees appreciate liars. In fact, we have strict punishments for anyone who breaches our trust." He leaned over his cane and his lips stretched out, inviting me to release my burdens. "If you continue lying, there's a chance I won't be able to restrain my overly enthusiastic friend from administering that punishment."

Dempsey's calm voice did more to expel the little ember of warmth in my chest than his threat to allow Dante to kill me. In fact, I hadn't noticed how my quivering had intensified since I'd seen the crime lord. But once I did, it only got worse. He truly deserved the legend he'd crafted.

The soft click of his tongue signaled he saw me fall into my fear, and his smile softened ever so slightly as he leaned back into his seat. "Now, please don't waste anymore of my time. We both know what you are capable of, and it is a rare and wonderful gift."

"Why did you have the cameras installed?"

CHAPTER 15

Dempsey tapped his cane against the floor and rolled its head about his hand. "I suppose our conversation can meander a bit before we reach our destination. But are you certain that's where you want to start?"

As my clattering teeth battered my sanity, I pulled my chin to my chest, signaling my affirmation. Ultimately, I didn't care why he altered his actions. Rather, I was hoping to prolong this terrifying conversation, hoping whatever drug they'd pumped into my body might fade, allowing me to access my gift. Despite it being the faintest of hopes, it was all I had in that pit of darkness.

"I can appreciate your position." That smile, framed by Dempsey's angular face, widened ever so slightly, becoming almost predatory. He laid his cane across the table and crossed his legs. "It was a shame you forced me to bring the cameras back, but the answer is straightforward. After your first dealer was rotated out, he informed me you caught an unusual number of last-second victories. Armed with that supposition, I dispatched a team of craftsmen to outfit one of the spare tables with cameras."

"You played a hunch?"

"No, the word of your initial dealer was simply the impetus to prepare the table." Dempsey's fingers drummed along his cane as his smile widened. "Despite my preparations, I planned to give you the benefit of the doubt, though I quickened the pace at which I replaced your dealers. Unfortunately, for you, they all echoed the suppositions of the first. Now, you can try to argue that you didn't cheat prior to reaching the final table. But given your victories, you won't succeed. Luck never skews that much in anyone's favor, not without assistance."

While fear still filled me, there was a bit of anger mingled with it. I'd dismissed a hunch as a possibility because of the optics with the rich. Yet here was Dempsey, telling me he didn't mind dealing with negative speculation. "You upended everything because I was lucky?"

Dempsey's left hand turned toward him, and he silently studied his fingernails. After an extended amount of time, he looked past me. "Isaac, please arrange for a manicure."

"Yes, boss."

The crime lord laid his right hand across his cane as he twirled his other hand. "You say it was luck, but when you combine that unnatural streak with how you won the tournament, you can't argue with me. I caught you cheating."

My quivering lips drew to a line as my gaze crept up to his nose.

With a wry chuckle, Dempsey slapped the table and perched on his seat's edge. "Marcus, considering your current circumstances, the why is ultimately not important. The fact is, I have video evidence that your last hand started with the eight of clubs and nine of diamonds. However, after the river, the ace of spades had taken the place of your nine."

Once more, he allowed a silence to emerge and hang in the air until my gaze fell to the table.

He laid his elbows on the solitary piece of furniture and clasped his hands under his chin. "Since every swap of a deck came with a new color or design, we're certain that you couldn't have palmed that ace. The only way you could have gained the card needed to beat Patrick was to wield real magic."

Despite latching onto magic, Dempsey's logic was sound. As fury and anger swirled in my chest, they helped calm my shaking body, blunting the cold. It wasn't much, but it was something. And for this to work, I needed more time. Seeking to prolong our deadly conversation, I pivoted to an alternate reason he might have felt slighted by my lucky streak. "Was Patrick one of your surrogates?"

"Do you honestly think I would have employees in the tournament?"

"Why wouldn't you?"

"Your fellow attendees wouldn't appreciate me stocking the field like that."

"It doesn't cost you anything to enter a few of your own players, especially if they're skilled enough to challenge for the final table."

"What would that do for me?"

"If they reach the top ten, you reclaim their entrance fee. But as long as we're being honest with each other, I can't see you not ordering some of your more skilled employees to take part in your tournaments. It's just good business."

Dempsey's smile altered slightly. Instead of evoking images of someone I could trust to ease my burdens, I saw a parental grin highlighting pride in a clever answer. Despite my precarious situation, I could tell I'd risen in his estimation. Why was I trying to gain real recognition from this mafia don?

But the man just beamed as he dropped his hand into his lap. "No, he wasn't one of my employees. Unfortunately, none of my people reached the prize this year." Dempsey shifted slightly in his seat as he smoothed his jacket. "It's nice to see that you can be quite insightful."

"That's not entirely true. If I'd let Patrick win, I wouldn't be here."

"You're both right and wrong."

"What do you mean?"

Dempsey pulled his cane off the table and studied the pommel before lifting the stick to look down its length. "While I'll agree that you wouldn't be here, you'd be in a worse position."

"How's that possible?"

Dempsey thumped his cane on the floor as he leaned back into his seat. "From the moment I ordered the cameras installed, your old life ended." He thumped the tip of his cane against my chest as his smile widened. "Believe me, this outcome was the best thing for you."

"How is this what's best?"

His lips quivered ever so slightly. Just as quickly as the motion came, it vanished. Almost as if having to explain his words bothered him. He eased the cane's tip on the floor and leaned over it. "My boy, my dealers thought you might be cheating me."

"I wasn't."

"Irrelevant. I've collected dealers with sharp eyes and quick wits. They know what to look for, and more importantly, they know what I do with those I suspect are trying to swindle me. When all the dealers who rotated through your table voiced the same concerns, I didn't have a choice. Without proof of your cheating, I would have let you go home and carry on with your life for a little while. But before long, one of my . . . associates would have resolved the issue."

My fingers curled into fists as the rage boiled in my chest. "I didn't cheat!"

Dempsey rolled his shoulders as he buried his eyes in a hand. "You keep claiming that, but since there were no cameras in place prior to the final table, there's no way to prove your claim. Therefore, I'm left to rely on my dealers' instincts. And every one of them insisted there was a chance you were cheating. I didn't have a choice."

My gaze rose and latched onto his calm gray eyes as they emerged from behind his fingers. "If my life is forfeit, why am I alive?"

With a soft gasp, both hands flew to his chest as the cane's pommel collided with his stomach. Instantly, his gaze flicked toward someone behind me as he rebuilt his emotionless mask. Without asking a question, Issac broke the momentary silence.

"We told him he was valuable to you, and escape would void that value."

With a curt nod, the full weight of Dempsey's emotionless glare loomed over me. He pulled the cane off his leg and leaned over it. "Given what you are, your life isn't forfeit, Marcus. It's simply no longer your own."

As I studied his lifeless eyes, I took a deep breath as I moistened my lips. "What makes me such a valuable commodity?"

Dempsey groaned as his head fell. "Marcus, I thought we agreed not to waste each other's time."

"When did we agree to anything?"

A groan slipped through Dempsey's mouth as he lifted the cane and struck the ground like a gavel striking its sounding block. As the hallow sound echoed inside the chamber, his back straightened. "Marcus, be careful where you tread. I'm sure this has been your most closely guarded secret. However, I have proof of what you are. And while your talents are exceptionally rare—in fact, I've only known a handful like you—those abilities won't be worth the expense if you continue your disrespectful behavior."

Had I been able to move, I would have fallen off the chair. In fact, I probably would have plowed through the building and its foundation. As it was, I simply tore my gaze away from the crime lord and stared at the ground, forcing my heart back into place. Once my internal organs settled, I moistened my lips and kept my gaze firmly attached to a rather unique tile from amongst its identical siblings. "Just because you have a video proving that a playing card changed, you're going to put aside your de facto punishment for cheaters?"

"That's correct."

The finality in his voice told me we were rapidly approaching the end of the conversation from his perspective. However, I needed more time for my warmth to swell. While I knew it would be foolish, I didn't see another option; I needed to stall for time. A bit more heat should allow me to overthrow the effects of the drugs and break free from my bonds. "I'm sorry if I'm beating this horse to death, but my head gets thick when I've been drugged."

"That's an unfortunate requirement for this conversation. Remember, I don't like others having more options than I do."

"Are you telling me that had I kept the nine, I'd be dead right now?"

Dempsey rearranged his chair to rest his left arm on the table. He let an intimidating silence build for a moment before he lifted the cane and dropped it, letting it settle to the ground while his fingers kept it from falling over. He repeated that motion several times before he shook his head. "You might still be alive for the moment, but it wouldn't last long."

"The slight gap in my execution aside, you risked killing a piggy bank on a hunch."

"That's a crass way to think of you and your fellow participants."

"Isn't it an apt description for you?"

His left hand clenched around his cane's pommel, and once more, he stepped into the role of a judge bringing a courtroom to order. As the last echoing sound died, he lifted my chin with the tip of his cane and glared into my eyes. "While the people who take part in the tournament are interchangeable to my bottom line, they are not objects. You will show them the respect they're due. Is that clear?"

"Fine, but my question still stands."

CHAPTER 15

"Remind me what it was," Dempsey said, removing his cane from under my chin.

"Why did you risk offending all your participants on a hunch?"

Dempsey thumped his cane on the ground twice, filling the room with discordant echoes. "Must you continue beating the corpse of this horse? My dealers thought you were cheating. That's all I needed to act."

"You have that much faith in your employees?"

"It's unflappable," Dempsey said, striking the ground another time, "provided they don't give me reason to doubt them."

I drew the mental image of my bonds changing into paper from the depths of my mind and probed the supply of heat coursing through my veins. Unfortunately, while it had grown, I still needed more. I kept my eyes focused on the tip of the man's nose as I moistened my lips. "Fair enough, but you dismissed everything, including my execution, because of the proof you obtained?"

Dempsey's shoulders slumped as he harrumphed. His fingers clutching his cane whitened as his other hand massaged his brow. "You keep getting hung up over the wrong details."

"What are the right ones?"

Another series of clangs echoed inside the small room as Dempsey slammed his hand on the table. "Your cheating is irrelevant. All that did was ensure you came under my scrutiny. The reason you didn't wake to find yourself dead is because you're capable of wielding magic."

I could see the utter belief in his gray eyes. His witch must have made him a true believer. While the things I can do appear to be magic, it's not that simple. However, Dempsey's belief was grounded by witnessing something that wasn't accomplished by some hidden trick. In his mind, magic not only existed, but he would do anything to surround himself with those who could wield it. People just like me.

With a wickedly cruel smile, he gripped both sides of the cane and rose from his seat. Pinning the cane to the table, he loomed over me with his smile taking on a predatory appearance. "Because of the proof you get to live."

I got to live all right; I got the chance to live as his personal slave. Despite all the liquid he'd dumped into my body, I felt like I'd been traveling across the Sierra without water for three days. As my rough tongue scraped my lips, Dempsey snapped, and a goon shoved a bottle of water into my mouth. As the water tumbled down my throat, I coughed and spat out the roughly supplied liquid.

Dempsey slammed his cane against the table as his gaze drifted to the goon trying to drown me. "Dante, that's not how you give our guest his water."

"Sorry, boss," Mr. Curious said as he put the bottle to my lips. When I opened them, Dante poured a mouthful in and removed the bottle from my mouth. I sucked my lips into my mouth, letting the water hydrate the cracked surfaces. Once I swallowed, I searched for the unique tile I'd studied earlier as I asked, "If you aren't going to kill me, what are you going to do?"

This was obviously the question he had been waiting for, as his voice softened, and he reclaimed his seat. "Well, Marcus, the answer depends on you."

I clenched my eyelids and scoured my body for the available warmth. While I found more than I had a moment ago, it still wasn't enough to escape my bindings. When I opened my eyes, I stared at my hands and realized I'd never unclenched my fists. As I forced my fingers open, my eyes crept up, searching for the man's nose.

CHAPTER 15

"What does it depend on?"

"Marcus, you'll be the author of your own fate," Dempsey said, pulling the cane from the table and laying it across his lap.

I opened my fingers as far as I could. "Right now, I don't seem to be able to do anything."

Dempsey raised a finger as he bent down to pick up a briefcase. He laid it down, unlatched it, and gripped the edges of its top. "I'm offering you a job."

The offer stunned me, like a slap in the face. As I sat there, silent and dumbfounded, the pain building in my chest reminded me to draw in a fresh breath. With each ticking second, I studied Dempsey's face and nothing there betrayed the sincerity of his statement. After a few ragged breaths, my breathing fell back into its normal cadence, and I snapped my jaw shut.

Hopefully, with a bit more time, I'd have enough heat to escape. While searching my body for every scrap of extraneous warmth, I shoved my head as far as I could. "What kind of job are you offering?"

Dempsey clicked his tongue as he opened the briefcase. "A man who gets right to the point. I like that." He withdrew two envelopes and laid them on top of the case after closing the lid. He leaned back in his seat, dragging the cane off the table. "But before we talk about the details, I have a couple of questions for you."

"What are they?" I asked, twisting my neck to glean everything I could from those mysterious envelopes.

"I'm fairly certain I know what your answer will be," Dempsey said, rolling the cane across his palm with his thumb. "However, it's important to be explicit. Are you a parent?"

The radical change in the topic was another slap in the face. When my mind stopped swirling, I licked my lips as I shook my head.

"I thought as much." Dempsey clutched his cane and laid it across his lap. "While I've never been blessed with children directly, I am a father of a sort. If you ever get there, you'll learn that raising children isn't easy. We must prepare our young for the world while also shielding them from all the wrong influences. They need constant guidance to make all the right choices. But after all the work, if you manage to guide them to a better life than your own, you've done something wonderful."

"And what does that have to do with me?"

Dempsey gripped both ends of his cane and flexed the slender shaft as his smile soured from the impudent question. "Your impatience is something we will have to work on, I see. No matter, I'm sure it's not the only thing that'll require some attention."

"I'm definitely a little stubborn."

"That's fine," Dempsey said, striking the floor with the tip of his cane. "Marcus, I am going to adopt you more or less. Thankfully, you're still young enough to learn the errors of your ways. You can still be guided down the right path."

"Given the laws surrounding adoption and adulthood, this sounds more like slavery."

This time, when the crime lord slammed his cane into the tile, I heard it shatter. When he released the walking aid, instead of falling over, it swayed in place. The man had driven it through the tile and into the subflooring. He pulled his hand back to his chest as he shook his head. When the red hue to his skin vanished, he plucked the cane from the ground and examined the tip. After a few moments, he sighed and tossed it behind me.

When the clattering finished, he laid his elbows on the table and supported his chin with his thumbs. "That was a vulgar thing to say. While Isaac hasn't returned yet, Dante was about ready to rip your head off. Just so you're aware, both were among my first employees. They are neither mindless nor automatons. I find them to be perfect examples of what I expect from my employees. Thus, they're always present during interviews such as this."

As a fresh silence enveloped the room, I stared at the threat I had just been given. Dempsey laid it down so thickly that had I been blind, deaf, and mute, I still would have understood him. It also squished some hopes I'd been tending. Specifically, accepting his employment only to find a way out later. If I accepted his opportunity, there would only be one way out.

My options were to meet the grim reaper or lose myself and accept his offer. On principle, I still didn't want to become Dempsey's slave, no matter his objection to the term. While he might have a problem with that word being spoken aloud, he couldn't prevent me from screaming it inside my mind. After another check on my supply of heat, I licked my lips. I was almost there.

"And what exactly would I be doing for you?"

"Why, whatever is asked of you, of course." Dempsey's voice had regained its normal tone. "You don't need to worry about the details right now. All that you need to know is that my employees are all well taken care of."

"And just what will happen to me if I were to refuse your, oh so generous, offer?"

However, instead of verbally answering, he reached into his coat and removed a simple black case. It was about eight inches long, three inches wide, and an inch thick. As soon as he placed it down on the table, he deftly undid the single latch, slowly opening it while ensuring I couldn't see its contents.

"You can always say no. I can't force you to take the job. That's one of the reasons why this country is so wonderful. You have the freedom to accept whatever employment you think is best for you. And if that is your choice, then my associates will untie you and escort you out of the building."

Before I could say anything, I caught sight of Dempsey's twitching finger. I licked my lips as my eyes fell to the obsidian case. With my attention fully on the black box, he removed something from it before closing the lid. He did a wonderful job keeping whatever he held hidden from me. "But for every decision, there is a consequence, and your cheating has brought you to this crossroad. Therefore, this is your other option."

As a new silence bloomed, he reached out and thumped a rather large bullet on the table as, with each passing moment, my new reality unfolded before me and my breath grew labored. Dempsey was showing me the exact bullet he planned to kill me with.

"And your choice couldn't be simpler." Dempsey pointed at the solitary bullet. "You can come work for me or embrace the fact that this bullet will end your life. Now Marcus, please do not take this personally. After all, it's just business."

CHAPTER 16

As I stared at the bullet looming before me, my mind dismissed all the other problems weighing me down. Ordinarily, given my circumstances, a bullet, no matter the size, wouldn't have been so hypnotic. However, Dempsey had ensured the hunk of lead and brass would consume every corner of my mind. In fact, it did such a good job it took the crime lord several polite coughs to regain my attention. The moment my gaze drifted back to Dempsey, I shattered the budding silence. "What are you talking about?! You just threatened to kill me! It's the definition of personal!"

One of Dempsey's hands flew to his mouth as if he were dabbing away a drop of blood. When he pulled his hand away from his lips, he folded his hands behind the threat as he offered me a wounded smile. "Believe me, Marcus, you're not in this situation because I dislike you."

"You want me DEAD!"

"Bah," Dempsey said, dismissing my fury with a simple wave. He reached forward and tapped the bullet's tip. "This isn't a threat to you as a person. Again, I don't know you well enough for this to be personal, not yet anyway."

The crime lord's finger bounced on the pointy hunk of lead as his eyes grew colder. "You're facing this crossroads based solely on your choices. If you choose correctly, there's a chance I'll learn who you are, and from what I've seen, you appear to be someone I could call a friend." He laid a finger on the small obsidian case and moved it from side to side. "The crux of the issue is that you cheated. That's why you're having to make a choice."

As I stared blankly at the bullet, I considered Dempsey's offer. No, this wasn't a genuine proposal, this was an ultimatum. I kept weighing my options, yet the more I examined them, the certainty of the road I'd take loomed over me.

"Oh, and before I forget," Dempsey said, twirling a finger over his head.

Instantly, ice water crashed down on me, reinvigorating my shudders and clattering teeth. As the cool air whipped past my now-soaked body, my temperature plummeted. "Why . . . why'd you . . . do that?"

Dempsey tapped the bullet's case with his index and middle fingers as his predatory smile widened. "You looked as if you were getting a little warm, and that would have stolen leverage away from me. But at the moment, I'm more interested in your decision."

That bucket of water sealed my fate. It extinguished all the extra heat I'd pulled together. As my teeth clattered, my eyes fell back to that massive bullet. "What would have happened if I'd just palmed the ace? We both know your other countermeasures prevented that, but suppose I achieved it. What would you have done?"

"Are you asking how things would have played out if, instead of being special, you were a common cheat?"

Not trusting my voice, I simply nodded.

"Well Marcus, we wouldn't be having this conversation," the crime lord said, crossing his legs and dropping his folded hands upon them. "While you would have walked away," he touched the tip of the bullet, letting his pearly white canines show through his smile, "you wouldn't have known what was waiting for you. Now, if you would be so kind, I'm in a bit of a rush, so I'll need your answer."

The impromptu bath limited me to two options: surrender my life or myself. I thought my principles were strong. I mean, I was the one who kept Matt from scamming those who needed help and protection. But staring up into the gray eyes of my executioner, I finally resigned myself to the only real option laid out before me. My eyes closed as my chin fell to my chest. "It would appear that you have yourself a new employee."

Dempsey clapped like a child seeing his presents laid out before him on Christmas morning.

"You have quite the recruiting technique." I twisted my head, searching for Dante or Isaac. "It's no wonder you have such quality employees."

"It does work rather well, doesn't it?" he replied, either missing or, more than likely, ignoring my sarcasm.

I kept my eyes focused on Dempsey's promised threat as I licked my drying lips. "I'll agree with you, if that bullet is truly dedicated for me."

As the crime lord plucked the bullet off the table, he spun the case around, laying the massive bullet inside before closing the box. When he pulled his fingers away, I noticed the plate embedded into the black surface. After he closed the latch, I read the word engraved on those stone slabs. It was the name I'd given for the tournament.

While my quivering eyes crept back up to Dempsey's chin, I cleared my windpipe and fought the sudden urge to vomit. Dempsey bought and prepared that case and bullet just for me.

He picked up the case and slipped it back into his jacket's inner pocket. "I have cases like this for all of my employees."

"That's mad. . . ."

Dempsey rose from his chair and dusted his clean arms. "You weren't wrong. For this recruitment tool to work, everyone needs to have this doom placed over them. Once my people begin their employment, their case ends up collecting dust inside my vault. As time progresses, everyone forgets about the doom hanging over their head. However, should any employee of mine try to betray me or fail in their job . . ." Dempsey patted his coat, letting the unspoken threat linger. "Well, they know what to expect. Motivation. It's the key for excellence at any job!"

"Everyone lives worrying about being assassinated?"

"That's not the point of these bullets." Dempsey shook his head as he slid his chair under the table. He tapped the back with his fingers as he rolled onto his toes. "They're judged based on their actions. You're free to do what you think is right. However, I hold them accountable for their choices."

"One and done, is that right?"

"When there's a sense of finality, one focuses their mind to reach farther than they ever could. Wouldn't you agree?" With a fatherly smile, he walked along the table, sat down on it, and withdrew both IVs. "Personally, we could stretch to new horizons if more businesses adopted that practice."

As I looked away from Dempsey's smile, I wondered what I'd accepted. No, I wouldn't and couldn't feel sorry for myself. That was the only thing that monster had right. I had made a choice. It hadn't been a good one, but it had been my choice. Still flashing me that genuine smile, Dempsey walked back to the other end of the table.

"Dante, now that we're all one big happy family, would you be so kind as to remove all of Marcus's restraints? And patch up the holes from the chemical one."

CHAPTER 16

"Yeah, boss," Dante said as he began loosening my bonds.

Once the bindings started falling, Dempsey pressed his fingers against the table and loomed over me. "Now Marcus, was this really such a horrible experience?"

He let a small silence linger, expecting a response from me, but I held my tongue and my head.

"As of this moment, you're now my employee with terrific benefits. What more could you want out of life?" As he looked at my dead eyes, Dempsey snapped, and he slid the briefcase across the table. "I can think of something that'll make you smile, your winnings. Well, a partial cash advance on them at any rate. I've already deposited the rest for you."

I thought I had everything figured out, but then Dempsey dropped that bombshell on me. He was going to let me keep my winnings from his tournament?! What was going on here? Something was wrong with the universe. He must have either read my mind or my surprise showed clearly on my face, because a warm chuckle filled the room.

"I just told you that you work for me. Why is it surprising that you'd get to keep the money? For a smart fellow, you seem to mis- understand what that means. Especially when you already worked out that I stock the tournament with top employees. Though you were mistaken about how much money they get to keep. Fair is fair. If my people win the pot, they get to keep most of it. After all, you earned it."

"But . . . I wasn't working for you when I won it."

"Which is part of the reason all of this unpleasantness was required," Dempsey said in a serious tone.

"But . . ."

"Don't worry about the fact that you cheated. Just don't do it next year, and there won't be a problem. Is that clear?"

"But . . ."

"How have you accomplished anything in life with such a limited vocabulary?"

His verbal jab was just what I needed to force the frustration and confusion from my mind. "You would have killed me if not for the last hand."

"That's correct. But I discovered you're a mage, so I arranged to employ you. What's making this hard for you to understand?"

"So just because I'm your newest employee, it becomes no harm, no foul?"

With a critical eye, he studied me for a moment. "You know, Marcus, I'm questioning whether this relationship will have any kind of longevity. It troubles me deeply when you have trouble grasping the simplest of concepts."

Dempsey silenced me yet again with nothing more than a glare and a slight wave of his hand. I had been so focused on Dempsey that I hadn't noticed Dante had finished untying me. I reached forward and grabbed the manila envelopes off the briefcase and looked them over.

The crime lord rapped his fist against the table, pulling my attention back to him. "As I mention, I'm in a rush, so I don't have the time to help you work through all your problems. Over time, you'll eventually figure it all out."

Dempsey walked back to me, but this time, instead of sitting down, he loomed over me and touched the envelopes. "For now, these two envelopes will be your life. The thicker one has all the paperwork for you to step into your new life as my employee, including a valid form of ID, your new bank, the cash advance, and an assortment of other requirements and goodies. Don't lose any of it. You'll need everything there to access your account with your winnings, minus my twenty percent."

I laid the first one on the table, tapping it with my fingers. "Why do I need a new ID?"

"While the bullet bears the name you gave me, you're being reborn, which means you need a new name. Though you'll have to open it to find out who you'll be from now on."

My fingers trembled as I lifted the flap of the thick package. I withdrew several stacks of money and placed them beside the other envelope. When I placed the final one down, I stared at the small fortune before me. "That's a ridiculous cash advance."

"Nonsense," Dempsey said as he leaned down, thumping a stack. "Considering you'll need new clothes, something to eat, and a temporary roof, I believe you'll get off to a great start with these funds."

That made a certain amount of sense, so I resumed my search. The next thing I pulled out was the paperwork for my bank and the authorization I needed to access the funds. Though that could wait while I used the cash. Aside from a folder chock-full of official papers, which appeared to be exquisite forgeries, the last thing to come out was my wallet. The worn leather felt good in my hands.

I dropped the now-empty folder onto the stack of cash and papers and opened my wallet. My eyes flicked to the revised driver's license. I yanked the card from the wallet and pulled it up to my eyes to ensure I'd read the name correctly. The card tumbled from my fingers and fluttered to the tiled floor. Though my falling stomach refused to abide by such a restriction.

Dempsey's predatory smile emerged as he retrieved my forged identification. He slipped the card back into my wallet and closed the leather bifold. "I trust you are fine with using your real name, Francis Harrison Bailey?"

With Dempsey looming over me, I finally understood how

expansive Dempsey's reach was. How was I going to escape a man who could discover the name I hadn't used since I'd escaped the fire that claimed the lives of my foster family over a decade ago? Despite the passage of time, those memories haven't dulled, though they weren't clear either. The fear of burning alive trumped my senses, right until I tripped and fell through an interior wall and somehow ended up landing outside. As the fire consumed the house, I had fled the scene long before the authorities arrived.

Despite the efforts of the firefighters, the entire house was lost, and besides me, nobody escaped. However, since everything burned to ash, including my foster family, the authorities assumed everyone, including me, had died. In the end, they had shelved the investigation since they couldn't discover how the blaze started. Having lost everything, I ran. Eventually, I ended up in a nearby city and did what I had to in order to survive. As the raging memories faded and my eyes resumed surveying the real world, a glimpse of the man who had rescued me from the streets replaced Dempsey, sending a shiver down my spine.

While Dominic couldn't compete with the crime lord's influence, power, or knowledge, both were key figures in my life. The difference between the two men stemmed from their knowledge of my gift. Back then, I hadn't even known what I could do. Ultimately, I had exploited Dominic's ignorance of my gift and eventually parted ways, somewhat amicably. With my freedom, I had leveraged the skills Dominic had taught me and my nascent understanding of my gift to grift my way to success. Unfortunately, Dempsey's hold on me centered around my gift. The only chance to escape the crime lord was in a body bag.

One second I stared down at the new identification, and the next I dangled from my neck. The wallet fell from my hands as my fingers dug uselessly at the digits squeezing me. Despite hearing

CHAPTER 16

something, the pressure on my neck stole my focus. A moment later, it vanished, and I collapsed into the seat. Dempsey picked up the wallet and placed it beside the stacks of money.

"We'll have to work on your manners, not to mention your patience." Dempsey reached out and laid a finger under my chin and lifted. When my eyes met his, he released me. "I do not tolerate rudeness. Employees who lack an ample supply of these qualities quickly find themselves unemployed. And I'm sure you understand that none of my former employees need to worry about unemployment benefits. Do I make myself abundantly clear?"

"Yes, sir."

"See? It doesn't take much to be polite." Dempsey tugged his jacket closed and buttoned it as he tilted his head toward me. "I'm in a terrible rush, so Dante will show you the way out and answer whatever questions you might have."

Immediately, the same goon, presumably Dante, lifted me to my feet by my neck.

THWACK!

Dante pushed me forward as he released my neck. Thankfully, I caught myself on the desk and glanced over at Dempsey, registering his scowl.

"Dante, you were warned about this behavior. Is our long friendship coming to an end?"

I glanced over my shoulder and got my first actual glimpse of the goon. There are a handful of times in life when your mental image of a stranger matches up with them in reality. While I've never encountered it, I've spoken with a few who have. And right then, my mental image for Mr. Curiosity, a.k.a. Dante, aligned perfectly with the mountain of muscle standing behind me.

Dante scratched the close-cropped hair behind his ear as his gaze flicked from me to Dempsey. "I'm sorry, boss."

"I'm not the one you need to apologize to."

Despite the man's bulk, the room didn't shake as he side-stepped the chair to offer me his hand. "I'm sorry for lifting you up by your neck, Francis."

Even though the living mountain offered me a genuine apology, I couldn't help but feel like he'd also threatened me. How could a man who had been cowed mere moments ago lace a threat inside of an apology? Though now that I saw the man, I'm glad Isaac kept him from breaking me in half. "Like the boss said, Dante, we're all family here."

With another paternal smile, Dempsey spread his arms out like a soaring eagle. "See, I knew we all could get along. Now Dante, you will lead our newest employee out of here."

I quickly shoved the money, paper, and my wallet back into the envelope. With the key to my new life in hand, I grabbed the other one and shoved both under an arm as I turned around. In the far doorway, I saw the other goon, presumably Isaac, and he was half the size of Dante. How could anyone that small override someone with Dante's bulk?

The other two people walking toward the exit were Dempsey and an older woman with wild hair. Unfortunately, before I could get a good look at her, she slipped through the doorway and vanished. However, just before Dempsey reached the door, he turned around and smiled. "Oh Francis, I hope you don't mind, but I assumed you would accept my offer. And I'm sorry to say that Bella seemed less than pleased when I mentioned that to her."

Those words made my stomach drop again. Bella had thought I was a good man. Now what would she think of me? Would she even speak with me again? As thoughts of Bella swirled inside my head, I dropped back into my chair.

"Goodbye, for now, my young friend." Dempsey flashed me

another warm smile as he walked through the door, with Isaac in tow.

Despite the terror Dante had instilled in me, I was thankful for the goon's help. I don't think I would have been able to get outside without him dragging me through the building. By the time we exited the structure, my legs were working, and I paused, letting the sun's light warm me up. After a few seconds, the living mountain released me, and my body fell like a chopped tree. Thankfully, I simply slammed into the exterior wall. As Dante started walking away, I cleared my throat. "Excuse me, Dante, but do you all still have my coat, watch, and phone?"

The man stopped, and I saw his mighty hands clench into fists the size of hammers. "When we're out of earshot of anyone else, you can drop the act. We both know we're never going to be friends."

"What about my stuff?"

"Do I look like your servant?"

"No, you don't." I used the wall to straighten up as the sun's warmth chased the cold away. "But you look like an inhospitable host."

The anger radiating from him was palpable and an excellent source of joy, which, in turn, helped warm my core.

"I'll see what I can find." The ponderous mountain hurried back inside, hopefully looking for my requested possessions instead of a good place to hide my body. But there was nothing I could do about him, so I opened the second envelope. However, once opened, the only thing inside was a photograph. I withdrew it and laid it on top of the manila folder to study the glossy eight by ten.

Even though the quality of the image was poor, the face, which occupied most of the image, captured my attention. The grainy lines in the photo told me this was an enlarged bit from a larger picture. However, despite the manipulation, I could still make out quite a bit of detail, enough that I'd be able to pick him out in a crowd. Whoever took this photo did so while studying his behaviors and patterns. Apparently, Dempsey was keeping tabs on the man, but I knew I didn't want to know the why.

My eyes drifted to the bottom edge of the page and read the few printed words. I quickly guessed they were the name that belonged to the face, Mr. Alexis Rene LeBlanc. What did you do to draw Dempsey's attention? As I sat there wondering who the man was and what he possibly could have done to merit this kind of scrutiny from Dempsey, I eventually turned the photo over. And on the other side, I saw more text and immediately wished I hadn't. What was there was an address, along with a simple command. Take care of the problem.

As I thought about what that command implied, I almost missed the door squeaking open. I hurriedly slid the photo back into its envelope before standing up to Dante's chest. And apparently my smile was more of a scowl than I'd thought, since he shoved a bundle into my chest. I draped the jacket on my thumb and patted the pockets, finding my watch and phone inside.

I could tell he wanted to turn around, but he must have received a warning to play nice because he held his ground, waiting in case I had any more requests. So, of course, I slipped into my coat and ran my hand through my hair. "I looked at the other envelope."

"Good for you."

I buttoned my coat and rubbed my arms. "What does 'take care of the problem' mean?"

"How stupid are you?"

I flinched at Dante's rebuke, even though I'd expected

something like it. "I've always been a solo act, at least . . . but that's not important."

Why was I flustered by the living mountain? I shouldn't have to explain why I didn't want to understand the command, but given the state of my life, I did anyway. "My life before today is radically different from whatever it's turning into. Historically, I've done nothing more than good old-fashioned breaking and entering, or con jobs. I'm a sweet talker, not a doer. So no, I'm not entirely sure what it means. And since Dempsey told me to address questions to you, I'm asking. What does it mean?"

The lines forming across the mountain's forehead told me he was struggling to contain himself. After several failed attempts to smooth the lines away, he stepped toward me and bent down, coming face to face with me. "That man has been interfering with the boss's business for far too long. And we couldn't get to him using the more conventional methods. You present a new means by which to remove the thorn. So remove the problem."

I wasn't intentionally trying to be thick. Well, okay, maybe a little. But I wanted this command to be explicit. I had to know where I stood with Dempsey. I needed to understand what my role was going to be. So I probed a little more. "And that would mean doing what?"

Dante's expression soured as his lips curled into a snarl. "You need to ensure that we never have to deal with him again."

When I remained silent, Dante spat on the ground right behind him as he slammed a meaty fist against the building. "Do I need to spell it out for you?"

"I would genuinely appreciate it, yes," I said with a vigorous nod.

Disgusted, he spat on the ground again. "Take him for a long walk on a short pier. Send him swimming with cement boots.

Teach him to push up daisies. How are those? Or do you still need me to dumb it down for you?"

"I have it."

"Good." Dante leaned over me and stabbed my chest with his meaty fingers. "Do you recognize where we're at?"

I looked about and swallowed a series of curses. "This is where we played the tournament."

"Then I'll assume you know where you have to go. Now, do your job," Dante stabbed my chest with a meaty forefinger. "Unless you're changing your mind and you're ready to die."

"I'm not suicidal."

"Goodbye," Dante said, spinning around and marching back into the warehouse.

Numbly, I checked for my keys and found them alongside my watch. With my stuff accounted for, I stumbled on my way to the parking garage where I'd left my car, rubbing my arms. The moment I was safe in the car, I turned the engine over and blasted the heater. I sat in silence, waiting till I was dry, warm, and my mind was clear. I tossed the thick envelope on the passenger seat and withdrew Alexis's photo. It's no wonder the crime lord was so eager to sink his hooks into me. I had the potential to be the perfect assassin. I was someone who would never get caught, since I would never leave behind any evidence. As I stared into the man's blue-green eyes, I pulled out my phone and called Matt.

As the phone rang in my ear, I wondered if I'd be able to do what Dempsey was demanding of me. Would my struggle for my life mean anything if I turned into an assassin? I couldn't do anything about the tears flowing from my eyes as I stared at Alexis's joyous eyes.

CHAPTER 17

Once I left the parking garage, the rest of the day was a blur. Looking through my memories, I can see the very broad strokes, but the details have deteriorated into nothing. For example, I remember getting my suit cleaned, but I don't remember where I went or receiving the freshly laundered clothes. With a full stomach, I know I spent some of my advance on a meal, but I don't remember what I had. Then when I woke up from a nap, I didn't recall pulling over to grab those forty winks. Ultimately, it wasn't until I found myself in a parking lot for a neighborhood playground that my mind started retaining everything.

As the night sky darkened, I retrieved my phone, hoping Matt had returned my calls or answered my texts. However, several hours after reaching out to him, he had not reached out to me. While I understood his petty act of revenge, he was picking a lousy time for it. Given my situation, and by extension his, we needed to talk. But as the seconds stretched into minutes, I stared at the last message I'd sent him and wondered if he'd gotten it.

Call me as soon as you can.

There wasn't a lot there, but diving into my situation with emotionless text wouldn't have helped anyone. I needed to talk to him, to warn him to keep an eye out for strange individuals, just in case Dempsey needed to satisfy his desire to punish me. He'd made it clear my gift gave me a little protection, but he hadn't mentioned Matt, and when I considered Dempsey's reach, I didn't think my friend would escape the man's wrath if he desired to flex his muscles. With a curse, I wrapped my fingers around the device and punched the steering wheel with my off-hand before tossing the cell onto the passenger seat and collected Alexis's photo and the remaining manila envelope.

I turned it over and studied the handwritten note containing the man's address. Was I really going to go through with this? If I didn't, the fact Dempsey had discovered my original name told me he'd find me no matter where I ran. While I might gain a few years of panicked living, wherever I ended up, I'd need to secure a plot, because the crime lord would find me, and I wouldn't live through that encounter. I pulled the stack of cash out of the envelope and thumbed through it, idly wondering if it would cover the cost for a final resting place.

I chased the morbid thought from my mind as I plucked a bill from the pile. Instantly, a bit of warmth seeped into it and the undulating paper rolled up, forming a simple ball-point pen. I quickly scratched Alexis's address on the envelope before shoving the cash and the photo back inside. After slipping the fresh pen into my jacket pocket, I opened my phone and searched for the address. When the pin appeared on the map, I quickly asked for walking directions. It didn't take long for the route to appear, and it would take me less than five minutes to reach the man's home.

I swallowed a groan as I switched to my phone's browser and started searching for what I could find about Alexis Rene LeBlanc, and based on the initial results, I learned a couple of things. The first was Dempsey's target had a relatively unique name. The other significant lead I gleamed from the results was he led an exceptionally quiet life. It was hard for someone to be this off grid unless it was the man's focus. Not that there was anything wrong with bypassing that corner of the world. I mean, I followed suit, though I could learn a few things from Alexis on that front. Why would Dempsey want him dead? He was nobody special.

Unfortunately, the answer to that question seemed like a luxury I couldn't afford. After several failed attempts to find anything out about him, I shoved my phone into a pocket and punched the steering wheel again, ignoring the horn. I shook my head as I pulled myself out of the car with the manilla folder tucked under an arm. As I stood there looking into the deserted playground, my foot lashed out, slamming into the nearest tire. With a curse, and a throbbing foot, I slammed the door and tucked the manilla folder into my coat after folding it in half. I took a deep breath and forced warmth into my suit.

"It's a shame to ruin such quality workmanship, but I have things I need to do."

I pulled the right half of the jacket across my body and held it in place as I lowered the other half, keeping my fingers away from the inner fabric. Once the last of the left front of my coat was pressed against the other half, I pulled my arms away and smiled when the fabric didn't budge. I pressed my fingertips on the seams running under my arms and as more heat flooded out of me, the material changed, becoming more elastic, giving me more range of motion. Finally, I pulled the ball-pen from my pocket and forced more heat into it. A second after the heat left my body, it undulated and expanded. As the colors faded to black, it grew in every dimension, contorting itself into a black fedora with a large brim. I put it on and pulled it down, bathing my face in shadows as I began sauntering down the sidewalk.

When I strolled past Alexis's home, I whirled about and scurried toward the bushes hugging the structure. I placed my hand on the earth beneath me and, with an expenditure of heat through a crystal-clear image, the ground lowered, creating a perfect little hiding hole. When the earth stopped moving, I twisted several branches to further obscure me from the casual view of any pesky neighbors and waited as the moon and stars traversed the sky. As I huddled in my personal foxhole, the wind nipped at my face despite the limited cover of the branches. Despite the brisk temperature, it was a tropical island compared to Dempsey's freezer.

There I was with nothing more than an exterior wall between me and Dempsey's obstacle, or my ticket to life. So close, yet a mile away from my destination. As I traced the wall, a battle raged between distinct parts of myself. The portion of my mind solely embedded in reason and an ally to my conscious pleaded with me to turn around and leave. They had already made a list of things to do, which would go a long way in preventing Dempsey's conventional methods of eliminating me, and the argument had weight.

Unfortunately, the bit of my brain responsible for staying alive had made an alliance of its own. It had paired itself with my desire to protect my friend, and they were quick to shred that list, rebutting every bullet point. The primary rebuttal revolved around not knowing how to protect myself from a sniper's bullet. But they didn't stop there. Eventually, they turned to rehashing Dempsey's ability to discover my legal name, something lost in a fire a long time ago. A man who could discover something dead and buried had the reach to find me wherever I tried to hide while learning that mythical defense.

As the plates of the mental scale teetered back and forth with the argument, my fingers retreated from Alexis's wall. While I lacked the conviction to press forward, I had ample warmth to carry out Dempsey's request. I simply needed to choose which path I would take. And while the righteous arguments continued to sway me away from the grizzly act, my self-preservation and desire to protect my friend kept derailing the arguments. When the end of the debate neared, I finally understood what Matt must have felt every time I sat him down and prevented him from violating my limits. Ultimately, I never swayed him. He simply accepted my demand.

How was I any different from Dempsey? While I hadn't forced my friend to murder anyone, I impacted his ability to make an unfettered choice. Ultimately, my dogmatic belief I was right didn't lessen that impact, rather it highlighted the similarity between me and the crime lord, and I promptly chased the comparison from my thoughts. Once it was gone, the remnants of my mind opposed to this grim act railed at the idea of becoming Dempsey's hatchet man. However, with each passing breath, the morals I'd clung to for so long began fading. There was no use fighting Dempsey. His empire was too extensive and far too powerful.

As my gaze drifted back to Alexis's home, a dull pain pulled my eyes toward my clenched fist. When had I done that? After a couple of thoughtful seconds, I released the breath I was holding and shook my fingers loose. As the blood resumed flowing through my hand, I fished the manila folder out from under my coat. With exaggerated motions, I unfolded it and pressed my fingertips against the small flap as I released a hint of warmth into the paper. When I pulled away from it, a soft glow illuminated the earth in front of me.

After looking past the bushes, I hunched down and licked my

lips. While the effect wouldn't last long and it was a trivial amount of light, there was enough for me to study the image again. Once I'd removed it, I looked past the distortions and studied Alexis's soul, or rather the windows, to his innermost thoughts.

Despite repeated alterations, there was enough clarity for me to see the twin sparks of joy and happiness in his eyes. The part of me who wanted to flee jumped on that acknowledgement, reclaiming the advantage. Yet the rest of me offered a simple retort. If you walk away, Dempsey will simply recruit two more people. One to finish the job and the second would reunite me with my personal bullet.

As the righteous portion of my mind waned, I resumed my final examination of the surveillance photo. Alexis's cheerful eyes were framed by shoulder-length blackish brown curly hair, loosely tied into a tail. While every bit of the man screamed happiness, the sole competition to his expressive eyes were the well-worn lips. There were so many hints of happiness etched around his mouth. And somehow, I could tell that those marks weren't the result of a singular moment. Rather, a series of happy moments from a life well lived. Alexis Rene LeBlanc was a good man. I couldn't run from it anymore. I'd been dispatched to take care of . . . No! Dempsey had demanded I assassinate a good man.

When the light died, I shoved the image back into the folder before cramming it all back into my jacket. I plopped onto the earth and stared up at the stars. What does that make me? I knew what Dempsey was. He was a monster, but I didn't want to answer the question about myself. I'd wondered if perhaps Alexis deserved to live more than either Dempsey or myself. After all, I was the one hiding in the shadows, debating with myself about committing murder. You could judge the value of a man based on the enemies they curated. I'd always believed that. So, if a man like Dempsey wanted Alexis dead, then he was an honorable man at worst or a saint at best. Either way, he didn't deserve to die.

Aside from Alexis's name and address, the only other text on the picture was the current date. Not only did Dempsey want me to kill Alexis, but he'd also given me a time limit. He'd provided me with less than a day to do what others couldn't. If I could accommodate his request while minding his insane deadline, I'd prove myself worthy of his mercy. If not, he'd lean into the wrathful side of his reputation. Or I was reading too much from a simple date.

That or he was placing way too much stock in what he considered magic. Though that was another oddity. That kind of fervent belief seemed at odds with his reputation. Yet, when I dared to look into his eyes, I'd seen his belief in magic. It was real, fundamental to him, and he knew that it would accomplish anything he desired.

In the end, it wasn't Dempsey's faith in my gift, or what I gleaned from Alexis's portrait, that swayed my decision. Ultimately, my choice was as simple as it was difficult. Either execute a good man or submit me and Matt to death. And as selfish as it was, I didn't feel like dying today or throwing Matt to the wolves. When the whimpers of protest vanished, a single question echoed through my mind.

Is it worth an innocent life?

Instead of answering, I busied myself with contemplating my "duty" to Dempsey. Without the key to Alexis's home, I would have to create an entrance. Fortunately, my gift made that a trivial problem no more difficult than breathing, provided I possessed enough warmth. The moment my skin touched the dirt packed beside the home, heat leached out of me, and the ground separated, exposing the foundation.

Taking another deep breath, I placed my hands on the home

slightly wider than my shoulders. While this would help to ground the image in my mind, I didn't strictly need the pageantry. All that was required was the simplest of connections, such as a single fingertip. And with such a connection, I could impose my will on the world.

However, anything that helped crystalize the mental image would decrease the required heat, and I didn't want to waste any. So with my hands pressed against the rough brick, I drew in deep breaths and duplicated Alexis's wall in my mind, save for a small hole resting between my hands. Then I envisioned it growing large enough for me to walk through. With the transition firmly entrenched in my thoughts, I gathered the required heat, mingled it with my desire, and pushed it through the mental picture.

Instantly, my fingers rocked forward as the wall vanished. After pulling my fingers away from his home, I shook them out as I peered into a deeper darkness. Thankfully, there was a single bright point in the distance. With a sigh, I withdrew a cheap pair of sunglasses from a pocket, and another pulse of heat flowed through my fingertips, imprinting my will upon the cheap gas station shades.

I slipped the altered glasses onto my face, but instead of muting the light, as was their original purpose, these intensified the ambient and lingering light, dispelling the deep darkness ahead. While that transformation required less heat than creating my door, it wasn't because it was simpler. Rather, it came from constant repetition. Unlike the first time, when I'd ended up in the ER from hypothermia despite warm weather, I could make these glasses while barely tapping into my supply of warmth.

Though even if it cost me more, it was a fair trade for the few minutes of unparalleled vision, which presented me with my first complication. I'd created the opening between the first floor and a basement. After a quick examination of the lower floor, I pressed my hands against the main level's flooring and released another burst of heat. And the exposed planks twisted in on themselves as they expanded and dropped into the personal foxhole, creating a rudimentary set of stairs.

I pounded the crumbling earth with my fist as I walked into Alexis's home. Despite my earlier and still correct claim that I wouldn't require more heat, I removed some of the cheap chemical ones I'd picked up. As I crept up the impromptu stairs, a pair of soft pops raced into the silent home. Heat poured into my fingers as soon as I extracted the pouches from their wrappings. With the excess, I poured a little heat into the soft material, making it tacky. I quickly pulled my jacket and shirt down to affix both warmers to my chest. With a wonderful supply of warmth flowing into me, I balled up the trash and siphoned a sliver of the extra heat into it and water dripped through my fingers.

Once inside the home, I flicked the remaining liquid from my fingertips before pressing one hand against the floor and the other against the wall. With another expenditure of heat, the floor snapped back into form as the opening vanished, removing any evidence of my entry. As warmth flooded into me, replacing what I'd spent, I turned around and studied the interior. Somehow, the spartan surroundings of the hallway complimented Alexis's simple smile.

I lifted the sunglasses, letting the darkness steal my sight, but after a moment, the singular point of light told me which way to go. With a steadying breath, I lowered the altered shades, I glided across the floor. When I neared a pair of doors, I heard bits of conversation seeping out from the doorway framed with light.

Did Alexis have a wife?

What about children?

Was this a conversation between a father and child?

An inferno fueled by indecision with a healthy dose of fear roared to life within me, keeping me from moving. After several frantic seconds, I inched closer to the source and pressed my ear against the wall, while the inner voice I'd expunged earlier roared back to life.

What are you going to do now? Will you be willing to include anyone else as collateral damage to become a Dempsey in training?

My eyes slammed shut as my imagination filled the unseen room with a cheerful man playing with his children while his wife watched from a nearby couch. Or was I blowing everything out of proportion? Alexis could be a single man at home watching a show or a movie.

Are they all worth your life?

I shoved the question from my mind and silently shuffled away from the opening. I filled my lungs with the stale air as I pressed my forefinger against the drywall. After applying some pressure and a touch of heat, the wall pulled away from my finger, creating a low-tech peep hole as I slid the glasses to the top of my head. When I brought my eye to it, I examined the room. My captive breath seeped out when I found Alexis alone in the room, facing away from me, engrossed in some TV show.

My self-preservation leaped for joy, while the righteous portion made its objection. Just because he was alone didn't mean he was single. His wife and children might be out of town. Are you sure about trading his life for yours?

As I watched Alexis toss some popcorn into his mouth, my mind flashed back to my conversation with Dante.

"*That man has been interfering with the boss's business for far too long.*"

If I were to balk at Dempsey's assignment for me, then he

would just send another one of his goons to finish the job. Plus, I would have that less-than-pleasant reunion with the rather large bullet. Of course, that's when another tidbit from that conversation resurfaced.

"And we could not get to him using conventional methods. You present a new means by which to remove the thorn. So remove the problem."

Based on Dante's demeanor, I didn't think those failed assassinations prompted any terminations, though I didn't think they were in my situation. It also made me wonder what they'd tried and how Alexis survived the attempts. I rubbed my eye as I swallowed the string of curses racing toward my tongue. If I hadn't just been tortured, threatened, and manipulated, I probably would have asked Dante to go into further details about what had happened. But I hadn't, and I was committed, and there would be no turning back.

I pulled the fedora off my head, crumpling it in my hand. As far as I was concerned, if I needed a weapon, I was doing something terribly wrong. However, I also believed in being prepared and collecting knowledge and experiences which might someday prove useful. And by happenstance, I possessed the perfect memory for this situation. Several years back, when I ran with Dominic, he'd insisted I learn how to assemble, disassemble, and use several handguns.

While my gift allowed me to create several workable facsimiles, perfected with countless repetitions, I preferred the elegance and durability of Glocks. So I summoned the detailed schematics from the depths of my mind and rapidly crafted the mental image. With the finished weapon in my mind, I kneeled down and siphoned the heat flooding into me from the hand warmers, mingling it with my will before imprinting my desire on the fedora. Instantly, the soft fabric was replaced with hard plastic.

When I opened my eyes, I stared down at the weapon, complete with a silencer. My fingers tightened around the gun's textured grip as I rose and brought my eye to the peephole. Thankfully, Alexis was still engrossed with his show. While it would be difficult, I wouldn't have to look him in the eye when I pulled the trigger.

I pressed my fingers against the wall and the hole widened, just enough for me to aim the gun. With the weapon trained on Alexis, I laid my finger on the trigger as I steadied the gun with both hands. This was it. There would be no coming back after I crossed this line. Alexis was already dead. I was simply cleaning up the mess created by Alexis's interference with Dempsey. I filled my lungs once more with the stale air and squeezed the trigger.

Thankfully, the muffled click announced I'd been successful with the silencer. The last thing I needed was to attract the attention of the police. Unfortunately, that was the only thing that went right. Instead of slamming into Alexis's head, it slammed to a stop when it drew near the man. It hung in midair, like a fly caught by a spider's web.

Confused, I repositioned my sights and squeezed the trigger. Or rather, that's what I tried to do. As panic swirled in my chest, I tried to turn around, only to discover my entire body was frozen. I couldn't move. Despite the frantic orders flowing through me, none of my muscles obeyed the commands, which spurred my fear to new heights.

What was going on?

I looked through the iron sights and saw Alexis rising. While facing his television, his arms appeared to be dusting off his chest as he shook his head. When he turned, his blue-green eyes found mine instantly. The fire burning behind those orbs raged, betraying the sight I'd seen from the photo. Instead of a joyous visage,

CHAPTER 17

all I could see was the gaze of an executioner resigned to the fact he had to carry out a duty he didn't want.

Alexis walked around his armchair and he stopped right next to the floating lead slug. He plucked the suspended round from the air and examined it. As he twisted the bit of metal, I realized the tip was flattened, as if it had slammed into something solid. But there was nothing there. Was this the real reason Dempsey had sent me here? Was this how the crime lord dealt with people like me?

Alexis dropped the slug and sauntered to the hole in the wall. After pushing the gun out of the hole, he ran a finger along the edge. For the first time since I fired the gun, I realized I didn't hear anything. Despite seeing the television on, nothing reached my ears. The fear continued swelling as Alexis's finger stopped probing the hole. Was he appraising my work?

As soon as his finger vanished, the room darkened. And in that instant, I realized what was happening. Alexis was just like me. We shared the same gift. He sealed the hole, leaving me in near darkness without the glasses that would have let me see. As it was, I didn't mind not being able to see the executioner fetch his axe.

CHAPTER 18

This wasn't fair!

From my earliest memories to waking up in Dempsey's freezer, I had met no one who shared my gift. I'd assumed I was a unique anomaly for the world. Then I altered one card, and Dempsey shattered the illusion I'd constructed. While I hadn't met the woman he employed, I knew she existed because someone had to help the crime lord construct his prison and develop his drug cocktail. After begrudgingly accepting Dempsey's offer, I came to Alexis's home to find he was just as special. I went from a happy and solitary existence to a member of at least a trio in less than twenty-four hours.

Why hadn't I listened to Matt?

As I continued my forced interpretation of a statue, I silently cursed everything from the number of people like me to my foolish attempt to assassinate one of us and everything in between. Between each bout of anger, my mind calmed long enough for me to marvel at Alexis's skills. Honestly, while we shared the same abilities, from our brief interaction, I knew he was far more adept at wielding it. While I'd thought myself a master of these abilities, his efforts proved how much of a novice I was.

While I understood how he sealed the hole, everything else made me wonder if we were truly capable of magic. Out of everything I had witnessed, the biggest mystery was the way he caught the bullet. His subsequent actions proved the only thing in the bullet's path was air. While that was my top question, one dealt with how he captured me. After all, he couldn't see me, which also meant he couldn't touch me. Both were crucial to imposing our will on the world. However, both acts upended everything I knew about our gift, and he did it in such a way that implied it was as simple to him as breathing was to the living. If he was capable of this, what were my limits?

As the question lingered in my mind, my feet started sliding across the polished wooden floor as if I was being dragged by my shirt or belt. Once I reached the middle of the doorway, I stopped moving and once again imitated a statue as the door swung away from me, allowing light to wash over me like water escaping a dam. When I stopped blinking, Alexis loomed over me, the light wrapping around him, casting his face in shadows, giving him the appearance of an avenging angel ready to wreak havoc amongst the guilty.

The looming herald of justice vanished when Alexis flipped a switch, letting light flood down upon us from several overhead fixtures, revealing his fiery gaze. He stood there in the doorway, weighing me as if I were a prized pig at the market. After a subjective eternity of scrutiny, the man pushed me back as he closed the door. When the doorknob clicked shut, he shook his head and pressed his back against it.

"Well," Alexis said with an emotionless voice as he folded his arms across his chest. "Despite your amateurish actions, I have to admit you're skilled." He wrapped his fingers around his chin as his lips drew into a line. "Unfortunately, you weren't as equally blessed with intelligence."

He pushed off the door with his shoulders and began walking

around me as if I was the local track. Every time he disappeared, I felt the weight of his glare as he studied every line of my body. When he finished his last lap, he plucked the gun from my hands. His fingers ran down its length multiple times as his eyes fluctuated from slits to saucers. After his examination, he slipped the pistol back into my grasp as he patted the back of my left hand. Then he reached down and grabbed a corner of my jacket. Despite the firm yanks, my alterations held, eliciting a surprised noise from him.

After a few more failed attempts to open my coat, he quickly switched to the other alterations he could easily examine. Despite his skill level, at that moment I didn't care about what he thought of my skills, not when there were pleasurable mysteries to work through, such as how he stopped the bullet? Not to mention how he immobilized me. Based on my understanding, what he did was impossible.

When a loud snap erupted next to my ear, my gaze whipped up to Alexis's harsh eyes.

The man laid my glasses on my head before leaning back against the door and folding his arms across his chest. "What am I going to do with you?"

He leaned forward and stabbed a finger against my forehead, pressing it back. However, despite the mounting pressure, my head wasn't retreating from the unyielding pressure of his finger. In fact, as the dull pressure turned to a slight pain, the entire back of my head screamed in agony. When he removed his finger, all the uncomfortable sensations vanished. "I'm going to remove the restraints from around your mouth, nothing else. You still won't be able to move, so don't think about escaping. I'm only doing this so you can answer my questions, but if you don't cooperate, I will silence you."

Instantly, I felt the pressure around my jaw vanish. As I flexed my jaw, I could feel the pressure everywhere else. It had been so slight I hadn't noticed it till some of it disappeared.

As Alexis's mouth curled into a warm smile, that cheer didn't dampen the raging inferno behind his eyes. Despite the conflicting emotions battling for my attention, he leaned forward and flicked my forehead. "Is that clear?"

"Yes," I said as my mind whirled for answers to a new litany of questions. Was that pressure the reason my muscles were quivering? How had I missed the pressure being applied? What did he do to me?

With a nod, he waved a hand in front of him, and the hardwood floor next to his feet bulged. It continued to expand until the shape of a stool emerged from the flooring. Then it popped up beside him and Alexis plopped himself onto the wooden seat. "As I mentioned earlier, you have talent, but you lack understanding to pair with it." A wry laugh escaped his mouth before he shook his head and massaged his temples. "Your actions tonight were as poorly conceived as a child shouldering a backpack in order to take the first steps up Mt. Kilimanjaro."

"What are you going to do with me?"

"Are you eager to face the punishment for your crimes?"

Feeling mentally drained and emotionally distraught, I attempted to shut my eyes. However, Alexis's binding stole that trivial decision from me. While I should have felt helpless, because I was, a rage boiled up from deep inside of my chest from the fear of looking up into the eyes of someone who held complete control over my life. "No, I've simply grown tired of feeling helpless."

"That sounds like a personal problem to me," Alexis said, dropping his hands into his lap.

My gaze crept back up to him as I licked my lips. "How are you doing this to me?"

If I thought the rage behind his eyes was an inferno a moment ago, the reaction to my question proved me wrong. As a silence bloomed between us, Alexis wrapped a hand around his chin while his eyes bored into mine. However, after a subjective eternity, the corners of his eyes softened, and his lips quivered. Then, out of nowhere, a deep belly laugh shattered the stillness. Several seconds later, as the laughter died away, Alexis wiped the corner of his eyes. With a click of his tongue, he whirled his finger in front of my face. "I've essentially wrapped you up in a cocoon."

"I figured that bit out. I'm curious about how you accomplished the feat."

Folding his arms across his chest, he offered me a friendly smile. But that's where the warmth ended. "Your question highlights your ignorance when it comes to forging."

"What?"

He reached out and pressed his finger against my lips. "Forget whatever questions are swirling through your brain. It's time for you to answer mine."

While his voice was calm, I could see the seriousness in his eyes. Between moments, he went from leaning backward to looming over me.

"Why did you even try to challenge me?" Alexis asked, his voice chilling to a degree that made me yearn for Dempsey's freezer.

The frosty air sent a shiver down my spine as my eyes flicked about, trying, and failing, to avoid his. "What are you talking about?"

"Surely you must have . . ." Alexis's thought died on his lips as he studied my face. In an instant, confusion seeped into his visage as he leaped off his stool, knocking it into the door behind him. As the seat settled on the ground, he grasped my coat and pulled me forward into his unyielding and invisible cocoon. "Are you trying to tell me you had absolutely no idea that I was a forger?"

"What's falsifying signatures have to do with anything?"

The shock and confusion fell away from his face, only to be replaced with a look of disgust. In a stern and commanding voice, reminiscent of a haughty teacher, he asked, "You don't know what a forger is, do you?"

"If you have a definition other than the legal one, then I don't."

The stool laying behind Alexis melted into the floor as he covered his mouth, muffling a sorrowful laugh. As the mocking mirth died away, the stool reemerged from the hardwood, presenting Alexis with a seat. Once reclaimed, he clapped his hands onto his thighs. "Then what on earth brought you here tonight?"

There it was. Here's my chance to embarrass myself. My throat tightened up, and not because of Alexis's constraints. Rather, I didn't like the idea of admitting the reasons I stumbled into his house. However, another part of me wanted to explain everything, hoping he might give me a chance to escape my predicament. If I could have shut my eyes, I would have. However, that was beyond my ability, so I took a deep breath and answered him. "I was forced into this situation by Bertrand Dempsey."

A visceral growl ripped through the room as his back straightened. "You're one of that man's assassins?"

The vitriol and revulsion dripping from his voice would've made me recoil in fear. Given my limitations, all I could do was pull my gaze away from Alexis.

"I guess so."

"What do you mean?" His hands once more grasped my jacket as he pulled me against the bindings for a second time. "You either are or aren't. How could you not know?"

While his voice still overflowed with wrath and disgust, a cautious curiosity tinged his words. I worked some saliva into my mouth. "He forced me into accepting this job."

"Okay," Alexis said, his voice warming, "I'll bite. How were you forced into this job?"

As I stared at the hardwood flooring, I took another deep breath and bit down on my inner cheek. While I wanted to melt through the floor and disappear, I quickly summoned the courage to answer him. "I was playing in his hold 'em tournament, and I had an extraordinary run of luck, which was taken by the dealers as a sign of cheating."

"You were trying to cheat Dempsey?"

"No, that's not what I said. It's what Dempsey's dealers claimed I was doing, but given this was Dempsey's tournament, they passed those suspicions along. That speculation spurned Dempsey to call a break in the game once we were down to ten players, which allowed him to install cameras. When it came down to the final hand, I was staring down elimination, and I was unwilling to accept second place."

"So you did cheat him."

"I wasn't cheating him personally, and don't forget, this was the only time I actually altered a card."

"Are you stupid? You actually tried to cheat Dempsey?"

"It's the only reason I'm alive."

Alexis slapped his cheeks, and his breath exploded from his mouth, like air escaping a popped balloon. "That doesn't matter, boy," Alexis said, scratching his head. "You cheated the worst man possible. But how did pulling it off keep you alive?"

"I changed one of my pocket cards into an ace."

Slapping his forehead, Alexis shook his head as he dragged his fingers down his face. "You forged one of your cards?"

"What are you going on about?"

Alexis lifted his shaking hands as he licked his lips. "We'll get to that later, but for right now, just answer my questions. Did you alter one of your cards using your body heat?"

"Yes, I did."

"What did you give yourself?"

"Full house, aces over eights."

Another bout of hearty laughter filled the hallway as Alexis began a slow clap. When he stopped punctuating his mirth, he laid his hands on his lap and scooted toward the stool's edge. "You willingly gave yourself a dead man's hand?"

"What?"

Alexis's hands slammed together as he pulled in a breath through his clenched teeth. "You're aware of the history of that hand, right? Or is this another area of your ignorance?"

"Despite playing several thousand hands of poker, I've never come across the term."

With a stifled groan, Alexis rubbed his forehead as the stool reformed under him. "You should know the history, especially given your circumstances." Alexis flicked my forehead as another bout of laughter filled the hall. "The tale surrounding that hand's name is rather infamous."

"But not overly famous, it would seem."

Alexis pressed his hands together as if he were closing a book. After a solid three count, Alexis winked at me before leaning forward to blow his breath across his opening hands. Once they were flat, a tiny collection of rudimentary stick figures flared to life across his palms. Eventually they all sat down at a table, with the last one sitting with his back facing me.

As they played poker, Alexis cleared his throat. "The tale revolves around an incident in 1876, where Jack McCall killed Wild Bill Hickok while he held that hand of yours." A second later, another figure appeared and leveled a gun at the one whose back faced me. When the gunman shot the man in front of me, Alexis closed his hands, dispelling the morbid play. "You are aware of the victim, correct?"

"He's some dead and famous cowboy, if my memory is right."

"It's a shame that our educational system is so flawed." Alexis rose and lifted my chin before grasping my shoulders. "The important part of the story is what Hickock was dealt before he was murdered."

"Aces over eights?"

Alexis stepped back and positioned his hand in front of his chest. Instantly, five large cards appeared hovering in midair between us. "While there is some debate over the actual composition of the hand," Alexis snapped his fingers and four of the cards rotated toward me, displaying their value, "there is a consensus that Hickock held two pair, black eights and aces."

"Huh, that's umm . . . that is interesting." I licked my lips and looked over the cards hanging between me and my executioner. "Why weren't you specific as to the aces he held?"

"It's because there's a debate on two of the cards in Hickock's last hand. The most trivial of which centers on the pair of aces. Some believe he held the black ones, while others argue one ace was a diamond or a heart."

"I'm surprised we know anything from that long ago."

Alexis shook his head as a twitching finger shot into my face. "However, the real debate is on the fifth card. There are some who will swear up and down it was a queen, while others claim the nine of diamonds."

"Really?" My eyes shot to the last card in time to see it transition from a royal figure into nine diamonds. "That's a claimed composition of that cowboy's last hand?"

The cards vanished as a thunderous clap reverberated off the walls. It didn't take long before Alexis's hearty laugh mingled with the rough echoes, blending into a melodious chorus. When the mocking tones died, he wiped a tear from his eye. "The card you forged was the nine of diamonds, wasn't it?"

"That's what I was dealt."

After another bout of laughter, Alexis rubbed his mouth. "Let me get this straight. You fled one version of the dead man's hand, only to wind up with another."

"You didn't mention a full house."

Alexis clapped my shoulder as his smile widened. "Only because you derailed the conversation. There are those who are convinced, or would just rather believe, that the third card was another ace. As a result, aces over eights is by far the most widely recognized version of the hand, despite the lack of historical evidence. In fact, most players I know consider it a bad omen."

Has this entire course of events just been a series of bizarre coincidences? Or had Dempsey arranged this outcome? When my mind finally pulled together all the stray thoughts into one intelligible, or mostly intelligible, pile, laughter was on the verge of bursting out of me like water from a crumbling dam. I fought to control myself, as I had zero reason to laugh. Eventually, I diffused the impending laughter and erected a massive wall separating me from it.

My eyes flicked up and latched onto my executioner's. "I guess it was quite the apt hand to make, considering the outcome." And when Alexis's smile curled up, the barrier I'd erected to keep me from embracing that awkward mirth crumbled and laughter filled the hall.

A second later, Alexis joined in, though neither of us knew what was so funny. After the infectious merriment ran its course, he rubbed his hands together. "Now that you've had your laugh, continue with your story and tell me what happened after you cheated."

The command chilled me to the core. Remembering what I had woken up to was enough to knock the remnants of the laughter from me and drop me into Dempsey's freezer. I didn't like the idea of admitting my mistakes to Alexis, but his authority prevented me from remaining silent. "There isn't much to tell."

"Then it should be a brief conversation."

"After giving him proof of my cheating and getting my victory, he pawned me off on one of his lackeys. While I believed I was being escorted away to collect my winnings, his goon seized the opportunity and stunned me before choking a cooperative me unconscious. The next time I woke up, I found myself effectively detained."

Stroking the left side of his chin, Alexis asked, "Given our abilities, how'd they manage to keep you detained?"

While the experience had been a first for me, it was obvious Alexis had some knowledge about imprisoning people like us. Was he trying to compare notes? "For starters, I came to in a rather spacious and cold freezer with a pair of IVs pumping saline and drugs into my veins."

With him leaning there against the wall nodding, I couldn't help but think of those old cartoons, where the weaker animal was examining the trap set by its predator. Specifically, I got hints of the large and speedy bird. While I don't remember any of the specifics, I knew the roadrunner always bested the coyote. The next time I ended up in a real-life cartoon, I needed to be the roadrunner. I was tired of being the coyote.

After a moment, Alexis locked his gaze upon my eyes and said, "That's a decent starting point for Dempsey. But you should still have been able to do some forging. Why didn't you forge a heat source into the lining of your clothing?"

"What are you talking about? If you're not talking about falsifying documents or records, what's forging?"

"We're not there yet," Alexis said, waving my question away. "Let's stick to my question. If they were freezing you, why didn't you create your own heat source?"

"I couldn't."

"Why? It's a trivial technique." He drummed his fingers along his thighs as he licked his lips. "Have you ever used hand warmers?"

"Yeah, I keep some electronic ones on me all the time. What of it?"

Alexis rubbed his eyes as he released his breath. "Think low tech. Have you used the ones that activate once you expose them to air?"

"Yeah, I've used those too." I thought about the squares attached to my chest. While I haven't created them or a facsimile, I added that to my to-do list. "In fact, there are a couple providing warmth to me right now, though I bought them before coming here. Unfortunately, despite my inexperience in making them, it wouldn't have worked."

"Why?"

"The IVs were pumping me full of drugs, which complemented the frozen atmosphere of the freezer."

"What do you mean?"

"Do you remember the IVs I mentioned?"

Alexis nodded as he gestured for me to go into the details.

"Whatever substances they were injecting into me, it prevented me from combining my will with anything more than a faint touch of body warmth. While I could find some warmth and access it, I couldn't put it to use."

"Interesting," Alexis said, rising to his feet. When he resumed his march around me, the stool melted back into the floor. After his second full revolution, he paused and stabbed my chest with a pair of fingers. "You're telling me that a drug prevented you from executing any forgery?"

"What are you talking about?"

"You weren't able to alter anything?"

With a mental shudder, I forced myself to think about Alexis's question. Ultimately, I focused on the tinge of shock lacing his gaze. Alexis hadn't expected Dempsey could restrain people like us. The ability to stop someone from . . . what had he been calling it, forging? Was I able to power a transformation right now?

I reached inside and mixed some heat with my will, and it worked. Alexis's imprisonment was strictly physical. However, because I was trussed up like a suckling pig, my ability to use my gift was effectively restrained since I needed to touch what I was affecting. Did Dempsey know more about people like me than Alexis? Or was it Dempsey's woman that knew more?

"That's correct, and as I was warming up to the point of being able to overcome his drugs, he had me doused with ice water."

Alexis's back straightened as his left forefinger rapidly tapped his lower lip. The soft sound of his tapping fingertip fell into a soft march while he stared down the hall over my head. "I wonder what drug or combination of drugs would net him that situation."

"You'd have to ask his witch. I'm sure she's the one who allowed him to discover the right brew."

Alexis's eyes whipped to mine as he leaned over me, his eyebrows threatening to leap off his face. "Dempsey's what now?"

"It's something I overheard my guards discussing. And based on Dempsey's deference about timing, I assumed his witch made the concoction coursing through me." I instinctively tried to shrug, but, like the rest of my body, my shoulders refused to comply with the command. "I guess I could be wrong, but it feels right."

"Did you catch the name of his forger?"

"He addressed his question to someone named Annabelle. But I couldn't tell you if that's his witch or not."

Alexis pulled himself up to his full height as he rubbed his chin, letting a silence wrap around us. As the seconds ticked by, my mind identified why Alexis's silences were more impactful than Dempsey's. Typically, there's always a little din in any silence, because of the laws of nature. However, at that moment, the silence suffocating me was perfect. There was nothing to distract my mind from the looming threat of my judge, jury, and executioner. How had he extinguished every sound? Or was my fear playing tricks on me?

"How are you doing that?"

Alexis's eyes flicked toward me as he waved my question away. "I'm the one asking the questions. Are you certain that his forger's name is Annabelle?"

"No. All I'm certain about is that when he prodded the IV with his cane, he asked her if there was time for a detailed conversation, and she supplied an answer. That's all I know about her. Are you suppressing sound?"

"Stop wasting my time with questions," Alexis said as he tapped the barrel of my pistol. "Let's jump to what brought you to my home, specifically why you agreed to kill me." His finger rose as if it were a conductor's baton preparing the orchestra to begin. "While I expect you'll respond with you didn't want to die, please don't lean on that trite excuse."

"It's unfortunate that you want another reason."

"That's all you can say?"

Pausing long enough to moisten my lips, I offered more from my inner debate. "Ultimately, I accepted you were a dead man walking, since you'd interfered with Dempsey's agenda. And to be blunt, I wasn't willing to die, nor risk my friend's life, in a vain attempt to protect a dead man."

Alexis's arms widened as his smile intensified. "Obviously, Dempsey hasn't been able to kill me. Why were you so sure of my fate?"

"He's already sent people after you, and he isn't one to forgive failure or give up."

Alexis's mouth opened as his lips curled into a devilish grin. "That explains a few things."

"Like what?"

Alexis waved away my curiosity and then tweaked my nose. "Since those would be private matters, let's stick with your story. Why would you expect your friend to be in danger?"

"Dempsey is ruthless, and he somehow discovered a part of my life that was long since dead and buried. When he's capable of that, I don't think discovering who my friends are is all that much of a stretch, and he still has to prove his ruthlessness."

"That's a rational justification," Alexis said, shoving his hands into his back pockets. "And it does complicate my response. However, while I can appreciate your ruthless logic, it's fundamentally flawed."

"How's that?"

"For the moment, let's say that you assassinated me. What about the next person Dempsey asked you to kill? Ultimately, that excuse will wear out since you're trading lives. Eventually, you'll murder someone who's guilty of nothing more than annoying Dempsey."

"You're not wrong."

"Then why'd you agree to become his pawn?"

I closed my eyes and drew in several breaths. Unfortunately, there wasn't anything for me to do but answer his question. "Because death doesn't free me from Dempsey's influence."

Alexis snatched my shoulders as he pressed his face to mine. "Are you telling me that you didn't accept your fate as Dempsey's tool? Are you suggesting that you were going to pretend to be loyal until you could escape?"

"Yes," I said, swallowing a curse.

Alexis released me and resumed pacing around me. "Normally Dempsey isn't that forgiving to people who cheat him." The man paused to my left and grabbed my shoulder. "Why are you still alive?"

"I don't know. He mentioned something about wanting someone else like me on his payroll."

"He wanted to employ another forger?"

"That's what he implied." But after a moment, I sighed and licked my lips. "Though I don't believe anything he told me, hence why I'm worried about my friend."

I would have continued, but Alexis beat me to the punch. "Well, that's because you don't know enough for it to make sense. That man could do some dangerous things if he ever got someone like you on his payroll." He paused for a moment as he ran his hands through his hair. "While, according to you and his men, he's already employing an external forger, it never hurts to increase one's assets. So let's keep him from getting what he wants."

"You're going to help me?"

But before he could answer, the gun resting in my hand transitioned back into the dollar it was at the beginning of the night. Alexis leaned forward and pulled the bill from my hand. Folding it in half, the man brandished it as if it were still a weapon. "I knew you forged the gun, but I'd assumed you used a toy as the base to get the mass in the right ballpark."

"While I don't go around with a gun all the time, someone took the time to ensure that I was deeply familiar with numerous firearms. As a result, I can make one from pretty much anything."

He slipped the money into my jacket pocket and patted my shoulder. "Your gaps in knowledge are maddeningly inconsistent."

With a soft chuckle, my lips curled into the first smile since the tournament. "Is that impressive or pitiable?"

"Both," Alexis said, rubbing an eye. "You have massive raw potential. The world is not ready for someone with your abilities to wind up as Dempsey's puppet."

"Does that mean you're going to kill me or do something else?"

Alexis shoved his hands into his pockets as he licked his lips. "Honestly, in our world, you would face an execution for the crimes you've committed tonight."

"You all go straight to execution? Don't you have some kind of jail or something?"

Alexis's hand drifted behind his back as he shook his head. "There is something along those lines for violations of our lesser laws. However, you've violated one of our major ones. And for any of those, there's only a single sentence: death."

If I could have fallen, I'm pretty sure I would have collapsed on the spot. I was astonished he could speak about any execution, let alone mine, so casually. While I'd begun to understand the world I belonged to, I hadn't expected to be thrust into a concealed realm, a world hidden from the ordinary. While I would have loved to explore the concept immediately, I figured there were other things I needed to sort out first, namely my future.

"You can't do that." My eyes bulged as sweat seeped from my

body. "I didn't even know about these laws, let alone this world until now."

"What you don't know isn't my problem." His emotionless words were like a slap across the face. His shoulders rose as his chest swelled. "Ignorance of the law isn't a valid excuse in this country; you're expected to educate yourself about every law, no matter how trivial. When you consider that, what makes you believe we should have any less of a standard when it comes to laws governing forgers?"

"You're a secret society!"

He raised a twitching finger as he clicked his tongue. While his words were devoid of emotions, his face embraced a serenity incompatible with the lifelessness of his message. After a few seconds, his hand drifted behind his back as he positioned his mouth next to my ear. "Arguing is meaningless. I've heard every possible excuse you could ever come up with multiple times."

"That's not fair!"

"Neither is a rogue forger who is doing things that make the rest of our lives harder." Hearing the derision in his voice, I could tell he considered me nothing more than a disobedient child. As he stepped back, his swishing index finger reappeared, laying down the silent beat for my remaining life. "All your exposure would accomplish would be to put magic back into people's minds. Let's see just how poor your education was. Have you ever heard of the Salem witch trials?"

My gaze lingered on the hardwood floor as I grunted in affirmation.

"Well, what you probably don't know, though hopefully you've put it together by now, is that some of those witches from back then were external forgers like you and me. However, they weren't the ones who brought the attention down on our kind.

They were innocent forgers who happened to be in the wrong place at the wrong time. A great number of innocent forgers were captured and burnt, but the rogue forgers who started the trials escaped." He paused, as if trying to keep control of his escalating anger. "Right now, I'm trying to decide what to do with you."

"There's no way you have the kind of authority to execute me."

As he shook his head, his face grew somber and calm. "Unfortunately for you, you tried to murder one of the few forgers in the United States that wields that kind of authority."

His revelation stunned me into silence. I couldn't even manage to mutter a curse, and at this point, that was all I wanted to do. How had I managed to anger two people with unchecked power and authority in their world in less than twenty-four hours? It must be some kind of record. No one was that unlucky.

Glancing around, I noticed that Alexis was no longer in the hallway, or rather, he was no longer in my line of sight. And that's when fear flooded through me. What would happen to me if he simply left me here?

"Alexis, where are you? What are you doing?" The responding silence sparked a mini heart attack. But when my heart slowed slightly, I risked another call to my executioner. "Alexis, please don't leave me here."

Alexis's fingers tapped my shoulder a second before his words drifted in from behind. "Don't worry, boy. I haven't decided what I'm going to do with you, yet."

He stepped around, smoothing his freshly dawned coat. "However, before I make that decision, I must iron out a few issues with Dempsey. Once I've addressed everything, I'll decide your fate."

The smile he wore on his face made me think of a ravenous lion staring down at a lame zebra. In that moment, I wished I knew who he pegged as the zebra. Me, Dempsey, or both of us.

CHAPTER 19

Despite the terror and fear swirling in my chest from Alexis's display of power, I wasn't eager to be left trussed up and alone in his home. As he loomed over me, I averted my eyes and cleared my throat. "If you're not planning on executing me before confronting Dempsey, would you bring me along?"

My would-be executioner stepped forward as he grasped my shoulders. Sardonic laughter washed over me as he pulled me onto my toes. "Why do you want to go with me?"

"I don't want to be alone."

Alexis released me, and I rocked back onto my feet. As my body stopped swaying, he tapped my forehead. "I was considering telling Dempsey and his lackeys that you were dead. That I killed you the moment you sauntered into my home, intent on assassinating me."

The simplicity of Alexis's response was another verbal slap. If Dempsey thought I was dead, he'd never be able to use that bullet he'd assigned to me. However, it did nothing to ensure Matt's safety. While my friend's safety was important to me, the mounting fear of being alone and immobile was rivaling it. It's not like I haven't been alone in my life. In fact, I've routinely enjoyed isolation. However, this was the first time I feared that situation. Nobody's confidence or courage can survive after meeting the likes of Dempsey and Alexis in such short order.

I looked up into Alexis's probing gaze and moistened my drying lips. "Please don't leave me here."

Alexis's fingers dug into my shoulders like a vise biting into a captive project. Yet instead of responding, he held my gaze and let a tranquil silence seep into the hallway. As seconds stretched into lingering minutes, I'd worried I poked the proverbial sleeping bear with my plea. Yet, as his predatory glare continued to loom over me, I didn't read any anger. Rather, there was a softness surrounding his eyes indicating he was weighing the pros and cons of the alternatives laid out before him.

As the stilted silence lingered, a couple of conclusions crystallized. First, the weight of his glare declared he was reweighing my worth. Granted, not much time had gone by since he'd last measured me, and I hadn't made the best first impression, but he seemed to be someone who rarely changed his opinions. So the fact Alexis was recalculating the risk-reward ratio of letting me live, or at the very least, allowing me to accompany him, spoke volumes.

Meanwhile, the second thought was much more simplistic. Alexis knew how to use silence like a physical weapon. With each passing second, the strain bearing down on me intensified, as if he'd been using me as a punching bag. As I stared into his predatory gaze, I knew there would be no debate over his decision. Live or die, it would be final. While the exhaustion from the mental and physical beatings were taking their toll, they weren't the reason an argument wasn't going to happen. I could have been in perfect health, and I would have accepted his proclamation because of his overpowering will.

Eventually, Alexis clapped my shoulders as his lips curled into a devilish grin. "I still think leaving you here and telling Dempsey you're dead is the best move I can make."

The bluntness of those words was like a dull knife plunging into my heart. "It might be good for you, but I doubt my friends would agree."

He bumped my chin with his knuckles as he gave me another wink. "Don't worry about it so much. While the boast would have been true enough, there might be a benefit or two in dragging you with me."

"What took you so long to land on a maybe?"

"Don't push your luck," Alexis said, pressing a finger into my forehead, tilting my gaze toward the ceiling. "You should learn to use your ears. I haven't finalized my decision regarding your fate. With that choice still outstanding, do you think I'd rush into something as trivial as where to park your butt?"

Yeah, that was a poor question on my part. So much for not adding to his list of justifications for executing me. "Answers are the only light when you're staring into the unknown."

"That's a decent saying," Alexis said as he patted my head, like I was an obedient puppy, "but it doesn't apply to your situation." After several seconds of tense silence, Alexis collapsed into an armchair that hadn't been there a moment ago. He steepled his fingers in front of his chest as he drew in several deep breaths. "No matter what your ultimate fate is, bringing you with me might intensify the message I deliver to Dempsey."

He slammed his hands against the wooden arms of his chair and hopped to his feet. Instantly, the mysterious piece of furniture melted back into the flooring as he loomed over me once more. "And those typically create a more lasting impression."

"Does that mean you'll take me along?"

"Isn't that what I just said?"

"I think so, but I'm not sure."

Alexis shrugged as he rushed to a small table and rummaged

through its drawers. After his brief search, he closed the last drawer and turned back to me, offering me a feeble smile. As he sauntered back to me, I could see the old-fashioned scales in his mind as he tossed this latest example of who I was onto the plate labeled with cons. It felt like Alexis was hunting for anything to add to that pile, be it a trivial lie or a reckless question, and I got the feeling I wouldn't survive for much longer once he finished his hunt. Held spellbound by those truth-seeking eyes, I almost missed his question.

"Can I trust you to behave yourself and be an observer?"

"Can I ask Dempsey a question or two before we're done?"

The moment the words tumbled through my mouth, I swallowed a curse with the latest stone I gave him. Though when I risked a glance at his eyes, I saw a glimmer of respect behind them. However, it was gone so quickly I thought I'd imagined it. Hopefully, he'd simply tossed the tidbit onto the plate bearing the pardon him label.

After another interminable silence, Alexis chewed his lower lip while he stabbed my chest with his fingers. "What questions do you have that would prompt you to voluntarily put yourself under that man's scrutiny again?"

"The day I stop asking questions is the day I'm due for the fitting of my pine overcoat."

My quip brought a small smile to his face, as well as teasing a wry chuckle. In response to the pleasant reaction, I felt a smile bloom across my face, which sparked a hearty belly laugh from my potential executioner. As the mirth settled down, Alexis wiped his eyes and thumped my chest with his fist. "Can you give me a little more than that?"

"My friend's safety, for starters."

Alexis clapped my shoulder as his head bobbed. "Fair enough.

I'll allow you to ask Dempsey your questions. However, I will not threaten him on your behalf. If you create additional problems for yourself, then you'll have to carry those burdens on your own."

"I can accept that." My tongue poked through my lips, moistening them as I drew in a deep breath through my nose. "Can I ask you a few questions before we get started?"

Contrary to the look he gave me when I expressed my desire to seek answers from Dempsey, this time, I got what I expected. His eyes narrowed into slits as he took stock of me. I was wondering if Alexis was capable of anything other than weighing people's actions and words. Yet between heartbeats, his eyes softened as he puffed out his chest. "And just what are you looking to ask me?"

As soon as the words reached my ears, I asked about the mysteries plaguing my mind. "How did you stop the bullet? How are you restraining me? And how are you able to impose your will on something that you cannot touch?"

His mouth straightened before curling into a wicked smile. As it continued to grow, his lips parted, revealing his pearly white teeth. After a few seconds of a terrifying silence, a slow chuckle filled the small hall. The combination of his toothy grin and sinister laugh made me recoil. Rather, I would have if I wasn't frozen in place.

As the hollow mirth died away, he stepped next to me and wrapped an arm around my shoulders, as if we were a pair of comrades preparing for a job. He stabbed my chest with his free hand as he pulled me closer. "You're getting ahead of yourself, my little would-be-assassin. Don't forget, your fate is still in flux."

"When is seeking knowledge a bad thing?"

He ran a hand across my jacket's buttons, and he must have undone my forgery because the garment fell away from my body. Then pulled back the shirt and retrieved the already cooling hand warmers. He placed both in his hand and slammed his other on top, like a magician seeking to collapse a pitcher or vase. And just like those purveyors of illusions who make the object disappear, the hand warmers vanished. However, I'm certain Alexis truly destroyed them.

"Boy, as I told you, your crimes are still pending. Just because you placed yourself in a terrible situation doesn't mean you get a free pass. Now I know I would have a hard time proving your guilt in a court of law. After all, there isn't even a murder weapon lying around." He tapped my coat as his smile warmed. "At least not one they can find."

"What does that have to do with my questions?"

"I'm not done," Alexis said, his finger twitching in front of me. "That's where my authority comes into play. After all, we both know the traditional legal system would have . . . a somewhat difficult time even holding you, much less actually punishing you. To be frank, in our world, that's not an issue, given that you've violated some egregious crimes."

"And what are those?"

"Akin to the crimes you're aware of, you're guilty of breaking and entering, assault with a deadly weapon, attempted murder. While the last one was committed via a mundane weapon, you created it with forgery. And that is the key to your biggest transgression. Using forgery in the commission of criminal acts is unforgivable. Before you object, those are why we face persecution throughout history. Without swift and severe punishment, we encourage people to violate the law. Because you risked exposing us to the wider world is the cornerstone for a potential execution."

Before I could object, Alexis waved his hand slightly, and just like that, my jaw was immobilized, and he continued as if I hadn't been about to object.

CHAPTER 19

"Now, before you can voice what I'm sure will be a very passionate objection. It is within my purview to put aside that judgment if I think you are willing, but more importantly are able, to learn from your mistakes and not fall down that path in the future." Alexis paused, letting his somber words linger between us. He must have dealt with people like me before, since his actions reminded me of a scripted response. "You expressed your willingness to learn from this mistake when you asked to go with me, hoping to ask Dempsey some questions concerning your friend.

"Then once I told you that you'd have to shoulder any additional burdens on your own, it didn't dissuade you. That was an excellent first step. However, it was only an initial one. There's still a long way to go before I change my mind."

He would never win an award for tact, but no one could doubt his honesty.

Alexis repositioned my jacket and brushed its clean surface. Though when he pulled his hands away, the flaps didn't budge. Had he redone the transformation he'd just dismissed? When he finished adjusting my coat, he stepped back and leaned against the door, folding his arms across his chest. "Now let me ask you this, boy. Since there is still the chance that I might have to execute you, why would I teach you something that could help you prevent me from doing what I'm required to do for those under my protection?"

And with another wave of his hand, I could feel that vice-like grip holding my jaw slacken and finally melt away. Instead of rushing to provide an answer, I took a few moments to loosen the muscles of my jaw. "So if you decide to let me live . . ."

However, it's not what he wanted to hear, though instead of gagging me with another binding, he simply spoke over me. "If,

265

and I strongly stress the conditionality of that word, you impress me, then I have the authority to set aside your execution, then I'll allow you to ask your questions. Keep in mind, in that scenario, while you won't die, you won't escape accountability for your crimes."

"What would the punishment look like?"

"It'll be whatever I deem necessary to balance the scales. Though you will learn how to be a forger. In fact, if I allow you to live, and you show an aptitude in forgery, I may handle your forging education myself."

I mentally licked my lips at the thought of such an opportunity. I didn't want to show him how desperate I was, though I'm sure he could read me like a large print book. After a few deep breaths, I got a strangle hold on my emotions, though I didn't trust my words, so I leaned into my meekest voice. "What do I have to do to convince you to let me live?"

"I'll be honest with you," Alexis said, rubbing his chin as his eyes pierced my soul, "I'm not sure you can."

With a ferocious slap on my back, he went on with a voice holding far too much sincere joviality. "Cheer up, boy, you're not dead yet. We have a long night ahead of us." With that, the warmth in his voice vanished like water down the drain. "Now answer my question. Can I trust you to behave on this little outing? Aside from asking your questions, will you act strictly as an observer?"

Great! Fantastic! So to recap my day, first I let a major crime lord get his talons into me. Then I agreed to dispense with a thorn from his side, only to have said thorn capture me instead and threaten to execute me because I had used my gift in my failed assassination attempt. If I was smart, I would simply have stayed here and waited for him to return. However, I couldn't be alone, and I had to ensure Matt wouldn't be punished in my place. "You have my word that, aside from my questions, I'll remain an observer."

"Excellent," Alexis said as he clapped his hands together before turning around, ready to leave.

After he took a few steps, I was ready to call out to him, but before I could, he seemed to remember I was still frozen in place, and he spun around. When he turned, he looked straight into my eyes, and I saw just how harsh they were. And with a voice that was even harsher than his eyes, he asked a question with just a hint of impatience. "Well, are you coming?"

Without waiting for my response, he spun about and left.

CHAPTER 20

While Alexis was obviously a great . . . what did he call people like us? Forgers, that's right. While his abilities outpaced mine by a wide margin, he seemed to be slightly absentminded, evidenced by his agreeing to take me with him but leaving without releasing me. Although I had no right to be upset, I couldn't prevent the plume of anger from billowing up when I saw him disappear.

Given how he affected the world without touching what he wanted to alter, a portion of my mind wanted to attribute genuine magic to him. However, the more rational part of me knew how our shared gift worked, and I quickly dispelled the notion. That was until I whirled about and brushed my lips with the back of my hand. Instantly, my body froze, not because of Alexis's intervention but rather from the awe of how he used his power.

It took me several seconds, but I eventually forced myself forward with a pair of unsteady steps. Eventually, my legs stopped trembling as I raced after Alexis. When I rounded the corner at the end of the hall, I found him holding his front door open, his foot tapping away faster than the wings of a hummingbird. "It's about time you started moving. For a second, I thought you'd changed your mind about joining me." He patted the door's exterior as he walked through the opening. "If you're still interested, stop wasting my time. We have too much to do with far too little time to accomplish it."

I lifted a hand as I took a step toward him when something yanked me forward. Before I could regain my balance, the hidden hand of Alexis redoubled its effort, forcing my feet to stumble as I strained to stand up while skittering through the open doorway. The moment I was outside, the door closed, though it wasn't slammed shut, and I was pulled forward like a leashed dog refusing to follow its owner. I swallowed a litany of curses as I stumbled toward the truck Alexis climbed into. It wasn't until the truck's engine roared to life that I found my footing, falling into a stilted gate at odds with my racing heart.

"You're going to want to hurry," Alexis said as he leaned through the open window. With a wink, he slapped his vehicle's door. "Unless you believe you can keep up with a truck."

Another batch of curses bubbled up to my tongue and promptly died as the truck crept forward. While I processed the situation, the leash's slack vanished and pulled me into an all-out sprint. Thankfully, I closed the distance as the truck pulled out of the driveway. Though with every step, that unseen tether shortened. As my fingers brushed the vehicle, I wondered if this kind of lesson was typical for him. If it was, I didn't want him to be my teacher, no matter how skilled he was. Even if this was his way of teaching me humility, he was being cruel.

Of course, when Alexis's truck started rolling away from me, I worried he'd changed his mind about executing me. The threat of losing my footing and falling only to be dragged behind the truck compelled my legs to move at a speed I never thought possible. As the truck's pace quickened, I slapped my hands on the rear gate. With a leap and a pull, I tumbled over the bed's wall. However, before I could gather my thoughts, the leash shortened, and I slammed into the rear of the cab.

I pushed myself into a sitting position with my back pressed firmly against the cab while my racing heart pumped adrenaline throughout my body. Despite the rough treatment and being severely out of breath, there wasn't anything to worry about. When I finished my quick self-evaluation, I pulled the last two hand warmers from my pocket and affixed them to my chest like I had before. As heat flooded into me, I crumpled the trash and siphoned a trivial amount of heat, turning the plastic wrappers into a handful of water.

As the liquid seeped through my fingers, I noticed a wraparound headset lying next to me. When I reached for it, the small device leaped off the truck's bed and hovered in front of me. When my fingers touched the headset, I plucked it out of the air and examined it before slipping it over my ears.

"Did you just make this?"

"I'm impressed," Alexis said, "though it took you long enough to grab the headset."

I rubbed my neck as I turned to look through the cab's rear windshield, finding Alexis's blue-green eyes filling the rearview mirror. He held my gaze for what felt like an eternity, but when he shifted his focus to the road, I dropped onto the bed's floor. "It took me a little while to catch my breath and make sure I didn't get any surprise cuts, scrapes, bruises, or broken bones."

"I'm sure you're less than pleased with your recent treatment. However, I won't apologize. Given the circumstances of our meeting, I am sure you can appreciate my unwillingness to completely trust you. Hence the gag in the house and the leash as we walked outside. Just don't get the wrong idea. You were never in danger of being dragged to death, and don't bother lying about the fear.

That kind of self-deceit will ultimately derail the exercise. I know you were worried about it because everyone I put through that stunt is. While you potentially have more raw talent than anyone I've worked with, human nature is one of the universal constants of life, like taxes and death."

Stunt? That was a stunt? He hadn't intended to drag me. If that was true, then Alexis certainly knew how to motivate people. Did he put everyone through this? Or was it just the tough cases like me? While I was dissecting the latest tidbit from my psychotic instructor, he continued speaking as if we'd simply been discussing an upcoming trip to the grocery store. "Now I'm fairly certain you don't know where Dempsey lives. But I've been wrong a time or two before, so if this is one of those times, please tell me."

"No," I said, rolling to my knees. As the wind whipped through my hair, I stared into Alexis's reflected gaze. "You're correct. I only met him inside the warehouse."

"I figured that."

"Where are we going?"

Alexis's eyes flicked up, locking onto mine for a second before giving me a knowing wink. "Fortunately for you, his home isn't a secret."

My forehead touched the pane of glass as I mentally screamed. Was that simply a test?

"I've never had a reason to bother with him until you waltzed into my life. He does not know what I am capable of, which is the only reason he thought someone like you could kill me."

I rolled over and dropped to my butt as I tapped my head against the back of the cab. "Won't his security be problematic?"

When a warm chuckle emanated from the headset, I popped onto my knees and peered through the glass to find a smile tugging at Alexis's eyes. "Why would it be a problem?"

Shaking my head, I sat back down and stared at the sparkling lights hanging in the dark sky. As I lost myself in the beautiful arrangement of light, I rested my head against the cab. "If his security isn't problematic, why have you left him alone?"

"Before tonight, Dempsey hadn't bothered me or anyone I'm responsible for. As a result, I was willing to allow the mundane world to police him as they would anyone else. However, you've confirmed that my assumptions were wrong, and now that I'm aware of his machinations, I'll make him regret that he ever met you."

With a wry chuckle, I pulled my legs against my chest and wrapped my arms around them. "What are you planning on doing?"

"I'm not sure."

My head turned toward the glass as I started tapping it with a finger. "We're heading to his home to confront him, and you aren't sure what we're going to do?"

"I have a rough idea," Alexis said, as his fingers whitened around the steering wheel. "Besides, no matter which path I travel, they all begin with the same first step."

"Which is?"

Alexis shook his head, and despite the empty road, he guided the truck onto the shoulder. Once parked, he turned around, and the glass separating us vanished while he removed his headset. "We can't educate Dempsey about his mistakes without removing him from his home."

"And you say security won't be an issue?" I whirled off my butt and grasped the new opening as I leaned into the cab. "I've seen the kind of men he employs for security. They're all well-trained thugs. You're glossing over something that you shouldn't."

Alexis shook his head as he pressed a finger against my

forehead and pushed me back. Instantly, the truck was made whole, and he put his headset back on and resumed driving. "I've already said his security won't be a problem. Dealing with them will take me a minute or two. And while I'm busy dealing with them, you'll be staying right where you are. The only difference that'll matter to you is where your leash will be tethered. For now, sit back, relax, and enjoy the scenery. If I tried explaining everything to you, you'd strain your brain trying to juggle it all."

Before I could reply, the slight pressure of the headset vanished. Reflexively, my hands flew to my ears, only to confirm the device was missing. As the wind whipped past me, I slumped down, sinking into the corner of the bed nearest the driver's seat. After a few minutes of the wind's constant roar threatening to deafen me, it lessened. Either that or I simply filtered it into white noise and a strange silence settled over me, forcing me to criticize my foolish life choices.

However, it wasn't a lengthy list, and due to perfect hindsight, my embarrassment was thorough. When I grew tired of berating myself, my mind drifted to the mental puzzles Alexis presented me with, primarily his ability to affect the world without touching his target. Of the now several examples of this ability, I looked at something that was already on my short list to figure out before I met this master, protecting myself from a gunman. Despite the mystery behind the how, the fact Alexis achieved it spurred me toward the goal. And given my recent experiences, I was motivated to unravel that skill.

As I worked through the ways to achieve a similar feat, I kept butting up against the same problem. How had Alexis's protection affected something moving too fast for him to see? Even if I developed something that protected me from guns and other less violent projectiles, all the options I could think of were limited to fabric placed between me and the attacker. While it should work, that's not what happened in Alexis's home. My bullet had slammed into something a good few feet away from him. Somehow, he created an invisible wall that caught the bullet.

No, Kevlar or some other protective fabric wasn't the ultimate answer. To consider this puzzle resolved, I needed something or a combination of things to protect me from every aspect of a surprise attack. More importantly, while the fabric would prevent the most serious side effect of getting shot, there were other problems that normally paled in comparison to dying, like bruising. If complaining about a massive bruise after surviving a gunshot sounds petty, then I'm glad to be petty with this mystery.

Yet no matter what I thought about, I kept circling back to the simplicity of Alexis's solution. While I could add layer after layer of fabric to solve all my problems, the protection would leave me unable to move, which created a different and more serious problem. Whatever solution I might end up with, I had to remember Alexis already solved the puzzle, or one of them at any rate.

While there are always multiple paths to any journey, if you have to carve out your own road, you're doing something wrong, more often than not. So I retrieved the memory of the failed shot and studied every aspect. All the mechanics on my end were perfect, from the trigger pull to the flight of the round. It wasn't until the bullet's journey came to an abrupt halt everything went wrong. As I rewound the memory to when the hunk of lead stopped, I thought about its misshapen form. It had mushroomed out as if it had slammed into something. Yet nothing stood between Alexis and the barrel.

Despite rewatching the point of impact a hundred times, the futility of assaulting that brick wall left me with a pounding headache. So I switched to another of Alexis's mysterious flexes, his binding me without seeing or, more importantly, touching me. I mean, he had detained me before rising out of his chair. Everything about our shared gift told me that was impossible. However, it had happened. Something allowed him to affect the wider world from a distance and passively. Could the ultimate answer to both puzzles be related?

Were the transformations Alexis performed tonight typical for him? Or had he simply been trying to flaunt his superiority? Granted, he was vastly superior to me, but were his actions as commonplace for him as breathing was for me? While my work was nothing more than rough stick figures in comparison, Alexis's efforts had more in common with masters like Picasso and Monet. While I'd have to get the answer from him, I don't think anything he did was something he hadn't done countless times before.

There had to be something more to both mysteries. Aside from the distance and the lack of a touch, another similarity between the two transformations was the invisibility of whatever affected the world. While enough microscopic things might secure me, I doubted any number could deform a bullet. In the end, the only thing that made any sense was if Alexis had turned the air into hardened steel. But that wouldn't work, air was too porous. . . . Unless he turned one molecule into millions and then altered their properties. Could the answer really be that simple? Was it possible? I almost laughed as a potential solution filled my mind. Had Alexis somehow learned how to forge air?

I considered the possibility. Air was technically made up of molecules just like everything else. But given how easily we walk through it, I never thought about trying to manipulate it. Did he manage the feat by focusing on a single molecule? Would that allow him to affect things from a distance and without a line of sight? I mean, ultimately, everything and everyone is connected by the surrounding air. Could it really be that simple? No! It had to be something else; there was no way the answer could be that easy.

But what if it was that simple?

The best magic tricks were always deceptively simple. It seemed to be an unwritten rule of the universe. The more complicated you tried to make something, the more spectacular its inevitable failure. I pinned the thought into the depths of my mind. I had to test the theory. With a deep breath, I concentrated on my left hand and pictured a marble, about the size of a dime, made entirely out of air, specifically condensed air. But when I tried to fuel the transformation, nothing happened.

What was I missing?

Before I could try again, the truck pulled to a stop. Did the two of them live that close together, or had I just been so absorbed with the puzzle I hadn't noticed how much time had passed? As I tried to stand, I abruptly came to the end of my leash and stumbled ungracefully back into a sitting position. How had he fixed my leash like that while driving? Wait, that was a dumb question, given what I'd already seen him do.

With every passing second, I was truly beginning to learn just how little I knew about my gift. Until recently, I hadn't even known it had a special name. I finally looked around and was only able to see a handful of houses. None of which were terribly close to each other, but more importantly, I saw no sign of Alexis. He wasn't in the cab. While I could search for him, I didn't need to. He was off to get Dempsey.

Instead, I refocused on working with air. What did I do wrong? Normally when I tried to transmute something, I just had to focus on what my intended result was, but that hadn't worked. Was working with something as sparse as air so different? I was not trying to make something from nothing. That wasn't possible. While I could not see the molecule, it was there. Ultimately, I sought to take an air molecule, something I couldn't see, and manipulate it. As I thought about it, I realized I sounded a like a blind man trying to perform lifesaving surgery.

With a deep breath, I flipped my script. Instead of focusing on my goal, I focused on my starting point, a single molecule of air. With that initial image, I doubled its size and squeezed it. Then I did it again, and again. I kept repeating the process until the image in my mind reached the size of a dime. Instantly, a trivial portion of body heat rushed out of me, and when I opened my eyes, I felt the weight of the marble resting on my palm. With another expenditure of heat, I colored the swirling air with a hint of yellow.

I rolled the marble around my hand and then picked it up with my thumb and forefinger. As I stared into it, I noticed the swirling air forming conflicting eddies, giving the sphere the appearance of a miniature gas giant. Seconds later, I felt the rippling pressure of the air as it struggled to escape the bindings. I closed my fist around the marble and grinned just as something slammed into my shoulder.

"Hey, boy!"

With a broad smile, I whirled around, tightening my grip on the marble as I hopped to my feet. "Please stop calling me that. I have a name."

Despite returning my grin, Alexis's shaking head told me I was pushing my luck. "Not yet, you don't. Like I told you earlier, I'm going to leave you in the truck. Is that clear?"

"You use air to achieve things I've always thought to be impossible, don't you?"

"Excuse me?"

Since I really wanted to discuss that topic, I took his question as permission to continue rather than a veiled attempt to silence me. "In order to protect yourself from random assaults and when you restrained me, you were using air to achieve both results. Weren't you?"

While Alexis obscured his reaction well enough, he didn't compare with the likes of Tyson or Patrick. The soft sparkle in his eyes confirmed my guess. I'd been right. He used air in his transformations. With a harrumph, he stepped toward the truck, grabbed my jacket, and pulled me down. "How did you come to that conclusion?"

"Alexis, you didn't answer my question."

Nodding his head, Alexis released me and gripped the bed's rail. As he drew in a deep breath, Alexis's fingers began drumming out a soft beat. "You're right. I didn't answer your question. At least not directly. And that's more than I'm willing to give you. Stay here while I collect our crime boss."

"Whatever you say," I said as Alexis nodded and turned around. However, before he took a second step, I grabbed his shoulder. "Before you go, would you mind taking the harness off me?"

"Why would I do that?" Alexis asked as he peeled my hand off. He turned around and leveled a glare at me that could have instantly bored through a sheet of tungsten. However, if I backed down now, I knew I'd never be able to resist his scrutiny. So I lifted my hands, indicating my willingness to surrender, though I took great care not to drop my trophy as I suggested a compromise. "If I'm not here when you get back, I won't fight you when you come to execute me."

"I'll hold you to that oath, boy."

With that, he turned around and walked toward the house.

Between a pair of heartbeats, Alexis vanished. Note I didn't say stepped behind a bush or some other shrubbery. He disappeared. Yet another impressive demonstration of his skills. And just like that, more questions flooded through my mind as I wondered where he was and how he would get in and out of Dempsey's home without sparking an alarm.

I hopped off the truck and sauntered around it. My lips curled into a wry grin as I thumped the bed's rail. With another thump of the truck, I resumed pacing around Alexis's vehicle. As I walked, I slipped the yellow sphere into my pocket and created two more: one forest green, the other a dark red. As I lifted the crimson orb to my eye, Alexis's voice reached my ear.

"You better get into the cab. Our friend needs the entire bed for himself."

I dropped the marble into my pocket as I ran around the back of the truck and scrambled into the seat. As the click of the buckle resounded about the cab, I looked through the windshield to find Alexis jogging toward me with Dempsey floating over the ground just past his right shoulder. What can't he do? When he reached the cab, Dempsey's body floated over the truck and settled into the bed.

Once the criminal mastermind was secured, Alexis slipped into the truck and turned the engine over. Instantly, it roared to life. In contrast to how we left his home, Alexis simply withdrew his foot from the brake, allowing the truck to gently creep forward. Puzzled, my gaze drifted to him, where I found a finger pointing to the windshield. I dutifully obeyed and found a chunk of the truck was missing. Despite roughly a third of the engine missing, I still heard its roar, and equally important, we were still inching forward.

Only the sheer awe of what I saw kept me from asking the

initial list of questions. What's happening? Where's the rest of the truck? How is it still running? However, the curiosity gave way to fear and panic as more of the truck vanished. I snatched his wrist and pulled him toward me. "What did you do?"

"Show me how clever you can be. Try to figure it out on your own."

"But the car is disintegrating."

With a sigh, Alexis slumped into his seat as he gripped the steering wheel with both hands. While keeping his grip, he extended a finger. "The truck is not disintegrating. If trying to decipher that is too hard, try explaining how I pulled Dempsey from his heavily guarded home without raising an alarm."

"That depends."

"On what?"

"The answer can change depending on how you got inside. So how did you get into the house in the first place?"

Laughter filled the cab as more of the vehicle vanished. He released the wheel and crossed his arms over his chest. "That's a good question, boy."

"Well?"

Alexis turned his head toward me with a neutral grin plastered across his face. Unlike the harsh glares he'd thrown my way previously, this look felt akin to what a harsh, yet fair, teacher would give a student, searching for correct answers. Which meant he would not give me a hint. Unfortunately, my mind couldn't find anything that resembled an answer. I slammed my clenched fist into my thigh. "None of this makes sense. You have to touch whatever you want to alter, and you're not touching anything."

"And . . ." Alexis said, his hand spinning in a circular pattern, prompting me to make a connection.

"So how to do you forge something that isn't within your

grasp?" I asked, pressing my back into the truck's seat in a vain effort to prevent the oncoming nothingness from reaching me.

Alexis laid his hands on the dash, despite the advancing nothingness as he said, "I had the same question when I started my training with my master."

With the rapid approach of the devastation, I peered at him from the corner of my eye. "Did you say master?"

"Yes, and if that word contains too much baggage for you, substitute 'teacher' in its place, and you're mostly there."

Those words were like a wrench tossed into the gears of a clock. They gummed up my thoughts, and everything else fell from my mind. Despite the vehicle disappearing around me, I stopped struggling. I lifted my hand and displayed the red marble of compressed and swirling air. "That implies you've decided to teach me. Hopefully, proof that I've mastered forging air will encourage your decision."

Through a smirk, he calmly reached out and plucked the small marble from my palm. Lifting it to his eyes, Alexis studied the whirling contents as the steering wheel vanished. "This is impressive work, boy. Unfortunately for you, I haven't decided your fate yet. I was encouraging your endeavor by telling you I asked a similar question when I was learning how to wield my abilities. Though the chances of your surviving the night are growing."

Grumbling under my breath, I turned my attention back to the disappearing vehicle, and with a start, realized my legs had already disappeared. Yet I could still feel my toes. I gripped my slacks and cocked my head toward my door. "What's happening, Alexis?"

He tossed the red sphere up and caught it as he clicked his tongue. "You'll see in a few seconds. Just be patient."

A new sense of dread coursed through my veins as my fingers

started turning white around the gray fabric of my pants. As we continued to disappear, I kept pushing against the seat, trying to delay the inevitable outcome of the implacable march. Just before my face went through the invisible barrier, I cursed my inability to push myself through the back of the cab. Then the nothingness swallowed me, condemning me into the unknown.

CHAPTER 21

After the nothingness swallowed me, the missing windshield hung in front of my face. And on the other side of that glass, instead of seeing Dempsey's neighborhood, I saw massive stalactites and stalagmites jutting out from the rock like the teeth of a massive predator. Unfortunately, given the darkness and how Alexis achieved this feat, it really felt like we were sitting in the mouth of a giant beast.

I pressed my face against the passenger window to study what I could in the dim light. After a subjective eternity, I turned back to Alexis, grasping his arm. "Where are we? What was that? Was that teleportation?"

Soft laughter with hints of warmth and joy filled the cab, conflicting with the ominous nature of the artificial beast.

My face reddened as I released him and inched into the door. "That is, would you please tell me what happened?"

Alexis glanced at his rearview mirror and turned off the car, letting a silence surround us for several seconds. "As far as where we are, the genuine answer is unimportant. For the sake of brevity, you can consider this to be one of my many safe houses. It can and sometimes does fulfill that purpose. For your other questions, you can consider that to be teleportation by the strictest of definitions. After all, we're almost fourteen hundred miles away from Dempsey's home."

"But how . . ." My eyes rapidly blinked as my gaze drifted back to the mighty stone structures. "How did you do that?"

The window rolled down as he jerked his thumb over his shoulder. "You're getting ahead of yourself." He exited the truck and leaned in through the open window, flashing me a devilish grin. "Though provided you get the chance, it's something you'll learn how to do."

His renewed jab at my predicament yanked my attention away from the simplistic beauty of the cavern's structure. I unbuckled the belt and leaned forward, forcing an emotionless smile up at him. "You can make all the jokes you want about my future, Alexis. However, you've overplayed your hand. I already know that you're going to put aside my execution. While I'm a little less sure about if you'll take me on as your student . . ." I paused long enough to let my face take on an impish look. "Though I'm sure you'll probably call me your apprentice."

His fingers drummed the opening as his smile soured. Something, presumably his knee, thumped the truck, creating the illusion of a heartbeat for the monster whose mouth we occupied. After a few more false heartbeats, a silence emerged before Alexis chased it away. "You're getting cocky again, boy."

With my smile widening, I slipped out of the truck and walked around the engine, stretching my arms and sides. "Not really. If you hadn't already decided, you would have laughed off my request to take the leash off back at Dempsey's home." Twisting my neck, a handful of soft pops filled the chamber. "However, you gave me the chance to hang myself."

"What are you talking about?" Alexis asked as he turned around and stared up into the monster's upper jaw.

"What's the old saying, 'trust, but verify?'" I slammed my hands together, punctuating my question.

CHAPTER 21

"It's terrifying how inconsistent your knowledge is." With a snap of his fingers, twin blooms of light filled the cavern.

I rubbed my eyes as they adjusted to the sudden light. "One of two things happened while you grabbed our friend," I said, pointing toward the truck's occupied bed. "Either you removed the leash, or you simply lengthened it enough to give me the illusion of freedom. Ultimately, it doesn't matter which one you did. You gave me a test, and when I saw the glint in your eye as you returned, with Dempsey trailing you, I got all the corroboration I needed."

"Hmm . . ." As the gears in Alexie's head whirled, the phantom heartbeat resumed. "Let's say you're right. If I trust you, why wouldn't I have just given you the answers to your litany of questions?"

"I never said you trusted me." I flicked the truck's body as I sauntered to the rear of the vehicle. "You don't have to believe someone to verify their words and actions."

A wry chuckle replaced the false pumping heart as he walked to the cab. "Touché. Though it doesn't discredit my question."

I leaned on the truck and peered down at the unconscious crime lord. With a few deep breaths, I pointed at Dempsey as my smile continued to grow. I pulled the other two forged air marbles from my pocket and brandished them. "Because students or 'apprentices' learn better when they're forced to figure out a problem on their own, or at least that's what teachers or, as you call them, 'masters' claim."

"Say that's true." Alexis's cautious grin turned into a genuine smile as he ran his hands through his hair. "Why did I give you a straight answer concerning how we got here?"

"You did, and you didn't," I said, pocketing my two trophies. Alexis would have to improve his bluffing skills if he wanted to terrify Dempsey. While he sought to trip me up, I saw where he was heading, so I simply skirted his trap. "You gave me a straight answer about the end effect, not about how you managed it."

"That's a real dissection of words."

"It's a skill honed to perfection at the poker table."

"You have a lot of debates while playing cards?"

"No," I said, stepping up onto the bed's step and grasping the rail. With my smile stretching across my face, I leaned back. "However, I've learned how to read people's faces and isolate their tells. And I've already discovered enough of yours to see where you're heading."

"Is that so?"

"Yes," I said as I pulled myself forward and thrust my open hand toward him. After a minor exchange of heat, a fourth marble of swirling air appeared on my palm. Though this time, I made it the size of a quarter and shaded it a burnt orange. "And my guess to the reason you won't give hints about how we got here is it's too complicated to experiment with." I shook my new toy. "It's not like it's a marble of air."

With a smile of his own, he thumped the side of his truck and walked toward the center of the chamber. "Good for you, boy. You've got quite the head for reasoning on your shoulders. It'll be a pleasure to teach you the craft."

"Can I get a hint at least?"

With a hearty belly laugh, he stopped in the middle of the cavern and shook his head while turning back to face me and the truck. "Not now. Before we get to the implementation, you'll have to study lots of theories."

"Why?"

"Because, as with anything, there are a multitude of ways to achieve the same thing. None are inherently better or worse, easier or harder than the other. It's just a matter of preference."

"Then why do I have to learn all of them?"

"You need to be aware of them." Alexis pressed his fingers to his chest as his head cocked to the side. "I'm only a master of the techniques that I use, but I'm aware of the basics of others. That knowledge aides my expertise not because they're complimentary but rather because I can be more flexible in how I achieve my end goal."

He clapped his hands and extended two fingers before twirling them toward the cavern's roof. Instantly, Dempsey's body rose into the air, and Alexis looked at me with a twitching finger. "However, right now, we have a more pressing matter to deal with than your desire to learn."

As the crime lord's body rose, I reached out and poked his temple. "Is he still asleep?"

"It's a little sounder than sleep." With several gestures, Alexis guided Dempsey's sleeping form toward a large slab of stone rising out of the ground beside Alexis. Once the crime lord hovered over the new bed, Dempsey drifted down to the harsh yet polished surface.

"What are you planning on doing?"

Alexis walked around the criminal and touched his ankles and wrists. Promptly, bands of stone wrapped around the crime lord's body. He quickly retraced his steps to Dempsey's head and reached down, grabbing the stone and adjusting it as if it were a hospital bed. Once he had it at the right angle, he walked in front of Dempsey and signaled for me to join him. "We're going to have a frank conversation."

When I reached him, I pointed up to the twin plumes of light. "How'd you make those?"

"Irrelevant at the moment." He stepped closer to Dempsey and placed a finger on the man's chest. "Are you ready to begin?"

"Do you want a private conversation with him?"

"No," Alexis said, snapping his fingers. Before I could react, a set of massive hands dragged me between the two men. When the phantom grasp released me, a smaller set, presumably Alexis's, gripped my shoulders. "I'd rather you be one of the first things he sees. The shock of seeing us together in a strange location should shatter his confidence. Wouldn't you agree?"

The words sliced through me, triggering my memory of waking up in Dempsey's freezer. Despite the warmth from the hand warmers, my body chilled a few degrees as I reflexively stepped away from the unconscious crime lord. Unfortunately, Alexis pushed me back to where he positioned me. Both men were powerful, just in different ways, and I was just a pawn caught in the middle of their struggle.

"There's some truth to what you said." I took a couple of deep breaths as I laid a hand over one of the warm lumps beneath my jacket. "But I'm not sure how wise it actually is."

"I've only been this sure of a few aspects of my life. And every one of them turned out to be a cornerstone used to buttress everything."

"A yes would have been fine." Another belly laugh rolled over the cavern, and somehow, despite the seriousness of what was happening, it brought a slight smile to my lips.

Alexis bent down as he placed his fingers under Dempsey's nose. "Remember, you're going to be my apprentice, and that means you're under my protection."

As I nodded, Dempsey's head lurched while he tugged at his stone bindings. When he stopped thrashing, he licked his lips as his eyes whipped about until they landed on Alexis. Instantly, they grew, threatening to pop out of their sockets. With several labored breaths, Dempsey cleared his throat as his eyes narrowed

CHAPTER 21

to deadly points. "How long do you think you can hold me in my home?"

Alexis spread his arms out like a mother preparing to embrace her wayward child as his head swept about the cavern. "Last I checked, you didn't build your home a mile below the earth's surface. Though I suppose I could be wrong."

With deliberate motions, Dempsey turned his head and studied everything, taking mental notes on the various jutting features of the cave. Once he finished cataloguing his surroundings, his eyes fell upon me. Yet, instead of launching into a tirade, he simply stared at me.

Just a few hours ago, I would have wilted under that harsh glare. In fact, my body still wanted to crumple. That's when I realized Alexis had bolstered my conviction and confidence by weaving his restraints about my legs. That guaranteed a couple of things. First, I wouldn't turn my tail and run. And second, no matter how severe Dempsey's eyes became, I wouldn't collapse into a puddle.

When he realized I would not back down, he shook his head. "I'm disappointed in you, Francis Harrison Bailey."

Dempsey's voice possessed quite the range, though right in that moment, he sounded like a father disappointed in his child's unfortunate decision. He expressed his disapproval and brought his gray eyes back to Alexis's. They held each other's eyes for several seconds, each attempting to gain control of the strained silence. Unfortunately for Dempsey, when you woke up restrained like he was, you lost a fair amount of credibility. Though to Dempsey's credit, he eventually realized he'd never gain the advantage, and I saw the change and filed it away.

When you strap someone to a table, you don't expect that individual to appear more dignified than the captors, especially when they're wearing pajamas. However, despite all the disadvantages arrayed against him, Dempsey did appear to possess the most dignity in the cavern. As he laid on the stone slab, his gaze eventually drifted back to Alexis, as his bored voice rebounded off the stone walls. "If I'm not at home, where am I?"

"Don't worry, Dempsey," Alexis said, grasping his hands behind his back. "We're safely beyond any prying ears."

"Which is where?"

Alexis released his breath as he rubbed his eyes. "We're about fourteen hundred miles away from your home."

Fear flickered across Dempsey's notoriously calm eyes. Though he quickly reinforced his unflappable mask as his chest swelled. "And how would you have abducted me in the middle of the night?"

"As easily as you breathe," Alexis said, shrugging, as he regrasped his hands behind his back. He took a step closer to the bound crime lord and licked his lips. "Dempsey, bypassing your security was as difficult as donning formal wear. I waltzed through your home and into your bedroom with the greatest of ease and in the blink of an eye."

Dempsey's lips curled into a snarl as a growl tinged the frigid air. "That's not possible!"

Alexis took another purposeful step toward Dempsey, the sound of his boots echoing ominously in the dimly lit room. He raised his hand, fingers curling with calculated precision. In response, the polished slab rumbled and crept up Dempsey's body. Dempsey's panicked screams pierced through the tense silence as he desperately thrashed against the encroaching bonds.

The scent of fear permeated the room, while the unyielding liquid stone continued its relentless advance, inching up Dempsey's trembling form. Its motion ceased when it covered enough of Dempsey's body to pin him against the unyielding surface. The scene was now frozen in time, the air heavy with tension and the sight of Dempsey's newfound prison.

With a rueful shake of his head, Alexis reached out and pressed his index finger against the crime lord's forehead, silencing Dempsey's screams. Alexis straightened his back as his hand returned to its twin. "You see, unlike my new friend here, I am a true forger. And I've been perfecting and expanding my skills for longer than both of you and your parents have been alive. I can do things you wouldn't be able to dream of. For example, abducting you from your bedroom without raising an alarm or manipulating stone to form a tomb."

For a moment, I thought Alexis's words had had their desired effect, because I glimpsed absolute terror etched into Dempsey's eyes. But then the despicable man must have found a trace of the fire inside. "Since you wield magic, how do I know this isn't just some sort of illusion? After all, that's within your capabilities."

With a stiff nod, Alexis started pacing around the stone slab. "That's a reasonable question to ask with people like me." When he returned to Dempsey's view, he offered the encased man a predatory smile as he twirled a finger. "I suppose you could call out for help."

As if on cue, Dempsey screamed for his security, but the only response was his own echo and a suffocating silence.

Alexis let the stillness linger as he loomed over the powerless crime lord. "While I won't stop you from crying out, I can tell you it won't do you any good." Alexis stepped back and raised his arms like a raptor preparing to catch its prey. "We aren't in your home, and there's no way your people can find you here. Believe me Bertrand, you're out of your depth with me."

Alexis's absolute confidence must have shattered Dempsey's

legendary resolve because the once ruthless crime lord was now a hollow shell of whom terrorized me. And from all appearances, Alexis was in no hurry to put the criminal out of his misery as he allowed the silence to stretch out. Judging from the worry lines spreading across Dempsey's face, uncertainty was something he was unaccustomed to. As Dempsey's fear and desperation continued to build, Alexis resumed his walk around the stone slab.

"Now, as you've realized, you are quite helpless. And since no alarm was raised, your empty bed won't be noticed for some time. So if you want to have any hope of a continued existence, you'll answer all the questions put before you." Alexis stopped in front of Dempsey and gripped the crime lord's chin. "Do you understand?"

"Yes."

"Excellent," Alexis said, releasing Dempsey as he resumed his circular walk, though in the opposite direction. "First question, why did you want me dead? I cannot recall ever interfering in your business, so why?"

Despite the fear swirling behind Dempsey's eyes, I could see a well-known emotion competing with it, stubbornness. However, eventually, the terror overpowered its opposition, though his clenched mouth showed he was going to choose his words carefully.

Unfortunately for the crime lord, when Alexis came back into view, he reached out and pressed a fingertip onto Dempsey's chest. In response to the simple touch, a cry of pain tore through the cavern. What did he do? Was that another use of our gift? If it was, wasn't that just as illegal as what I did earlier? I was going to have to figure out these new laws, or I'd waste the clemency Alexis had given me.

Alexis pressed his finger into Dempsey's chest as he leaned closer to the once stoic crime lord. "I asked you a question,

CHAPTER 21

Bertrand. Don't forget that you've already agreed to answer me, so stop wasting my time and my patience. Once they're gone, you'll discover what I'm capable of. Is that clear?"

Instead of the piercing eyes that had pinned me into my chair earlier today, I saw eyes filled with nothing but terror. I couldn't make out the mumbled answer, but obviously Alexis could. "Now, let's try this again. What is the real reason you wanted me dead?"

"You . . . You have been interfering with my business; you just haven't known about it. Francis over there wasn't the first of your kind I've tried to recruit."

Alexis inched forward, his finger digging into Dempsey's chest. "I know our friend here walked into your tournament. But how are you finding the other forgers?"

The vitriol dripping from Alexis's words scared me. I wanted to flee, but instead of obeying my mental commands, Alexis's bindings brought me closer, allowing me to hear Dempsey's soft reply.

"A man in my position has the resources to scour not only this city but others as well. I simply keep my ears open for interesting stories."

With a deep breath, Alexis licked his lips as his teeth ground together. "How long have you been searching for forgers?"

"I've always searched for people capable of genuine magic."

I thought Alexis might make another objection, but he simply asked his next question. "What brought our kind to your notice in the first place?"

Dempsey hesitated for only a second, but it was a second too long, and he cried out as Alexis filled his body with another round of pain. When the cries died off, Alexis leaned close to Dempsey. "I thought you remembered our agreement to answer whatever I put before you."

"I'll never give you the answer to that! No matter how much pain you pour into me."

"Why?" Alexis asked, as his forefinger dug into Dempsey's chest.

"Because they aren't my answers to give."

Alexis silently studied his captive before stepping away from him and clasping his hands behind his back. "I believe you would endure any kind of torment I could imagine, and I would get no closer to an answer. Fine, I'll not ask you to reveal anything about your witch to me."

As Dempsey heard those words, I thought the flowing fear would wash us away like a bursting dam clearing the riverbanks. Seeing the intended reaction from Dempsey, Alexis leaned right next to the other man's ear and spoke so softly I almost missed the words.

"Bertrand, it wasn't all that difficult of a leap to make." Alexis thumped the crime boss's exposed chest as he shook his head. "How have you been so successful if a simple, logical conclusion spikes your fear like that? Now that I know how you noticed our world, tell me who was the forger I denied you access to. Why was he so special?"

"You and your kind are all special, don't you know that?"

"Of course I do!" Alexis slammed his hand against the stone beside the crime lord's head, cracking it. When he pulled his bruised hand back, he waved a finger under Dempsey's nose. "But why was this one specifically so special to you?"

"Her name was Julia Santiago." Dempsey's initial words were more forceful than they were a moment ago, but his voice quickly dwindled as he continued his explanation. "She wasn't as powerful as your friend over there, or you, apparently. But she had power all the same."

"Power you wanted to harness for your own gain, no doubt."

"Of course," Dempsey said, closing his eyes, "do you know anyone who would relinquish access to power and the profits it brings willingly?"

Alexis began chewing his lip in thought, and I saw a specific question swirling through his brain, but after another moment, he skipped to another train of thought. "Fine, keep your secrets." Alexis pressed a hand to his chest as he snapped a finger. Instantly, Dempsey's eyelids opened, and Alexis put his face next to the criminal's "So I kept you from getting forgers, and ultimately, when you finally had a name to chase, you wanted to stop the interference. I'll assume your witch was involved in most of this up to then. But why did you send Francis here after me?"

This time, when Alexis mentioned the witch, Dempsey kept his face impassive, though he'd already surrendered that pot. "I sent him after you, hoping that a wizard would have better luck eliminating you. Two of my men had already failed using more conventional methods."

"Those were because of you?"

"That's what I told you," I said, before clamping my hands over my mouth.

Alexis walked back to me and patted my shoulder. "You relayed secondhand knowledge." He pointed a finger at the entombed crime lord and flashed his widest, predatory grin. "He provided me with hard facts."

"Such as?"

"First," Alexis said, thumping my chest, "conventional methods must refer to a sniper."

"That's a stretch," Dempsey said, licking his lips. "There are other conventional ways to remove you from the world."

Alexis nodded as he paced up to Dempsey and laid a fingertip on the man's chest. "While that's true, I've had some rather large caliber bullets slam into the protections I employ on two specific occasions." Jerking his other thumb over his shoulder, Alexis leaned closer. "Our young friend ran into the same barriers when he tried to shoot me."

Dempsey looked away from Alexis as he asked, "What else did it tell you?"

Alexis dug his fingertip into the crime lord's chest as he crept closer. He released a pent-up breath as he shook his head. "That you're considering employing new methods of terminating people who've crossed you, and you no longer care about potential collateral damage."

His chest swelled as the rest of his hand joined his digging finger. The moment his fingers and palm rested on Dempsey, Alexis's skin glowed a brilliant pale yellow as an acrid scent filled the room. In the following moment, Dempsey's scream threatened to shred my eardrums. Undeterred, Alexis kept his hand in place for several seconds. When he pulled it away, the cavern swallowed the criminal's lingering echo. After several tense seconds, an unnatural stillness filled the chamber.

"Now I know those shots were meant for me. At the time, since I was in a crowd, I thought the shots were meant for someone else. And that's a decent reason to force your newly recruited forger into an assassination attempt, though my guess is there was more to it than that." Alexis's glowing hand lowered to an unmarred section of Dempsey's chest. "I'd be willing to bet your witch suggested it to you."

When I woke up in Dempsey's freezer, the crime lord had worn an unreadable mask, something he'd spent a lifetime crafting. However, after the short meeting with Alexis, that emotionless persona was shattered, and his emotions were flittering in the wind like tattered flags for the world to see. While fear had been motivating the crime lord, that was being pushed aside by hatred. The glow around Alexis's right hand vanished as he patted Dempsey's cheek like he was a good little puppy.

"Thank you for the confirmation."

I looked at Dempsey's chest and saw the burned flesh shaped like Alexis's hand. What had he done to Dempsey? Could he alter himself?

Alexis placed his hand back on the exposed burn and leaned closer to Dempsey. "Here's my million-dollar question. Why is this forger or witch or whatever you call her so important to you?"

"I thought you weren't going to pry into that subject," Dempsey said through a feral snarl.

Alexis removed his hand and paced around the stone slab. When he walked away, my eyes bulged when I saw Dempsey's undamaged clothing. Did Alexis just undo the branding?

When Alexis was halfway around the table, he broke the brief stillness. "I'm not asking you to betray any confidences. I wanted to know why she's important to you. Though I also want to know why she wants me dead so badly."

"I want you dead!" Dempsey railed against his stone bindings, and after several failed attempts to pull his hands free, blood trickled down his underarm. "I want the pair of you dead! I'm the one in charge!"

Alexis stepped back into view and twirled a finger, instantly silencing the crime lord. With a step away from the silent criminal, Alexis spun toward me and beckoned me forward. "Come here, boy."

As I inched closer, I pointed at Dempsey's furious eyes. "Given that his eyes are open, did you just silence him? Or are you preventing him from listening to us as well?"

Alexis's lips curled into a tight smile as he lifted a hand and snapped his fingers. Somehow, the resulting thunderclap was incongruent with the simple act. Yet as the thunderous chorus rebounded against the cavern's walls, my feet slid across the smooth ground despite my lack of intent. When I came to a rest, Alexis grasped my upper arms. "No, he cannot hear us. For the moment, our conversation is completely private." His fingers dug into my arms as he sighed. "Given how far I've pushed him, I don't think he'll provide me with anything else that's useful. It also means you might not get the answers you're hoping for. Do you still want to dig your hole any deeper?"

I looked over Alexis's shoulder and studied the raging eyes looming over us. Even though the fire behind them frightened me, I was no longer terrified of Dempsey, like I was during our chat in the freezer. Don't get me wrong, even with the clemency from Alexis, I still had to worry about the bullet the crime lord had reserved for me. However, I needed answers. So I looked back at Alexis and swallowed the massive lump in my throat. "I don't have a choice but to ask my questions, and he's the only one who can provide the answers."

With a nod, Alexis released me and gestured to the captive criminal. "Then feel free to take center stage."

Despite the suggested command, I stepped closer to Alexis while keeping my gaze fixed on Dempsey. "Can you tell me how you inflicted pain with a touch?"

"No."

Inching closer to Dempsey, I peered over my shoulder. "What about the branding? I didn't imagine that or the smell. You branded him, and then in another moment, every trace of the wound and damage you inflicted was gone, save for the smell."

Alexis leaned down and pressed the same finger he used

against Dempsey on my back. "You're inquiring about skills that are well beyond your capabilities. Not to mention flirting with the edges of the law."

My eyes flicked to Dempsey as I took a step away from Alexis and shoved my hands into my pockets. "If my intent is flirting with the law, why were you allowed to play with those same boundaries?"

"Because of my position. I'm responsible for the forgers in the country. As a result, there are times I must act with impunity to ensure the safety of those I protect." Alexis rose and pressed his palm against my back. With a grunt, he shoved me closer to the criminal. "Don't think you have the same carte blanche to deal with Dempsey as I do. If you try to imitate my tactics, then the clemency you're receiving will vanish. Is that understood?"

A shiver raced down my spine, and I couldn't decide if Alexis's soft-spoken words or the chill wrapped around us caused it. As my lips moved, nothing came out of them. The man truly had a personality demanding both respect and obedience, no matter how quietly he spoke. I snapped my useless lips shut and nodded.

"Then ask your questions," Alexis said, folding his arms across his chest as he circled the slab to stand behind Dempsey. "There's still too much to do for us to waste time dawdling."

I looked over my shoulder, licking my drying lips as I gripped my neck. "What if he refuses to answer my questions?"

Alexis leaned over Dempsey's shoulder while staying out of the criminal's line of sight and smiled one of his predatory smiles, displaying far too many glistening teeth. "Then I'll remind him it would be in his best interest to answer your questions just as he answered mine. Though remember where his line is. That's a line he's willing to die for. Also, be respectful should you discover others."

As I nodded, Alexis twirled his fingers, releasing the criminal from his invisible prison. Promptly, Dempsey launched into a tirade, promising me a future filled with all sorts of evil, some of which seemed rather unlikely or flat out impossible given the circumstances. I tried to give him the time he needed to work out his pent-up frustration. However, as I grew tired, I glanced at Alexis, and his finger crept toward Dempsey's chest.

The moment Alexis brushed his fingertip against Dempsey, his cries were so feral I had to clamp my hands over my ears. Once the echoes died to a whimper, I massaged my ears while Alexis casually brushed his fingers on his coat. While the whimpering was gone, grunts of anger returned as the bound criminal fought against his unrelenting bindings. After his failed struggle, Dempsey swallowed his pride, yet he mustered up enough anger to glare at me as if he were pressing a weapon to my head. "What do you want, dead man?"

While I knew Dempsey couldn't escape, I still didn't want to get too close to him. So I rubbed my chin as I inched closer. When I was within arm's reach, my initial question flew from my mouth. "How extensive was your check on me?"

"What are you talking about?"

I leaned forward, letting my nose hover just above his as I drew in several deep breaths. "How deeply did you dig into my life?"

"You cheated me!"

The suddenness of Dempsey's harsh response, in addition to its vitriol, forced me to step away as I rubbed the inside of my ears once more.

When the echoes died off, the crime lord's eyes narrowed, and he continued with the same fire but with a softer voice. "I know everything there is to know about you."

CHAPTER 21

I took a step forward, thrusting a finger in his face. "Have you investigated and targeted anyone in my life?"

A scoff broke the momentary stillness before a horse chuckle chased it away. "Do you think I'd put anyone else under the same scrutiny as you? You were the one who cheated me!"

I grabbed Dempsey's night shirt and pulled him up, letting the rough stone bite into his skin. "Did you make a bullet for my friend?"

As blood began pooling around the stone edges, an invisible force struck me. Reflexively, I released him and massaged my stinging hands. With a brief glance up, I saw Alexis shaking his head and mouthing 'don't do that.'

Licking my lips, I stared into the twin whirlpools that were Dempsey's gray eyes. "Are you targeting my friend?"

"Matt has nothing to worry about. While the life of a two-bit criminal might be relevant to you, he's inconsequential to me. You're the one who cheated me and is now betraying me. The moment I'm free, the case containing your bullet will be handed over to a troubleshooter who will ensure you meet your punishment. Your death will be the end of it. So don't worry, your friend is safe from my retribution."

My gaze fell to the floor as I chewed over those callous words. While he confirmed I'd be looking over my shoulder for the rest of my life, at least Matt wouldn't share my fate, provided Dempsey was as honest as his reputation made him out to be. When pain lanced up from my palms, I glanced down at my hands and found my nails digging into my skin. With an intense effort, I spread my fingers wide as I latched onto Dempsey's hardening glare.

"Did you really talk to Bella?" While I'd been curious about this ever since he mentioned it to me in the freezer, I wasn't sure why I asked the question. Though Dempsey's scoff and Alexis's gasp told me everything I needed to know about what they thought of it. I pushed their reactions from my mind and drew my thumb across my lower lip. "Did you talk with her after you abducted me?"

"Yes," Dempsey said, his eyes narrowing into slits, "I spoke with my niece."

I pressed my hand on the cracked stone and pressed my face next to his. "What did the two of you talk about?"

"About you being my newest employee, of course. I thought we . . ."

I pushed myself away from Dempsey and glanced at Alexis, who immediately pressed his finger on the crime lord's chest, eliciting another series of deafening cries. When the sounds of Dempsey's agony died, I stepped forward, grasped his shirt, and yanked him into the stone restraints. "What did you really talk about?"

When another wave of hatred flared behind his eyes, I flinched. Though I quickly corralled my courage and inched forward, tightening my grip on his shirt as a growl emerged from my throat. "What's the truth, Dempsey?"

"As soon as I had you escorted from the main hall, she rushed down to demand what was happening to you. She wanted to know why I didn't present you with your winnings like I'd done with her the year before. I explained that you and I had something special to discuss, and so while I was busy with the remaining guests, my men would entertain you."

I released Dempsey's clothing and brushed the wrinkles away. "Did she believe you?"

"No," Dempsey said, barring his teeth, "she didn't. She wanted to know what was so important to discuss. I told her we were going to speak privately about the employment opportunity we discussed earlier."

"What was her reaction to that?"

CHAPTER 21

"She called me a liar before collecting her winnings and storming out. Her little spat created a controversy amongst the remaining finalists, presenting me with a mess to clean up. But what can I do? She's family, or at least she was."

I gripped Dempsey's neck and squeezed, not enough to choke him but enough for him to fear I'd go too far. "What does that mean?"

"Given her connection to you, I'll have to deal with her," Dempsey said with a gasping voice.

Who did he think he was threatening? Was the crime lord trying to regain a semblance of control after waking up completely outmatched? Despite my trembling knees, my face contorted into a sneer as I tightened my grasp ever so slightly. "Given that you've admitted lying to me, what makes you think you're walking out of this cave alive?"

For the first time, in what was probably at least a decade or two, fear washed over Dempsey's features. His eyes flicked about, searching for help, but when he couldn't find it, his quivering eyes came back to me as a quiet plea escaped his lips. "Neither of you has the fortitude to kill indiscriminately."

While that statement rang true for me, after the conversation with Alexis, I wasn't so sure Dempsey was safe from him. While Alexis might present a friendly and civilized face to the world, there was a part of him that could hand out death. Dempsey's plea consisted of hollow words whose purpose was to convince himself that he was safe.

"Define killing, Bertrand," Alexis said, breaking the budding stillness.

As he walked around the stone slab, Dempsey railed against his stone restraints, searching for Alexis. "What are you talking about?"

A predatory smile spread across Alexis's face as he stepped

beside me. "I want you to give me your definition of the word. That way, we're all on the same page."

Dempsey's silence emphasized how far he'd fallen from the man who had loomed over me in his freezer, and it added another layer of terror within me.

"No answer." Alexis reached out and pressed a fingertip against Dempsey's exposed chest. "What do you think would happen to you if Francis and I simply left? Specifically, when you're discovered missing. I guarantee you no one will ever find you in this place."

"Annabelle will," Dempsey said, forcing a frail sternness into his words. "She's always able to find me."

My eyes bounced between the two men as I inched closer. "Is that something your witch can do?"

"While you're the first to enter and escape my home without raising an alarm," Dempsey said, his voice regaining his reputational coolness with every word, "this isn't the first time I've needed to be rescued. After that debacle, Annabelle cast a spell on me, and now she's able to find me wherever I am in the world."

I grabbed Alexis's elbow and pulled him away from Dempsey. "Is that something we can do?"

"While I might face some discomfort in the short term," Dempsey said, flashing us a broad smile, "I won't be here for long. And once I've rejoined my men, I'll use everything within my power to lay waste to both of you and everyone you hold dear."

Alexis glided back to the slab, slamming it with his fist like a ten-pound sledge, knocking off a chunk of the stone. "While I can't prevent Annabelle from eventually finding you, I can delay her long enough for nature to take its course." Alexis pressed his fingertip into Dempsey's chest, and it began to glow the same light as before. "Do you know what'll happen if we abandon you?"

CHAPTER 21

"You cannot stop her magic," Dempsey said between cries of pain.

"Bertrand, I promise you that you'll die of dehydration long before your witch breaks through my defenses." With a sigh, Alexis withdrew his finger, revealing a patch of scarred flesh.

"If I die," Dempsey said, spittle flying from his mouth with every syllable, "I go knowing both of you will join me in short order. And given your skills, my men will switch to other methods that are less discriminating than a bullet, increasing the damage done to your loved ones."

Alexis shook his head as he placed his fingertips on Dempsey's forehead. "I'm sorry, but I'd rather not deal with your tongue while we plan our next steps. Goodbye, Bertrand."

Instantly, the crime lord slumped in his stone prison. As he turned around, the stone returned to its original shape, including absorbing the broken piece on the ground. With a snap, the unconscious crime lord rose from the polished slab and drifted into the cab of Alexis's truck. Once he secured Dempsey, Alexis spun and clapped my shoulder. "Don't worry, I'll figure out a way to keep you alive."

"Were you serious about leaving him here?"

Alexis's back straightened as he walked back to the vehicle. "It was my original idea." Alexis paused, thumping the hood with his hands. He glanced back at me and pointed to the passenger's seat. "Though I was surprised that you threatened him with it before I got the chance."

"What are we going to do?" I asked as I hopped into the truck.

Alexis opened his door and pounded the roof with his fist. "I don't know. If I left him in that tomb, his personal forger would have breached my safe house, and while I'd survive the loss, it would have been a major inconvenience, especially since I was bluffing about keeping her out."

I slapped my thighs and threw my head against the headrest. "That brings us back to the question at hand. What are we going to do with him? We can't kill him because of the potential collateral damage, and he's too slippery to get arrested."

"It's worse than that," Alexis said, running his fingers through his hair. "He has enough connections that the police wouldn't arrest him unless they caught him in the act. And even then, they'd still try to avoid putting the cuffs on him. Though his lawyers would ensure he'd get away with anything short of murder."

I clasped my hands over my mouth as I stared into the phantom maw of the beast through the windshield. "What do you think would happen if we arranged that situation?"

Alexis put a knee on his seat as he grasped my shoulder. "What's tumbling through your mind?"

Twisting in my seat, I lifted my forefinger. "We need to remove the threat that Dempsey poses to us and the people in our lives."

"Yes."

"If we kill him, directly or indirectly, those orders will get sent out," I said, extending a second finger.

"I would agree," Alexis said, slipping into the car. He turned the engine over and closed the door. "Though you still haven't provided an option to our current predicament."

I lifted a third finger, turning toward the truck's bed. "People like him don't do anything themselves. They use intermediaries to isolate and protect themselves from legal actions."

"What are you getting at?"

I clenched my fingers and looked into Alexis's eyes as I ran my tongue along my teeth. "How do you think his underlings or associates would react if he was caught red-handed, standing over a dead body with the literal smoking gun?"

CHAPTER 21

Alexis released the brake, and the car started inching forward. "But as you said, men like Dempsey don't get their hands dirty, so it's a moot point."

"We'll circle back to that," I said as the vehicle started vanishing. "For now, let's assume Dempsey got caught in that situation. What do you think the fallout would be?"

"It would upend his life." Alexis folded his arms as our bodies started to disappear. But after a few seconds his head shook back and forth as he grasped the steering wheel. "It might derail a few things. However, it won't remove the bounty on your head, and we'd need someone who was willing to die." He slammed his palms against the wheel and looked down at me with a sorrowful smile. "No, the best path forward is to keep moving him so that his witch is always a step behind. After a week or so, he'll just be a high-profile missing person."

Once the vehicle reclaimed its place in Alexis's driveway, I grabbed his forearm, tugged it off the wheel, and beckoned him to lean in. Once he parked the truck, he obliged me, and I explained my plan. While there were some gasps of disbelief and brief protests. In the end he sat up rubbing his chin. As a silence stretched out, I studied the still body in the bed and asked a final pair of questions. "What do you think? Do you think it's worth trying?"

Several seconds later, he turned to study Dempsey with me as he answered, "If you're willing to risk it all, then we might have a workable solution."

CHAPTER 22

After clapping my shoulder, Alexis climbed out of his truck. As he stood in the pale moonlight, he twirled his fingers, and Dempsey's body vanished. I whirled back to stare at him, and as I clambered out of the vehicle, I forced my jaw shut. However, before I rounded the truck's engine, Alexis had opened the door and waited for me to enter, but instead of entering, I grabbed his arm and pulled him closer. "Do you think we can pull this stunt off?"

"Oh, this is by no means something that I would take on lightly." Despite the halfhearted smile, he pushed me inside before leading me to a room next to the entryway. Upon entering the new chamber, he thrust a pair of fingers toward the empty couch and Dempsey's body appeared as if he'd been carelessly dropped onto the cushions. Alexis quickly pulled me into a conspiratorial hug as he prodded my side. "Have you already lost confidence in this scheme of yours, boy?"

I wasted no time in freeing myself from his grasp and facing him. "When will you start using my name?"

"Once you've progressed far enough," Alexis said as his hands slammed together. Before the sound could echo off the walls, a rift opened behind him. "Hop on through. Your idea requires a tremendous amount of preparation."

"How much of your hand movements are for show?" I asked as I approached the circular hole.

"All of them," Alexis said, shoving me through the opening, "and none of them. Unfortunately, we don't have time for a deep dive into the mechanics of forgery that would explain the apparent contradiction."

Once I regained my footing, I pulled up to my full height and studied my newest surroundings, only to realize I'd been here a few moments ago. I turned in time to see Alexis walk through his rift, joining me in the massive cavern. "I was appreciating your work."

Alexis's finger flew up, twitching as he brushed past me. "While I appreciate your quick wit and the resulting questions, your apprehension for following directions doesn't bode well for your graduating past the appellation of boy."

As I sauntered over to the empty slab, I rested my fingertips on the polished surface. "Can you do everything I'm assuming you can?"

"I'm not sure what you assume I can do."

My eyes slammed shut as I pinched the bridge of my nose. While the man could probably dispense with me in countless ways, he had more in common with a teacher than someone wielding the authority of a judge, jury, and an executioner. "Is what I've witnessed you do tonight something trivial, or have you been straining to achieve it all?"

"I've done everything up to now countless times before."

"Okay, so nothing you've done is out of the ordinary. That's good and terrifying to know." I turned back to the open portal, licking my lips. "But why did we leave here just to come back without Dempsey?"

"Did you pay attention to your own plan?" Alexis asked,

patting my back. Before I could reply, he squeezed a shoulder and waved a hand at the opening. As it dwindled to a point, he snapped his fingers and two chairs rose from the earth, flanking the smooth slab. With another snap, a new portal emerged right behind each seat. "The only way your plan has a chance of working is if I appear to be home, and that's difficult if my truck's absent."

"That's a fair point." I peered through the portal nearest me, finding a forest lit by the midday sun. When I glanced at the other, I found a simple yet modern kitchen. With a click of my tongue, I walked closer to the gateway leading to the vibrant patch of trees. "Though that doesn't explain why you left Dempsey behind."

"While I admitted not being able to obfuscate his forger's ability to find him, there are still more defenses built within my home that don't exist here." When he turned me around, he must have seen the confusion pouring out of every pore, because wry laughter filled the stone chamber. "That's a fancy way of saying his forger can't take Dempsey without me knowing about it."

"Oh, how's that work?"

"Stop looking for secrets in every word, boy. You're not ready." Alexis reached out and patted my head as if I was a cute dog with sad, bulging eyes. "All that matters is that Dempsey's unconscious, and without my intervention, he will not wake up on his own. With him secured out of our way, we'll be free to handle all our preparations for your festivities."

"Despite your confidence that his witch can't free him without your knowledge, aren't you worried that she'll still free him and unravel our plans?"

Alexis glanced at his watch and shook his head. "Given the hour, we have a decent amount of time before that becomes a worry." He clapped my back and guided me to the chair next to the opening leading to the forest. Once he shoved me into the seat, he turned around and walked forward, the stone parting ahead of him and then sealing up in his wake.

"Now you're showing off."

A hearty belly laugh washed over me as Alexis claimed his seat. He scratched the corner of his mouth as he looked past me. "Normally, I wouldn't even think of showing you anything like what I'll have to for this plan to succeed. Much less condone explaining some of the details behind it, but this isn't a normal situation."

I grabbed the stone slab's edge and leaned forward with widening eyes. "You're going to teach me some tricks, aren't you?"

Alexis shook his head while lifting a hand. "While your solution is more than a little convoluted, I think you're right. It's the best way to undermine Dempsey's power and influence." Alexis laid a hand on the stone and pulled it up, drawing an axe from it. He laid the tool down between us and pushed it toward me. "While there's a chance to break a fair amount of his more professional criminal ties, I doubt it'll shatter all of them. However, it should be enough for our purposes."

I grabbed the axe and studied it. Despite the newness of the tool, it felt like it had been well used for more than a decade. And when I pressed my finger against the blade, I could feel how fine of an edge it was. Placing it down, I looked over my shoulder. "So while you do the cool transformations, I'll be out there collecting some firewood?"

"Given my knowledge and skills, with enough time, I could execute this plan without help."

My gaze drifted back to Alexis as I wrapped my hand around the shaft. "How about when you factor in the looming time constraints?"

"There's no chance." Alexis wrapped a hand around his chin as he leaned his elbows against the slab. "I'm going to need help, and I don't have the opportunity to reach out to those with the needed experience."

"Does that mean you're going to teach me some tricks?"

Alexis snapped, and an invisible force wrapped around my mouth. As I reached up to struggle with nothing, he reached out, slapping my hands down. Then, with a beckoning finger, something dragged me into the stone, and it gave way like soft putty. It quickly engulfed my legs before solidifying.

"This will be tricky, but with a little luck, we should be able to pull it off." He lifted a twitching finger as he leaned forward. "To achieve success, I'll be exposing you to subjects that you're ill-prepared to comprehend. If you don't do exactly what I tell you and, more importantly, when I tell you, I'll cut my losses and figure something else out that might not be as equitable for all involved. Do you understand?"

I nodded.

"Good," Alexis said as he moved the axe to the side, while placing his other hand on the table. This time when he pulled his hand away, roughly two dozen small stones trickled out of it. He plucked one from the pile, and it altered into a sealed hand warmer, like the one I'd affixed to my chest. "How are you at making these?"

I pulled my jacket and shirt aside, displaying the fresh hand warmer stuck to my chest. "They're a relatively inexpensive source of heat, but I've never made them, not when most places offer them for sale."

He tossed the sealed one next to the axe before sliding the remaining stones toward me. "If you're aware of them, why do you lug an electronic one around?"

CHAPTER 22

"Free is better than cheap," I said, pulling the small device from a pocket. "While I have to charge this after each use, it doesn't require any body heat. Provided the battery is full, they provide far more warmth with the flick of a button."

Alexis rapped his knuckles against the stone wrapped around my legs, and immediately it receded, freeing me. "Just because something is free doesn't mean it's good for you. While you continue to change these stones into sealed hand warmers, I'm going to prepare some hot tea." He jerked a thumb over his shoulder as he rose. "Would you like some?"

"We're under a deadline," I said, gesturing between us, "and you're going to make tea?"

"It's another source of warmth, and we'll need all we can get." He walked to the opening behind him and paused halfway through it. "If you're not much of a tea drinker, I have coffee and hot chocolate; they all get the job done. The hand warmers seep through from the surface, but the drinks will work from within. You'd be amazed at how often that pairing will simplify your life or save it, depending on the scenario."

I grabbed a stone from the slab and forced heat through the mental image of a hand warmer. When my transformation was done, I added it to the one Alexis created and plucked another stone from the pile. "That makes sense, though I hate to admit that it's something I never connected."

"That's a yes to the tea." Alexis walked through the opening, and as soon as he was on the other side, it closed. Then a small opening formed in the middle of the table and two porcelain mugs slid out while Alexis's voice filled the chamber. "Talent, you have in spades, yet I can fill a thimble with your common sense."

"Hey!"

"I'm going to have an uphill job training you, provided this craziness goes according to plan," Alexis said as he slid more things through the opening. "How many stones do you have left to alter?"

"I just started, and I've never done this before," I said, tossing another freshly altered stone onto the growing pile. "Though each of these is taking more than a trivial amount of heat to make."

"That's due to your reliance on the electronic gizmos," Alexis said, sliding a few canisters and a couple of steaming pitchers out of the opening. "The more you do it, the easier it will become."

When the small portal popped out of existence, another large one opened beside the empty chair, and Alexis slipped back into his seat. The moment he settled across from me, he picked up one of the steaming kettles and poured the hot liquid into both mugs. With a fatherly smile, he slid one toward me. "This is black tea sweetened with a little honey."

I accepted the mug and took a sip. While there were some bitter tones cutting through the heavy dose of sweetness, I let the warm liquid linger in my mouth before swallowing it and letting the warmth fill my core. "It's not too bad."

Alexis peeked over his mug and asked, "What's wrong with it?"

"I like your definition of little," I said, tapping my drink before taking another sip. "Though despite the addition of honey, it's still bitter."

"Sorry." Alexis took a swig from his own mug before brandishing it like a weapon. "I prefer stronger tea, particularly when I'm doing something crazy. And given our pressing need, I heated some concentrated tea. Unfortunately, that naturally comes with bitter notes. However, with the dose of honey I use, typically it doesn't bother me."

I swallowed more of the liquid warmth and peered into

Alexis's eyes as it slid down my throat. As it resupplied my body with precious heat, I wrapped my fingers around the warm mug, letting the heated porcelain soothe my fingers. "Now that we've secured an ample supply of heat, what's up next?"

"We prepare our victim."

After we finished all our errands, we sat beside the stone slab and stared at the pile of raw components needed for my plan. I slid my cup toward Alexis while laying the axe down beside the pile. He promptly touched the tool, and it seeped back into the slab while he refilled my cup. When he finished, I added a couple dollops of honey and took a long pull of the steaming beverage. "How are we going to knit all that together?"

Alexis smacked his lips as he brought his steaming mug to his face. He drew a plume of steam into his nose before draining his mug while he tossed a spent hand warmer over his shoulder. "We don't have access to enough heat for me to fuel the forgery that we need."

"Then why did we go collect all of this? What are we going to do now that we wasted our time?"

"We haven't, and we're going to do something I'm not happy about," Alexis said as he laid the empty cup down. "Despite my experience with the field, I'd have to be standing in the middle of a bonfire, to hopefully have access to all the heat we require."

I laid my cup down and dropped my head into my hands. "If that's true, are we going to abandon the plan?"

"No," Alexis said, snatching another hand warmer. He quickly popped the wrapper and pressed the pouch to his neck as he stared at the ceiling. "What it means is we'll have to tackle the forgery together, and we'll have to have a massive heat source to boot."

I peered into the mug and licked my lips. "I didn't taste any booze or hallucinogenic compound in this, but you never know."

"What are you going on about?"

I laid the drink down and swabbed my ears with my fingers. "I'm sorry, but did you say we?"

"Yes, boy, I said we," Alexis said with a sigh as he grabbed the kettle. After refilling his cup, he doctored it with a large shovelful of honey. After he stirred the drink, he brought it to his nose and inhaled a lungful of his tea. "Do you have a problem learning a new skill?"

"Absolutely not." I grabbed a couple of hand warmers, freed them from their wrappings, and affixed them to my chest. "You'll never have to worry about me refusing to learn something new. But based on what you're saying, it sounds like we'll be working on a forgery together."

"Yeah, there's a special technique that allows us to do that."

"That's possible?"

As Alexis's hearty laughter filled the cavern, the steam from the cup wafted across his face. When the echoes of mirth faded, Alexis laid his mug down and clapped his hands. "I keep forgetting that you're about as knowledgeable as a newborn babe."

"Hey!"

"Settle down," Alexis said, wrapping his fingers around the porcelain mug. "It isn't an insult, it's a fact. But yes, you and I, as external forgers, can funnel our body heat into any other forger."

"Given what you said, wouldn't we still need more heat?"

"We're going to need a bonfire, or a forge, one or the other." Alexis stood up and walked to one end of the slab and pulled up another bit of stone, creating a spherical firepit. After opening a small portal, Alexis pulled several pieces of firewood from it and piled them up in the pit's bottom. Once he laid the last one, the small portal vanished, and the logs burst into flames. "Thankfully, the transfer isn't strictly linear. Despite attempts to figure things out, we've never been able to understand why heat offered in this manner is always magnified."

"Seriously?"

"Yes, and don't go prying for more information. This is essentially a doctorate level course that you're getting exposed to, without the benefit of the backing theory as we understand it." As the flames intensified, Alexis dragged the spherical pit a few feet away from our components and stepped between the two stone structures. "Given our constraints, I'm going to talk you through the process. Thankfully, with your natural skill, I'm pretty sure you'll be able to pull it off."

"You think you can talk me through it without the required experience?"

"Yes, considering I'm the one who teaches this to externals when they're ready."

"Oh, okay," I said, sipping my tea.

"Unfortunately, if your plan is going to work, this is our only play." Alexis plucked his drink off the slab and gave me a salute. "Drink up and whatever you do, don't skimp on the heat sources. For the foreseeable future, it's better that we run our bodies too hot than play it safe."

Rubbing my mouth with both hands, I peered down my fingers as my tongue probed my cheeks. "What do you mean?"

While the escaping steam tumbled up Alexis's face, he drew in a mouthful of the warm vapor. "You know that at a certain temperature the human body stops functioning, correct?"

I nodded.

"While we can escape most of the ill effects of high body

temperatures through forgeries," Alexis said as his fingers around his mug whitened, "there are chances for complications."

I leaned away from him and the looming fire as I pushed my tea away. "Then why would we risk it?"

Alexis laid his cup down and started picking up hand warmers. With a series of methodical motions, he opened the package and affixed them to his body. After the fifth one, he grabbed the sixth and flashed me a sorrowful grin. "Given what we need to do, we'll be better off trying to ride our body's limitations. I figure if we shoot to skirt a temp of a hundred and eight, we should pull this off."

With a nod, I grabbed a few more hand warmers and followed suit. As I fixed the fourth one on my arm, I raised a finger. "What else is there for me to learn?"

With a small scowl crossing his lips, Alexis stuck the sixth one to his side and plucked a seventh from the pile. He waved the unopened package at me as if it were a weapon. "You'll learn everything I know about forging later and over many years, provided we survive this mess. However, I need you to focus on my instructions as you dabble in things well above your understanding."

"Can you try to explain some of the theory behind what we're doing?"

"No." Alexis's tone let me know I wasn't going to get anything else from him. He snatched the last warmer from the slab and unwrapped it. With a shake, he pressed it to his neck and gave me a withering glare. "You'll learn more than you need to throughout the night. And with every extra question, you're delaying and endangering your plan."

"Okay, I'll keep my inquisitive nature in check."

"There is nothing inherently wrong with being curious, boy. In fact, that's how we find our limitations and define our abilities.

Just make a mental note of your questions and, in time, we'll go through them if we survive."

"Oh, that's a warm and fuzzy attitude."

Alexis grabbed the slab and pulled it up to his waist, and the collection of raw materials drifted toward him. Once everything was within easy reach, Alexis pressed his hands on the pile as his chest fell. "Alright, get behind me, boy. It's time for your crash course. And yes, if you don't follow my instructions to the letter, you can die doing this."

"What?"

Without pulling his hands from the pile, he looked over his shoulder. "Do you see why I normally wouldn't even consider exposing you to this technique without years of study under your belt? And that assumes you've been an exceptional student."

With a shudder racing down my neck, I walked between Alexis and the blazing fire. It didn't take long for the heat to roll off the blaze and amplify the effects of the hand warmers and hot beverages. I widened my stance and got comfortable. "I'm all ears."

"Okay," Alexis said, turning back to the collection. He took a deep breath and closed his eyes. "The first step is pretty much what you expect with any forgery. Gather all the warmth that you plan to give me."

After taking several deep breaths, I tagged all the spare heat coursing through my body. Once I finished identifying it, I opened my eyes. "Done, what's next?"

Alexis's head swept back and forth as he pinched the bridge of his nose. "You don't have to check off every step in the process." He placed his hand back on the pile and his chest swelled, like a balloon testing its limitations. "After doing that, place your hand somewhere on my exposed skin, like the back of my neck. Before I try to tell you the next steps, make sure everything is ready."

I followed Alexis's orders and laid my hand on his neck as I gathered all the heat I could spare. Then, considering what we were trying to do and the numerous heat sources available, I pulled a bit more. Not a lot, but more than I originally planned. Despite Dempsey's bullet hanging over me, I didn't want to flirt with hypothermia. "What's next?"

"You need to focus your mind on the part of your hand that is touching my skin." Alexis said, rolling his shoulders, forcing his neck against my hand. "And as with all forgery, you need a pristine mental image for this to work."

"You just lost me," I said, licking my lips as I inched closer. "What kind of picture am I supposed to form?"

Alexis's chest swelled as his head tilted back. "You're going to create a mental picture of a tunnel leading from your hand and ending in my neck. I'll agree this is more of an abstract image, but you can get a clear enough picture in your mind."

"Alright," I said with a shrug as I closed my eyes and chewed my lips. "I think I have a starting point."

"Good," Alexis said, as the sound of moving stone thundered in the chamber. "The next step is to force the gathered heat through the tunnel. The only caveat here is you must do it slowly."

"Why?"

"Because if you don't keep it slow, you'll end up creating a fireball instead of a heat transfer."

"Oh, fun," I said, furrowing my brow. While the abstract image was simple to create, when I swirled the heat with my will, the resulting combination didn't have the expected results. "Is there anything else? Because I can't power this heat transfer."

"Are you feeling an absence of sensation?"

"Yeah."

"Good, you're on the right path. Keep doing it, and you'll

know everything is fine when the heat lingering around your funnel suddenly drains from you. When that happens, don't fight the
swiftness of the transfer. Instead, allow it to happen or you'll just
waste part of the heat you're attempting to give me."

My eyes snapped open as I rolled my head. "Which is it, rapid
or slow?"

"You're overthinking this," Alexis said as the slab rose higher
and drifted closer to him. "Simply push slowly in the beginning.
However, once the heat is flowing, don't interfere with the swiftness of the transfer."

I closed my eyes and focused on the mental connection
between us. It took all my concentration, but eventually I felt the
heat begin to seep through my palm and flow into Alexis's neck.
After a handful of heartbeats, the gathered heat rushed through
the funnel. As the transfer neared the end of what I had prepared,
it didn't stop. While I was confused, I wondered if this is what
he meant about the not so linear nature of the transfer. After a
few additional heartbeats, I fell to my knees yet somehow main-
tained contact and the transfer with Alexis, despite the odd angle.
However, I stopped worrying about the unexpected nature of the
transfer when the world went black.

Sometime later, I woke up when Alexis jostled my shoulder
and handed me a steaming mug. "You gave me too much heat.
Be more careful in the future. Fortunately, I was able to use the
excess to make our forgery a permanent one."

Gripping the mug with one hand, I rose to a sitting position and
rubbed my throbbing head. "I didn't think that was part of the plan."

"Drink up." Alexis tapped the mug in my hand and dropped
into a seat that emerged from the stone floor. "Even with the

heat transfer, I didn't think we'd have enough warmth for that purpose. However, you gave me more than enough."

"How will it hold up long term?"

Alexis's head turned toward me as he flashed me a patient smile, like what a father would give to a struggling child. "In my youth I was an extremely talented doctor, and as such, quite a student of anatomy. With the abundant supply of fuel you provided, I made a perfect forgery. It'll hold up just fine."

I took a swig of the hot tea and sighed. A moment later, I rubbed my face and felt a line of lumps running down my arms. "I have two questions for you."

"Just two?"

"Let's start with those," I said, pulling my shirt away from my chest, and noting the additional hand warmers. "First, what happened?"

"You transferred too much heat, a potential pitfall even for those who possess the proper training. It's far too easy for a forger to forget the required heat to power the transference."

"Oh," I said, taking another sip of the steaming tea. "Is that all?"

"No," Alexis said, twisting toward the fire and extending a beckoning finger. Instantly, the spherical firepit obeyed his command and drifted closer to me. "However, besides that misallocation of body heat, you also assumed the external heat sources would mute the ill effects. As a result, after the transfer, you collapsed, and I was forced to return some heat after I made our prop."

Alexis pulled a poker from the ground and moved the logs about, teasing brighter flames. Once he was satisfied with the increase in heat, he slammed the tool into the ground and refilled my empty mug. "What's your other question?"

With another pull of the steaming liquid, I could feel my core warming back up to a normal level. "How close was I to dying?"

CHAPTER 22

He tapped an armrest with a fingertip, and in response the stone split, forming a small opening. After taking another sip, Alexis placed his drink in the custom cup holder and leaned forward on his knees. "As I said, it was an honest mistake, though you're fortunate that you didn't follow in the footsteps of other reckless forgers. Fortunately for you, I didn't pass out from my forgery, though, truthfully, it was a close call."

"You nearly passed out?" I asked with rising alarm.

With a small chuckle, Alexis said, "Yes. This was the most dangerous part of your plan, well dangerous from the forging aspect. I shouldn't have to tell you what would have happened to both of us had I passed out."

"I would have died," I said before downing the rest of my cup.

When he saw the fear in my eyes, he finished his thought. "But I didn't pass out, and I kept you from dying because of your enthusiasm."

"So what now?"

With a fatherly smile, Alexis said, "We set the stage for the closing act of this drama." He rose from the chair and extended his hand toward me. "Come, we have far too much to do to prepare."

"Are you sure about this plan?"

"Despite the issue with the transfer," Alexis said, bending down to grab my shoulders, "this is a decent plan, convoluted but decent. Don't worry about potential dangers. No plan survives its implementation." He dragged me to my feet and clapped my back. "Fortunately, I'm ready for whatever wrinkles come my way."

I forced my lips into a halfhearted smile and looked at the dancing flames. "Let's get started then."

CHAPTER 23

Alexis sauntered to the large bay window and laid his fingers on the glass. He allowed a silence to build as his fingertips turned white. After several tense moments, he spun around, grasping his hands behind his back as he marched toward me. "While this plan of yours has taken a lot out of us, I want you to know I didn't accept this course of events just for you."

"Then why?"

"I accepted it because of the threat Dempsey poses to the people I'm responsible for, including you."

"No pressure," I said, stepping back and bumping into the wall opposite the bay mirror. The burden of his scrutiny bore down on me like a thousand-pound weight. My legs trembled as I clenched the muscles, trying to prevent myself from collapsing into a puddle. "I'll do my best."

With a chuckle, he placed his hand against the wall, and a portal appeared beside me. Several heartbeats after the rift opened, Alexis grasped my shoulder and squeezed. "All any of us can do is our best. Keep the goal at the forefront of your mind."

"And what's my goal?"

He clapped my arm and flashed me a lopsided grin. "Ultimately, I can't answer what your motivation is." He thumped his chest with his fingers as his smile widened. "For me, I'm doing this for the hope that you and every forger in this country will be free from Dempsey's meddling hands."

"That does sound like a decent reason." I reached out, grasping his arm and pulling him closer to me. "But I'm terrified about what we're about to do."

"I'd be worried if you were calm." Alexis stepped through the opening and turned around, blocking my view of the other end of the tunnel. "Pay attention and don't forget about everything we discussed. If you're late with any of the preparations, this will be for naught."

"Are you certain about your projections?"

A soft laugh slipped through the portal as it diminished. "While I'm not the Master of Illusions, my simulations are usually accurate enough to satisfy all but the most exacting of tacticians. Now prepare yourself and be ready."

When I remembered how to breathe, another message from Alexis thundered through the front room, rebounding off the walls. Each syllable sunk the overall message into my brain, like a brand searing an owner's mark into his cattle. "Don't forget, even with a promise of clemency, your fate rests upon a knife's edge. If you stray too far in either direction, you'll find yourself lost to us all."

As the second stretched out into minutes, little marbles of colored air tumbled from my fingers and rebounded off the floor, vanishing as they soared over the hardwood. Unlike earlier that evening, I didn't mind being alone in Alexis's home despite the looming threat of our plan. I gripped the latest marble and stared at the swirling orange hues. It's amazing what a little knowledge can do for your life.

Unfortunately, the impending risk to our plan kept me from focusing on anything other than the most trivial use of the newest skills I'd developed. While it was worth perfecting my transformations with air, after the hundredth or maybe the thousandth, it was becoming monotonous. After dropping my latest marble, a sigh rushed from my lips as I withdrew my phone and checked the time.

With a groan, I shoved the device back into my pocket and I positioned my hand next to my chest with my palm facing the ground. Closing my eyes, I started creating marbles and letting them fall. At first, I created a new one once I heard the first bounce off the floor. However, after a few seconds, I created a steady stream of them. When I stopped the flow, I opened my eyes and smiled at the rainbow strewn about my feet.

I quickly dropped to my knees and started gathering all the loose bundles of condensed air, dispersing each with a touch. Once most were gone, I rose, stretching my sides. Like Alexis had said, repetition was key to mastering a new technique. The rapid creation and destruction of the marbles made the process more natural, and after that batch, I knew creating them had become as simple as breathing.

Of course, all that practice made me realize just how unskilled I had been before meeting Alexis. He'd made many comments about my ignorance, even comparing me to a baby. When he'd lobbed them at me, I thought he was simply insulting the man who had wanted to kill him. However, after everything else, I realized he was simply making an accurate comparison to highlight my ignorance of this hidden world. I'd been skating around this world's periphery for some time, somehow just keeping out of its reach.

I grabbed another marble and tossed it into the air as I

wondered how my life would be different if I'd stumbled into someone like Alexis years ago. As my mind started crafting a narrative of that hypothetical life, a revving engine shattered the tranquility wrapped about Alexis's home. As soon as I adopted a proper stance, preparing to flee or fight, a massive SUV plowed through the bay window.

For the first time in my life, the world seemed to slow to a crawl. In that instant, I felt like I'd be able to count every shard of shattering glass, every bursting fiber from the wall's timber, and each clump of drywall as it hung in the air, like a photograph of a cresting wave. Despite the promised devastation, I could see the beauty in the unfurling chaos, and for a singular moment, I saw it all.

But before anything else could happen, time resumed its normal cadence, and the promised violence washed over the room like the wave washing away a child's sandcastle. Once the initial devastation was complete, a figure emerged from the vehicle and stalked through the debris, entering Alexis's home.

It was Dempsey, and rage filled those stormy gray eyes. Despite Alexis's assurance, the crime lord was standing in front of me, and his desire for revenge seeped from his every pore. With legs accustomed to polished floors, Dempsey clambered over the rubble and stumbled into Alexis's home as he withdrew a large pistol from under his jacket. As he scanned the devastation, he tapped the barrel against his leg, but when he found me, his eyes narrowed into slits as he leveled the gun at my chest.

Before I could react, three gunshots filled the room, and my body collapsed. As I laid there, blood seeped out of the bullet holes and the crime lord stalked over to me. Once he loomed over me, he kicked my crumpled form with his shoe. When I didn't move, he squatted down and pressed the gun into my temple.

CHAPTER 24

The crime lord looked over his shoulder and flashed me a wide smile as he snapped his fingers. Instantly, a shimmering barrier flared up between him and the car. "Do you think the three shots are sufficient? Or do we need to add one or two more?"

I twisted the doorknob and eased open the closet door, and the image I'd been watching winked out. "It's scary how much you look like Dempsey," I said walking into the devastated room.

With a wide smile, the faux Dempsey rose, spreading his arms wide as he walked across the debris scattered across the floor. "We discussed the illusion I'd be wearing before I left. Didn't you remember that detail?"

"I remembered, but that doesn't mean I was ready for it," I said, pointing at my lifeless doppelgänger before I looked at my chest, brushing it where Alexis had shot my double. "Or for witnessing someone shoot me three times."

Alexis wrapped his arm around me as he tapped the barrel against my chest. "Technically, you weren't shot, but I understand what you mean." He thrust the weapon at the body and asked, "However, my question still stands. Do you think our decoy needs any more bullet holes? Or do you believe that's a substantial amount of damage?"

My spine shivered as Alexis's arm tightened around me. "That should be enough, but can I ask you a question?"

"Provided that it's brief."

"For something that was never alive," I said, lifting a trembling finger toward my copy, "it's bleeding as if it was alive before you shot it."

"That body was never alive. There was never any brain activity," Alexis said, clapping my back as he sauntered over to the room's entrance and pulled Dempsey's unconscious body inside. "Just accept what I've told you."

"How will something that's never been alive fool any court of law?"

Alexis holstered his pistol as he guided Dempsey into place. "Stop trying to pry secrets out of me, boy."

"I'm not seeking secrets behind what you've done," I said as my hands shot up, highlighting my willingness to abide by his decisions. As Alexis planted the crime lord's feet on the debris a few feet from my doppelgänger, I licked my lips and inched forward. "The answer I'm hoping for is how you expect a judge or a jury to consider murder when the victim was never alive to begin with."

Alexis's head shook as he positioned Dempsey's arm in the body's general direction. With a sigh, he drew his weapon and walked around to put it into Dempsey's hand. "While I'd been hoping to create a temporary body that would revert to its original form . . ."

"You mean the tree I chopped down from that forest halfway around the world?"

"Yeah," Alexis said, patting the crime lord's stomach, "though I'm not sure why that bothered you so much."

"Why couldn't I grab a log from a nearby forest?"

"Under the original plan, something that foreign would have amplified the assumption that Dempsey arranged for the evidence to be stolen."

"Then why'd you alter the plan?"

Alexis shrugged as he adjusted Dempsey's grasp on the pistol. "We've discussed this, but to rehash it, I never thought we'd get enough heat to create a lasting duplicate." With a shrug, Alexis tightened the criminal's grasp on the weapon. "However, thanks to all the heat that you poured into me, there was an ample supply. As a result, I took a snapshot of your body, down to the molecular level. With that perfect image, I created a clone that will fool any insistent scientist.

"No one can identify our friend there as anyone other than you. And to answer your observation about the realistic bleeding, that's getting to some techniques that are inappropriate for you to know." Alexis finished wrapping Dempsey's hand around the pistol and walked back behind the crime lord to position the pistol in the rough direction of the doppelgänger. "Does that look good enough?"

"It should fool Dempsey."

"Good," Alexis said, pointing at the closet as the illusion wrapped around his face vanished. "Get back in there and don't come out. In fact, don't do anything that might let anyone know you're in there."

"Are you sure about this next step?"

With a wide smile, Alexis walked over to his place beside the double and dropped to his knees. "Boy, it's a little late to ask that question. Now get inside and don't ruin all our hard work."

I turned and stared at the devastation, highlighting the worst of it with a few gestures. After making a full revolution, my eyes dropped to Alexis, and I inched away, asking, "If the timing isn't perfect, do you think all this will be worth it?"

CHAPTER 24

As his snap thundered through the miniaturized battlefield, something grabbed my collar and dragged me back into the closet. The instant the door closed, the wall became transparent, at least from this side, giving me the perfect seat for the last act of this drama. Alexis turned toward me and, with a smile plastered on his face, he winked before his voice emerged from the ceiling. "If all I have to do is clean up broken glass and repair a damaged wall, I'd consider it a fair price to pay, even if the timing is less than ideal."

As soon as the force released me, I rushed to the two-way wall and watched the barrier separating Dempsey's vehicle and the rest of the room vanish. I clenched my fist and tapped the invisible divider. "I hope you're right."

After giving me a thumbs up, Alexis stretched out his hand and clenched it as if he was grasping a pistol. With a deep breath, he shifted his arm and Dempsey's outstretched limb followed. When both arms stopped moving, Alexis squeezed his finger, and in response, the gun in Dempsey's hands fired. I'm not sure how Alexis aimed it, but the shot was perfect. While he insisted on this detail, Alexis's positioning resulted in the bullet simply grazing his upper arm. With a loud cry, Alexis clamped his hand on the flesh wound, stifling the blood flow.

"With that, the curtain has finally lifted," I said, massaging my temples.

Alexis looked at me and gave me a curt nod as he snapped with his injured arm.

"What's happening?" Dempsey asked as his body quivered and took a step away from Alexis. The crime lord looked from the dead body to the wounded Alexis, and then to the gun in his hand. "Where am I?"

As Alexis tightened his grasp on his wound, he flipped onto his butt and scurried away from Dempsey. "I didn't think you got your hands dirty anymore. Why did you have to kill him? Why are you trying to kill me?"

Dempsey took a step forward as the trembling pistol steadied in his grasp. As he drew nearer, the crime lord's eyes narrowed to slits. "What are you talking about?"

As blood seeped between Alexis's fingers, he heaved several deep breaths as he pointed at my doppelgänger mingled with the debris of the accident. "Why'd you race down here to kill both of us?"

Dempsey's gray eyes roiled with rage as he stepped toward Alexis. "I don't know what's going on here, but since my traitor is already dead and you're wounded," Dempsey pulled the slide back to confirm that a round was chambered. He leveled the pistol at Alexis and inched forward as a sadistic grin spread across the criminal's face. "I suppose it makes sense to complete the removal of a thorn from my side."

"You won't kill me as easily as you did the boy," Alexis said as he twirled his injured hand and the barrel jerked away from Alexis. Thankfully, Alexis took advantage of the distraction and hopped to his knees before diving away from the crime lord. As his shoulder hit the ground, a barrage of gunshots thundered through the room. Fortunately, Alexis had rolled to his feet as the last echo died and he was already facing the armed criminal.

Unfortunately, Dempsey was faster than we had thought. In the blink of an eye, the crime lord went from facing away from me to staring right at me. As Alexis collapsed to his knees, I studied the gray eyes looming over him. In that moment, instead of the emotionless face I saw in the freezer or the face of terror in Alexis's cavern, I found a hint of what looked like excitement or joy behind those eyes. Ultimately, it didn't matter which emotion it was, either proved how depraved the crime lord had become.

CHAPTER 24

Dempsey added his other hand to the pistol as he stared down its iron sights. "You're a crafty fellow, but you can only run so far."

Wry laughter rushed from Alexis's lips as his legs propelled him away from the man wielding the pistol. "You only have so many bullets, and you squandered your aim on the boy."

As Dempsey's cold smile grew, he leveled the pistol at Alexis and pulled the trigger. However, when the striker hit the bullet, the gun swerved, and the shot slammed into the wall a few feet from me.

Dempsey twisted the handgun as he shook his head. "I guess it'll be a little trickier to remove you from my side." He repositioned the weapon and flashed a wicked grin. "I'm sure your luck will run dry before my last shot."

Where are the cops? Should we have lingered a little longer before releasing him?

Looking down at Alexis's wounded body, Dempsey took one tentative step toward him. But a moment later, he confidently closed the distance and lifted Alexis by his shirt. "Maybe you can prevent me from getting a clean shot at a distance." He pressed the gun into Alexis's shoulder. "Though I don't think you'll have the same luck from point blank range."

Watching my great plan unfold, I couldn't stop thinking about how it was going to get Alexis killed. As the fear grew in the back of my mind, I realized my heart was about to explode when the police burst into the room. Why didn't we hear the sirens? And as if in response to my mental question, sirens filled the evening. Had Alexis done something to prevent us from hearing them? Did it matter? As the police swarmed the crime lord, I fell to my butt and let my head bang onto the opposite wall. While I could hear everything, the words failed to imprint themselves in my memory.

The only thing I could remember was the broad description of them calling Dempsey a crazed lunatic. At least that was what I hoped the cops were saying as they handcuffed the once-mighty crime lord. Hopefully, those cops would spread the news and it would consume the city like a wildfire purging a dying forest. The dutiful officers had everything they could ever want to force Dempsey into a dark cell somewhere. And none of his lawyers or well-placed connections could or would do a thing to save him. He was going to be arrested for murder and attempted murder.

As I watched Emergency Services treat Alexis, he appeared to be okay, despite refusing to leave his home. As the cops and paramedics canvassed the crime scene, I relaxed, knowing Alexis's bullet was no longer something I had to worry about, and it appeared I'd receive clemency for the crimes I had committed. As my hazy focus returned to the unfolding scene, I watched the medics patch his flesh wound while the cops questioned him.

After they finished with him, I was forced to wait and watch the police and medical personnel as they completed their duty. However, the eeriest thing I saw that night was them removing my corpse from Alexis's home. I finally understood the adage about someone walking over your grave, and the shiver that sent down your spine. When the last of the policemen finally left, Alexis made a beeline to my closet's door but came up short as an officer returned with a few more questions to ask.

EPILOGUE

After what felt like an eternity, Alexis stepped back into view through the transparent wall, sporting a sling cradling his wounded arm. He eased the closet door open and leaned against the doorframe. "Are you ready to go?"

"Go where?" I asked, stepping away from the injured man looming over me.

Alexis peered into the small room while rubbing his chin. "Did you want to sleep in here?" He rapped the wall with the knuckles of his good hand. "I understand that it's an exceptional space, but I believe you'll find it a little cramped."

I stepped forward, licking my lips as I rubbed my secondhand clothing. "No, I'm ready to step out of this space. Despite looking larger than it is, I'm getting a severe case of cabin fever."

"That's understandable, considering your only form of entertainment was watching the police manhandle your corpse. Though given your recent activity, it's not likely to change anytime soon."

"Yeah, that's not funny," I said, stepping closer to Alexis.

"You cannot walk through this door." Alexis rapped the frame as he flashed me a lopsided grin. "Given the giant hole in my home, there's a chance someone would catch a peek at a walking dead man, which would undo all the work we accomplished tonight."

"That sounds fair," I said, rubbing my hands across my face. "But if I can't walk out the door, how am I going to get wherever I'm going?"

Alexis pushed off the doorframe and placed his hand on the interior wall. Within moments, the transparency vanished as a circular rift opened in front of me, revealing a simple wooden table and its complementary chairs. "Haven't you seen enough of my skills to answer your own questions?"

"Where's that?"

"It's my primary panic room, though it'll serve as your world while we work out our next steps of your life."

I rubbed my upper lip as I studied the spartan furnishings in the room through Alexis's portal. My gaze drifted to him as I stepped away from the opening. With a gulp of air, I thrust a finger at the strange room. "Before you usher me inside, can I have my phone?"

"Didn't the police take it?"

"No," I said, trying to peek over the man's shoulder, "I slipped it into the couch."

"You're dead!" He stepped closer to me and thumped my chest with two fingers. "Who could you possibly want to call?"

I rubbed my chest, where he prodded me and dropped my head. At that moment, I understood I wouldn't have much privacy soon. After all, he was escorting me to my prison. "I have a couple of people I need to speak with before disappearing."

"Who?" However, before I could reply, he let out a tiny gasp as he lifted a twitching finger. "Would it be Bella and Matt?"

"Yes, I need to reach out to both of them and let them know I'm alive."

Alexis's eyes dropped into his hand as an irritated growl laced his voice. "Didn't I hear Dempsey say Bella is his niece?"

"Yeah, she bears that burden."

A loud scoff rebounded off the cramped confines. "After all we did to kill you, while ensuring you walked away from it, you want to advertise your perfect health to a member of Dempsey's family?"

"She can't stand her uncle." I stepped toward the portal and tapped the edge of the wall. When the solid thump filled the room, I slipped my finger through the opening and felt the sudden temperature change. I yanked my hand free, shaking it. "In fact, she'll probably jump for joy when she finds out that her uncle is being locked up, despite the false pretenses."

Alexis gripped his chin with his good hand as his lips wrung together. After several seconds, he snapped his fingers and a moment later my phone drifted into the room, settling into his open hand. "You want to bring her into your confidence?"

"We had something at the tournament," I said, extending my open hand.

"What about your friend?"

"He's always been a confidant."

With a nod, he placed the phone into my outstretched hand and stepped out of the doorframe. Then, as he pulled the door closed, the portal to his panic room sealed. Before the door shut, he snapped once more, and a pen and notepad appeared on the floor. "I'll give you a few minutes. But before you're done, jot down those numbers."

"Sure thing," I said, navigating my phone. I quickly called Matt, but he didn't answer. So I hung up and sent him a brief yet encrypted message.

Okay, will reach out again soon.

When I returned to the contact list, I thumbed through it until I found Bella's entry. I pressed the call button and brought it to my ear and listened to the rings while I waited for her to answer.

"Hello," Bella said, her sweet voice slicing through the silence. "It's nice to hear your voice."

"Is that you, Marcus?"

Her dulcet tones teased a smile as I rolled my shoulders. "It's me. And before you ask, I'm okay, and we have a lot to talk about."

"We certainly do," she said with a warm laugh.

WHERE TO FIND ME

www.stevenmeehan.com:
This is my escape from the drudgery of my daily grind. Inside those digital pages, you'll find with the various thoughts and questions that swirl around my mind, and even original stories. While those tales are limited to a thousand words, aka flash fiction, it's my hope that they provide you with a momentary break from your busy day. While those form most of my posts, they are not the limits of what I like to talk about or share. Besides the above, I also share my opinion on everything from a topic that won't leave my mind to the stories I'm consuming no matter their form, and even some of my artwork. The last thing you'll find littered about each page is the quotes. While they're taken from seemingly random sources, each of them made me think, laugh, or simply entertained my mind.

www.patreon.com/stevenpmeehan:
For those who enjoy my writing, this gives you the opportunity to support me and delve further into my work. Not only that, but every patron has an opportunity to shape the stories I bring them monthly. Come join the community and you'll receive three original stories every month and the ability to choose their genres, a first look at my artwork, access to my Discord server, and potentially insight into my writing.

Printed in the USA
CPSIA information can be obtained
at www.ICGtesting.com
LVHW031931111024
793587LV00013B/208